MILLIONAIRE DAD'S SOS

BY

ALLY BLAKE

MILLS & BOON

First published in Great Britain 2010
Large Print edition 2010
Harlequin Mills & Boon Limited,
Eton House, 18-24 Paradise Road,
Richmond, Surrey TW9 1SR

© Ally Blake 2010

ISBN: 978 0 263 21234 1

Harlequin Mills & Boon policy is to use papers that are
natural, renewable and recyclable products and made
from wood grown in sustainable forests. The logging and
manufacturing process conform to the legal environmental
regulations of the country of origin.

Printed and bound in Great Britain
by CPI Antony Rowe, Chippenham, Wiltshire

This one's for Veronica, my constant companion
through the writing of this book—
from bump, to blinking into the light,
to becoming my beautiful smiley girl.

PROLOGUE

WWW.CHIC-ONLINE.COM.AU

News just in…

The cameras were out, the paparazzi waiting, seamstresses across the city ready to copy whichever designer frock they were about to be dazzled by, yet all were sorely disappointed when so-fabulous-it-hurts, thinking man's It-Girl Meg Kelly—the youngest, and we think most adorable, offspring of one-time uber-financier, some-time squillionaire, KInG of the corporate jungle Quinn Kelly—failed to show at the opening of hot new nightclub Bliss.

But wait, there's more!

Sources close to the family say she hasn't slept at her apartment or her folks' pad, the stunning Kelly Manor, the past two nights. And her familiar classic red convertible, often seen parked out front of Kelly Tower—the home of

*titanic family biz the Kelly Investment Group—
is nowhere to be seen.*

*Where has Brisbane's favourite daughter dis-
appeared to?*

*Could she be—gasp!—in hiding, nursing a
new nose job? Has the nicest girl in town finally
shown a kink in her squeaky clean armour by—
eek!—blowing off her host? Is her vanishing act
a sign that her Herculean father is not as recov-
ered from recent heart problems as the family
would have us believe?*

*Or—bless her little heart—has she run off with
the studly Texan oil baron seen visiting the family
manor last week? Oh, please, let that be it! Can
we possibly hope this means the last of the Kelly
kids has finally found true love at last?*

*Take our online poll for a chance to win a copy
of bestseller* Long Live the King: An unauthor-
ised biography of Quinn Kelly!

CHAPTER ONE

'OF ALL the resorts in all the world, why did she have to walk into mine?'

Zach Jones stood in the shadows of a lush potted palm in a dark corner of the Waratah House lobby, narrowed eyes locked on the figure skipping down the wide stone steps leading away from the main building of the Juniper Falls Rainforest Retreat.

There weren't many reasons why his resort staff would contact him directly, *ever*, his reputation being that he was akin to a bear with a sore tooth at the best of times. That was as kind a character reference he could have hoped for, considering his years of unequivocal lack of co-operation with the press.

Despite all that, the rumoured arrival of the woman currently whipping off her cap and trying and failing to tuck her mass of dark curls beneath it had been deemed important enough to give the bear a nudge.

The bear was thankful they had.

After his daily run, he'd lain in wait for her to show her face. In the end he'd missed out on that privilege. She'd scooted through the lobby, head tipped down. Nevertheless, he'd recognised her in an instant. There wouldn't be many a red-blooded man in this corner of the world who would not.

Even though she was dressed down in shorts, vest top, sneakers and cap rather than her usual society princess razzmatazz of designer frocks and diamonds, there was no mistaking her. Not with those sexy dark curls, that hourglass silhouette in miniature, the kind Zach couldn't help imagining just begged for fifties-style dresses and high heels to make the most of it, and the ridiculously confi-dent, rock-and-roll sway of those infamous hips.

The woman who'd sent his staff into a tizz the moment she'd zoomed up to the front gates of the resort earlier that week in a growling red con-vertible filled with designer luggage and equally designer friends was none other than Meg Kelly.

'Dammit,' he said loud enough a group of guests heading out the doors gave him a sideways glance. He slid deeper into the shadows, a place he'd always found far more comfortable than being under any kind of spotlight.

Much less the kind of spotlight Meg Kelly seemed to carry on her person, such was her magnetism for the kind of rabid media attention usually reserved for royalty and rock stars. That kind of attention made her exactly the kind of guest most resort owners would give their right arm for.

Not him. Not now.

She disappeared for a moment behind a fat spray of red Waratah flowers and he felt himself leaning to catch her coming out the other side. He rocked himself back upright and planted his feet into the marble floor.

She popped out eventually only to bend from the waist to tug at the heel of what appeared to be brand-new sneakers, her shorts curving tight over her backside, her thigh muscles tightening, her calf muscles lengthening.

He glanced away, but not soon enough to stop the quickening in his blood. He ran a hand over his mouth, his palm rasping from the effects of three days' worth of stubble growth, and told himself it was the after-effects of his run.

He glanced back out of the window only to have his gaze catch on the sliver of pale, soft skin that peeked between the back of her shorts and her top... Was that a tattoo?

His eyes flicked to the heavens and he drew in a deep breath through his nose, attempting to temper the swift kick of attraction.

Not her. And most certainly not now.

The little-known truth that he'd stayed put in the one place for the past few months, rather than jet-setting about the globe in a constant effort to exponentially expand his empire of international resorts, would be enticing news for the kind of gossip-hungry media for whom Meg Kelly was the poster girl.

As far as he was concerned they could all go jump. Not since he'd jumped off the merry-go-round of foster homes and orphanages he'd grown up in had he let anybody tell him who he was, who he was not, how low he might fall, or how high he dared reach. His successes and mistakes were only his own to judge.

And of all the successes and mistakes he'd ever accomplished in his life the reason *why* he was now stuck in the middle of nowhere was the most inviolable yet.

In fact, he'd missed a call from his 'reason why' already that morning, and now she wasn't answering the mobile he'd bought her specifically so they could *always* be in touch.

Then his man on the ground in St Barts had left a message saying the government was playing hard ball on signing off on the final inspections of his latest resort site. And then there was Meg. All that before the day had even officially begun.

He didn't see how this week could get any worse.

Meg couldn't imagine how her week could get any better.

'Ouch, ouch, ouch!' she barked as a blister spontaneously popped up on her right heel.

Okay, so a handy supply of Band-Aids might have made it ever so slightly better, but everything else was heavenly. She simply shifted her stance to compensate and breathed deep of the glorious fresh air, sunshine and fifty acres of beautiful resort and her world was close to perfection again.

The breath turned to a yawn, which turned into a grin, which she bit back lest she be caught laughing to herself in the middle of the patch of lawn in which she'd come to a halt. Apparently she'd already been declared AWOL by the gossip hounds today—she didn't need to add loony to the list.

A funny sensation skittered down her back.

Years of experience gave her the feeling she was being watched. She did a casual three-sixty-degree turn, but in the early morning, the resort grounds were quiet and still and she was all alone. It was probably just the rising sun sending prickles over her pale skin, and teasing her curls into damp springs on the back of her neck.

Another deep breath, another blissful smile as she skipped onto the immaculate lawn, which she figured would be kinder on her feet.

If her big brothers could see her now—up and at 'em before the birds, in a jogging outfit of all things—they'd be in hysterics. She wasn't exactly built for the great outdoors and her way of life meant that the only time she ever saw a sunrise was when she'd yet to go to bed the night before!

But this week she wasn't Meg Kelly, socialite. This vacation was not about to turn into some last-minute Kelly Investment Group junket in disguise. This week, thanks to her angelic best friends, she was just a girl on a summer holiday.

Sure, when Rylie and Tabitha had turned up on her doorstep two days before, told her they'd cleared her schedule, shoved her into her car and demanded she drive them to a wellness resort high in the hills of the Gold Coast Hinterland, she'd had a moment or two of panic.

Events had been planned. People had been counting on her—dress designers she was meant to be wearing, charities whose events she was attending, local businesses she was turning out to endorse, the several staff she kept in gainful employ, the women and children at the Valley Women's Shelter. There was such inertia to her life it was almost impossible to bring it to any kind of halt.

But even after Tabitha had explained that the 'wellness' in wellness resort was more about detoxing one's life by way of eating granola and valiantly trying to put one's left ankle behind one's head while meditating thrice daily, and not so much code for cocktails, chocolate fountains and daily massages at the hands of handsome Swedes she'd soon begun to warm to the idea.

As the city lights had dropped away from her rear-view mirror and the scent of sea air had filled her nostrils the idea of getting away, of having one blissful, dreamy, stress-free, family-free, paparazzi-free, drama-free week had almost made her giddy.

Not that drama, paparazzi and family issues bothered her. They'd been par for the Kelly course from the day dot.

Though, when she thought about it, the past few months had been particularly dramatic even for her family—engagements, elopements, near-death experiences. The kinds of things that made the paparazzi that touch more overzealous, and a touch harder to avoid when she tried to sneak away for much-needed private time.

Meg shook off the real-life stuff creeping up on her and glanced back at the main building. Still no sign of the girls. Her girls. Her support crew. The ones who'd obviously sensed she was floundering just a very little even if she hadn't uttered a word. Girls who were right now both probably still fast slept in their snug, warm beds.

'Cads.'

She headed off; this time with slower, shorter steps in the hopes the girls would catch up. Soon. Please!

A resort staff member passed, smiling. 'Good morning.'

'Isn't it just?' she returned.

His smile faltered and he all but tripped over

himself as his neck craned to watch her while he walked away.

Meg's smile turned wry. So the cap and sunglasses and still-so-white-they-practically-glowed sneakers she'd bought from the resort's well-stocked shop the night before might not fool everybody as she'd half hoped they just might.

It had been a long shot anyway.

Meg stood happily at the back of the morning jogging group—primarily a group of middle-aged strangers in an impressive array of jogging outfits—collected on the track that ran along the edge of the overhang of thick, lush, dank, dark rainforest.

In an apparent effort at warming up, Tabitha lifted her knees enthusiastically high while jogging on the spot. Rylie, the Pilates queen, stretched so far sideways she was practically at a right angle. Meg, on the other hand, tried not to look as dinky as she felt without her ubiquitous high heels.

'Now that man is worth the price of admission all on his own,' Tabitha said between her teeth.

'Shh,' Meg said, only listening with half an ear as she tried to make out what the preppy, bouncy 'wellness facilitator' at the front of the large group was saying. 'Please tell me she didn't just say we're jogging four kilometres this morning!'

'She said five.'

Meg slid her sunglasses atop her cap and gaped at Tabitha. 'Five?'

'Five. Now pay attention. Hot guy at six o'clock. He's been staring at you for the past five minutes.'

'Not news, hon,' Rylie said, touching the ground with her palms and casually glancing between her legs before letting out a long, slow 'I take that back. This one is big news.'

Meg rolled her eyes. 'I'm not falling for that again.'

'Your loss,' Rylie said.

A husky note in her best friend's voice caught Meg's attention. 'Fine. Where?'

'Over your right shoulder,' Tabitha said. 'Faded T-shirt, knee-length cargo shorts, sneakers that have pounded some miles, cap he ought to have thrown away a lo-o-ong time ago…'

Rylie laughed, then gave Meg's leg a tug so her knee collapsed, turning her whether she wanted to or not.

Meg didn't even get the chance to ask Rylie

what was so funny. She didn't need to. There was no way any woman under the age of a hundred and twenty was going to miss the man leaning against the trunk of one of the massive ghost gums lining the resort's elegant driveway.

He was tall. Impressively so. Broad as any man she'd ever met. His chin was unshaven, the dark curls beneath his cap overlong. With the colour of a man who'd spent half a lifetime in the sun and the muscles of a man who hadn't done so standing still, he looked as if he'd stepped out of a Nautica ad.

She tucked a curl behind her ear and casually bent down to tug at her ankle socks, not needing to look at the guy to remember exactly what she'd seen. Her hands shook ever so slightly.

He was the very dictionary definition of rugged sex appeal. For a girl from the right side of the tracks, a girl who was a magnet for stiff, sharp, striving suits, a girl whose planner had become so full of late she had to diarise time to wash her hair much less anything more intimately en-joyable, he was a revelation.

She glanced up as she stood. He hadn't moved an inch.

The skin beneath her skimpy clothes suddenly

felt hot, and the fact that it was thirty-odd degrees and muggy had nothing to do with it. She was a Kelly, for Pete's sake. It took something *extra* extraordinary to make a Kelly sweat.

Though she couldn't see his eyes beneath the brim of his soft, worn cap, she could feel them on her. Her right shoulder tingled. The sensation moved up her neck. It finally settled in her lips. The urge to run her fingers across them was so strong she had to curl them into her palms.

Then he finally moved. He pressed away from the tree and shifted his cap into a more comfortable position on his head before crossing his arms across his chest. His strong, tanned, brawny arms. His broad chest.

She breathed in deep, releasing it on a long, slow, deliciously revitalising sigh.

What if *this* was what she needed more than even a holiday right now? More than granola or t'ai chi. More than early-morning jogs or internal reflection classes. A little bit of something for herself.

Could she? Should she? Considering every step and every misstep she experienced outside the walls of her family home somehow ended up being known by the whole country, it took some-

thing *extra* extraordinary for her to put herself
out there. The lanky stranger who would not take
his eyes off her was exactly that.

She took another deep breath, faced him
square on and gave him an honest, inviting, un-
ambiguous smile.

Needless to say, after all that build-up, it was
more than a bit of a shock when she didn't get
one in return. *Nada.* Not a twitch, a nod, not any
kind of acknowledgement that he was paying
her any attention at all.

Her cheeks heated from the inside out, her fingernails bit into her palms, and her lungs
suddenly felt very, very small.

Meg fair leapt out of her skin when Tabitha
leant on her shoulder and sighed. 'Imagine,' she
said, 'if we hadn't kidnapped you to this place
this moment never would have happened.'

'I'm trying my very best to imagine it right
now,' Meg said on a mortified croak.

Pathetically late though the attempt at saving
face was, Meg let her gaze glance off Mr Tall
Dark and Silent Rugged Man, then up into the
sky as if she were pondering the time and using
the sun as her guide.

'I might well be seeing things,' Rylie said,

finally upright and now staring brazenly at the silent stranger, 'but isn't that Zach Jones?'

Meg grabbed Rylie by the hand and spun her around to face front. All the while her wits began to return and synapses connected in the back of her brain. 'Why do I know that name?'

Rylie said, 'He was a rower years back. Olympic level. Keeping it up too, by the looks of him. Now he's a businessman. Big time. Owns this place, in fact, as well as a dozen-odd of its like all 'round the world. Self-starter. Self-made. Renegade. Refuses to list his company on the exchange. Not all that much known about him otherwise. He somehow manages to live under the radar.'

'Single?' Tabitha asked.

'Perpetually,' Rylie said with a grin.

'Perfect.' Tabitha grinned. 'Your dad'll hate him.'

Meg turned on her. 'So?'

Rylie said, 'She has a point. You don't have to limit your dating schedule to charming, skint, ambitionless, undemanding men to get back at Daddy.'

Meg's right eyebrow tweaked to a point. 'I actually *prefer* to spend time with men who don't consider bragging about that day's corporate buyout fit for pillow talk, thank you very much. I get enough of that around the family dinner table to find it in any way an aphrodisiac. The only way my father comes into it is that at least men not on their way up the corporate ladder never try to get to him through me.'

Tabitha mirrored her expression. 'Whatever you say.'

Meg poked a face, then looked decidedly back to the front of the group.

What she didn't say was that the men she favoured also weren't the types to press for any kind of commitment. They weren't in any rush to start families of their own. One less pressure to concern herself with.

Besides, it had been a long time since she'd bothered doing anything extreme in order to get through to the big man herself. What was the point? It had never worked anyway.

Rylie pushed in tighter, her voice a secretive stage whisper. 'It has to be him. Zach Jones. He's notoriously impossible to pin down. He's one of those ungettable interviews that would take a girl like me out of Sunday morning fluff TV into the big leagues. I wonder what he's doing here rather than flitting around the world buying up great wads of prime real estate like it's going out of fashion? I smell a scoop.'

Meg shook her escaping curls from her cheeks and peeked out of the corner of her eye one more time.

He'd tilted his head up ever so slightly. Sun-kissed skin was smoothed over the most immaculately masculine bone structure Meg had ever seen. The shadow of three-day growth covered a jaw that just begged to be stroked. And his lips were so perfectly carved she struggled to take her eyes off them.

All that perfection somehow managed to pale in comparison when she finally saw his eyes.

They were locked on hers.

Dark, dangerous eyes, too far away for her to make out the colour, but she had the feeling she could have doubled the distance between them and still been hit by the thwack of awareness behind them.

She sucked in a breath, thick with tropical humidity that caught in her throat. And a trickle of what was most definitely sweat ran down her neck and between her breasts.

Zach Jones.

His name buzzed about inside her head in her

father's most frosty voice as he flapped the *Financial Times* in a way that meant he was not happy. '*He got too big, too quick. Stubborn fool is overreaching. One of these days he'll land flat on his face. Mark my words.*'

Meg didn't know about overreaching, but she did know that her father didn't give a damn about *anyone* below a certain level of accomplishment—client, competitor, offspring...

She swallowed.

There was no flirtation in Zach Jones's gaze. No measure of awe about who she was. Just copious amounts of brooding intensity centred in those unfathomable dark eyes. Despite it all, the backs of her knees began to quiver.

He blinked. And rolled his shoulders. The first sign he wasn't as nervelessly blasé as he was making out.

The very thought made way for an unimpeded rush of sexual attraction to slide through her, like a waterfall breaking through a dam of knotted foliage that had held it back a decade.

The ferocity of her reaction had her literally taking a step back. The blister on her heel popped, again. A hiss of pain slid through her teeth as she hopped madly on her good foot.

The man took a step towards her, a hand appearing to flicker in her direction. The tension curling inside her ratcheted up a notch and a half and she knew her sudden breathlessness had far less to do with her stinging foot, and more to do with the stranger in her midst.

Thankfully she caught her balance all on her own, and the man unclenched from his ready-to-pounce position.

She spun back to face front. 'When are we going to start running, for Pete's sake?' she whispered through her teeth.

Rylie reached out and pinched her hot pink cheek. 'Look who's suddenly Miss Eager Exerciser.'

'You bet,' she said, shuffling from one foot to the other as though she had ants in her pants. 'Bring on the lactic-acid burn!' Better that than having to endure the feel of the man's burning eyes on her back.

She shook out her hands, attempting to shake off the fidgets. It wasn't as though she hadn't been rebuffed before. It came with the celebrity package as much as being excessively adored. It just thankfully generally happened from afar. By strangers. Whom she didn't have to look in the eye and pretend it didn't sting.

'Meg, he's coming over!' Tabitha said so loud those straggling nearby must have heard.

'We'll leave you to it, then,' Rylie said cheerily. 'I'm counting on you to get me the exclusive!'

'No, no, no!' Meg begged.

But it was too late, they were off—Rylie the runner, and Tabitha the gym junkie. There was no way Meg was keeping up with them, even with the amount of adrenalin pouring through her body as she stood all alone in the middle of the dirt track, Zach Jones making a beeline her way.

CHAPTER TWO

MEG jogged for almost five minutes before pulling up to a walk. By then she was already wishing she'd brought a better bra, a hairband and a scooter.

The rest of the stragglers passed her by, including the wellness facilitator who had been bringing up the rear.

All bar one.

She could feel a male presence tucked in behind her. She could hear the heavy pad of his large feet on the compacted dirt path. Dragging in deep, unfit breaths, she caught his scent on the hot summer breeze—expensive, subtle, and wholly masculine.

All this from a man who'd managed to get under her skin in half a second flat. A man who'd rejected her come-hither smile in even less time. Sheesh. The sooner she found out what he was after and got rid of him, the better.

She said, 'Are we there yet?' just loud enough he could have no doubt she was talking to him.

'Do a U-turn and ask me again,' a deep voice rumbled beside her. A voice that matched the rest of him so perfectly that if she wasn't gleaming with perspiration from the effect of it she deserved some kind of medal in self-control.

Meg pinched her side with the hopes of fending off an oncoming stitch and the slow burn of attraction that was infusing her in one fell swoop, and turned.

At a distance Zach Jones was something. Up close and personal he was too beautiful for words. Her breath shot from her in a discombobulated *whoomph*.

She concentrated on the slight bump of a once-broken nose, the different angles each of his dark brows took above his hooded eyes, the stray sun-kissed flecks within his dark hair, lest she be overwhelmed by the whole.

'Please don't hang back on my account,' she said, oft-practised casual smile firmly entrenched. 'My pace is purposeful. Those chumps up ahead don't realise how much more one can appreciate the scenery by walking.'

He said, 'I'm fine right here.'

If she didn't know better she could have taken those words a whole other way. As it was she had to give her heart a mental slap for the unwarranted little dance it was currently enjoying.

'Excellent,' she said. 'We'll walk together. Scenery is always more enjoyable when you have someone to share it with.'

And then neither of them said another word for a whole minute. The unmistakable tension was almost enough for Meg to start jogging again, despite the fact that she'd barely caught her breath.

'Would I be right in thinking you're not a big runner?' he finally said.

After Meg's laughter died down she waved her hands in the direction of her well-tended curves. 'Do I look like a runner?'

Given the invitation to do so, the man's eyes travelled down one side of her body—over her borrowed hot-pink short shorts and black T-shirt with sparkly designer name splashed across her chest—and up the other. Given the chance, she looked into his distracted eyes.

Deep, dark, soulful brown they were, with the kinds of creases at the edge that she just knew would make a girl's heart melt at ten paces when he smiled. *If* he smiled, which she realised he still was yet to do. In fact, he carried with him the distinct impression of a frown.

Finally, and none too soon, Meg managed to duck out of the heady cloud of attraction to hear cymbals crashing inside her head. They warned of impending doom.

There was no doubt he was intentionally at her side. He'd had to have waved the wellness facilitator on to get her alone. But it was becoming increasingly clear he wasn't exactly over the moon to be there. On both counts she was clueless as to why.

She worried the tiny chip in her front right tooth with her tongue, an old habit that re-emerged only when she felt as if things were slipping out of her exacting control. An old habit she worked hard at keeping at bay.

She curled her tongue back where it belonged and answered her question herself. 'Between us, running's not my forte. I'm more of a yoga girl.'

Sometimes. Every now and then. Okay, so she'd taken a couple of lessons with Rylie once.

'Yoga,' he repeated, his eyes finally, thankfully, leaving the contours of her body and returning to hers.

She shouldn't have been so thankful so soon.

For in those dark, deep, delicious brown eyes she saw that he had seen the equivocation in hers.

She dropped her gaze to the fraying collar of his T-shirt lest he see the surprise in her eyes as well. She'd had a lifetime in which to perfect the art of being Meg Kelly, public figure. Her front had been demonstrably shatter-proof. *Two minutes* after meeting her, Zach Jones had seen right through it.

Who was this guy and what did he want with her?

'Downward dog? Upward...tree?' she shot back, arms swinging in what she knew was a terrible impression of something she'd seen on TV once. 'Okay, so I'm not a yoga fanatic or a runner. I'm more an eat-chocolate-for-breakfast dance-it-off-in-your-living-room kind of girl. Either way there is no way on God's green earth I'll be catching up to the others any time soon. So please go ahead. Jog. Be free.'

'Between us,' he said, leaning in, his voice dropping to a conspiratorial tone that sent her blood pressure soaring, 'I've already run five K today.'

'Oh.' Oh, indeed. 'So what brings you out here again?'

All she got for her blunt question was an out-held hand. 'I'm Zach Jones.'

Meg twisted her body to slide her smaller hand into his. Even the coolest of customers usually gave themselves away when shaking her hand. A nervous vibration here, a sweaty palm there. She was extremely adept at ignoring their nerves.

With Zach Jones they never eventuated. His grip was warm, dry, strong, masculine and wholly unmoved.

Remarkable, she thought. More than remarkable. The man was perspiration-inducing, utterly gorgeous and wholly unsmiling even though he had the kind of warm, open, likable face purpose built for the function.

And don't forget, she reminded herself, *beneath the casual curls, the sexily shabby clothes, and the body of an Olympic god, Zach Jones is an alpha in beta camouflage. So not worth worrying about.*

So why was she still holding his hand?

Because it really is so very warm, dry and blissfully enveloping, that's why.

'I'm Meg,' she said, pumping once more, then letting go.

At the last second she held back her surname. As if there was a slim chance she'd been reading too much into every cheek flicker, or lack thereof, from the very beginning. Maybe he was just some cute guy too shy to chat her up even though he had a thing for girls with impossibly curly hair and a glaringly obvious lack of sporting prowess.

'It's a pleasure to meet you, Meg,' he said, his mouth quirking at her omission.

Argh! What was she thinking? He knew. Of *course* he knew. She'd have to go further than the Gold Coast to find a man who didn't know who she was. A man whose mind wasn't already made up about her before they even met.

She squeezed her eyes shut a moment. Using a technique they'd encouraged in internal reflection class the day before, she searched for her centre. Patience thin, she failed miserably. Instead she went with what worked in the real world: she summoned her inner Kelly and looked the guy dead in the eye.

'So, Zach Jones, from what I hear around the traps you own this joint.'

The full-frontal approach brought out a combative glint in his darker than dark eyes. If possible it only made the guy more tempting. Warmth curled through her empty stomach.

But rather than doing the polite thing and answering her charge, he ignored it and asked, 'How long are you planning on staying?'

Frustration began to war convincingly well with attraction. In response, her practised smile only grew wider.

'A survey?' she said, lobbing it right back in his corner. 'Aren't you the hands-on boss?'

The most sensuous mouth she'd ever laid eyes on kicked into a sexy almost-smile, creating an arc in his cheek that hinted at so much more, but still it never quite reached his eyes. He didn't believe her devil-may-care performance for a second.

'How long?' he repeated.

'We're here the week.'

His eyes skimmed the empty path ahead. 'We being?'

Something in his tone gave her the sense the impending doom wouldn't be impending that much longer.

She casually lifted a foot and stretched her…whatever the muscle that ran down the front of your thigh was called. 'Two of my closest mates gave me this holiday as a present. Rylie Madigan and Tabitha Cooper.'

At the last second she threw out their full names on a gamble, for Tabitha, with her ex-

Prime Minister dad, and Rylie, with her job on TV, were almost as recognisable as she was.

Her fishing paid off. He breathed deep, his fists bunched at his sides, and the sexy hollows in his cheeks grew their own hollows.

'So you go home…?' he said.

'In a few days.'

He nodded, breathed out deeply, apparently most satisfied that she'd be out of his sight as soon as that.

Whoa. That was harsh.

Even though beneath the bright smiles and fancy clothes she was a tough cookie—she had to be in order to survive being a Kelly—it turned out she was still just a girl whose pride could be hurt like anyone else.

Okay, so there had been a time before she'd toughened up. A time when she'd been in danger of imploding under the relentless pressure. A long time ago, a lifetime really, in some perverse effort to get her father's attention she'd let things go far too far. It had scared her enough to buck up and take control over her image, her life. To figure out how to use the process that used her.

Any naivety she might have had was lost for ever, making a certain amount of cynicism unavoidable. On the upside she was no longer easily fazed. By anything.

Yet somehow this guy was getting to her.

Frustration finally won out, bringing with it a desire to share the pain. She lifted her chin and breathed deep of the tropical air. 'I have to say you picked a gorgeous spot here. I could really get used to it. Who knows? We may stay longer yet.'

His eyes slid back to hers; dark, gleaming, shrewd.

She raised both eyebrows. *Now what are you going to do about that?*

What he did was smile.

Naturally it was everything she'd imagined it might be and so much more. The latent vitality his physique hinted at shone from his eyes when he smiled. It made him appear playful, warm, engaging. Her knees turned to jelly. Her resolve turned to mush.

She opened her mouth, ready to ask him outright what the hell was going on when he placed his bare hand in the small of her back and gave her a light shove. She was so surprised she gave a little yelp.

Through the thin cotton of her T-shirt his fingers were hot. Insistent. Touching her without fear or favour.

Only when she looked up to see a small tree in the middle of the path did she realise he was merely stopping her from thwacking into the thing.

And even after his hand moved all too easily away, and even while he was making her feel more and more out of step with every step in his presence, she could still feel the hot, hard press of Zach Jones's hand against her skin.

Now why did he have to go and touch her?

A simple, 'Watch out for the tree,' would have sufficed. Instead, constant glimpses of that tattoo peeking out from the rise of her shorts had been like a magnet.

Now he had to do this thing with the sensation of that soft warm skin imprinted on the tips of his fingers.

Zach curled said fingers into his palm and took a small step to the left to add a little more physical distance between himself and the woman at his side. The woman whose very proximity could expose everything he'd worked so hard to keep preserved. Protected. Pure.

He stretched out his shoulders and shot her a sideways glance. He had to concede that for a woman who appeared to bloom under the spotlight like an orchid in a hothouse, in person she was smaller, more low-key, and more approachable than he'd expected her to be. Funny, mischievous, switched on...

He actually had to remind himself her father was Quinn Kelly, one of the most patronising men he'd ever had the displeasure of dealing with in the early stages of his business career. No doubt there would be a good dash of spice beneath the sweet. That kind of bite had to be genetic.

As for the rest of her?

His gaze lingered on her mouth before skimming over her pale bare shoulder, down her slim arm, over her Betty Boop hip, before being drawn back to that mouth.

Surely lips that lush could not be the real deal. Soft, pink, curving up at the corners even when she frowned as she was doing right then. Those lips alone were enough to make sure half the men of Brisbane thought themselves in lust with her. The other half simply didn't read the right papers. And as it turned out *his* body didn't give a hoot if they were genuine. Saliva gathered beneath his tongue. He swallowed it with such force his throat ached in protest.

His gaze moved north only to be reminded of

those infamous blue eyes. The colour was mentioned every time her name was spoken aloud. The second she'd turned them his way he'd known why. They were startling—glinting, bright, sapphire blue. The kind of blue that looked as if it could cut glass. The kind of blue that could make even the most disinterested man dive right in and not care if he drowned.

Luckily for him the fact that his hormones had so spectacularly tuned into Meg Kelly's siren song was not going to be a problem to add to the reasons why he needed her as far away from there as possible. He'd long since been wise to the barb of wanting someone that would never be his to have. He had the relentless dislocation of his childhood to thank for that vital life lesson if for nothing else.

There was no getting away from the fact that she was trouble. Add friends who were of all people a TV reporter and an ex-Prime Minister's wild child to the mix and his day had just got a whole lot worse.

It was time to turn things around.

'Ms Kelly,' he said, making sure she knew without a doubt he knew who she was, 'I need you to tell me what you and your friends are really doing here.'

Her hands clenched so tight at her sides her knuckles turned white. Whatever else she was, Meg Kelly was smart. She had clued onto the fact that he wasn't about to roll out the red carpet.

'Whatever do you mean?' she asked, her spicy core all too evident in her tone.

'Wouldn't you all prefer somewhere more... rousing in which to spend your vacation?'

She afforded him a glance. There was nothing he could pinpoint to say it wasn't a perfectly amiable glance. Yet he felt the smack of it like an arrow between the eyes.

'I'd say a five-thirty wake-up call is about as *rousing* as I like things to get when on holidays,' she said.

His cheek twitched. He corralled it back into line. 'Perhaps. Yet neither you nor your friends fit into our usual demographic of guests looking to shed a few pounds, get back to nature or affect a mid-life change of life.'

He turned to find she had come to a halt. Hands on hips. She said, 'Now why would you think that we aren't here to replenish our emotional wells just as it suggests on the brochure? Is my jogging prowess really that atrocious?'

Her answer was entirely reasonable, her tone

playful even. But in the end it was those most famous of eyes that gave her away. Inside she was readying for battle. A battle he had no intention of letting her win.

He took a slow step inside her personal space, forcing her to tilt her head to look up at him. He could feel the breath from those sweet lips brushing over his chin. His blood accelerated with the kind of urgency it hadn't felt in a good many months.

'A private island off the Bahamas,' he said. 'A yacht on the Mediterranean. Las Vegas. You could be in any of those places within twenty-four hours and no jogging would be required.'

'Well, now, *Mr Jones*,' she said, her voice low and deliciously smooth. 'I'd think twice before making that your new resort motto.'

Again his cheek twitched, and again he caught it just in time. He leaned in as close as he might without risk of contact. Her chin shot up, her jaw clenched, her stunning blue eyes flashed fiercely.

His skin warmed, not like a man with a serious purpose, but like a man in heat. He pulled hard at a hunk of leg hairs through his shorts.

'Then what do you think of this one? My resorts are places of private contemplation and rejuvenation, not celebrity hunting grounds. If I see one film camera, one news van, anything that looks like a long lens glinting through the underbrush—'

'Then what?' she said, sitting on enough steam to cut him off. 'You'll assume it's somehow our fault and kick us out?'

God, how he would have loved to have done just that. But negative publicity would bring as much attention to the place, and to him, if not more.

'Of course not,' he said, turning down the heat. 'I'm only concerned that your privacy remains upheld as much as I am concerned for the privacy of all of us staying on the resort grounds.'

She watched him for a few moments, her eyes flickering between his as if she was trying desperately to figure out his angle. She could try all she liked. She would never know. Her jaw clenched tighter again when she realised as much.

Then with what appeared to be an enormous amount of effort she breathed in, breathed out and smiled so sweetly his whole body clenched in anticipation.

'So no drunken nudie runs across the golf course. No demanding that everything we eat is first washed in Evian. No insisting a documentary crew follow our every move for a new reality TV show. Then we can stay?'

He lifted his eyebrows infinitesimally in the affirmative. 'That works for me.'

She lifted hers right on back. 'Truly, Mr Jones, the further away you stay from the marketing side of your businesses, the better.'

Then *she* took a step closer, this time purposely invading *his* personal space. He dug his toes into his shoes to stop himself from pulling away from the rush of her body heat colliding with his.

'This is your lucky day,' she said. 'Because I am here for a holiday, not to be caught out in my bikini for next month's *Chic* magazine gossip pages. This is my first real vacation in a little over two years, and I need it. I really do. So for the next few days I have every intention of having a fun time with my friends. Right here.'

She pointed at the dirt and looked up at him, daring him not to believe her. But even though she appeared to be the very picture of candour, he had too much at stake to care.

'And your friends—?'

'Exist entirely independently of me.'

It was not an ideal answer, but he'd done all he could do without holding her down and forcing her to give him her oath in blood. He said, 'Then I bid you have a wonderful stay for the remainder of the week.'

She nodded. And when she finally took a slow step back he felt as though a set of claws was unwinding from his shirtfront. The waft of hot summer air that slid into the new space between them felt cool. Cooler at least than the remnant reminder of her body heat.

She started to walk away, talking back to him as though expecting him to follow. 'You know, there is something you could do to make sure my stay is wonderful.'

Negotiation? This he could do with far more panache than stand-over tactics. In three long strides he was back at her side. 'What's that?'

'The mini-fridge in my room is stocked with nothing but bottled water. I'd re-e-eally like you to add some chocolate to the menu. And coffee. I'm not fussy. Instant's fine. Not you personally, of course. You still have to catch up to the group ahead to survey them as to why they're here and to wish them all a nice stay too. They are already about a kilometre ahead of you so you'll have to run your little heart out to catch them up.'

And then Zach laughed, the sound echoing

down the unoccupied tunnel ahead. Well, that was the very last thing he'd expected he might do after he'd first answered his phone that morning.

While her forehead frowned, her mouth curved into a smile. A smile with no artifice or strategy. A smile that reminded him of one she had aimed at him while he'd been standing in the shade of the gum trees awaiting his moment to strike. A smile that even from that distance he'd recognised as being loaded with pure, feminine summons.

He swallowed the last of his laughter and cleared his throat before saying, 'If you *had* read the brochure you might have discovered that this here's a health resort.'

'So that's a no?' she asked.

'Unfortunately, that's an absolute no.'

'Oh, well. I guess it never hurts to just ask nicely. Right?'

The hint in her tone—that he might have caught more flies with honey—was as subtle as a sledge-hammer, but by the time he realised it she'd lifted her feet and jogged off along the trail, her dark curls swinging, the small muscles of her thighs and calves contracting with each charmingly wonky step. If she made it back to the main house before lunch he'd be very much surprised.

Zach slid his mobile phone from his pocket, called the resort's manager and asked him to contact the wellness facilitators to send someone to escort her back to the resort.

He flicked to his inbox. No new messages. No more missed calls. His frown lines deepened so severely he wasn't sure they'd ever fully recover.

Then he turned tail and ran in the opposite direction.

He concentrated hard on the *whump whump whump* of his feet slapping against the compacted dirt. Better that than let himself get caught up in that earlier moment of unmistakable invitation. Or the lingering spark.

He pushed himself harder. Faster. Till sweat dripped into his eyes. It didn't help.

Maybe if she'd lived down to his expectations and been the ditzy powder puff he'd fully assumed she'd be, that'd be the end of that. Instead he couldn't let go of the fact that despite her reputation she'd been out there at six in the morning with no entourage, no make-up, no airs and graces, no expectation of special treatment.

A woman who hid a sharp tongue behind her soft lips. A woman whose wickedly intelligent eyes could make lesser men forget themselves.

Zach pushed till his muscles burned.

Forgetting himself was not an option. It would mean forgetting a little girl who had no one else left in the world to protect her bar him.

His daughter. A daughter only a handful of trusted people even knew about.

No one else *could* know. Not yet. Not now.

She was so very young. Her life so recently upheaved. It was all he could do to keep her safe.

To do that he had to keep her from those in the media who would carelessly make bold, loud assumptions about her future before she ever had the chance to find her footing in the present.

He knew full well how even the most innocent of comments at that age could influence how one thought about oneself. He'd met more than one person in a position of power who'd taken some kind of sick pleasure in telling a lonely orphan kid that he was nobody and would grow up to be even less. Decades on he still remembered each and every one.

He'd never forgive himself if that happened to her because of her relationship to him. And that meant keeping her identity concealed from those for whom Meg Kelly was their most prolific source of sustenance.

Eyes on the horizon, he ran until his shins ached, his heels felt like rock, and his body was drenched in thirty-five-degree sweat.

He ran until the ugly faces from his past became a blur.

He ran until it no longer mattered how long he'd now been in lock-down in this middle-of-nowhere place trying to make his round life fit into a square hole.

He ran until he was too exhausted to be concerned that he was trying to be a father when, having never had one himself, he had no real clue what the word meant.

He ran until he could no longer quite remember the exact mix of colours it took to make up the most bewitching pair of feminine blue eyes he'd ever be likely to see.

CHAPTER THREE

POST-BREAKFAST, post long hot shower, make-up done, hair coiffed, and changed into a vintage pink designer sundress—the exact kind of body armour she'd have preferred to have been wearing when meeting the likes of Zach Jones— Meg's skin still felt all zingy.

Not good zingy either. Uncomfortable zingy. Miffed zingy. It didn't take any kind of genius to know it was all *his* fault.

Standing in front of Waratah House she held the resort map in front of her, turning it left ninety degrees, then right. Rylie and Tabitha thought she was taking a nap, as they were. All the zinging made that absolutely impossible, so she'd snuck out.

'Excuse me?' she said to a passing couple. 'Do you happen to know which way's north?'

The gent pointed without even thinking. Amazing. Then his hand remained outstretched, his mouth agape even after she'd hit the bottom of the wide steps and was heading north towards the bulk of the resort, her ballet flats slapping against the stone path.

Her calves were so tight she winced with every step. The blisters on her heels stinging as if they were teaching her a lesson for not wearing high heels.

Message well and truly heard, she wasn't going to push her luck by going the week without her beloved caffeine as well. She was going to find something sweet and dark and rich and bad for her if she had to hike down the mountain, flag a passing truck and barter her shoes for some at a local milk bar.

The fact that what she craved sounded a heck of a lot like Zach Jones only made her walk faster.

It really was the strangest thing. She was used to people bending over backwards to get her endorsement, to have her wear their product, mention their charity, look sideways at whatever they were touting. Not that she ever agreed unless it was something she'd advocate even without being asked.

Zach Jones, on the other hand, had all but suggested he'd really prefer it if she and her friends would just clear off. To Las Vegas, no less. As far, far away from his resort as possible seemed to be his main point.

Far, far away from him.

Yet there was no mistaking the zing of electricity when he'd touched her. No denying the way the tension vibrating throughout him had melted away when she'd made him laugh. No confusing the way he'd taken his time getting to know her body when she'd unthinkingly told him to take his fill.

And absolutely no doubting, whatever beef he had with her, it was very *very* personal.

She was nice, for Pete's sake! She worked her backside off. She was kind to small animals. She gave everyone a fair go. Why shouldn't she expect to be treated the same way?

It was as though the guy had been given a torch and a map pointing him right towards her Achilles heel—a terminal relic of a childhood spent doing whatever it took to get even a hint that her father cared. *That* heel couldn't be soothed with antiseptic cream and Band-Aids.

'Grrrrr!' she shouted to the wide-open sky.

When she glanced down a group of guests in matching pale green Juniper Falls Rainforest

Retreat brand tracksuits doing t'ai chi on a mound of grass were looking her way. From nowhere one of them pulled out a mobile phone and took her picture.

It shouldn't have surprised her. It happened every day.

But being on holiday she'd been silly enough to let down her guard. Enter one tall, dark, handsome businessman and her usual cool had gone up in smoke. She had to pull herself together quick smart.

The kind of attention that followed a down-and-out It Girl was far worse than for one who went about her business with cheerful grace. Not only would that adversely effect the family— God, the horror of ever being on the end of *that* conversation—the one part of her life that was truly her own, her one beautiful unspoiled secret, her time volunteering at the Valley Women's Shelter, would be gone.

Zach Jones was a very lucky man. They both seemed to want the same thing—for this next week to be drama free. She'd just have to keep Rylie away from Zach, Zach away from Tabitha, and herself aware of the whereabouts of all three so that she could relax. Ha!

Meg picked what felt, and tasted, like birdseed from between her teeth. If she was looking for a reason to really not like him she realised she had one. It was his fault her belly was full of nothing bar raw oats bathed in pale soy milk, bite-sized chunks of some mysterious organic fruit and a green drink so thick and speckled it looked as if it had been scooped out of primordial ooze.

She needed chocolate. And coffee. And bad.

She pulled herself together and waved cheerfully to the group. 'Good morning, all!' she called out.

A few people waved back. Several more mobile phones went click-click before the wellness facilitator clicked his fingers loudly and reminded them it would be best to leave their mobiles in their rooms while working towards a mind free of distractions.

Then she skipped up the path as fast as her sore muscles and flat shoes would carry her.

Skirting the eastern edge of the resort grounds, Meg passed an array of cosy guest bungalows peeking out of the edge of the rainforest. One was completely covered in creepers, the next had been built on stilts above a bounty of ferns. Another bungalow had obviously been built around an existing tree. Each was more charming than the last. But unless the ginger-bread house from Hansel and Gretel appeared next she wasn't slowing.

Coffee, chocolate, coffee, chocolate, chugged in her mind along with each step. The large out-buildings she'd seen on the map had to contain food for the staff. Food she planned on sweet-talking her way.

A handful of minutes later Meg's foot slipped a tad and she realised she was no longer on the white stone path that guided guests everywhere around the resort. Thicker, less perfectly trimmed grass slid underfoot. And the rainforest encroached more tightly on all sides.

She was so hot she was puffing like a steam train. Her brow, her underarms, and the spots behind her knees were slick with sweat. And she realised she had no idea where she was.

A gap appeared in a moss-covered rock wall peeking through the underbrush ahead. A faint path had been beaten into the grass at her feet by regular footsteps so she did all she could think to do and followed.

Barely a dozen steps beyond she found herself in a garden—tiered, and lush with wildflowers in the most amazing, vibrant colours the likes of which she'd never seen.

And beyond that…

A house. But what a simplistic word for the structure crouching silently before her.

A large octagonal structure had been built tight against a rising embankment. It had a pointed thatched roof and more windows than walls. Rope bridges led from the yard up to the front door, and then again from the front door to several separate enclosed rooms scattered haphazardly about the hill face. A meandering creek ran beneath, and a wide deck wound around the lot.

Her brother Cameron, the engineer, would go absolutely nuts for the place. She just stood there and admired the heck out of it, not noticing a rhythmic squeaking sound until it stopped.

She glanced towards the space where the noise had been to find a young girl staring at her. Her small hands were wrapped about the handles of a swing, legs locked straight as she used her feet as a brake to halt her progress through the air. Her long dark hair was pulled back by a yellow headband and flickering in the light breeze.

She must have been six or seven, around the

same age as her brother, Brendan's eldest girl, but with her loose footless pink tights and pink floral shoes browned by mud she was deliciously messy where Violet and Olivia were always picture perfect. As always happened when unexpected thoughts of her favourite girls came to her, Meg's heart gave an anguished little skip. The skip was always part love, part fear.

Right now they were such innocents. But without their mum around any more to give them balance they were becoming deeply indoctrinated into the Kelly way of life. Meg's greatest hope was that somehow, some way, they would have a choice in how their lives turned out that she'd never had. And that being the granddaughters of Quinn Kelly didn't eventually smother those sweet natures for good.

'Hi,' the young girl said, and Meg blinked to find herself on the other end of a long, flat, intense stare.

Shoving her concern for the next generation deep down inside where it couldn't shake her, she took a deep breath and smiled.

'Hiya,' Meg said.

The little girl shuffled her feet through the muddy ground till her legs dangled beneath the rubber swing and her hands slid down the chains. 'I'm Ruby,' she said.

'It's a great pleasure to meet you, Ruby. I'm Meg.'

Ruby's mouth twisted as she fearlessly stared Meg down. Meg bit back a smile. She was being sized up.

When Ruby came back with 'I'm seven and a half,' she knew she'd come up to muster.

'Seven and a *half*? That's impressive. I'm a tad older than seven too, and I'm lost. Any chance you can read a map?' Meg waved hers back and forth.

Ruby merely blinked at Meg, giving her time to work out the answer for herself.

'No?' Meg slowly tucked the map back into the front of her dress. 'Fair enough. I couldn't read a map at seven any better than I can now.'

From nowhere her father's voice came to her. *How simple do you have to be not to be able to tell up from down, girl?* She placed a hand over her thudding heart and begged it to calm down.

And for good measure found herself, once again, cursing Zach Jones.

It was *his* fault the resort menu contained nothing remotely normal, thus sending her out into the blinding heat in search of sustenance. It was his indifference that had made her crave comfort chocolate in the first place. He'd started the chain reaction that was bringing up long-since-buried feelings now fanning out like a swarm of angry bees whose nest had been poked with a really big stick. She had no idea what one was meant to do to mollify angry bees, but as for her...

Her hand fell limply to her side as she sniffed the air. 'What's that heavenly smell?'

'Chocolate muffins,' Ruby said. 'My nanny cooks them. I don't like muffins much.'

'You don't like muffins? And you call yourself a seven-year-old!'

Ruby's mouth quirked ever so slightly. Her eyes narrowed for several moments before claiming, 'My dad likes them so I get her to make them for him so he can take them to work and I just eat the leftovers.'

'I see.' Meg licked her lips and looked to where the smell was coming from. The sight of that dramatic dwelling reposing peacefully, silently, privately within the forest had her letting out a long, slow, soothing breath. 'That is one amazing house you have there, Miss Ruby.'

'It's not mine. It's my dad's.'

Meg's eyes swerved back to Ruby to find her toes had slunk together, her chin had dropped and her whole body had curled into itself.

With Violet and Olivia firmly in mind, Meg made sure she had the girl's full attention before she said, 'You have your own bedroom, right? Fridge privileges. Access to the TV remote.'

Ruby thought a moment, then nodded.

'Then that means it's your house too.'

Ruby looked up at the house thoughtfully. Meg did the same, wondering how close the kitchen might be. And if she might be able to outrun the nanny. Then it occurred to her—it was mid-morning on a weekday.

She spun back to Ruby. 'Shouldn't you be at school?'

Ruby's mouth puckered into a defiant little pout and her chin lifted a good two inches. 'I have a sore throat.'

Meg's eyes widened as she let her gaze run over the swings, and the Frisbee resting next to them on the lawn. If the kid had a sore throat she'd give up chocolate for ever. Still, Ruby's rebellious streak hooked her. Maybe the kid was more like her than her nieces after all.

'A sore throat, you say.'

Ruby nodded, then added a couple of terrible attempts at a sniffle for good measure.

'You know what?' Meg said, tapping her chin with her finger. 'When I was seven and a half and got a sore throat, I found the days went so much quicker if I actually went to school. I know, sounds crazy, huh? But truly, by the time I got home I'd forgotten all about my throat and why it felt sore in the first place!'

Ruby eyed her down a moment before admitting, 'It has been a very long day.'

Meg laughed before hiding it behind a cough. 'Okay, now the lesson's done, you didn't hear this from me. But if I did stay home from school I let my mum smother me with ice cream and tuck me up with blankets on the couch while I watched daytime TV. That way she knew where I was and I felt better at the same time.'

Ruby blinked, but her expression didn't change a jot as she said, 'My mum's gone.'

'Gone?'

Ruby nodded.

And then Meg knew from the look in the kid's eyes 'gone' meant she wasn't coming back. She took a step towards the small girl and knelt down in front of her. 'Oh, sweetheart.'

Why God let some kids grow up so quick she'd never understand. Now she *did* understand.

Now she did understand the sore throat all too well. Classic 'get Daddy's attention' manoeuvre. But come on, what kind of father didn't give his little girl attention when he was the only thing she had left?

The guy obviously had no idea Ruby's attention-seeking behaviour could escalate so fast and in ways more dangerous than he would ever believe possible. Then again, maybe he knew, and maybe he simply didn't care.

Meg nibbled at her bottom lip as she glanced back to the house. This wasn't some shell-shocked urchin at the Valley Women's Shelter happy to have a pair of warm, comforting arms around her no matter who they belonged to; this was a spunky, healthy-looking kid, surrounded by toys in a multimillion-dollar home. A home Meg was currently trespassing on.

She stood and took three steps back. 'Sweetheart, I'm sure your dad knows where the ice cream is kept too.'

This time at mention of her father Ruby sat bolt upright. 'He's busy. He has an important job with lots of people counting on him. He works all week while I'm at boarding school and only comes home weekends when I come home. But I could go get him now if I really wanted to. To tell him about my throat and all. I just don't want to.'

'He works at the resort?' Meg asked. The imaginary huffy bees were back, swirling about her head with increased volume and intensity.

Ruby said, 'He owns this one and lots more all over the world. He's going to take me on his plane and show me all the others one day. He promised. Just not right now. I have school when I'm not sick. But some day.'

Meg heard not much more than *blah blah blah* as she stared down at Ruby. The dark hair, the wary dark eyes, the natural intensity that even a supposed sore throat couldn't dampen. Once she saw the similarity it was so blaringly obvious she felt like a fool for not noticing it sooner.

Her blood pounded so loudly in her ears her voice came out rather more flat than she would have liked when she said, 'You're Zach Jones's daughter.'

Ruby's eyes flashed with the first spark of real enthusiasm and Meg knew she was right even before the girl said, 'Do you know my dad?'

Did she know Ruby's dad? Not a jot.

Zach Jones had a daughter. A daughter whose mother was gone.

Hang on, he had a daughter with a mother Rylie hadn't even known about and Rylie was such a proficient muckraker she probably already knew who really killed JFK and was awaiting the right moment to reveal all.

He had a daughter who was at home sick, or pretending to be. And the only reason Meg saw that Ruby might not want him to know was in case he only proved to her he didn't give enough of a damn about her to care.

Meg's fists clenched at her sides, a scene to end all scenes threatening to erupt from within.

She'd seen it time and again listening to stories told by countless women at the Valley Women's Shelter—men, focused on themselves, on their work, on their local bar, who blithely disregarded their children's need to be loved. Hell, she'd seen it with her own eyes. She'd felt it with her own heart.

Thankfully she'd taken measures in order for it never to happen to a child of her own. Conclusive measures. Unfortunately none of that helped her from feeling threadbare watching neglect happen to someone else.

Her gaze cleared to find Ruby was still looking up at her with her father's uncompromising gaze. And while she knew the second she'd found out who Ruby's dad was she should have walked away, she still said, 'As a matter of fact I met your dad only this morning.'

'What did he say about me?'

What did he say? Well, he was actually pretty darned arrogant. He said back off. He said lie low. He said...

Meg's fingers unfurled from her palms. He'd said he was determined that the privacy of *all* staying at the resort remained upheld.

He was talking about himself. Him and his anonymous daughter. A daughter who no longer had a mum.

She closed her eyes to hide the mortification that she had beamed her flirty little smile at a man who'd lost his...wife? Lover? Ex? What did it matter? He'd lost the mother of his child.

Far too many adult-only concepts to share with a seven-and-a-half-year-old.

Instead, she gathered up her cheeriest smile and said, 'I'm such a yabberer I'm sure I didn't let him get a word in edgewise. If he'd had the chance I'm sure he would have said plenty. How could he not? A daughter who lets her nanny make chocolate muffins even though she doesn't like them but her dad does. You're a gem!'

Ruby tried for a smile herself, but her slight shoulders drooped, giving her away. Meg's heart twitched far harder than she liked for the little girl. She couldn't let herself get attached. There was no way it could end well.

She opened her mouth to say her long-overdue goodbye when something out of the corner of Ruby's eye had her springing from the rubber seat like a jack-in-the-box. 'I have to go!' she shrieked.

Meg glanced up at one of the small detached rooms to see the wooden blinds snap shut. A flash of silver hair, not dark and curling, meant her heart didn't stop, but it certainly thundered hard enough for her to know she'd pushed her luck far enough.

Ruby took a last quick step forward. 'You won't tell my dad I was on the swings, will you?'

Meg laughed. 'Not a chance.' Probably best for her continued health if she didn't bring any of this up with the man at all.

'I won't tell him you were here either, okay?' Ruby said.

Meg laughed again. 'That would be fine with me.'

Ruby gave a quick, sweet, girlish wave, and then ran off towards the flickering blinds and freshly baked chocolate muffins, her long hair swinging behind her as she skipped up onto the longest rope bridge and was soon consumed by her astonishing home.

Meg spun on her heel and vamoosed back along the makeshift path, through the gap in the rock wall and out onto the manicured grass of the resort proper. She headed in a direction she thought was probably south. If it wasn't, someone would put her to rights soon enough.

Her breaths shook as the adrenalin she'd held at bay finally spilled over.

What if when she'd smiled her flirty little smile Zach had smiled back? What if when she'd made him laugh she'd let herself join in? What if when he'd touched her he'd liked it too much to let her go? What if things had happened between them and she'd gone in deep before he'd decided to let her know that he had a little girl?

It had taken her nearly thirty years to get to the point where she finally felt as if she had a handle on her celebrity. There was no way she would knowingly expose a child to it.

It gave her the perfect excuse to wash her hands of the whole situation, get on with her holiday, and forget the lot of them even existed.

Damn him! He'd started this. By including her in his convoluted duplicity he'd made her a part of it. And having met Ruby, talked to her, looked in her eyes and seen herself mirrored right on back she couldn't let it go.

He might not know it yet, but Zach Jones needed her help. And for the sake of a bright, sweet, adoring little girl who needed him it appeared he was going to get it.

CHAPTER FOUR

MEG rushed to find the Wellness Building to meet the girls for that day's internal reflection class. While they tried to locate their *chi* she had every intention of pretending to meditate while dreaming up the perfect way to broach the subject of his daughter when she bumped into Zach Jones again.

With an objective in sight, despite the flat shoes and sore muscles, she had a decided spring in her step when she rounded a thick bank of head-high reeds.

Until she came face to face with a human rear-end.

Male it was, bent from the waist. Knee-length khaki cargo shorts sculpted a magnificent rear belonging to a tanned, solid man fiddling with something in a cooler. And even though she couldn't see the colour of his hair, or the breadth of his shoulders, or the shape of his arms or any of the other bits that seemed to be permanently imprinted on her mind, she knew it was Zach Jones.

Her heart hammered in her ears, and her palms grew slick. She and *chi* might well be incompatible, but there was simply no denying this man's life force was so potent it radiated from his very pores.

He stood, stretching out his limbs. Sunlight glistened lovingly off the expanse of perfectly sculpted muscle, as he was naked from the hips up.

His large hand was wrapped about a condensation-covered bottle of beer. He tilted his head and downed half the bottle in one slow go.

Meg's gaze remained stuck on the muscles of his throat, pulsing with each large swallow, with each heavy thud of her heart against her ribs.

Once done, he let out a deep, satisfied *ah-h-h* that seemed to echo across the distance between them, then he wiped a tanned, muscular arm across his forehead. He might as well have been sliding that arm around her waist for the reaction that shuddered through her.

'I must have done something horrible in a previous life to deserve this,' she murmured beneath her breath.

As though the slow, hot, summer air carried her

whisper to him too, he stilled. Then his body twisted at the waist until his eyes locked on hers.

The colour of expensive dark chocolate. The colour of strong espresso coffee. Right there in those eyes she saw everything she hungered for. Unfortunately half a second later she also caught the full force of his disapproval simmering beneath the urbane surface.

Then she remembered why.

She'd been seriously kidding herself in thinking she might be able to convince this man he needed her help. If he had any idea she'd stumbled upon his daughter he'd probably already decided which exact spot in the surrounding rainforest would be the best place to hide her cold dead body.

Her tongue darted nervously out to slide along the chip in her tooth. His gaze slipped to watch the movement, his dark eyes turning almost black.

She was pinned to the spot, unable to move as he reached out and grabbed a T-shirt from beside the cooler, then slid it on in that particular way men did such things. The soft cotton casually sculpted his muscles and if at all possible he was even more intimidating fully dressed.

When Meg finally found her voice again she said, 'This isn't the way to the Wellness Building.'

'No,' Zach said, his deep voice rumbling through her very bones. 'It's not.'

She frowned. 'Where am I exactly?'

'The lake.'

'There's a lake?' she asked. 'Wow, I really don't know how to read a map.'

'I'll give you a hint,' he said. 'It's the big blue bit at the bottom with "Lake" written in the middle of it.'

Her cheeks, if possible, grew warmer still. Her voice was dripping with sarcasm when she said, 'Thanks. You are as ever the gracious host.'

'Was there something else you wanted from me?'

'Look, you can relax. I really didn't mean to invade your beer-drinking time. Stumbling upon you was pure accident.'

'Obviously fifty acres isn't quite as much room as it sounds.'

'So it seems.' She began to back away. 'If you'd be so kind as to point the way—'

'I was just about to head out for a row. Want to join me?'

Her feet stumbled to a halt. 'Excuse me?'

While his eyes seemed to skim the view behind her in search of prying eyes, he waved an inviting arm towards the end of a jetty that was shrouded in tall reeds wilting in the heavy heat. 'After many months of wrangling with a guy on the end of the phone, my old row boat has finally arrived from a storage lock-up in Sydney and I'm taking her for a spin. You game?'

Game for *what*? Concrete shoes? A speedboat containing Rylie, Tabitha and their ready packed bags? Or worse, an intimate boat ride with a man whom she couldn't want; who didn't much like her; who still managed to give her uncontrollable stomach flutters that only grew more intense with each and every meeting.

A whimper from her self-preservation instincts had her licking her lips in preparation to say thanks but no thanks, until her mind filled with the memory of a sprawling house in the forest, and a lonesome, brown-haired girl with his eyes.

The most decisive reason for her to walk away was the one reason she finally could not.

'Sounds lovely,' she said with the distant but polite smile she used on those who shamelessly accosted her in the fruit and veg section of her local supermarket asking for an autograph.

His eyes darkened all the more, as though he knew it too, but he still slipped the strap of the cooler over his shoulder, then turned and walked towards the lake.

Meg did all she could do and followed.

Once she rounded the thick reeds she saw a small, fat, wooden boat bobbing merrily on what turned out to be a massive lake. The boat's mission-brown paint was faded, the red floor was scratched and fatigued, and the benches had seats worn into them from a lifetime of accommodating bottoms.

It was ancient and imperfect. So not the kind of sea-faring-type vessel any of the men in her family would be caught dead in. She loved it.

She crouched down and ran a hand over the stern to find it smooth and soft. 'She's really yours?'

She glanced up to find Zach watching the rhythmic movement of her hand. She curled her fingers into her palms and pushed herself back to standing.

He had to bend past her to unhook the rope from the jetty. She leant back to give him room, but not far enough not to catch his scent. She breathed it in. She couldn't help herself. It was drinkable.

He wound the rope around his hand and elbow, muscles contracting with every easy swing.

'*Marilyn*'s been a faithful companion since I was about eighteen.'

'*Marilyn*? Are you serious?'

His cheek twitched into one of those almost smiles that gave a girl unfair hope there might be more to come. 'She came with the name.'

'Sure she did. You haven't thought to trade her in for a fancy schmancy yacht with all the trimmings?'

'I've got one of those too. A hundred footer moored off St Barts right now.'

'The *Norma Jean?*'

And there it was. The holy grail. His mouth tilted into a slow smile complete with brackets that arced around his beautiful mouth and creases fanning out from the edges of his delicious dark eyes. Boy, were they worth the wait.

'I called her *Lauren.*'

'Bacall?'

'It was my mother's name.'

Of course it was. Meg looked down at her shoes instead of into those too discerning eyes. 'And a tad extravagant to use for a paddle about the lake.'

'Just a tad.'

She glanced up, and for a brief moment Meg swore she saw a glint warm his dark eyes before it was gone. He ought not to bandy those about unless he meant them. It was hard for a girl not to get ideas.

Zach threw the rope into the boat, then held out a hand. Unless she wanted him to know her mouth turned dry at the thought of him touching her again, she had no choice but to take it.

A slide of natural warmth so out of sync with the constant cool in his eyes leapt from his hand to hers. She gripped on tight as she stepped into the wobbly vessel, but the second she had her backside planted on a bench she let go.

He stepped in after her and tossed her a cosy, red-checked, woollen blanket. It was too soft to be freshly washed, too fluffy to be new. It was the kind of thing a man might keep at the end of his bed, or the back of his couch. She imagined it covering his long bare legs as he lay back—

She cleared her throat. 'What exactly am I meant to do with this?'

'Slide it beneath your backside or you'll get splinters,' he ordered. 'That or that dress of yours will be shredded.'

Of course. So what if it carried a faint lingering scent of him—he hadn't given it to her as some sort of come-on. It was near forty degrees out! She lifted her backside and planted it back on the folded blanket.

'This too,' he demanded, throwing her a soft khaki fisherman's hat, which was frayed to the point of falling apart.

She gripped the hat between tightly coiled fists. All that commanding was beginning to get on her nerves. Her voice was sugary sweet as she asked, 'And where, pray tell, am I supposed to put this?'

His hands stilled. He glanced up. The smile hovered; the glint loomed.

And it hit her as if the lake had suddenly thrown up a tidal wave over the boat. Zach Jones might prefer her to be far, far away, but a certain part of him took a purely masculine pleasure in having her close by.

She licked her suddenly dry lips and blinked up at him. The smile faded and the glint disappeared without a trace.

'Just stick the thing on your head, will you?' he growled.

'Aye aye, Captain,' she muttered.

The hat smelled like the sea and fitted over her head like velvet. Atop her sateen cocktail dress it must have looked a treat.

He slapped an old cap atop his curls, shoved a

foot against the jetty, pushing them off before easing down onto his own bench.

She tucked her knees tight together and pretended to pay attention to the ripples fanning out through the flat silver water, and not how close his knees were to hers, as he picked up the oars and pushed them effortlessly out into the lake.

Within seconds the wilting reeds shielded them from the rest of the world and they were alone.

The sun beat down upon Meg's back, making her glad of the hat. The soft swish of the displaced water created a slow, even rhythm. And as Zach built up a sweat every breath in gave her a fresh taste of his clean cotton clothes and some indefinable heat that was purely him.

Like this, all easy silence, all effortless masculinity, it was hard not to imagine he might be exactly the kind of guy she could happily spend oodles of time with. A beautiful sailor who slept in late, didn't believe in making plans, and just went with the flow.

It was hard to believe he owned and ran a huge multinational business that no doubt took long hours away from home. That took the kind of relentless ambition that meant everything else in life came a distant second. Family included.

Her brother Brendan was trying to do the single father thing. Running the Kelly Investment Group and raising two young daughters. And though she'd never tell him so to his face she knew in her heart the half of his life he was letting slip from his grasp was his girls.

Zach's eyes slid from some point over her shoulder to find hers. His dark, deep, unfathomable eyes. Their gazes held a beat longer than polite. Two beats. She held on, trying to sense regret, bereavement, concern for his little girl. All she got for her trouble was the sense that *she* was getting more entangled by the second.

She breathed in slow and deep through her nose. Could she ask him about Ruby now? Should she? Would she be doing it to be helpful? Or did she know he'd react badly, so she could use Ruby to save herself from feeling the way she did when he looked at her like that?

In the end she lost her nerve and said, 'So you've been on two runs today and now rowing. I feel tired just thinking about it.'

He went back to staring at the water. 'I like to be on the move. Eyes forward, nothing but the wind and the sun to keep me company. It clears the head. If you don't run or do yoga, what do you do?'

Mmm. She had proven that day that exercise made her hurt, and wobble and crave sugar.

'To clear my head?' she said. 'Disco music.'

One dark eyebrow rose and his hot, dark gaze slid back to hers. 'Disco?'

'Blaring from my iPod directly into my ears. Ten seconds into any Donna Summer or Leo Sayer song and the rest of the world fades away.'

They said music soothed the savage breast, and so it had done for her, many a time in her teens when she might have otherwise given in to mounting frustration with her life and done something she'd later regret. Ultimately disco could only soothe so much hurt.

'Even if you're lying on the couch your feet can't help but bop. Your head clears of everything but the music. It's kind of like exercise only more relaxed.'

When he merely blinked at her she gave him her 'greeting line' smile, with a full showing of teeth, twinkling eyes and dimples. 'You're going to give it a go the moment you go home, I can tell.'

And while most people, even members of her own family, could no longer tell when she was 'on' and when she was just being herself, the slow rise of the corner of his mouth told her she hadn't fooled him for a nanosecond.

How did he *do* that? How was *he* able to see straight through her? Again she felt exposed, as if she'd walked into a ballroom with her dress tucked into the back of her undies.

He stopped rowing and the boat's sleek glide slowed so that she rocked forward on her seat.

'I'm game. I'll give disco a go,' he said. 'But only if you take the oars right now.'

She imagined splinters. She imagined aches in even more as yet undiscovered muscles. She imagined her hands brushing against his as she took him up on his offer.

'I'll pass.'

Zach laughed. The column of his throat moved sexily beneath the sound. It faded all too soon in the wide-open space, and his eyes once again grew so dark they drew her in while they pushed her away.

She wondered if he could see the same impulse in hers.

She wondered what might happen if they both pulled at the exact same time.

His large hands curled back around the worn old wooden sticks and he slid the oars back into the water, pushing off with such grace and power Meg was sent to the back of her seat. Smart move. Pushing was much more sensible.

A cooling wind fluttered past her warm face. Streaks of gold dappled the rippling silver water where the sun burst through fluffy white clouds. The edges of the lake were completely obscured by the thick, green rainforest spilling into water.

Time stretched and contracted. She realised she had no idea how long she'd been gone. Or why he'd taken her out there onto the lake alone in the first place.

'I don't mean to say this isn't entirely pleasant, and so generous for the owner to give me such a personal tour of the blue bit on the bottom of the map,' she said, 'but how long were you planning for this outing to be?'

'We can turn back now if you're getting too hot.'

Only then did she even consider that, while he looked like a sun god, she must have looked an utter treat—in his floppy hat, her hair plastered to her face after her hike to the end of the resort and back, her Irish skin pink as a rose.

She wasn't used to feeling so discomposed; her voice was rather sharper than she intended when she said, 'I'm only thinking of you.'

He raised a solitary eyebrow. 'You're thinking of *me*?'

More than you know. 'Many a poor fellow has ended up reportedly engaged to me after spending far less time in my company, and I have been made quite aware how highly you regard your privacy.'

'I do at that. Which is why I have not left any stones unturned in an effort to protect it. You needn't worry on my behalf.'

'I need not?'

His cheek twitched. 'The forest has eyes. Trackers flushing out the perimeter in search of poachers.'

'Poachers? There's nothing for miles bar a few birds, some lizards and a bunch of resort guests in matching tracksuits.'

And then she got it. Her jaw dropped. 'Are you saying you have people posted about the place to ward off anyone turning up here to take a photo of *me*?'

'We both know it's not you I am trying to protect.'

His gaze was steady. Not a hint of humour. Not a hint of a smile. While Meg's cheeks grew so flushed even her teeth began to feel hot.

Ruby.

Of course. This, *all* this, the thoughtful blanket, the helpful hat, the beautiful scenery, the long brooding looks, were all about his daughter.

He wasn't thinking of her at all.

Zach couldn't remember a time in recent history when he'd been so furious. And mostly with himself. For since the moment he'd turned and found Meg Kelly standing on the jetty in her completely inappropriate pink party dress he'd thought of nothing but her.

He hadn't been exaggerating when saying he rowed to clear his head. The sport had saved him from being just another scrappy, angry kid with a chip on his shoulder and had turned him into a man who knew how to focus, create goals and push himself to the absolute limits to achieve them.

He needed a clear head now more than ever. The St Barts government was still playing hardball with the building inspections on his latest site. It was balanced on a knife's edge with his only achievable contributions controlled by the whims of local telephone operators. Because he was trying to run a multimillion-dollar international business from a laptop and a three-room bungalow in the middle of nowhere.

For Ruby. So she could be in a familiar place. So she knew her world was solid and secure. Ruby, who, despite his best intentions, had been compromised.

When Ruby's nanny had called to say she'd had a visitor he'd almost popped a gasket, believing the woman had blatantly gone out of her way to punish him for not bowing and scraping and rolling out the red carpet. When he'd calmed down he'd realised the only way she could possibly have found Ruby in such a short amount of time was by stumbling out of the forest in one great cosmic accident.

Either way, rather than putting himself as far from Meg Kelly as he could, he now had no choice but to be on her like a rash until the day she left.

So as far as he was concerned Meg Kelly could sit out in the hot summer sun all day, her knees knocked in chagrin, her ridiculous dress getting splattered with water spray, his dilapidated green hat sloping low over her face, leaving only her down-turned mouth in sight.

Except of course it had only given him enough time studying that mouth of hers to know it was all natural. And so was she. Her skin was as pale as it ought to have been with a smattering of freckles across her nose make-up couldn't, and needn't, hide. Her curves were as God gave her with apparently a little bit of help from occasional disco. The woman was pure, wholesome femininity and irrepressible audacity and ingenuous sex appeal.

He was beginning to wonder if she'd been sent to test him. After dedicating his entire adulthood to purely selfish pursuits, was he really man enough, strong enough, self-sacrificing enough to resist her? To put aside his needs for the needs of one girl?

When Ruby had landed on his doorstep, her small hand held tight in the hand of a weary-looking social worker, she was alone in the world, orphaned and in shock. She'd been on the verge of replaying his cold, lonely, disjointed past through her future. There was no way he could let that happen to her and look himself in the mirror ever again.

But had he been the right person to save her?

He let out a long, hard breath and realised that beneath the brim of his hat Meg was watching him. Those sharp blue eyes constantly calculating.

He should have known better than to believe what he'd heard about her in the press. Assuming she'd be a lightweight adversary had been a huge tactical error. It served him right that it had come back to bite him where he'd feel it most.

The ante had been upped. It was time he showed his cards.

He used the oar on the starboard side to head the boat back to civilisation. 'So, Ms Kelly.'

'Yes, Zach.'

'What possessed you to trespass inside my private residence this morning?'

'Your yard,' she shot back as though the words had been waiting to explode from inside her. 'I never went any farther than the very, *very* edge of your yard. Once I knew it was yours I was out of there.'

'I don't give a flying fig if you were sitting on my rooftop. What the hell were you doing so far from the boundary of the resort that we now have to have this conversation?'

'Please,' she scoffed, her voice cool, her eyes electric. 'It was an honest mistake. It's not like there's a ten-foot-high electric fence separating the two.'

'There's a rock wall and a whopping great big gate!'

'A gate? Not today there wasn't.'

Zach swore beneath his breath. That meant Ruby had been out again. What would it take to make the kid understand that it was for her own safety that she stay put and not gallivant about the resort? Hell, all he wanted was to keep her clear of those who would have her believe that because her childhood had not been perfect she was damaged from the start. He was fast running out of ideas.

The boat rocked beneath them as he pulled harder on the oars. Meg's hands whipped out to the sides and held on tight.

'For a woman who thinks lying on the couch listening to disco is a form of exercise, the hike to my place makes no sense.'

'Fine,' she said, throwing her arms in the air, rocking the boat so that he had to steady them with some fancy flicking of the oars. 'I was casing the grounds in search of chocolate.'

'Give me a break—'

She lifted her chin as though a haughty bearing could make the words seem less undignified. 'I warned you. Caffeine is a staple in my diet. And

I never expected to have to go cold turkey this week. So actually it was all your fault that I ended up there.'

His laughter again came from nowhere and again surprised the hell out of him. And a few local birds that screeched as they scattered from the treetops nearby.

Gorgeous, plainspoken and stimulating. Delilah herself couldn't possibly have been more tempting.

Thankfully he'd long since proven himself invulnerable to the lure of apparently easy promise. He'd learnt early on not to trust the feeling as far as he could throw it. So long as the bright, breezy, easy warmth in this corner of the world hadn't rotted away his indoctrinated dubiousness he'd be just fine.

CHAPTER FIVE

'ZACH,' Meg said, and by the tone in her voice Zach wasn't sure he'd be keen on what came next.

'Okay,' she continued, 'I was hoping to get around to the fact more gracefully, but since I have no idea how long you intend to keep me hostage out there let's get to the point. You have a seven-year-old daughter named Ruby who, it seems, nobody knows anything about. There. Now it's out there. So what do we do from here?'

Zach slapped an oar into the water at such a rough angle it covered them both in wet spray. 'Don't get cute, Ms Kelly.'

She waved a hand across her face as though swatting away a fly. 'Stop being so formal. I've practically been in your house, I'm on first-name basis with your daughter, and you've seen me in this hat. Call me Meg.'

Through gritted teeth he said, 'If you saw

yourself in that hat you wouldn't be half so concerned.'

She blinked up at him. Hell. So much for proving himself invulnerable. Now she was sitting there gawping at him as if he'd outright told her how lovely she was.

'Okay then, *Meg*,' he said, his voice coarse, 'if formalities are now to be tossed aside, then I'll be blunt.'

'All this time you were being polite?' Something in his expression must have made her catch her tongue. She mimed zipping her mouth shut. That mouth…

'I want you to tell me in avid detail about every second you spent in my daughter's company. And don't miss a moment.'

She blinked at him. 'Relax, Zach. We didn't talk about sex, drugs or rock and roll if that's what you're worried about.'

Sex? *Drugs*? He ran a hard hand over the back of his neck, which suddenly felt as if it were on fire.

'She's seven, for Pete's sake. The *High School Musical* soundtracks are as extreme as her rock and roll tastes go.'

She hooked a thumbnail between her teeth and looked up at him from beneath her thick dark lashes. His gut sank so fast he pressed his feet into the bottom of the boat. What wasn't she telling him?

By age seven he'd already stolen his first pack of cigarettes, he'd kissed his first girl, he'd been hit so hard by one so-called parent he'd gone to school with a hand print bruised into the back of his thigh.

He'd known Ruby barely seven months. There was a fair chance he didn't know his kid at all. His voice was unsteady as he said, 'Ruby's situation is…sensitive, therefore it's imperative that I'm kept informed.'

'Just informed? Not present? Not available? Not her first port of call?'

The riddles finally became too much and his frustration got the better of him. 'Meg, I'm her father. If I don't know everything I'm going to imagine the worst and then go quietly out of my mind.'

A smile spread across her face—a radiant thing that made the sun beaming down upon the lake pale into insignificance. 'Well, now, that's just about the best news I've heard all day.'

He shook his head, hoping for clarity. None came. 'What on earth are you talking about?'

'The fact that you *want* to know is a good thing. A wonderful thing.'

She even reached out and patted his hand, as if he'd accidentally given her the password to a treasure he didn't even know existed. It wasn't the kind of touch he wanted from her.

'Then hurry up and tell me.'

'I'm not going to break her confidence that way. Come on.'

Zach glanced at the clouds above Meg's head. Who in heaven had he screwed over to be made to live through this day?

'Trust me,' she said, 'every girl needs her mysteries, especially from her father. It's character building. So long as she knows you care enough to *want* to get to the bottom of them, to the bottom of her, then you have nothing to worry about.'

Nothing to worry about.

She couldn't possibly have known that of all the four-word combinations that could placate his exasperation with her, that was it.

Still, time and again in his life, just when he'd begun to get comfortable, that was when fate pulled the rug out from under him. Foster families he'd felt as if he'd connected with had let him go. His knee had given way a week before the World Championships and he'd been forced into early retirement from competitive rowing. The momentum and success of his resorts had him finally living his life in such an easy groove, then along came Ruby.

He couldn't accept things could be that simple. That certain. There always had to be a catch. What was he missing?

Aw, hell.

'What did you tell your friends about her?'

'Nothing!'

'One thing I've learned from Ruby is that girls like to talk to their friends. A lot. About everything.'

'We do. A lot. But here's the thing—I have the feeling the reason you accosted me this morning was tied up with wanting to keep your private life separate from your working life. And Ruby would naturally be a big part of that. Right?'

He didn't say no.

'If so, believe me, I'm not going to be the one to out her. She's your only secret kid, I assume. Lone heiress to all this?'

Zach still didn't say no.

Meg said, 'Well, I know better than anyone

what she'd have in store for her if the world found out. I wouldn't bring it on any young girl.'

Crazy as it sounded, he believed her. 'Thank you.'

'My absolute pleasure.' She smiled. That lush mouth. Those stunning blue eyes. He had a sudden need to know what they'd look like bathed in moonlight as she spilled apart in sheer pleasure in his arms.

He hooked the oars back into their loops and aimed for the resort, and every stroke felt as if he were pulling them through wet cement. 'You seem perfectly comfortable in the limelight. Are you implying that's all an act?'

'Oh, no, did that just sound all woe is me? Please tell me it didn't. Don't get me wrong, I know I'm blessed in, oh, so many ways. And I am perfectly at peace with the contradictions that came with being notable. But I wasn't born twenty-nine and world wise. You haven't heard the story of my glittering debut?'

Zach shook his head.

'Well, here it is. I must have been three at the most. My father was giving a press conference to announce that he'd bought the George Street building in which the Kelly Investment Group was housed and was renaming the thing Kelly Tower. Mum had taken us all along to see him in action. All trussed up for the big occasion, my hair in ringlets, wearing my favourite navy velvet dress and black patent shoes, I got away from her. I made it to the podium mid-announcement, clambered up, tugged on my father's trousers and whistled through the gap in my front teeth that I needed to tinkle. Needless to say my father wasn't all that impressed at being upstaged, but the press ate it up. I haven't been able to tinkle since without the world knowing about it.'

Her smile was cheeky, but as he seemed able to do with this woman from the outset he felt the undercurrent stronger than the surface words. On the outside it was a cute story about a girl and her dad. For her it was a story of innocence lost.

He pulled the oars harder through the water. 'Just because a spotlight follows you doesn't mean you have to perform for it.'

She raised both eyebrows in challenge. 'You really believe that? Do you really want to know the God's honest truth? Or are you pushing my buttons in an effort to continue to punish me for the whole Ruby thing?'

He felt a smile coming, but this time didn't bother trying to put a stop to it. 'Both.'

'Fine.' She took a breath. 'The only reasons I am telling you any of this is recompense for Ruby. Okay?'

'Okay.'

'Fame is a funny old thing. It's not like I've done anything to deserve being remembered. I haven't invented something, or cured anything or broken any world records. But my name has brand recognition, which gives me not only a certain power, but responsibility as well. Say the name Kelly and what do you think?'

Wealth. Charm. Beauty. But also excessive influence. Secrets. Lies. Scandal. Everything he wanted Ruby nowhere near.

She didn't wait for him to answer. 'I had to figure out early on how to deal with all that baggage. I have no interest in running the company like Brendan. Or owning the city like Cameron. And the rush Dylan feels every time a new client is lured into the KInG net is a mystery to me. I wouldn't even begin to know what drives King Quinn himself. But what I can offer with a splash of perfume, a flash of designer skirt and a dash of feminine glamour is a much-needed counterpoint to the excess of testosterone my family exudes. A way to use some of that power for the greater good. And, boy, am I good at it. So good I could sell tickets. But unless you know a guy with a good line in wigs and fake noses it's twenty-four hours, seven days a week, barely a holiday in sight.'

'Why do it at all?'

She blinked, clearly thinking him obtuse. 'For them. For each other.'

'For your family?' That kind of self-sacrifice was something he was only just beginning to understand.

'Jobs change. Friends come and go. Family is where you begin and where you end. My brothers may appear to be the kings of the jungle, but deep down they have the hearts of big kittens. They need me as much as I need them. And no matter what part we play all of us are working towards the same goal.'

'The succecss of your father's business.'

'No. For our family to be happy. The business success is a side effect. I certainly don't dance to my father's tune, if that's what you mean.'

'Is that what I said?'

She frowned deeply. 'It's what you intimated,

isn't it? To be fair, I did once. Then a time came when I became a right little tearaway. The things I got up to would make your eyes water. Then I grew up. Took charge of my life. And decided making love and not war was the only way forward.'

'Who knew the life of a society princess was lived on the front line?'

Her frown faded away, but her eyes remained locked on his, a tad wider than normal, as though she couldn't quite believe she was telling him all of this. 'You can mock me all you like, but in offering a corner of myself to those who are interested, I am able to use my money, my influence and my time helping some of the less trendy, less telethon-appropriate organisations I believe need all the help they can get, which is extremely satisfying.'

'I wasn't mocking you. I—'

What? *Envy you your infamously close family?* Like hell he was going to tell her that.

Not knowing how to ask, he instead said, 'Moving on.'

'Excellent idea.' She let out a deep breath and leant forward, just a touch, but enough that when her mouth curved into an all-new smile, a luscious, flirtatious, brain-numbing smile, he felt it like nothing else. If her life really was lived on a battleground, that mouth was as good a weapon as they came.

'Am I off the hook?' she asked.

He slowed his strokes, not quite ready to return to land. To real life. To the other side of the battle from her.   'Just one last thing. Tell me how you got the chip in your tooth.'

She crossed her eyes as her tongue slid to the gap. His hands gripped the oars for dear life.

'It's so tiny. How did you even notice it?'

'I happen to be an extremely perceptive man.'

Her eyes slid to his, warm, tempting, wondering just how perceptive he might be. Unfortunately he was perceptive enough.

As she slid her tongue back into her mouth her teeth scraped slowly over her lips and her nostrils flared as she let out a slow, shaky breath. He knew he wasn't the only one feeling the impossible zing between them. He also knew she was wishing with all her might that he hadn't noticed a thing.

She tilted her chin up a fraction before shaking her hair off her shoulders in a move meant to distract him from the fact that for the first time since he'd met her she was no longer looking him in the eye. 'How else would a party girl chip a tooth but on a glass of champagne? On the upside, it was truly excellent champagne.'

He laughed softly as he was meant to do. Her eyes flickered to his and her smile was grateful.

After a few long, loaded moments, Meg asked, 'I just… I'd like to know one thing too. Did Ruby tell you I was there?'

He shook his head. 'Her nanny.'

She nodded, then looked down at her paint-chipped fingernails with an all-new smile on her face. A secret smile. An honest smile. One reserved for Ruby.

And from nowhere Zach felt something the likes of which he'd never felt in his entire life— the most profound kind of pride that a woman such as her thought so highly of his little girl.

Meg's tongue kept straying to the itty-bitty chip in her tooth.

What had she been thinking, fessing up to all that guff in some great unstoppable stream of consciousness? Nobody wanted to see the workings behind the wizard. It ruined the fantasy. It seemed all she needed was a man who looked her in the eye and asked about the real her, and it was fantasy be damned.

Thank goodness she'd been rational enough to pull back when she had. There were some parts of her life not for public consumption.

If she wanted to continue volunteering at the 'less trendy, less telethon-appropriate' Valley Women's Shelter she had to keep it underground too. Every woman needed her mystery, and every public figure needed their sanctuary, even if it meant she had to truss herself up in a blonde wig, red liptick, brown contacts, and tight second-hand acid-wash jeans circa 1985.

If she was to remain Brisbane's favourite daughter she had to pretend the part of her life in which she'd attempted to leave the spotlight had never happened. She felt lucky much of her memory of that time was a blur of flashing lights—from the nightclub, the police car, the hospital.

As to the way she had finally taken control of her life? If she planned on going through life with a spring in her step and a smile on her face she knew it was best not to revisit the choices she'd made back then ever again.

It was done. It was for the best. Move on.

So Zach Jones—stubborn, pushy, scarily in-sightful Zach Jones; the guy who saw through her so easily that every time they met she had to chase him deeper into the darkest recesses of herself in order to drive him back out—could just take a step back.

Besides, her big mission had been to sort him out, not the other way around. *He* was the one with the rebellious daughter. *He* was the one who'd lost someone close. *He* was the one who needed help.

As she'd seen real social workers do, she started slowly, easing her way to the point so as not to scare him away.

'So Ruby was home sick from school,' she said. 'Does that happen a lot?'

Zach's cheek clenched and the look in his eyes made her wonder if he might not be deciding whether Operation Dispose of Meg might have to be put into action after all.

'I ran away from home once when I was a little older than her,' she pressed. Though she kept back the part where she got to the corner of the street, sat there for a good hour before she went home, only to find nobody had even noticed she was gone.

'She told you she had a sore throat?' he asked, taking baby steps her way.

'She sure did.'

She bit her lip. Argh! Had she broken a confidence? No, she'd told Ruby she wouldn't tell her dad she was home from school, and that had been taken out of her hands by the nanny. Phew. She'd make sure the kid knew it the next time...

Only then did it hit Meg there wouldn't be a next time. She believed Zach wasn't kidding when he said he'd hired security to case the perimeter of the resort, so he'd probably already commissioned twenty-foot-high fences around the house as well.

If she were in Zach's shoes she'd keep his kid as far away from her as she possibly could.

Still, the thought of never seeing Ruby again made her heart give an all too familiar little twinge. But this wasn't about her. Then again, maybe, just maybe, as a nice little side effect, if she helped Zach get Ruby on track then she could stop those darned heart twinges for good.

He watched her with those clever dark eyes that made her feel as if she were melting from the inside out and he rowed.

She merely sat there and waited.

It paid off.

He took a deep breath, narrowed his eyes, then with all the enthusiasm of a man with a knife

pressed to his ribs to make him talk, he said,
'She rang Felicia this morning, claiming a sore
throat. Felicia called a cab to bring her home.
When I heard my first thought was that it was a
ruse. Then I wasn't sure. Do you think…?'

He shook his head and pressed the oars deeper
into the water.

It more than paid off. Had Zach Jones just
asked her for advice? She was shocked it had
come so easily. But boy, was she ready to—

Who the heck was Felicia? Another woman in
Zach's life? Meg wrapped her fingers around the
bench to stop from tipping right off. 'Felicia is…?'

'The nanny.'

She all but laughed with relief. When Zach's
eyes narrowed, she babbled, 'I had a nanny once.
I told her I was adopted. She told a friend, who
spilled the news to the press. Wow, I'd completely forgotten about that. Mum was so upset.
And my father…' She shook her head to clear
that image before the rest of the memory filtered
through. 'Let's just say no more nannies came
through the place.'

Zach's eyes widened a fraction. He really had
no clue that young girls were as much about
sugar and spice as they were about snakes and

snails and puppy dogs' tails. It only made her more determined to make him see.

'Don't get me wrong. Other kids adored theirs,' she continued on. 'Tabitha still sends hers cards on Mother's Day. Does Ruby get on with Felicia?'

He waited a beat then nodded. 'She taught at Ruby's school for over twenty years. She's seen it all. I poached her earlier this year when Ruby came to live with me.'

'Well, that's great, then,' she said, her finger fiddling with her bottom lip as she frantically thought through what tack to take next. 'A girl needs firm boundaries as much as she needs her space.'

And then it hit her. Ruby hadn't always lived with him.

Where had she been? With her mother? Had they divorced? Had they never married? Had they been in love but couldn't live together? Was he still in love with her now? Was that where his innate darkness sprang from? There was no denying her heart hurt just thinking about it. It hurt for Zach. For Ruby. It was much easier letting it hurt for them than in any way for herself.

Now Meg needed to know the whole story so badly she could taste it. She held her breath.

'That's enough,' Zach said, and Meg's finger stilled. 'I have no idea how we started talking about this in the first place.'

Enough? They'd barely begun! She didn't have half the information she wanted—no, *required*—in order to help.

'You brought it up,' Meg shot back.

'I— What?' His oars paused mid-air.

'If you'd been sensible enough to ignore the fact that I happened upon your backyard, then we might never have had to have this conversation.'

'Why do I get the feeling you're used to getting your own way?' he growled.

'Ha! I have no idea because it certainly ain't true. I have three bossy older brothers and a father who thinks everything I do is a complete waste of time.'

Meg's eyes slammed shut and she bit her lip, but it was far too late. She'd said what she'd said. Somehow he'd done it again—given her all the rope she needed to hang herself.

She opened one eye to find him sitting ever so still, the oars resting lazily in their slips, dripping lake water over the bottom of the old wooden boat.

He was quiet for so long Meg could hear the sound of wings beating in the forest, the soft lapping of water against the side of the boat, and her own slow, deep breaths. Then he put the oars back where they were meant to be and pushed off.

He said, 'Ruby attends a local weekly boarding school.'

Meg could have kissed him. Right then and there. She had no clue why he'd let her off the hook when she'd been pressing herself into his personal life with barely concealed vigour. All she knew was that if he looked her in the eye rather than at some point over her shoulder she would probably have gone right ahead and kissed him.

'Where Felicia used to teach,' she encouraged, her voice soft, her words clearly thought out before she uttered a single word.

The muscle beneath his left eye twitched. Then as he pulled the oars through the water he said, 'It's barely a ten-minute drive from here. The same one she was attending before her mother passed away a few months ago.'

And there it was.

Meg's hands clasped one another so tight her fingers hurt. Ruby's mum had been gone only a few months. Oh, that poor little creature. No wonder he wanted to keep Ruby wrapped up in cotton wool. The fact she was able to go back to school at all was amazing. As for Zach…

She opened her mouth to ask how he was doing, when he cleared his throat and pushed the oars deeper into the water, sending them spearing back towards shore.

He said, 'This isn't the first time since she moved in with me that she's had a sore throat, a finger that twitches so hard she can't write, a foot so itchy she can't walk. So far all she's needed is a day at home and she's been right for another few weeks. So all in all I think we're doing okay.'

Doing okay? He cared. He considered. It was important to him to be a good father. In her humble opinion Zach was doing everything in his considerable power to do right by his little girl. And just like that all sorts of bone-deep, neglected, wishful, hopeful feelings beat to life inside her.

'Zach, I had no idea,' she said as she tried to collect herself. 'Truly. I'm so sorry about your wife—'

He cut her off unceremoniously. 'Ruby's mother and I knew one another for a short time several years ago when I was visiting with a view to building this place. I didn't even know Ruby existed until after Isabel died.'

'So you weren't—'

So you're not still in love with her, was what she was trying not to ask.

'We weren't,' he said, insistent enough Meg had the feeling he'd heard all too clearly nonetheless. 'I was in Turkey when my lawyer contacted me with the news. After much legal wrangling I met a social worker here, at the house. And I met Ruby. She had one small suitcase and carried a teddy bear wearing a purple fairy dress under one skinny arm. I never expected her to be so small—'

Zach came to an abrupt halt, frowned deeply and glared down into his lap.

The backs of Meg's eyes burned. It took her a few moments to recognise it was the sharp sting of oncoming tears.

She never cried. Ever. Never sweated, never blushed, never cried. The moments she'd let herself succumb to her emotions were the times she'd been most deeply hurt—by careless whispers of envious types, by stories of horrendous depravity at the Valley Women's Shelter, even by herself. But this guy tugged shamelessly at hidden parts of her that didn't know the rules.

She blinked until the sensation went away.

'We're both trying to get used to our new living situation. To each other,' he went on, his voice raw, his eyes staring at some point on the bottom of the boat as it drifted steadily on. 'The last thing we need at this point is for her existence to come to the attention of the press. You obviously do know what they can be like. She needs to find her feet without constantly looking over her shoulder. She'll trip. She'll fall. She'll be hurt even more.'

He lifted his dark eyes to hers. There was a newfound lightness within them that came with getting everything off his chest. But the second he remembered he'd been divulging his story to her, it was gone.

'Meg,' he said, his voice rough, beseeching.

She breathed deep to calm her thundering heart and said, 'I know I haven't done much to make you believe this, but you really can trust me. I'm exceptionally good at keeping secrets. You have no idea how good, which only proves my point. I'll not breathe a word.'

'I truly hope so.'

She smiled. He managed to do a shadow of the same. And in that moment of silent communion something rare and magical was forged between them.

It felt a lot like trust.

CHAPTER SIX

THE boat bumped against solid ground.

Meg flinched, her flat shoes slipping on the wet wood, but she caught herself in time. She'd been so engrossed in Zach, in his story, in the man, she hadn't even noticed the head-high reeds encroaching.

Zach tied them off. He threw the cooler onto the wooden deck, then leaned over and held out a hand.

She took it, the loaded silence of the lingering moment of amity still making her feel all floaty and surreal.

Once on the jetty she took off his hat, ran a quick hand through her messy curls and handed it to him along with his blanket. He wrapped his hands around both, but didn't tug. Meg looked up into his dark eyes.

Her heart felt heavy in her chest. Her body felt heavy on her legs. The only thing about her that felt light was her head. Which was probably why she said, 'Now that I know everything there is to know about you, are you finally going to give in and stop stalking me?'

His dark brows rose. His voice, on the other hand, deepened. 'Is that what I've been doing?'

She said, 'Either that or fifty acres *really* isn't quite as much room as it sounds.'

From nowhere his head rocked back and he laughed. The sexy sound reverberated deep in her stomach, leaving it feeling hollow. As it faded to a smile in his eyes it left a new kind of warmth in its place she wasn't sure what to do with.

'I like you better this way,' she admitted.

'What way?'

'Not bossing me around. You should try that more.'

He gave the blanket and hat a tug. She shuffled forward a step before letting go and he threw them lazily onto the cooler.

He looked back at her. The earlier glints in his dark eyes had been mere imitations of the glints glinting at her now. The kind of glints she now wished she'd not wished for. They were dazzling, they were blistering, they were completely incapacitating.

His voice rumbled, low and deep. 'By that

logic if I continue that way you'll only like me more.'

'You can't argue with logic,' she said, trying to sound pithy; instead she sounded as if she was flirting. Which, of course, she was.

How could she not? He was glinting and smiling, and somehow, whether by her brilliant psychological tactics or by his choice alone, she'd been allowed to see a little of the man behind the mask.

What she saw there she liked.

And by the look in his eyes what he saw in front of him right at this moment he liked right back.

Meg licked her lips. His hot gaze trailed slowly down the curves of her face until it landed square upon her mouth. His eyes turned dark as night and he breathed out. Hard.

Despite knowing that what was about to happen was reckless and pointless and born of nothing more concrete than the ephemeral connection of confidences shared, Meg just stood there, her entire body vibrating in anticipation.

Zach slid his arm gently around her back, with such little pressure she had time and room to curl away.

She knew she should. She thought to the very

last she would. She was *always* the one to back away first before anything truly serious came to bear. But her toes curled into her shoes and she held her ground.

Zach's brow creased for the briefest of seconds as though he was surprising even himself before a small smile eased onto his mouth. Hers lifted in its image.

Then he pulled her in close. The warmth of his sun-drenched body pressed through her dress until every inch of skin, exposed and concealed, felt as if it had begun to glow.

Her hand fluttered up to rest against his chest to find it hard, fit, unyielding, everything she'd thought him to be. Only now she knew that beneath the tough exterior beat the heart of a man whose primary goal was the protection of a little girl.

He leaned down and moved his lips over hers. He tasted like chocolate muffins. She was toast.

The kiss was slow. Dreamy. As if he had no intention of missing out on experiencing every single nuance.

It took about three and a half seconds before Meg slid her arms around his neck and pressed up onto her toes to get closer to him. Sinking against him. Soaking up every bit of him that she possibly could.

With a groan that reverberated through her body like a little earthquake, his strong arms wrapped so tight around her he lifted her off the jetty as though she weighed nothing at all.

The kiss deepened. And deepened again.

His tongue eased into her mouth, caressing the edges of her teeth, sliding over the tiny chip in her front tooth, sending delicious shivers through her, touching her tongue for the briefest of moments before it was gone.

She was breathless and hot. Her skin hummed. Her insides ached. Her toes curled. Her lungs burned. And the kiss continued as beautifully indulgent and unhurried as it had begun.

Until her flat shoes slid from her feet, landing on the jetty with a soft slap, leaving her feet bare, and leaving her feeling exposed. Completely at his mercy. And finally her senses came swarming back.

She pulled away. Ever so slightly. But he felt it. Slowly, gently, he placed her back on the jetty. And they uncurled their limbs from around one another.

Only once there was enough space for a

summer breeze to slide between them did Zach say, 'I'm not sure where that came from.'

'I am,' she said, her cheeks pinking the second the words left her mouth. But it was the truth. She'd wanted to do that since the moment she'd first seen him.

It got her a slow, easy smile and a nod. The moment of accord, of finally admitting to each other what they both felt, was even more formidable than the kiss itself.

'I'd better go,' she said. 'My posse will be moseying back to camp any time soon.'

She reached out and rested her hand on his arm. His skin was so warm, the energy coursing through him so vital, her heart rate rose in direct response.

'I'm really sorry about Isabel,' she said.

His mouth quirked, but he didn't smile. And she wondered if he'd been hoping the kiss would wipe everything else from her mind. She wasn't about to tell him how close it had come.

Instead, she squeezed his arm again, and said, 'But I'm not worried about Ruby. I have no doubt she's in good hands. She's really lucky to have you.'

She lifted her hand in a small wave, then gathered her shoes and jogged up the jetty, her mind already playing over the fib she'd have to create for Rylie and Tabitha to explain where she'd been, what she'd been doing, and why she was floating an inch off the ground but couldn't quite remove the frown from her forehead at the same time.

Later that night, once Rylie and Tabitha were snoring lightly in their rooms Meg lay on her bed, wide-awake, her mobile phone warm in her palms.

She'd been tossing it from hand to hand for a good couple of hours, ever since she'd got off the phone from saying goodnight to Olivia and Violet, Brendan's girls.

They'd sounded bright, cheery, happy. What had she expected? They were seven and four, and they had ponies, ballet lessons, piano, rock climbing, Chinese and French lessons, summer trips around the world with their grandmother, twenty-year-old nannies who spoilt them rotten, and a dad who clearly wrestled with the amount of time he spent at work while they grew up without him there to see it.

But as she lay back on her bed, the pale summer moon spilling light through the far window creating a hypnotic play of light and shadow on the ceiling, the fairy dust cleared from her eyes and Ruby's small face looked back at her instead.

She'd seen so much of herself in the kid's mutinous streak. That spark could be so easily deflated. Or worse, it could spin out of control. She hoped not. With all her might. Not just for Ruby. But also for Zach.

Big, bad, daunting, noble, solid Zach Jones.

Growing up in her family, the only kind of masculine strength she'd understood till she met him had been overt. Overpowering. Uncompromising.

Zach's strength came from somewhere much deeper. A place he didn't feel compelled to proclaim to the world. The fact that she'd been allowed to witness it in the revelation of how he'd changed his life for his little girl made it that much more compelling. It was like seeing a fireman rescue a kitten from a tree.

She'd hate to see all his good work go to waste. But since Zach's parenting skills were now obviously nothing like her father's, Ruby might not need the intervention her adolescent mutiny necessitated after all. She struggled with deciding what to do.

One thing she knew had been a bad decision on both their parts had been that kiss.

Her fingers lifted to stroke her lips as they must have done a few dozen times that afternoon. She could still taste his sweetness, sense his warmth all around her, feel his hardness imprinted on every inch of her body as if it had happened mere moments ago.

Soft, dreamy, luxurious, deep, unguarded, magic.

And indefensible. Because Zach Jones had a child.

When she'd ruled out any chance of having kids of her own, kids who—just because they were hers—would never live up to her father's expectations of them, it had never occurred to her that she might one day meet a man who came with kids of his own. Her usual types were never that proactive.

Then Zach had to come stomping into her life, shaking loose old choices she'd never thought she'd have to revisit again.

But no. Her nieces were living proof of why she'd done the right thing.

They seemed fine, now. But they were little kids. They ought to wear gumboots and get into mud-pie fights, not wear dresses and tights and patent leather shoes when playing in the backyard.

The pressure for them to live up to her father's

unwavering ideal of what a Kelly had to be was mounting. And soon they'd be old enough to feel it. Soon they'd be old enough to know.

There was no way she'd wish that pressure on any child. Not by blood, and not by association. Because she knew the consequences.

She threw her phone across the room and it landed with a thud on a couch in the corner.

She tried humming Stevie Wonder to clear her head, but it didn't work. Zach's deep voice rang louder still.

She liked the guy. She adored how he kissed. She was smitten with his efforts to do right by Ruby. And she was in his debt for letting her get away with the unforgivable slip about her exceedingly private dealings with her father.

But she wasn't any good for him any more than he would be good for her. He might not see it yet, but he had the natural inclination to be some kind of dad. He'd want more kids down the line, and with her insides the way they were she could never give them to him.

Meg turned on her side, tucked her thighs against her belly, and slid her hands beneath her pillow. The sheer curtains over the ceiling-to-floor windows—chosen especially to *not* let a girl sleep in when there was jogging to be done—flapped under the soft push of air-conditioned air.

Out there, in that big, rambling, amazing house of his, Zach would soon be asleep. She wondered if he dreamt. What he dreamt about. And more importantly, who.

It had long since been dark by the time Zach stepped foot in the place he'd called home for the past few months. He was humming as he shut the front door. It took a few moments until he realised it was KC and the Sunshine Band. Classic disco.

Throwing a full set of keys onto the sideboard rather than a simple hotel card still felt strange.

Being shuffled from foster home to state institution and back again, he'd hit a point where he'd simply stopped feeling connected to places, to possessions, to people. Living in this large, rambling house, sleeping in the same bed every night, seeing the same faces every day, he felt the return of the natural desire to preserve those connections. Along with that came the niggling fear that it all might yet be taken away.

'Good evening, Zach,' a voice called out to him in the darkness.

He jumped. 'Felicia. You took a year off my life.'

'Working to all hours will do that to you far more quickly,' Ruby's nanny said. 'I'd say you are a prime candidate for attending one of those wellness programmes that are so trendy nowadays.'

Zach gave her shadowy figure a flat stare. 'If I'd known you had such a funny bone I'd have left you in that draughty old school.'

The older woman patted him on the arm.

He glanced down the dark front hallway towards the bright haven of the warm family kitchen, his nose catching the delicious concoction of homey smells that meant there were leftovers waiting for him in the oven. 'Is she still awake?'

He felt her shake her head. 'Out like a light the minute her head hit the pillow.'

'Have you heard any—?' He stopped, hoping he wouldn't have to put into words the wretched sounds she screamed out every few nights.

'Not a peep. What with her sore throat I'd say she needed the rest.' She tossed her large book bag over her shoulder. 'Goodnight, then. I'll see you in the morning.'

He heard her meet up with one of the rotation of night staff who escorted her back to her own bungalow down the way, their voices trailing into the distance until he was left with silence.

Rather than heading for the beguiling scent of zucchini quiche he took a left. The light from the kitchen faded the farther he moved through the house.

He reached Ruby's bedroom door and stared at her name spelled out in big pink letters, his ears straining to hear the sound of her sleeping breaths.

He could have been home hours earlier. Certainly before her bedtime. Instead he'd remained shackled to his workstation in the Blueberry Ash Bungalow he'd taken as his office, telling himself Ruby wouldn't have expected him home as it was still officially a school night. The truth was the thought of having to question her, to chastise her even, for skipping school had left him in a cold sweat.

She was seven, for Pete's sake. He was thirty-five and operated a massive multinational company. There wasn't anyone on earth who had a hope in hell of intimidating him. Yet from the day he'd first looked into those all too intelligent brown eyes he'd lived with the fear that, though he'd *never* abandon her, there was always the chance she'd decide she did not want him.

He ran a hand over his face, the pads of his fingers rasping against the day-old shave, before resting his palm on the cool wood of her bedroom door.

The instinct to press open the door, sneak in and check on his daughter, to let himself believe she slept because *he'd* made her feel safe, was so strong. Yet every night he managed to talk himself out of it.

He might wake her. She might see him and expect her mum and become distressed. He might get used to her being there.

Yet this night the urge felt different. Not nearly so complicated. Today his knowledge of what a girl needed in order to feel safe had been increased tenfold in one short conversation with the most unlikely source—Meg Kelly.

She'd been so confident that Ruby needed her space. And just as sure that it was okay for him to impulsively not want to give it to her. And even more than okay that Ruby knew it. His instincts were spot on. Maybe he did have it within him to do this right after all.

He wrapped his hand around the door handle.

Good hands, Meg had called them, and with enough vehemence he'd let himself believe it too.

He went in. Even in the darkness there was no mistaking the big white bed jutting out into the centre of the largest bedroom in the house. He might have gone overboard with the rocking horse, the padded window seat, the library stacked with *Saddle Club* books, the tea-party table, the twenty different dolls, but he'd taken note of every lick of advice from Felicia and her other teachers who'd known her the past couple of years and let his International Resort Decorator go crazy, no expenses spared.

He took a few steps into the plush-carpeted room until moonlight spilling through the faraway window gave him enough light to see that beneath the pink-and-white lacy bedcovers lay a skinny, young girl.

A handful of days had passed since she'd been home for the weekend, but he was sure she'd grown. Her dark hair splayed across her pillow with such perfection it was as though someone had brushed out every strand. Her face was smooth and unlined. Her breathing even and un-worried. Her throat not bothering her a bit.

Before he knew it was coming he smiled wide. Cheeky kid. She even had her nanny fooled. But Meg, considering her more recent experience

being a daughter, had seen through the subter-
fuge in a second.

He took another step closer until he was near
enough he allowed himself the small gesture of
wiping a long, straight lock of hair from across
her eyes.

Ruby stirred. Mumbled a bit. He froze. But
she soon resettled—taking up the whole bed,
one arm flung over her head. Exactly the way
he'd always slept.

His heart slammed against his ribs. This
creature was his daughter. His responsibility. His
only family. If anyone did anything, said
anything, printed anything that made the au-
thorities even *think* about denying her to him…

Before his throat clogged so tight he couldn't
breathe he spun on his heel and walked from the
room.

'Daddy?' a soft voice called when he was a
metre away from being home free.

He turned; Ruby was sitting up, a shadow in the
darkness, as he must have been to her. He found
his voice for her. 'Yes, honey?'

'Nothing. Just checking.'

Checking to see he was real.

Checking to see he was still around.

Checking to see he hadn't disappeared right when she was getting used to him being there. God, how he knew that feeling. That loathsome, sinking, hollowness when someone you trusted to love you left without looking back.

'I'm here,' he said, his voice gruff. 'I'm not going anywhere. You can go back to sleep.'

By the slow, even breaths coming from her bed, he knew she already was.

He closed her door and paced into the kitchen where he leant his hands on the island bench in the middle of the huge room.

Felicia had left out his newspapers. Beside them sat a permission slip from Ruby's school for an upcoming field trip, and a spaghetti jar overfilled with a mishmash of local wildflowers. He imagined Ruby picking them for Felicia as an act of contrition, and Felicia falling for the sore-throat stunt all the harder. Smart kid.

He played with the rubbery, cream petal of a waxflower. Working in solitary, coming home late to a dark house, eating leftovers, keeping his weekends completely free to spend them at Ruby's beck and call within the confines of a handful of safe places; this was the inflexible life he'd chosen. This was how things were going to be for the next dozen-odd years. No more hands-on business, no more travel, no more adult company?

Meg Kelly's lovely face swam all too easily back into his mind.

For the first time since he'd set foot in the door—but certainly not the first time that day—he remembered the kiss. God, the delights he'd found within that mouth. It had drawn him in like a siren song he could no longer resist. But her warm skin, and her goddess curves and her instant response had made it impossible for him to tear himself away.

He pushed away from the island and moved to the oven to grab his dinner. Oven mitts the last thing on his mind, the ceramic quiche tray burnt his fingers. He let go and it smashed to the floor. Egg and zucchini and cheese flew everywhere, splattering the wooden cupboards and embedding themselves in every bit of slate-tile grout it could find.

He swore at the great mess profusely but sotto voce, always remembering Ruby was asleep down the hall. He flipped on the tap and shoved his stinging fingers beneath the cold-water stream.

What the hell was he thinking? Kissing Meg. Confiding in her. Her pretty words might have sounded believable at the time, but Meg Kelly could yet bring down his carefully balanced house of cards with one word whispered in the wrong direction. Her best friend was a journalist, for Pete's sake! Dammit. That mouth of hers could prove to be his downfall in more ways than one.

He turned off the tap, wiped his hands down his trousers when he couldn't find a handy tea towel, and set to cleaning up the mess.

After cheese on toast for dinner he signed Ruby's permission slip with a flourish so fierce he tore the paper.

He'd let himself be wrapped around a female finger for the last time. The next time Ruby tried to pull a stunt like skipping school, he *would* talk with her. He would grow some backbone and set some boundaries.

Apparently boundaries were something young girls needed. Or so some would have him believe.

CHAPTER SEVEN

IN LIEU of the dawn jog, the next morning Meg slid notes beneath the girls' doors saying she was taking the hike through the national forest instead and to meet her at the rendezvous point at seven.

After finally falling asleep some time after two she needed the extra hour to recuperate. But that wasn't why hiking was suddenly her new favourite pastime.

She was avoiding Zach.

After the dreams she'd had, G-rated dreams of white picket fences and yellow Labrador puppies with herself in an apron washing dishes while looking out a kitchen window at a yard full of kids, she needed to put as much of the fifty acres of resort land between her and Zach Jones as she could.

She stood at the back of the thankfully large hiking group, decked out in what seemed the most appropriate hiking attire she had, twisting her crazy morning hair into two thick plaits, determined not to let the humidity beat her, ready to put aside the past couple of days and start her holiday anew.

'Good morning,' a deep voice rumbled beside her.

She snapped her eyes shut, not needing to look up to know who the voice belonged to. That tone alone could make her skin hum no matter what it said.

'So where are the other two musketeers this fine morning?' he asked.

Thankful for the excuse not to look him in the eye, she glanced over her shoulder to find the path behind her empty. She said, 'Still snug in their warm beds, I expect. Who knew I'd turn out to be the energetic one?'

Who knew? They knew. And that was why they weren't coming. Oh, no…

In an effort to be honest with her best friends while still keeping from them everything she was unable—or not yet ready—to share, she'd been brief when mentioning her run-ins with Zach. Obviously too brief. Her insouciance hadn't fooled them for a single second. They knew something was up, and being her best friends they'd optimistically assumed her reticence meant true romance was in the air. They were leaving her alone so that it might flourish.

Being stuck with Zach looking all scruffy and gorgeous, with no buffer to keep her out of harm's way, was all she deserved.

She tied off her second plait then glanced at him causally from the corner of her eye, catching sight of yet more cargo pants, yet another sexily faded T-shirt, a tattered old backpack snugly attached to his back and the same well-worn cap she'd seen him wear before.

Her perusal ground to a halt when it reached his mouth. Her own turned as dry as dust as their kiss came rushing back to her in Technicolor. She licked her lips, then croaked, 'Please don't tell me I've accidentally done something else that would necessitate you tailing me?'

'Now what could possibly make you think my presence here has anything to do with you?'

Before she could come up with a succinct retort, the wellness facilitator called out, 'Today the crew heading up our new St Barts resort are joining us to see how we Aussies do it. So let's lift our feet, keep up a super pace, and ooh and ahh at the local flora and fauna like we've never seen anything so fabulous!'

'You're here to train your next crew?' she said, mostly to herself.

'Beautiful *and* brainy. Who knew?'

Zach tugged on one of her plaits, shot her a grin that was complete with the glint that made her common sense unceasingly fall to pieces, pulled his cap lower over his face then jogged ahead.

With the words *beautiful and brainy* ringing in her ears, she stared at his back until he was swallowed by the forest.

Amazing. He was well over six feet tall, with skin like bronze and the build of a world-class athlete, yet he clearly had no clue *that* was why half the people in the group would be wondering who he was. It wouldn't matter if she was sitting in his lap or a million miles away.

Meg hitched her shiny new Juniper Falls backpack into a more comfy position on her shoulders, took one last glance back at the empty path, then followed on as the group turned off the running track.

They soon found a network of wide wooden walkways with the kind of gentle slope built to accommodate every level of trail rambler and

Meg was truly surprised to soon find herself contentedly lost in the rhythmic pace of her feet.

Before long they were ushered through a gap in the railing as they headed off the main tourist trail. The path became instantly less clear-cut, less regularly tramped, and the gentle path gave way to one in which they had to walk single file, at times grasping at vines to pull themselves up the face of a steep rise.

Sweat dripped down the sides of Meg's face, down her spine and behind her knees. She could feel spirals of her hair plastered against her cheeks and the back of her neck. When she licked her lips she could taste salt. She gave up trying to hear the guide over her laboured breathing and just climbed.

Meg wasn't sure if she'd picked up her pace or Zach had slowed, but somehow right when she needed leverage to step over a particularly slippery-looking rock as she picked a path across a slow-moving stream, his hand was there to help her leap across to the opposite bank.

'Thanks,' she said, her voice rough from lack of use. 'Are we there yet?'

From her view of his profile she caught his smile, this one complete with eye crinkles. Her heart skipped a beat, which, considering her fitness level and the uneven ground, was not smart.

'Not far now,' he said, his voice as clear as if he'd been standing still the past half-hour.

'If I have a complaint do I really have to write to management?'

'Hit me. I can take it.'

'Are the super-early starts entirely necessary?'

The smile spread to laughter as though it was the most natural thing for him to do. 'The days get hot very quickly around here.'

'I'm not sure I believe that makes a lick of difference to your sadistic timetable planners.'

The eye crinkles deepened. 'That's because you're too smart for your own good.'

'Mmm. So does that mean you actually believe in the stuff you're spouting? Inner health, inner happiness and all that.'

His eye crinkles faded as he gave her question consideration. The guy listened, seriously listened, to what she had to say. Most men in his position patted her on the head as if she were a clever puppy before deferring to her brothers, not caring that she might be a woman with ideas and opinions and more street smarts than they had in their little fingers. No wonder she was finding it harder and harder to pull herself away from this one.

He said, 'I believe that what you put into your life is what you get out of it. Treat it well, it'll treat you well. Surround yourself only with positive people and they'll affect your life positively. Fill your body and your mind with rubbish and rubbish is all you can ever hope to be.'

Meg let those pearls sink in and then kind of wished she hadn't asked. Because it shed a new light on how she must have appeared to others. And to him.

She attended parties to keep her profile current, so that meant she was a party girl. Nothing deeper. Nothing more. And it was entirely her own doing.

She kept hush-hush the best parts of herself; the truth about the number of women at the Valley Women's Shelter she'd secretly helped over the years. That way *nobody* knew the real her. Not her family. Not even her friends.

For years she'd thought she had the best of both worlds—public affection and private fulfilment. But Zach's words made her wish *someone* knew. They made her wish he knew. The urge to just blurt it all out then and there was a powerful thing.

But then what? He was too perceptive. He'd wonder why she needed to spend time with battered women and displaced children in particular, and why she'd even hidden the fact in the first place.

Nah. Better to keep things as they were. Best not to discover people might only be attracted to the light, bright, amusing, easily palatable version of herself. Zach included. She wasn't sure she was prepared to know the answer to that one.

Realising the silence was stretching on far too long, she forced a dazzling party-girl smile and said, 'So you are what you eat?'

His cheek lifted. 'In not so many words.'

'By that logic if I go home right now and marinate myself in chocolate and red wine, then at the very least I'll die tasty.'

He laughed softly, before saying, 'You can't argue with logic.'

Meg's breath caught in her throat. He'd just had to go and use the last words she'd said to him before they'd kissed, hadn't he? Her heart beat double time. She breathed deep to control it before she keeled over.

Perhaps he hadn't realised what he'd said, because he just turned and followed the group.

Or perhaps the kiss hadn't affected him nearly as much as it had affected her.

Good, she thought. *Fantastic even. Fan-bloody-tastic.*

Now they were descending again. Single file. Meg was caught behind Zach, so naturally while she ought to have been watching her feet she watched him instead. The spring of curls against his tanned neck. The athletic ease with which he strode the trail.

Surely he'd felt *something* when they'd kissed. She'd felt magic.

When her foot half missed a stepping stone, she stumbled and caught hold of his backpack for support.

'You okay back there?' he asked, snapping a hand behind him to cradle her hip.

She closed her eyes against the flow of feeling rushing through her that felt more tangible and immediate than mere magic. 'Mostly.'

'Take my shoulders.'

'Why?' she asked.

He glanced up at her, his dark eyes shadowed beneath his cap. And she was certain his voice dropped a note or two when he said, 'Because it only gets riskier from here.'

'I'll be fine,' she said, her voice husky.

'Meg—'

'I'm not completely inept, you know. I may not know which direction I'm heading, but I can put one foot in front of the other without falling flat on my face.' *Most of the time.* 'I can do this on my own.'

Ignoring her outburst, Zach simply took her by the waist and physically lifted her and placed her to the left of the path so that those behind her could get past.

Once they were alone with their group bundling down the descent in front of them, Zach said, 'Relax, Meg. I'm not offering you anything more than a hand down the mountain.'

Meg swallowed, the lack of saliva making her throat scratch so she winced. His dark eyes slid down her face to rest on her lips. His grip tightened. Infinitesimally. And she felt in his touch the same confusion of want and restraint surging through her body.

Triumph coursed through her. He'd felt every bit of enchantment in that kiss that she had.

Triumph fast turned to confusion. What was she meant to do with the knowledge that helping her down the hill wasn't all he wanted to give her any more than that was all she wanted from him?

In the quiet that followed Meg realised the group had moved far enough away that birdsong came back to the forest. The water in the stream they had crossed bubbled melodiously about the fall of rocks unable to completely block its path.

They were to all intents and purposes alone. Anything could happen. Like having photos of 'Meg Kelly and friend' getting up to no good being splashed all over the Internet within hours. For that he'd never forgive her.

She took his hands from her and pressed them back to his sides. 'Thanks for the offer, but I just slipped a little on some moss. I'll pay more attention to where I put my feet.'

His eyes finally, thankfully, skimmed from her mouth back to her eyes and his hands moved to grip the straps of his backpack. 'Just be careful, for my sake. I don't need you slipping and breaking a bone.'

'God, no. The press would be all over this place like a rash. Which is, of course, the last thing we want.'

'We want?'

'Yes, *we*. As in we agree that it's Ruby who's

front and foremost in our minds when we happen upon one another.'

Ruby who should be reason enough we never happen upon one another again.

After one final dark glance he nodded, then turned and headed down the ragged path.

'Keep up,' he called without turning, 'before we have to send out a search party for you again.'

'A search party? Please,' she called back as she walked unsteadily down the trail.

Had he just said 'again'?

Five long, hot minutes later, the descent evened out and the path became made up of wide, neat steps carved into layers of grey rock.

The group spread out, walking in clumps. The scurrying, flapping, whistling noises of the forest had been overtaken by the nearby sound of rushing water. The overgrown forest cleared to reveal a vertical slant of wet rock that was so high Meg had to crane her neck to see the sliver of sunlight above.

'Hold onto the handrails, step carefully, and prepare yourselves for something fabulous!' the guide called out.

Meg followed Zach into a gap in the rock. And

darkness. And sudden dank coolness. The sweat covering her whole body brought her skin up in goose bumps.

Bit by bit, step by slow step, Meg's eyes became used to the gloom. Up ahead, through the bobbing heads of her fellow hikers, there was light. Eerie, green light.

Then suddenly she stepped onto the edge of a high-domed cave. At her feet lapped a pool of bright green water clear enough to see the floor was made of a tumble of smooth stones of all shapes and sizes. Above, through a gap way up high in the ceiling, a stunning, glowing, white sheet of water splashed magnificently into the deep centre of the pool. It was literally one of the most beautiful things she'd ever seen.

'I give you Juniper Falls,' Zach said from somewhere to her right.

Meg couldn't think of a thing to say back. She just let it wash over her—the noise, the colour, the primal violence and beauty of it all.

'Worth the early start?' Zach asked some time later.

'And then some,' she said, drawing her eyes away from the spectacle to give him a quick smile.

A couple of nearby camera flashes went off.

She took a step away from him, her eyes instantly scanning the crowd for the offender. But everyone was ogling the waterfall, not their blurry shapes in the semi-darkness.

'Photos don't do it justice,' he said. 'Just look, listen, absorb, get your fill. You won't forget. This moment will be with you for ever.'

While Zach kept his gaze dead ahead, and despite the splendour raging in front of her, Meg's remained locked on him.

As though he knew just what she was taking her fill of, he turned to look at her. His brows came together and his right cheek creased into a sexy arch, questioning her. She shook her head, shrugged. What could she possibly say?

His eyes left hers to rove slowly over her face as though he too was taking the chance to memorise every centimetre.

He was right—it was a moment she knew she would never forget.

The group spread out, some continuing around the other side of the pool, others finding patches of sunshine so they could sit and relax. A few game souls took off their shoes and waded into the shallows.

'Coming?' he asked, holding out a hand.

'How about you point the way to the best spot, then you can get back to work?'

His eyes narrowed, then he looked about and saw the camera flashes for what they potentially were. He took a slow step away from her. And even though she'd been the one to encourage the move, her heart clenched just a little in her chest.

He curled his hand back to his side as he pulled his old hat farther down over his eyes. Then he gave her a long, straight look. 'As it turns out I have a little time to spare for my guests if you'd care to follow me.'

She swallowed and nodded. Then followed him to a large, mostly dry rock on which sunshine dappled through the ferns above. Meg settled herself onto it with a thankful sigh.

'Is the water warm?' she asked.

He stood, towering over her. 'See for yourself.'

When she leant over and whisked her hand through the clear water the illusion firmed. It was warm enough to swim in, but cool enough to soothe her hot hands.

Zach filled his flask with water, then his tanned throat worked hard as he chugged it down. When Zach saw her eyeing his drink bottle with her tongue practically hanging out of her mouth he handed it to her.

Her lips hovered where his lips had been. She imagined she could smell chocolate muffins. She closed her eyes, all but groaning as the blissfully cool liquid slid down her scorching throat.

Zach's voice was loud enough for those nearest to hear when he went all 'tour guide' on her and said, 'The pool is fed by the falls and the overflow creates an underwater spring to the south, which feeds into a stream that heads off into the national park. With the constant pummelling, the floor at the centre of the pool is the softest sand you'll ever feel.'

She put the lid back on his flask and handed it to him, their fingers sliding past one another as they exchanged the bottle from her hot hand to his.

'So you've swum here?' she asked, looking back out into the pool, tucking her shaking hand tight into her lap.

'Once or twice.'

'I can't imagine when you'd find the time. What with running a trillion businesses and looking after you know who.'

She felt him draw back. She'd been discreet.

But it hadn't mattered. The withdrawal of all that lovely warmth stung.

And shocked her sensible. Even though they were both on the same side in wanting to protect his daughter, while it was her wish, it was his mission in life.

She slung her backpack onto the rock between them, the most substantial wall she could mount on short notice, then said, 'I'm sorry. I won't bring that subject up again.'

His voice was low and intimate when he said, 'Meg, I wanted to—'

She flapped a hand between them. 'It's fine. I understand.'

'No, I don't think you do,' he said. 'I wanted to tell you… She made me pancakes.'

Meg's eyes slid to his, envy and delight spilling through her in tandem. 'She did? When?'

'This morning. Before she went back to school.'

'Jeez, she's an early riser. Like father like daughter, I guess.'

He glanced at her with an expression she'd never seen on him before. As if he'd thought the same, but couldn't be convinced that it wasn't just wishful thinking. It got to her, like an arrow straight to the heart.

'Were they any good?' she asked, her voice reed-thin. 'The pancakes.'

'Atrocious.' He laughed softly.

'But you ate them all,' she said, knowing the answer before she even asked the question.

He nodded once. 'I certainly did.'

The arrow in her heart stabbed a little deeper.

She tried to imagine her own father eating pancakes she'd made. Unless they'd been fit for the table of literal kings he would have taken one look and fed them to the dogs. And he would somehow have made sure she knew it too.

She swallowed down the heady mix of new good and old bad feelings rising far too quickly inside her.

'She asked after you, you know,' Zach said, glancing away from her to stare out at some vague spot in the distance.

Meg raised her eyes to the roof of the cave to hold back the encroaching sting. If he knew what was good for him, the guy should really stop talking. Now.

She knew what was good for her and still asked, 'What did she say?'

'Young girls need their mystery. Or so I've been told.'

'Hey now,' she laughed, taking a quick moment to brush a finger under her eyes, 'that's not fair. I was being nice giving you all that secret girls' business insight, and now you're using it against me.'

'Fair enough,' he said, 'then I will tell you that it was something you said to her yesterday that had her heading off to school today like she had the wind at her heels. So thank you for that too.'

Wow. She'd done that? She gave him a nod. It was either that or croak out, *You're welcome*.

'Mr Jones,' a woman's voice with a lilting foreign accent said from between them.

Meg flinched and dragged herself out of the cloud of intimacy that had wrapped itself around them like a slow, thick, enshrouding fog shifting across the pool.

She turned to find a stunning redhead, her hair neat as a pin, her Juniper Falls uniform pressed, not a lick of sweat anywhere. Meg ran a quick hand over her fuzzy plaits and so wished she hadn't. It would have been better not to know.

'Claudia,' Zach said, his voice so cool and aloof Meg was surprised to remember when he'd last used that tone of voice with her. 'What can I do for you?'

'Sorry to interrupt, but the St Barts group had a few questions about the morning they wanted to run by you while we had a moment's respite.'

'Of course. Claudia, this is Meg, a guest at the resort. Meg, Claudia will be my St Barts manager,' he explained.

'St Barts? You lucky duck,' Meg said with the instant return of her practised smile. 'And thank you, Zach, for taking the time to explain how the waterfall works. It was most informative.'

Claudia gave her a short smile, then headed off to join the St Barts crew.

Zach looked across at her with a kind of smile she was having more and more trouble resisting. 'Most informative?'

'Well,' she said, 'it was.'

Zach stood, yet he lingered.

'Go,' she said, shooing him away. 'Please. I'm not going to fall into the pool and drown and cause you endless hassles. I promise.'

His brow furrowed, then he said, 'No, that's not… I was going to ask if I'll see you tonight.'

'Tonight?' Her heart beat so hard in her throat she was certain it must have been obvious to everyone in sight.

'You are coming to the luau, are you not?'

'The what?'

'There's a clearing at the west corner of the lake on which we've created a beach. The staff put on a controlled bonfire there once a week. Have you even read the brochure?'

'I glanced at it. Briefly.' Trying to find chocolate, trying to find the Wellness Building. Both times she'd only found more of him. 'Look, I'm not sure what our plans are for tonight—'

'The St Barts team will be there tonight so I was thinking about putting in an appearance. For their sake,' he said. Adding, 'There'll be marshmallows.'

She couldn't help herself. She licked her lips.

And he laughed. Throaty, loud laughter that resonated through her bones as though her marrow were a twanged guitar string.

'Real marshmallows?' she asked, her voice comically low, amazed at the cool she could still find within herself when she needed it most. Thank heavens for her years of training. 'Or soy-based, gluten-free, sugar-free sticky balls?'

'Real marshmallows. Bags and bags of them. Pink and white. Sticks supplied if you're a toaster.'

'Sure I'm a toaster. You?'

'All the way. But just in case you need something to keep you going until then...' He tossed her a small package wrapped in the ubiquitous Juniper Falls pale green. He tipped his cap at her, then bounded across the rocks to join the St Barts crew.

Meg tore it open to find herself holding a small packet of M&Ms. She laughed out loud, then pressed her finger to her mouth before her fellow hikers discovered her laughing to herself and realised they ought to have been paying more heed to the frizzy brunette in their midst.

CHAPTER EIGHT

ZACH stood on a corner of the lake's beach not lit by the blazing fire, feet bare as the day he was born, dressed top to toe in linen he'd ironed himself, and a hot pink lei someone he didn't recognise had thrown over his head.

'You're a fool,' he muttered to himself for about the seventh time in the past ten minutes. 'You and Ruby might have had a good morning because of something *she* said, and maybe you can't get that kiss out of your mind, but by poking your head out of your perfectly adequate cave again and again just to get another glimpse makes you a damn fool.'

His hands gripped the lei, crushing the flowers, but before he had the chance to whip it over his neck the sound of female laughter split the night.

Glitter twinkled in the darkness. Three distinct voices wafted towards him, followed by three female forms. The other two must have been her friends. All he saw was Meg.

Her dark hair had been pulled back into a slick ponytail. Huge hooped earrings hung from her ears to her shoulders, encrusted with more diamond dust than most women would ever own. But it was the dress that had him clenching his fingers into his palms.

Fire-engine red it was, made of some sparkly material that clung to her torso like second skin, cinching tight at her waist then billowing all the way to her ankles. Her shoulders were bare, her décolletage on display within a deep V, and around the middle she was tied up with a big red bow.

Never had he been given a gift quite like that. He'd obviously kept the wrong friends.

She leaned in as a staff member explained the 'no shoes on the beach policy' for the luau, and without hesitation she rested her elbow on someone's shoulder, hitched her voluminous skirt as high as her knee and proceeded to uncurl a good metre of red leather strap wound about her calf.

Zach closed his eyes and prayed for mercy.

When he opened them it was to see Meg, barefoot, bouncing onto the sand with the exuberance of a puppy. Mid-twirl he got a load of the back of the dress—she was completely bare from a small clip at the back of her neck all the way to her waist. It wasn't quite low enough to give him a glimpse of the tattoo he knew was there, but low enough he ran a hand hard over his mouth.

He knew what it was about her that had him tempting fate. For the past twenty years he'd spent every waking minute dedicated to turning himself from a kid with nothing into a ruthless business-man. For the past several months he'd had to com-pletely strip away that part of himself in order to pour all of his energy into becoming a father.

Meg Kelly simply let him feel like a *man*.

It was energising. It was addictive. It could so easily prove to be his undoing.

Look at her, he said to himself. *The diamonds, the flashy friends, the artless va-va-voom. She revels in the flash and flare of public life. And look at you, hiding in the shadows.*

In allowing this infatuation to continue he was setting himself up to lose too much—he'd cer-tainly lose Meg, and there was every real pos-sibility he might yet lose Ruby. As for the fact that he could look in the mirror and see a guy who'd learnt from the alienation of his past? Gone.

Convinced beyond a shadow of a doubt leaving was the right thing to do, he took one step in that direction when a local reggae band on the other side of the fire struck up their steel drums with a little 'How Deep Is Your Love' Bee Gees action.

His eyes searched for Meg's. She looked up and clapped, radiating pure joy as he'd known she would when he'd put in the request with the entertainment director.

Her gaze began flicking back and forth across the crowd and he knew too that she was looking for him. Instead of sliding deeper into the shadows where he belonged, his feet held firm until her eyes found his.

She smiled with her whole body—ravishing red lips, sparkling blue eyes, the happy shrug of her creamy shoulders. A deeply felt attraction slid through him like slow, hot lava. God, it felt good—like gut instinct, abandon and release. Feelings he'd never allowed himself to come close to feeling for another person his whole adult life.

She made a beeline his way, her friends following in her shimmering wake.

'Zach,' she said on a release of breath when she was close enough he could see the firelight flickering in her eyes.

'Good evening, ladies,' Zach said, purposely including all three. 'Don't you all look beautiful this evening?'

One gave Meg a small shove forward. 'Don't we just.'

Meg glared at her friend, while Zach pretended not to notice.

'Ready for a big night?' he asked.

'I heard rumours of a marshmallow roast,' said the brunette. Tabitha.

'Bring 'em on,' said the blonde, her voice wry.

The hairs on the back of Zach's neck twitched under the blonde's incisive gaze. That one was the journo. At the very least she knew that *something* was happening between her friend and him. She who probably kept a lipstick camera and microchip microphone on her person at all times.

Meg slapped her friend on the arm, which he approved of heartily. 'Don't pay any attention to Rylie. She doesn't understand that sweets belong to their own food group the way some of us do.'

When her eyes slid back to him, she let them flick to her friends and with a small shake of her head told him not to worry. He was safe. Ruby was safe.

Then a small smile hooked at the corner of her mouth. *Thanks for the M&M's*, her eyes said.

He blinked back, *My pleasure.*

'Are they actually serving drinks from coconut shells?' Tabitha asked, then she was off.

Rylie, on the other hand, had her hand clamped over Meg's arm as if they'd been soldered together.

Meg blinked at him, her mouth curving in apology. The St Barts crew were a hopeless cover. She knew he was there for her. And while she'd made it perfectly clear to him on more than one occasion that she understood why they should remain miles apart for Ruby's sake, she'd come. The both of them needed their heads read.

'I like the choice in music,' Meg said over her shoulder as Rylie pulled her away. 'Yours?'

'Disco,' he said. 'It's my secret passion.'

She grinned. It lit up the night. And then she was gone.

Zach slid his hands into the pockets of his trousers. He'd put in his promised appearance, meaning he could walk away. Ruby wasn't home so he could slink back to his bungalow and work himself late into the night till his eyes burned and his back ached and he was too exhausted to think about anything but sleep.

He could do that, but instead he decided to stay a little longer. Listen to some Bee Gees.

Drink some punch. Eat a marshmallow or two. See where the night took him.

Damn fool.

Meg sat on a straw mat next to Rylie, drinking a mocktail and pretending to watch Tabitha lead a conga line around the fire, but whenever she had half a chance her eyes sought out Zach.

The moment she'd first seen him standing with the fire at his back, feet bare, watching her with the kind of intensity that took her breath away, her skin had warmed as though she'd stepped too near the flames. Even wreathed in hot-pink flowers he was the most wholly masculine creature she'd ever known.

Dark hair slicked back, clean-shaven, and wearing a pale grey linen suit, he *finally* appeared how he should have all along—like the kind of man her father would know by name.

That first moment when she'd been allowed to dream he might be something he was not hadn't been fair. If she'd first seen him looking like this then maybe she would have had her guard up and have avoided this whole mess from the outset.

Who are you kidding? she thought to herself on

a slow release of breath. In cargo shorts and a soft faded T-shirt he was beautiful. In a perfectly cut suit he was devastating. A woman would have to be made of far sterner stuff than she to skim past such a creation.

'You having a good time so far?' Rylie asked.

'Mmm?' Meg said, turning to Rylie with the straw of her third pineapple mocktail bitten between her front teeth.

'I feel like we've barely seen you enough to make sure you're actually relaxing as promised.'

Meg raised an eyebrow. 'If you actually turned up to any of the scheduled events rather than leaving me to fend for myself that wouldn't be the case.'

'I'm here now.'

Meg bumped her friend with her shoulder. 'So you are. And I'm glad. This is fun. Especially since Tabitha is so on form, and thankfully not trying to rope us into her insanity.'

'Too true. And, now that I am here, is there anything you'd like to catch me up on? The weather, perhaps? Petrol prices getting you down? Anything happen in the past couple of days you'd like to let off your chest?'

She knew what Rylie was asking. And it was

fair enough. They were best friends. Had been since school. Maybe she could give her a little sugar, so long as she gave nothing away about Zach or Ruby. But to do that she'd have to give too much of herself away as well. The myriad reasons why she couldn't just throw herself at him and be done with it went deeper than even Rylie knew.

'The weather, then,' Meg said, tilting her head towards the heavens. 'Look at that sky. Have you ever seen so many stars? Hasn't this been the most beautiful night?'

Rylie paused a long moment before glancing across the fire towards the man they were both pretending not to be talking about. 'Absolutely gorgeous.'

On a sigh Meg said, 'You have no idea.'

A gorgeous man and a gorgeous dad. It was the second part that was making it so easy for her to fall for him, while also making it impossible for her to have him.

She'd never gone through the grieving process the doctors had warned her she might when she'd convinced them to give her the operation that would take away her chance of conceiving a child. All she'd wanted was to do whatever *she* could to stop her father from ever getting the chance to bully another kid again.

She was beginning to fear that was what the faint but now constant ache in her heart was—fissures that had existed in her happy facade since the morning she woke up in Recovery. Only now, as she understood fully for the first time what she'd given up, those fissures were turning into cracks big enough to split her in two.

'Can you do me a favour?' Meg asked.

'Anything. Always.'

'I don't want to be missing any more. In the press, I mean. Dylan texted me today. Apparently the snippet *Chic* ran online a couple of days back has grown legs. I'd rather not be hounded by people with mobile cameras any more than usual this week.'

'I'll get onto my contact at *Chic* and give them the word,' Rylie said. 'Where do you want to be instead of missing?'

Here. 'Anywhere but here.'

'May I ask why?'

Meg tucked her chin against her shoulder and glanced at her friend. 'I wish I could tell you, but it's complicated.'

'Okay, for now. I'm not so silly to think wheatgrass juice is the reason you're glowing like you are. Tell your man he can do as he pleases, I'm looking the other way.'

Meg gave Rylie a quick hug.

Tabitha chose the perfect moment to twist her way out of the line and head on over, laughing as though she could barely draw breath.

'You are a maniac,' Meg said, her voice still slightly ragged.

Tabitha slumped down onto the straw mat beside them. 'Every party we ever have from now on should be exactly like this.'

'With nobody we know as guests and no alcohol?' Rylie asked.

Tabitha shrugged. 'Why not? I know the wellness class we took the first day was all about finding balance, but sometimes I think you need to let yourself go completely *off* balance too. It's a yin and yang thing.'

Off balance. That was the term Meg had been reaching for to describe how Zach made her feel.

He was intensely private while her life was splashed about the papers so regularly she might as well have been living in her own reality TV programme. He saw family as something to safeguard, not to flaunt. His life was so far removed from her own as to be completely foreign.

This was a man trying so hard to be worthy of his daughter, if he knew how low she'd sunk, how desperate a measure she'd taken in order to pull herself back out into the bright lights, would he understand? Or would he think her ridiculous? Hopeless? Weak? All the things she'd been told she was by the one man who ought to have been her fiercest champion. If even her father couldn't see the good in the real her, what hope did she have with anyone else?

He shifted in the firelight, all shadowy angles and dark good looks.

This man had given her chocolate when she'd needed chocolate. He'd given her disco when she'd needed disco. Would he, *could* he, be the one she could trust to accept her just as she really was?

'As much as it pains me to admit,' Rylie said to Tabitha, 'you may be onto something with this *off balance* thing.'

'I hear that,' Meg whispered.

When the party had well and truly wound down, Zach found Meg standing by the bar alone—a bright red firecracker amongst the few shadowy forms lingering till the end.

'Did you get your fair share of marshmallows?'

he asked when he was close enough to breathe in her subtly exotic perfume.

She turned to him with a coconut shell curved into her palm and a straw in her mouth. That mouth. If Zach had ever had cause to believe in heaven and hell that mouth was enough to convince him of both.

'I've eaten far more than my fair share. But it's too late. There's no getting them back now. You had a good night?'

'Tonight hiding in plain sight finally caught up with me. My right hand is bruised from pressing local flesh all evening.'

Her eyes smiled as she sucked on her straw. 'So how was it being Mr Social?'

'One couple had me pinned for half an hour trying to get me to join their pyramid scheme.'

She laughed so hard she tucked her drink to her chest so as not to spill it. 'If you want I can give you some hints on how to extricate yourself quickly and politely so that they leave thinking you were lovely but somehow certain they'd better not go near you again.'

'You are a woman of many hidden capabilities, Ms Kelly.'

She raised one thin eyebrow. 'And then

some. Now come on, you must have met some nice people.'

'I did.' Most were surprisingly decent. Warm, welcoming, enthused that he'd seen such value in their beautiful region to create the resort. He said, 'One local businesswoman had some fantastic ideas about marketing local produce around the country using the resort label. I might even look into it while I'm here.'

She grinned. 'I told you schmoozing had its perks.'

'So you did.' He glanced around. 'Where are your chaperones?'

'Rylie needed her beauty sleep and Tabitha practically had to be carried back to the room, she so wore herself out dancing.'

When she smiled at him she made him feel as if he were sixteen again with possibilities he'd never even imagined opening up before him. He felt as if he could take on the world. He felt as if he were standing on unstable ground.

He waved an arm away from the bright bar. Together they walked around the edge of the beach to a place the firelight didn't quite reach.

She slid her bare feet sensually through the sand. Her fingernails and toenails had been repainted blood-red. She smelled of jasmine. Her skin glowed warm and creamy in the firelight. Escaped tendrils of her hair flickered away from her lovely face in the light summer breeze. Heat curled deep within his abdomen.

His voice was rough when he said, 'I've had a question I wanted to ask you all night.'

She clutched her coconut shell to her chest and looked at her feet. 'And what's that?'

'Did you seriously have *that* dress in your suitcase this whole time?'

She laughed. 'A girl never knows when she's going to need a party frock. Besides, the girls packed my bags for me. You'll be shocked to discover coming to a wellness retreat was their idea.' She glanced sideways. 'You look very smart yourself.'

He puffed out his chest. 'I always do.'

'Mmm. But there's just something extra special about you tonight that I can't put my finger on.'

She put her finger on the fullest part of her bottom lip instead. The urge to drag her into the reeds and finish what they'd started the day before, to give in and let instinct and abandon bring release, was almost overwhelming.

Until she asked, 'So did you choose hot pink for your little necklace there?'

Zach glanced down at his shirt only to be reminded of the wilting lei. 'Give me a break—everyone got one coming in.'

'Do you see me wearing one?'

'They must have run out before you got here.'

'Likely excuse.' She slid the straw into her mouth and grinned.

And now you're flirting, he said inside his head. *Of course you're flirting. Just look at her. I mean, really look at her.* He did. She took his breath away.

They hit the far side of the fire and as one took up residence on an empty straw mat. The bonfire no longer blazed, but embers glowed red-hot at the base of the gently licking flames.

'It's very quiet out here all of a sudden,' she said, her voice soft.

'I think we may officially be considered stragglers.'

'Most socially uncool.'

'No need to panic quite yet. We won't be the very last. I'm told there's always one fellow hanging about ready to douse the fire once all's said and done.'

'Then our party reputations will live to see another day!' she said, but he saw in the flicker of her eyes that she heard what he'd really been telling her. They had a chaperone of sorts after all.

She crossed her legs frog style, sitting her drink on her far side and laying her hands in her lap— they fast disappeared into her ample skirt—as she looked into the fire.

Silence stretched between them. He wondered if she could feel the same electricity running up and down her arms that was creating havoc over his.

When she blatantly asked, 'So where's Ruby tonight?' he knew without a doubt that she was well aware.

CHAPTER NINE

THE fact that Meg had to be the one to remind him of the participant in their relationship who wasn't there brought Zach solidly back to earth.

Habit had him slamming his lips shut tight. But then Meg tucked loose strands of hair behind her ear and shot him an encouraging smile. And he couldn't deny, even to himself, that talking to her helped. More than talking to Felicia, or the teachers at Ruby's school, or the social workers who came to the house once a week.

Maybe it was the fact that she would be leaving in a few days. Maybe it was because sometimes she seemed to understand Ruby more than even he did. Or maybe it was because he simply enjoyed talking to her.

For whatever reason, he said, 'She's sleeping over at her friend Clarissa's house. Her first sleepover since moving here. She was so excited when the invitation came through this morning I couldn't say no.'

'Did she tell you about the invitation before or after she made you pancakes?'

He thought back. 'After.'

Meg laughed softly. 'Getting you all nice and buttered up before going in for the kill. I love it.'

The affection in Meg's voice didn't surprise him, but again it moved him. Because of this woman, parts of himself he'd thought long since turned to dry ice had begun to melt. And he wasn't the only one.

He patted the chest of his jacket and felt inside the card Ruby had presented to him that morning. A card she'd made, addressed to Meg. He'd brought it with him with every intention of giving it to her. He even got as far as reaching inside and touching the pink cardboard before his fingers curled into his palm.

Even as he'd slid the card into his jacket earlier that evening, he'd known he couldn't *ever* tell Meg about the card.

Letting Ruby develop a fondness for her was a bad idea. A kid could only have the object of their affection snatched away from them so many times before they learnt it hurt less to simply never form attachments at all. It was his duty to protect Ruby from that kind of hurt as well. As such he could only in good conscience encourage friendships he knew would last.

Meg turned to him with a wide, lovely, genuine smile, and he wished he could be as conscientious with himself. He let his hand slide out of his coat pocket, empty.

She waggled a finger at him and said, 'If I didn't know better I'd think you've read the book after all.'

'Which book is that?'

'*How to Father a Girl.* It's extremely hard to track down and even more difficult to decipher. Lots of hieroglyphics and double talk. But you seem to be following along beautifully.'

'I don't always get that same feeling from Felicia.'

Meg raised an eyebrow. 'Do tell.'

He baulked. Then convinced himself that while keeping Ruby a step removed was one thing, sharing pieces of *his* experiences was fine. In fact, so far it had done him nothing but good. 'She seemed to think I ought to keep Ruby home from Clarissa's because a) she did have a sore throat, or b) she'd been hamming it up. Either way she should be spending the weekend in bed.'

'You overrode the nanny?' Her eyes widened. 'Brave man.'

Zach laughed. 'Letting Ruby have some fun felt right.' He scooped up a handful of sand and let it run slowly through his fingers as he remembered. 'Then after it was settled, for some reason I winked at her. I've never, not once in my entire life, winked. Didn't even know I knew how. And you know what the rascal did?'

'What?'

'She giggled. No more amazing a sound have I heard in my entire life.'

Meg pulled her knees back to her chest and wrapped her arms around them. 'I knew it,' she said on a sigh. 'You've so-o-o read the book.'

Zach brushed the sand from his hand and glanced at her from the corner of his eye. In the semi-darkness the angle of her body was outlined in gold from the dying fire—all curled into itself like a ball of shimmering red fabric. It wouldn't matter who her father was, or the size of her trust fund, she would draw the eyes of those who knew quality when they saw it wherever she went.

He took in a deep breath, wood smoke tickling the back of his throat. 'I may be faking it well enough to fool you, and perhaps even Felicia and Ruby. But the grim truth is I know next to nothing about kids, and less about girls.'

'Many, *many* eons ago little Zach was seven.'

'That is so. Yet my hope is that Zach at seven and Ruby at seven have very different experiences.'

'Why's that?'

The night was so quiet, the fire so mellow, the air so warm, Meg's voice and presence in the darkness so reassuring. The uncomfortable truth of his childhood balanced on the tip of his tongue for a moment before he swallowed it down. He didn't talk about it. Didn't even like thinking about it. If having stopped flying to the ends of the earth and back meant all that purposely lost baggage might yet catch up with him…

He said, 'She's a girl, for one thing.'

Meg laughed and it echoed through him hollowly. All that virgin trust between them had been built for nought if he could still feign his feelings so easily. But it was too late to tell her now. The moment had passed.

'To tell you the truth,' she said, 'what girls think, what we like, what annoys us, what we want isn't really all that different at Ruby's age or mine.'

'And that is?'

She laughed again. This time he was quick enough to close down the exposed parts of himself so, instead of it making him feel so cool and alone inside, her laughter skittered hot and fast across his skin like sparks from the fire.

Her knees fell towards him, her hand reached out to give her balance and he could see more of her face in the firelight. 'Better I don't say. The more you think you know about womankind, the more you realise you don't know. I'm not being any help to you at all, am I?'

'You are. More than you know.'

'Really?' The flicker of surprise in her voice caught him off guard.

'Really,' he said, infusing the word with as much gravity as he could.

She watched him for a few long, hot moments before finding the fingernails of her right hand unexpectedly intriguing. 'Well, of course I'm helping. I was a seven-year-old girl a lot more recently than you were a seven-year-old boy.'

'That'll be why.'

She smiled. He caught it at the fire-lit edge of her

profile. A sexy curve of her mouth, a softening of her wide blue eyes. Heaven help him, he could have kissed her then and there. In front of the lingering fire-douser and anyone else who'd cared to hang about once the food and drinks were gone.

Then she had to go and ask, 'Did you always want kids?' and it was as good as a cold shower.

'Never.' The all too illuminating answer shot from his mouth like some kind of penance for his earlier cowardice. But it was out there now. So he went the only way he knew—forward.

'My lifestyle was not conducive to kids. Or a family of any sort. I was on a plane twice a week. I've lived in hotel suites my whole adult life. The only real-estate I've ever owned was commercial. Any relationships I've had had to fit into that way of life, period.'

'And when you first found out about Ruby?'

'When my lawyer rang with the news I thought it was some kind of cruel joke. But when I hung up the phone it felt as though I'd been waiting for that call all my life.'

'Simple as that, she changed your mind?' she asked, her voice gentle.

'In a heartbeat. It's the strangest thing, but now I can barely remember my life without her.'

The fire crackled as a log split and those above spilt into the gap. Zach came to from far, far away, a whole other lifetime. He glanced across at Meg. Her face tilted to watch the sparks that fluttered up into the darkness. Without the play of expressions that continuously gave her away, he had no idea what she was thinking.

'How about you?' he asked on a whim.

She licked her lips and her brow furrowed for a moment before she turned to him with a breezy smile. 'Kids? Gosh, no. Wherever would I find the time?'

'You're just saying that to make me feel better for admitting I felt that way.'

'Not at all. I promise.' Again he thought he caught a hint of a frown, but it was too dark to really tell. Whatever it was it was soon swallowed by the kind of overbright smile he knew better than to trust. 'Don't get me wrong—my nieces are two of my favourite people in the entire word. I love them to distraction. But it's not on the cards for me.'

'Why?'

He could tell she was really looking at him, and he wished there were some way of turning on a light. Of looking into those bright eyes and knowing what she was thinking before she said it. Being a step behind felt...disquieting somehow.

She eventually said, 'Even apart from the whole cameras-outside-your-front-door thing, the life of a Kelly kid is not an easy one. The pressure to be the best, the brightest, every day a winner is immense. And that's not changing any day soon.'

'Your nieces are going through this now?'

Again she paused. *Come on*, he thought, *I could do it, so can you.* 'I find myself quietly sabotaging the process wherever I possibly can. I sneak them junk food when their dad's not watching. I teach them swear words in French, which my father doesn't speak. If I babysit I let them wear pyjamas all day. I let them be kids.'

'Talk about maternal instincts,' he said with two raised eyebrows.

She stared at him as if he had grown horns. As if he was missing the point entirely. Then her hand moved to rest on her belly. She scrunched her hand into a fist before looking away and reaching out to grab her toes.

'Instincts or no, unlike you I'm hardly going to have one appear out of the woodwork so that's the end of that.' She shook it off. Literally, her whole body gave one great shiver, before she said, 'Okay. Moving on. Here's something *you* can take to the bank. You ready?'

'Always.'

'Meg's crash course on Raising a Girl 101. Ruby will make friends you don't like, she'll see movies that'll make your eyes pop out of your head, listen to music that makes your ears ache, she'll diet when she doesn't need to, and eat ice cream for breakfast, and she'll meet boys you wish had never been born. Roll with the punches for your own sake. And for hers, let her know no matter what happens she always has a safe place to go home to.'

He nodded, though his head was reeling with points one and two, much less the rest. 'That's why I took on the house here. To give her somewhere near her familiar haunts to come home to.'

'Nu-uh, Mr Jones. By home, I mean *you*. This is the clincher, the one thing you should get tattooed to your arm. No matter what happens, no matter what she does, always, *always*, make sure she knows you love her. That's what will keep her coming home.'

Zach realised he was holding his breath. But he didn't let it go until his lungs began to burn from inaction.

Love. *Love*. Love? The more times he said the word, the less sense it made.

What did he know about love? He'd fed Ruby, clothed her, given her shelter, filled her room with trinkets, let her have her little rebellions as some kind of compensation for not having a mother. But love?

If his own childhood had taught him anything it was that love was a sham. A fickle fairy tale. If loving someone as much as he'd loved some of his foster parents didn't ensure they loved him back, what was the point?

He breathed deep and buried his face in his palms. What a hypocrite. He'd been busy convincing himself he was all about the fatherly care, when all the while he was actually dolling out the same kind of veiled neglect of his childhood without even realising it.

That poor, *poor* kid. Baking him pancakes, picking him wildflowers. At least she was trying to show him she loved him. While he hadn't given her a single clue that he loved her too.

He loved her. Of course he damned well loved her. He'd have been some kind of fool to have changed his life so completely had he not.

He blinked into the fire. Stunned. Apparently

never being shown how did not make him as incapable as he'd always believed.

He glanced at Meg. Their gazes tangled a moment longer than could ever be considered merely friendly.

Meg raised her eyebrows. 'Are you okay?'

'Terrified,' he said before he could censor himself.

She laughed softly. Sadly even. 'Then you know you're not perfect. You know you have limitations. That's a good thing. Believe me. What happened to Ruby's mum?'

The last part came so out of the blue it shocked Zach right out of his funk. 'Cancer. It was quick. Ruby didn't even know till it was all over.'

'No! Oh, the poor pet. And Isabel had really never told you about Ruby?'

He shook his head. 'Our relationship had been casual. It ended as easily as it had begun. Still she was very clear in her will that she wanted me to have custody. For that one fact I have to forgive her the rest.'

'Was it really that easy? I know I'm speaking out of turn, but even I don't feel like *I'm* ready to forgive her and I didn't even know the woman.'

She hadn't even had to tell him so. He'd seen

the fight in her eyes. Like a lioness protecting her cub. When had this fireside flirtation suddenly become so intense?

He said, 'Over something that important, it was either forgive or let it burn for ever. The choice was simple.'

One dark curl draped over her pale shoulder as she wrapped her arms tight about her knees again. And there they sat, in loaded silence for a good couple of minutes before she finally said: 'My father's sick. You've probably heard.'

He didn't nod. He didn't need to. A person would have to be a hermit, a far more dedicated one than he was, not to know Quinn Kelly had heart problems. 'How's he doing?'

She nodded vigorously. 'Exceptionally well, the old warhorse. So far as I know. He's retired. Plays golf a lot. Eats the kind of food your chef would applaud.'

'That's good news, then.'

She nodded, but it wasn't as effusive. She was a million miles away. 'It gets a girl to thinking.'

'About?'

She scrunched up her nose. 'Things far too blah to go into on such a beautiful night. I'm sorry. Where were we? Ruby.'

Back to Ruby. Always Ruby. It occurred to him then that she might be using his daughter as a shield as much as he had been. He couldn't help but wonder why.

'Meg.'

'Zach,' she said in a mock-sombre voice.

'Tell me.'

She focused on the flowers around his neck. 'It's just all this stuff that I haven't thought about in years that has shuffled up to the surface in the last little while. And then you sit there all noble, making forgiveness sound so easy when I just don't think I could—'

'Tell me,' he said again.

She blinked at him. All big blue eyes and down-turned mouth. 'I can't believe I'm about to... God, where do I begin?'

His voice felt unusually tight as he said, 'Wherever you see fit.'

'Okay,' she said with a hearty sigh. 'There's this one memory that's been playing on my mind. Years ago my father was given an Honorary Doctorate of Commerce by a university in Melbourne. He'd never gone to uni, never even finished high school, so it was a matter of immense pride. One of my brothers had scraped his knee or something equally boyish, so Mum waited at the hotel to be taken with them in the town car and my father drove himself, with me there, at my mother's insistence, to keep him company. This was years before GPS.'

She looked to him. Her eyes narrowed, almost pleading he get her to stop. He just nodded. *Go on.*

'Anyway, when he finally admitted he was lost he gave me the street directory and told me to show him how to get there. I'd never used one before, couldn't pronounce half the street names, so I read the map wrong and we were late. Less than five minutes, but late is late.'

She stopped again. Licked her lips. Her hands were shaking. The tension streaming off her was palpable. He could feel his pulse beating in his temples.

'What did he do?' Zach asked, half not wanting to know, half needing her to trust him enough to tell him.

'Before the engine had even come to a halt he turned on me. With such venom.' She shook her ponytail off her shoulder to hide the flinch as the memory came at her. 'I was careless, ridiculous, stupid and I had to find my own way back to the hotel to teach me to take heed of where I was and who I was with. By the time I made it to the hotel it was after dark, my mother was beside herself and my father had holed himself up in his room. His doctorate thrown onto the front table of the suite as though it was rubbish.'

Her eyes flickered to his—dark, grave, wounded. Eyes so beautiful they should never be made to look that way. His fingers curled into fists and adrenalin like he'd never felt shot through him.

'How old were you?'

'About Ruby's age. Maybe a little younger.'

He'd known it the moment she'd started telling the story. Hearing her admit as much still made him want to hit something. Or more particularly someone.

'It wasn't the first time,' he said matter-of-factly.

She shrugged and seemed to disappear even further inside her ample skirt. 'Ever since I can remember he'd always been distant. Working a lot. But the first time he took it out on me was the time I told my nanny I was adopted. I thought it was because I'd dare think not being one of them was a more attractive option.'

'And now?'

She let out a long, shaky breath. 'Now I

wonder if I had it all backwards. There have always been rumours...' She swallowed, and looked at him, her big, blue eyes begging him to say the things she couldn't.

Zach said, 'You mean his affairs?'

'Not the kind of thing a parent can keep from their kid when even rumours make the papers.' Her mouth twisted, but a gleam had lit her eyes, as though her strength was returning now she wasn't the only one bearing the load. 'I've often wondered if I was an afterthought. A way to keep their marriage together. If so, it worked. But while my mother never gave a hint of it, the only way I could make sense of my father's behaviour was that I was a reminder of the worst time of his life. That he regretted it. And regretted me.'

'Even if that's true it's not your fault.'

She shrugged. 'I know. I do. And I don't even care any more. At least I thought I didn't. I don't even know why I brought it up.'

Zach understood all too well. 'You've made it very clear exactly why I need to always put Ruby first.'

'I did? I guess I did. And don't you forget it!'

Her soft mouth turned up into the echo of a familiar smile. As they looked into one another's eyes the night stretched and contracted, and once again they communicated more in the silence than mere words could ever say.

Ruby's card began to burn a hole in his top pocket. If ever there was a moment for him to take a risk and give it to her…

And then she yawned. 'And on that note now seems like a good time to escort me back to my room.'

She flapped her hands at him. He pulled himself to his feet before pulling her after him. As they stood face to face her perfumed scent washed over him, delicate and delicious.

All he'd have to do was slide a hand around her neck and pull her to him and that mouth would be all his. The urge to kiss her, to take away the hurt, to give her something warm and wonderful to think about instead was overwhelming.

But she wasn't some gorgeous young thing putting her hand up for a one-night stand. She'd had an intense night. Her thoughts were so obviously still scrambled. He'd be taking complete advantage.

'One last question,' he said, his voice low and rough.

She raised one sexy eyebrow.

'It's about Ruby. I know, I know, I'm getting predictable.'

The corner of her mouth twitched as though she knew exactly what he was doing. 'Shoot.'

'Should I get her a pet? A rabbit maybe?'

She let go of his hands and backed away from the beach towards the resort, towards the end of the night. 'You can't get her a rabbit! They're a pest in Queensland. Start with a goldfish. Let her choose it. Let her name it whatever she wants. She'll be putty in your hands.'

He caught up in three long strides. 'You had a fish?'

'I was a terrible pet owner. I always forgot to feed them, and they had a habit of leaping from the tank in desperation to leave me. But Mum just kept on replacing them. A dozen fish must have died to save the poor woman from having to tell me what was happening.'

'What did you name your first fish?'

She bit back a smile. 'Luke Skywalker. I so-o-o wanted to grow up to be Luke.'

'And now?'

'Now I know better. Han Solo is the bomb.'

CHAPTER TEN

MEG felt more than a little shaky as she walked slowly beside Zach up the white stone path leading away from the lake back to the resort.

What a mess. The things she'd said, the things she'd admitted. So many years she'd kept them deep inside. And then along came Zach and her tightly reined-in emotions were in a tailspin.

There was only one conclusion. She was falling for him. She might as well have been running around with a pair of scissors in her hand. It was only a matter of time before she got seriously hurt.

She had no idea if it was ten at night or three in the morning. The moon told her nothing as she had no sense of direction. The grass was grey and dewy, low cloud cover hovered higher up the path, lending a magical feeling to the place. If she weren't feeling as highly strung as a thoroughbred she might even be able to enjoy it.

Instead all she could think about was the man walking silently at her side.

At the very least she knew he'd taken from her shambolic confession what she'd wanted him to—that the foundations of his whole relationship with Ruby were being forged *right now*. The good moments, the pancakes-for-breakfast moments, should be the ones she remembered too.

But even knowing she'd done a selfless thing didn't stop her from feeling like a bowl of jelly on a shaky table.

She slowed her steps before she tripped over her numb feet. Zach's slowed to match.

'Zach?' she said, her voice so croaky she cleared her throat. 'Can I just ask, the things I told you before, I—'

He shook his head and held up a finger an inch from her mouth. Her words dried up in her throat.

Zach's voice was deep when he finally opened his mouth to speak. 'My parents passed away when I was five years old. With no other family I grew up in a slew of foster homes and state-run children's homes—some fair, more atrocious. It didn't matter which, I was still pushed in and pulled out again months later, again and again, with no warning and no word as to why. I had no consistent contact with any one person—no supervisor, no parent, no other foster child—until the day I turned sixteen and I caught a bus to Sydney and began my life.'

Meg realised she was breathing heavily. 'God, you must think me a schmuck. Complaining about my father when yours wasn't even—'

'No,' he said with a stilling hand on her shoulder. 'Don't do that. No comparing. We each need to own what we've been dealt or we'll never be able to move on.'

She nodded. Then laughed softly to release the pent-up energy coursing through her starting at the point where his strong hand lay upon her bare shoulder. 'You're making me think I ought to have listened harder in wellness class.'

She shook her head, angry at herself for being flippant when talking about anything real. If there was ever a time to not go there, this was it.

She looked up at Zach—tall, dark, divine. 'Have you really owned your past?'

He made a clicking noise with the side of his mouth. 'Please. Why do you think I keep building bigger and better wellness resorts? I'm looking to prove I'm better than my past as much as the next man. But in the past few days I have come to understand a little more about what my foster parents went through. Not taking me in with open arms had little to do with me at all. They would have had to have been masochists to have given that kind of emotional investment to a child they knew would never be theirs. Knowing there's even a minute chance is akin to emotional torture…'

His voice petered off.

'But Ruby—'

'Might still not end up with me.'

'What?' Meg said, her voice like air. 'How?'

'We have up to a year for the state to decide if I am a fit guardian,' Zach said.

Meg's heart squeezed as she remembered the look in Zach's eyes when he'd said his life had changed in a heartbeat when Ruby had come along. The look in Ruby's eyes when she'd proudly said who her father was. 'How long have you had her so far?'

'Seven months, eight days.'

Meg bunched her dress to keep her hands busy lest she do something stupid like hug the guy.

She couldn't even imagine the daily torture it must be to have something so wonderful within reach, knowing it might yet be snatched away.

She glanced up at his beautiful profile. Okay, so maybe she could imagine it just the tiniest little bit.

She placed a hand on her heart. 'If there's *anything* I can do. Write a letter of recommendation. Talk to the judge. My family has connections the likes of which you wouldn't believe.'

Before he could be too proud to turn her down, she held out a hand close enough she could feel the warmth of his breath washing against her skin.

'Forget you're not a fan of hoopla. If you need to in order to fight for Ruby, use me for all I'm worth. My notoriety has to be good for something more than invites to every party in town, right?'

He wrapped his fingers around her hand, sliding them through hers until they were intertwined. 'I was going to say thank you.'

'Oh. Well, then, you're welcome.'

She glanced at him, the dark silhouette striding alongside her in the near darkness. Things were even more complicated than she'd imagined. A little girl. A custody battle. And all remarkably hush-hush. How he did it alone, with no family support and with such integrity, she had no idea.

'Is that why you don't do press? You don't like talking about your background?'

'I didn't like being judged for something I had no control over then and I still don't.'

'Why?'

She looked up at him too late to notice how tight his jaw had become.

'If people tell you you're crap often enough, you begin to believe it.'

'You don't think I know that?'

'I say don't give them the chance.'

'I say find a way to negate it so that it can no longer hurt you. There's nothing at all shameful about it. Who you've become is amazing.' She looked down at her toes sticking out of her Grecian sandals. 'I mean, the story of how you got here is amazing. Think about all the foster kids you could help if they knew how you'd pulled yourself up by your own socks to become who you are.'

'Not going to happen. I have to think of Ruby.'

'And what about her?' she asked. 'Are you ever going to tell her where you came from? And if you do will you swear her to silence? Or keep her locked up here for ever to protect yourself from the sting of other people's opinions?'

'What about your father?' he shot back.

'What about him?'

He pulled her closer, until they came to a stop. 'He's a bully. Hell, Meg, he was emotionally abusive to you. Yet of all the parts of your life on show, why has that never come out? Why not show other young girls that their own expectations of themselves are the ones that matter, not what other people think they should be?'

She tried to expertly extricate her hand from his, a move she'd pulled a thousand times, but it was as though he had been waiting for it.

He took her other hand so she was stuck facing him when he said, 'Forget Ruby for a moment—what about all the other little girls who read magazines and look up to you as a role model?'

That was what her volunteer work was for! So what if the girls whose hair she braided and the boys she played cops and robbers with didn't know who the woman behind the bleached-blonde wig and brown contacts was? At least she was there.

She itched to tell him so. To say out loud that working at the Valley Shelter was the most rewarding thing she'd ever done and that every moment she spent flirting with a camera lens so that her rotten bloody father got the chance to muck about with someone else's hard-earned savings felt more and more like hard work.

Especially when even having looked death in the eye it hadn't once occurred to him to make retribution.

But the old fear of being thought ridiculous for thinking herself more valuable than she was rose up her ankles, her calves, her waist, until it reached her throat and she sputtered like an old car whose engine would never again come to life.

'I do think of them,' she said. 'I am doing what I can. In my way. Just not the way you mean.'

He closed his eyes a moment and took a calming breath. He was probably counting to ten. Her brothers did that all the time.

When he opened his eyes they were deliberately calm. As such she wasn't nearly prepared for his next words.

He said, 'So you're not simply filling the void of not being loved by your father with being loved by the entire world?'

She coughed out an incredulous laugh, and dragged her hands from his to slam them onto her hips. 'Are *you* trying to tell *me* that giving up your life for Ruby isn't your way of making *someone* in the world love you back?'

Silence stretched between them as taut and dangerous as an overstretched rubber band.

Until Zach said, 'Maybe you're right. Maybe that's how this all began. But I do love her. And as soon as she comes home from Clarissa's, I'll tell her so because it's important for a little girl to know her dad loves her. Or so someone I trust told me.'

Meg shook her head. This was backfiring big time. If he pulled when she pushed she was never going to be rid of him. Instead, he was being gorgeous and warm and understanding and a tower of strength and a wonderful dad.

With a growl at the moon she headed back up the path again.

'Meg,' he said from behind her.

She waved a go-away hand at him.

He jogged to catch up to her, this time spinning her to face him with the gentlest of pressure at her elbow.

'Thanks ever so much for being such an enchanting escort, but I'm sure I can make it back from here.' She glanced at her surroundings to discover they had gone a ways past the Waratah House turn-off and had found themselves outside one of the lovely little bungalows on the way to Zach's place. A light was on over the porch.

'I could do with a coffee right about now— how about you?' he asked.

She whirled to stare at him. The moon was now almost completely obscured by cloud and his eyes were nothing more than patches of black within his shadowed face. 'Now what are you talking about?'

He waved a hand towards the bungalow. 'I use it as my office. Some nights I stay over rather than heading back to the house. So the pantry is well stocked with all sorts of delights, including coffee.'

'Oh,' she said, his meaning not even the slightest bit obscured by the fact that she couldn't see his eyes. He'd been leading her here the whole time. To his cosy, empty, private abode. Which had a bed. And coffee.

She licked her lips as her mind whirled a million miles a minute. 'And you kept this from me the whole time? The coffee part, I mean.'

His mouth lifted so the preposterously sexy arc in his right cheek put in a surprise appearance. 'I wasn't prepared to share my coffee with you then.'

'And now?'

He lifted a hand to slide it into the hair at the base of her neck, the tug of his warm fingers almost too much to bear.

'I'd say things have changed rather dramatically over the past few days. My eyes have been opened in more ways than one. And I only have you to thank. Coffee seems a meagre place to start.'

Meg swallowed, her mouth dry, her blood thundering in her ears until she felt the slightest bit dizzy. There were reasons, good reasons why this couldn't happen, only she couldn't remember one.

He slid his spare hand into his trouser pockets. She imagined she could hear the soft tinkle of keys somewhere on his person.

'Zach—' she said, her voice half appeal, half groan.

'Enough talk,' he said.

He leaned down and kissed her. And she was on her toes, reaching up to him even before he gathered her into his arms.

The raging heat of his kiss swept her away, spiralling her into the cosmos until she could no longer feel her feet. Could no longer remember her name.

Or why they hadn't been doing this all along.

Meg lay on Zach's bed, white cotton sheets tangled about her, his long limbs trapping her in his warm embrace.

She glanced at the clock on the wall. It was

only a couple of hours before sunset. Rylie and Tabitha would soon notice her gone. They'd assume where she was, and they'd be right. They'd known she'd end up here before she did. As apparently did Zach. It seemed everyone knew her better than she knew herself.

She tilted her head to watch Zach's sleeping face. The creases at the edges of his eyes had disappeared. His tanned skin looked radiant against the white pillow. A faint line curved down his right cheek, a reminder of the arc that grooved deep when he laughed. He was sleeping like a man with no worries on his mind.

She reached up and slid a curl from his forehead. He didn't stir.

Such gentle strength. She felt it infusing her more with every second she spent in his arms until she couldn't imagine when in her life she would ever have felt this kind of peace, this slowly budding confidence that if she looked deep inside herself she might not be afraid of what she saw.

The words spilled from her lips to his sleeping form before she even knew they were coming. 'I volunteer at the Valley Women's Shelter at least once a week. It's a halfway house for women

who've managed to break free of abusive relationships but have nowhere else to go. Most have
kids. Most have nothing with which to go it alone
bar the clothes on their backs. Many are so
battered and bruised they can barely talk.'

He shifted and she held her breath. He slid his
leg along hers, wrapping his arm tighter about
her, sending warm waves of pleasure all over her
body. But his eyes remained closed. She waited
until the sensations rolling across her skin dis-
sipated, and his breaths were once again even
and deep.

'I wear a blonde wig,' she whispered, 'contacts,
the kind of make-up you'd see in a bad eighties
movie, clothes I picked up in a bargain bin at a
thrift store. I can walk through a throng of paparazzi in front of my building and they don't turn
an eye. The guys at the shelter know me as Daisy.
They've never asked questions, just appreciated
someone giving their time to play with the kids
while the mums have medicals, or to just sit and
hold a woman's hand while they tell their stories
to the counsellors.'

She took a deep breath and let it out on a wobble.

'Compared with the level of abuse they've
been subjected to my dad constantly finding

new weird and wonderful ways of letting me know he didn't consider me worthy of the name Kelly was a walk in the park. But I still see myself reflected in their eyes when they talk about how hard it was to finally say "enough". I give cups of tea, and a shoulder to cry on and secretly stashed envelopes full of money to help them start a new life. It's the most worthwhile thing I've ever done and my name has nothing to do with it.'

She let her gaze amble over Zach's beautiful nose, his strong jaw, the smattering of dark hair curling over his chest.

'So there you have it. That's what I do to really make a difference. I just don't shout it out to the world. Not because I'm not proud, or I don't realise it's vitally important. But because it's hard, and it's private, and I do it for myself and for them, not for him and not for the cameras.'

'Thank you,' Zach said, and had it not been for the knot of sheets and his heavy limbs keeping her in bed Meg might well have leapt a foot in the air.

She placed a hand over her thundering heart. 'How long have you been awake?'

'Longer than you have.'

She lay back and blinked up at the ceiling. 'So, just now, you heard everything.'

'Everything.' He snuggled in closer and kissed her on the cheek, right at the edge of her mouth. 'And thank you for telling me.'

She turned to face him. His dark eyes burned into hers. She needn't have searched so desperately for what he was thinking—it was written all over his beautiful face. He did not think her ridiculous. He did not think her a mere party girl. He thought her pretty amazing.

'Thank you for listening,' she whispered before leaning in and placing her lips against his.

And they made love again. Slowly, gently, not once taking their eyes off one another.

A while later Meg fell asleep, knowing without a single doubt that she loved him. Knowing she was never again going to meet someone who saw her, really saw her, as he did. Who made her wonder if the day might yet come when she'd be brave enough to let the rest of the world nearer than skin deep too.

She fell asleep knowing Zach cared for her. Knowing he respected her. Knowing he'd made *love* to her.

She fell asleep knowing that, despite all that, Zach Jones and his gorgeous blooming little family only reminded her with stark, heart-wrenching clarity what she could never have.

As the sun rose through the bay windows of the bungalow, Zach stood in the bedroom doorway in last night's trousers watching Meg dress.

She stood by his rumpled bed, tying the bow on her dress, the muscles of her back working sexily, a small frown pinched between her brows, and her top teeth biting down on her bottom lip. He couldn't believe there was ever a moment when he'd assumed the Meg Kelly the country adored was all an act. In that moment she was so very, very real.

The diamonds, the flashy friends, the *va-va-voom*, they were the trappings of her life, but not why she was beloved. It came down to the fact that she was a warm, dynamic woman who bled like everyone else, and spent her life making sure those around her didn't hurt as much when they bled too. Whether it was a woman running from an abusive husband, her complicated family, his young daughter, a complete stranger who accosted her, camera in hand, while she vacationed, she had time, she had a smile, she had a way of making them feel better off for having met her.

His hands literally ached with the desire to haul her back into his arms and soak up every bit of vitality she could spare. But he needed to get home. To be there when Ruby returned. He had things to do. Things to say.

He pushed away from the door and slid his hand down her back, tugging at her dress until he could feel and see the trail of wild daisies tattooed across her lower back.

At his touch her head fell back in pleasure, her hair spilling over her bare skin.

'So what's the story here?' he asked, his fingers tracing the daisy vine, his breath tickling her ear.

She shivered. 'I got it when I was fifteen. Daisies were my favourite flower. Luckily they still are.'

'What? Fifteen? You need parental permission, right? Until you're eighteen?' *Please, God*, he thought, *let that be true*.

She smiled over her shoulder at him. 'Of course you do. Unless your father said no way in hell was his daughter getting a tattoo and you were me. Then you find a way to get whatever you want.'

Her skin was warm and soft until the tattoo made it feel ever so slightly rough. 'Did it hurt?'

'Like hot needles into the bone for two straight hours. Yuh-huh.'

'You really were a tearaway.'

'I could tell you stories.'

He placed a kiss where her neck met her shoulder. 'So tell me.'

She moved so that her hair fell over the spot he'd just been kissing. 'Another time perhaps.'

He pulled back. A sudden chill had come from her direction. He shook it off. Mornings after were always at least some level of awkward. She'd be all right with some space to process it all.

He searched for his shirt from the night before to find it crumpled on the floor. 'Give me a minute to find a T-shirt and I'll walk you back.'

She plonked onto the corner of his bed as she tied the straps of her shoes around and around her calves. 'Best not. The forest has eyes and ears.'

It struck him she'd once again gone there, to Ruby, so fast, and before he had. But then again there was so much about this whole night that had surprised him. Including the fact that eyes and ears no longer seemed such a threat as they had twenty-four hours earlier.

She had been right in accusing him of locking Ruby away to save himself from having to face the demons of his past. And while he didn't want to see Ruby hurt, ever, surely he didn't want her living the kind of emotionally and physically isolated existence he'd lived all the years before she brought him back into the light.

Meg stood, smoothed down her dress, slicked her hair back into a fresh ponytail and looked around to make sure she hadn't left anything behind.

'Come over for morning tea,' he said before he could stop himself.

Meg glanced up at him in obvious shock. She licked her lips before saying, 'And what, skip DIY Colonic Irrigation class?'

He laughed, but he was not to be deterred. 'Let's say around eleven.'

She watched him a few long moments. Her back was to the sun, so he couldn't make out the expression in her eyes. For the first time in hours a familiar hollowness began to expand inside him. He didn't know what to make of it, he only knew he didn't like it.

'Why?'

Good question. 'I promised you coffee last night and we never quite got there.'

'You didn't promise me anything, Zach,' she said, her voice gentle.

'Come over. Drink coffee. The rest we can make up as we go along.'

Another few protracted moments passed in which she just looked at him. Though it felt more as if she was looking through him, her mind a million miles away. 'Should I bring anything?'

The hollowness went away. 'Just yourself.'

She ran her hands down her dress again. 'Okay.'

'We'll see you then.'

She caught the 'we' loud and clear. He could see it in her sudden stillness. In the duration of her indecipherable stare.

'Just you,' he said. 'Not your family. Not your father. In the privacy of my home. I'm asking *you* to break bread with my daughter and me under comparatively conventional circumstances.'

She nodded. Then said, 'Fine. Till then.'

She leaned into him, her hand pressing against his bare chest as she placed a goodbye kiss on his cheek. He could smell the scent of the lei he'd worn the night before on her skin.

She moved back just far enough to look into his eyes for one dark, hot moment before she walked away.

CHAPTER ELEVEN

LATER that same morning Meg stood in the opening in the stone wall at the edge of Zach's backyard, her fingers gripped tight around a bunch of wildflowers she'd picked along the way.

'What are you doing here?' she asked herself out loud.

She couldn't answer that any more than she could figure out what Zach saw as the end play to all this. She'd made it clear kids weren't part of her life plan and that she wouldn't be the right kind of influence over his. Last night she'd let him off the hook in showing she understood why he would choose Ruby's privacy over any manner of relationship with her.

Last night…

She sighed. It ought to have been their swansong, and a beautiful swansong at that. If only he hadn't had some crazy idea she couldn't fathom. And if only she hadn't gone and fallen in love with the guy.

Her mobile phone buzzed in her pocket, scaring the bejeezers out of her, and fraying her very last nerves.

She ignored it as she had the last ten times it had buzzed that morning. The moment she'd got back to her room her family—who had mostly left her alone for less than half her allotted vacation time—had decided to rear their relentless heads en masse.

Dylan's voice message had appeared first, taking the edge off her long, luxurious, hot shower: 'Hey, kiddo. Tabby told me where she's taken you. Classic! By now you must be itching for something to take your mind off the boredom. Find a computer, RSVP yourself to the Shyler Benefit in KInG's name for the day you get back.'

No *goodbye*. No *if you happen to be free*. Just do it. She justly ignored him.

During breakfast Cameron's first text message came through: 'U have Dad's *The Iliad*? Urgent…ish. Rosie'd love to read it. What Rosie wants Rosie gets!'

From her newly mobiled-up mother: 'Love you. Miss you.' From her father? Not a whisper. All that water under the bridge and it still wounded.

Angry with herself for letting her father get to her by omission, when Brendan's number blinked on the screen five minutes later she ignored it. Voicemail gave her: 'Mum has a thing next Saturday night. The nanny's night off. You need to look after the girls. Confirm with my secretary ASAP.'

Dylan must have called again as his next message came through straight after: 'How do you feel about co-hosting the Queensland Fashion Awards? You love the idea. I knew you would. Call me ten minutes ago and I'll set you up with press to confirm.'

She'd somehow almost forgotten that this was what her life was like back home—non-stop motion, never saying no, doing everything to be appear cheerful and be inordinately useful. Everybody's favourite girl. She felt exhausted and underwhelmed just thinking about it.

Of course the fact she'd had less than two hours of uninterrupted sleep amidst one of the most stunning, tender, unsparing, magical, revealing nights of her life would likely have made aliens landing on her doorstep an underwhelming experience.

She looked through the brush to the hint of a

house beyond. To Zach. She breathed in deep through her mouth and out through her nose, her heart racing as if she'd run five kilometres that morning rather than tucking herself up under the bed covers and hiding the moment she'd snuck back to her room.

As she walked through the backyard a flock of pink and grey galahs settled in a nearby tree. Discarded by Ruby's swing were her skipping rope and a pink bike with a white cane basket and streamers on the handle bars. Had it really only been days since she'd been there before? It felt as if weeks had passed.

The thing that ought to have her walking away kept her moving forward: the chance to see them together. To see if he was as natural a father as she'd trusted. To see if Ruby was as doting a kid as she'd suspected. It would be akin to self-flagellation, but she had to know. To see if that kind of relationship really could exist.

Her phone buzzed again. She whipped it out of her pocket, switched it off and shoved it out of sight.

She headed up the rope bridge that led to the largest structure amongst the string of thatched-roof rooms.

A grey-haired woman came out onto the verandah, and she jumped in fright at seeing Meg bundling her way. 'Aren't you just as quiet as a church mouse?'

I'm as nervous as one, Meg thought. But she conjured up her second-nature Meg Kelly smile, designed to put others at ease, and said, 'I'm Meg. I'm expected.'

The woman's cheeks pinked. She even gave a small curtsy. 'Of course you are, dear. I'm Felicia, Ruby's nanny. You may as well make yourself comfy out here. Zach won't be long.'

Meg handed the motley bunch of flowers over to Felicia, whose eyes widened a tad before a smile snuck into her already copiously creased cheeks.

'How charming. I'll put these in water, shall I?' Felicia then turned and headed along the balcony and across yet another bridge and out of sight.

Feeling like a flibbertigibbet, Meg tugged at her floral peasant top making sure it remained demure, and smoothed down her tight, cropped jeans.

Footsteps came from behind her. She spun around and had to cling to the railing for support against the rush of heat that swept over her as Zach walked down the hall inside the house towards her.

His feet were bare below faded jeans that fitted snugly to his long legs as though he'd owned them all his life. A just as faded coffee-brown T-shirt made the most of his bronzed skin and his dark hair was still wet, as though he'd had a recent shower.

Her heart felt so full it didn't know what to do with itself. Beat? Go bust? Leap from her chest and into his arms?

As Zach hit the sunlight angling into the house she saw Ruby was hiding behind his legs. How alike they looked. Long, lean, dark good looks, fierce intelligence swimming behind their guarded eyes. But it was their natural connection that hit hardest. If he took one short step she would have banged into him, but somehow their rhythm stayed in sync. It was mesmerising. And unbearable.

'You came,' Zach said when he spotted her.

She shrugged, feigning nonchalance she was nowhere near feeling. 'I had nowhere better to be.'

He laughed. 'I won't be putting *that* on the brochures, I can assure you.'

'Smart move.'

They smiled at one another awhile and Meg took solace in the fact that she wasn't the only one who was nervous.

'Now, Ruby,' Zach said, gently uncurling his daughter from behind him, pulling her around in front but keeping two hands on her shoulders. 'You remember Meg, right?'

Ruby's dark eyes stared back at her, testing, deciding whether it served her to admit as much. Meg's heart performed the greatest twitch of its life. Zach had his hands full more than he even realised.

She leaned down to Ruby and murmured out of the corner of her mouth, 'You didn't happen to save me any muffins from the other day, did you?'

Ruby shook her head.

'Mmm.' Meg held a finger to her mouth. 'I'm guessing that's because your dad ate the lot.'

Ruby glanced up at him with wide eyes.

'Men,' she said, rolling her eyes. 'Promise me you'll never make the mistake of thinking they're at all complicated.'

'I won't,' were Ruby's first words. Bright kid.

'On that note,' Zach said, his voice a rumble that skittered along Meg's arms, 'I'll be back in a minute with real food. No muffins. Behave. Both of you.'

Meg smiled back.

He gave her one last, white-hot look before

heading inside, jerking her poor heart around all the more. How could he expect her to behave after that?

She sauntered over to a large square outdoor table sitting neatly in the shade of a massive cream, linen umbrella and perched her backside on the edge of a wooden bench seat.

'So, Miss Ruby,' she said, curling a finger at the girl, 'what's the plan for this morning?'

Ruby moseyed near and picked at a knot of wood in another chair. 'Since Dad got to choose who was invited over, I got to pick what we'd eat.'

'Fair enough. So what are we eating?'

Ruby eyed Meg down with wisdom beyond her years. 'I picked peanut butter on white bread. Dad thought you might like something else. I told him you'd like peanut butter on white bread.'

'Well,' Meg said, trying to keep her cool while the kid wrapped herself tighter and tighter around her heart. 'Would you believe that of all the food in all the world, peanut butter on white bread is exactly what I want?'

'I knew it. I liked your pink dress, so it made sense that if I liked peanut butter you would too. Ooh, wait there!' Ruby said, before tearing off inside.

'I'm not going anywhere,' Meg said to the empty doorway, her heart pressing towards the space where Ruby had been.

She shoved her face into her hands. She should never have come. She knew it would only make her love him more. Make her feel for his sweet kid. Make her wonder how she was ever going to go back to a life of smiling and pouting and pretending it was the greatest job on earth.

Unless this didn't have to end. Unless Zach had brought her here with completely non-altruistic intentions. Unless last night had meant exactly as much to him as it had done to her.

Ruby came running out of the house with something behind her back.

Meg sat up and physically wiped the hope from her face. 'What have you got there?'

'I asked Dad to give this to you yesterday but I found it on the hall table this morning. He must have forgotten,' Ruby said, sneaking up onto the bench beside Meg.

As Meg would have done with her nieces, instinct had her putting her arm around Ruby as she opened the gift. Pink cardboard was covered in scraps of cellophane, wrapping paper, leftover art-supply stuff. And inside Ruby had drawn a picture of a woman who could only be her. Brown curly hair. A pink dress. And a pile of chocolate muffins at her feet.

To Meg, it said in rainbow-coloured letters. *Love Ruby.*

Her breath got stuck in her throat. A gorgeous card that Ruby had made for her. A whole day earlier.

Zach hadn't forgotten to give it to her. He was so smitten with this kid there was no way. He was on a high from the smallest of advances they were making. He might even have believed he had her advice to thank for many of them. But deep down he had no intention of either he or his little girl getting too attached to her.

She breathed in and out and somehow managed to talk Ruby through all the delightful nuances of the present knowing Zach had never wanted her to have it.

It had been the smart move. The right decision. That still didn't stop her heart from shrinking until it felt three sizes too small.

'Are you both still in one piece?' Zach asked as he rejoined them.

Meg slipped the card beneath her backside,

looked to Ruby, held a finger to her lips, and said, 'Shh.'

Thankfully, Ruby just giggled.

Zach's smiling eyes were full of questions. Of devotion to his little girl. Of so much promise to be the most complete man she'd ever known. Only Meg knew that the promise would never be hers to see fulfilled.

All this and morning tea had only just begun. If she was ever going to get through this she'd have to give the greatest performance of her life.

Zach placed the tray of drinks and a platter of fat fruit and gleaming cheeses and exotic crackers on the table. Her motley bunch of flowers had pride of place in a skinny glass vase in the centre of the tray.

Ruby snuck up onto her knees and pulled out a waxy white flower from the bunch, tore off the stem, and tucked it behind her ear. She did the same for Meg. Then a third for Zach, who leaned down and let her do it.

'They're Ruby's favourite,' he said, running a hand over his daughter's hair.

Meg could have cried.

'Wait here,' Ruby said. 'I have more to show you.' She took off back into the house.

Zach grabbed some loose grapes and threw them into his mouth. He looked at her as if he knew some great secret, when she was the one sitting on the greatest of them all.

'You look ridiculous,' Meg said, staring at the flower. Anywhere rather than in Zach's warm eyes.

He grinned. 'So what were you two up to when I came out here?'

Meg's eyes connected with his and got stuck in all that deep, dark, beautiful, chocolate-brown. 'I have no idea what you're talking about.'

He stared into her eyes. 'You're a terrible liar.'

She blinked, desperately hoping he wasn't as clever as he thought he was. She looked away, and took a couple of strawberries from the platter. 'Ruby seems really happy.'

'I think she just might be. In fact, I think we both are. At the very least we're both now on the right path to get there.'

Zach leaned forward in his chair. His hands slid across the table until they were almost touching hers. She tried to keep her breaths steady.

'When you get home,' he said, 'you should talk to your father.'

She curled her fingers into her palms. 'About?'

'Meg,' he said, looking deep into her eyes, his

voice ever so slightly ragged. 'This is me you're talking to.'

She swallowed. She knew exactly whom she was talking to—the man who'd won her heart. She uncurled her fingers from her palms, slid her hand along the table toward his—

Footsteps sounded on the wooden balcony. They both looked up to find Felicia holding a landline phone. 'Sorry to interrupt, but it's Reception for Meg.'

Meg cursed Reception with every fibre of her being for their terrible timing. Then she realised she hadn't told anyone where she'd be. As if that would stop the Kellys. If this was Dylan trying to pin her down to a dozen PR jobs for the first dozen hours after her return she'd throttle him.

She took the phone, her tone cool as she said, 'This is Meg.'

'Oh, thank God.'

'Rylie?'

'Honey, you have to come back. Now.'

'What's happened?'

'It's Quinn.'

Meg's eyes slammed shut as wave after wave of anger rolled through her. Of all the moments the man could have picked to— The words clogged in her head and anger turned to guilt, which turned to too many emotions for her to keep up.

'Tell me straight,' she said, her voice astonishingly even. 'Is he—?'

'He's had another heart attack.'

'But he's alive,' she said.

'He is. Brendan called my mobile when he couldn't get through to yours. Tabby's packing your stuff and we can be at your car in fifteen minutes.'

'I'll be there.'

She pulled the phone from her ear and suddenly didn't know what to do with it.

Zach was already beside her, sliding it from her shaky grasp. Then his warm arms were around her, pulling her close, wrapping her tight.

'What do you need me to do?' he asked, her ear against his chest feeling the rumble of his words.

I want you to love me. I need you to let me go.

She said, 'I have to go home.'

Home. Her life. Her father. God, could this be it? She realised she had begun to tremble.

Zach, on the other hand, was in complete control. He had already eased her down the bridge and across the yard before she even knew her feet were moving.

'But Ruby,' she said.

'Felicia's looking after her. I'll explain later that you had an emergency and had to go early.'

'What about her peanut butter on white bread? She was so excited.'

His arm at her back slid around her waist until he was cradling her and pressing her forward at the same time. She let him. Let herself steal as much of his kind of strength as she could get while she had the chance.

'Felicia's a pushover,' Zach said. 'Ruby probably has that all the time and they simply don't tell me. Feminine mystery. I'm learning to live with it.' His voice grew deep and close as his lips settled on her hair. 'Now stop worrying about us, and just walk.'

When she tripped over her own feet for the third time, Zach picked her up and carried her. She wrapped her arms about his neck and snuggled in. If he didn't care who saw them like that, then neither did she. It cushioned the several kinds of dread inside her as nothing else could.

He put her down when they reached the garage behind Waratah House. Her momentum propelled her to Rylie, who gathered her up and swept her into the tight back seat of the already packed Jag.

'Take care of her,' she thought she heard Zach's deep voice rumble as the engine gunned.

Rylie said, 'Never fear, Mr Jones. We always do.'

The car backed out of its spot, and Meg looked up to find Zach was a silhouette already too far away for her to see his eyes. Already too far away to thank him. To tell him…anything.

Tabitha drove them out of the high white gates, while Rylie held her hand in the back seat.

It must have been a good deal over an hour later, though it only felt like minutes, when they rounded the final bend of the Pacific Motorway to see the towering silhouette of Brisbane's glass and chrome skyline.

Kelly Tower—the home of the Kelly Investment Group—stood out tall and majestic, a gleaming reminder that she was nearly home. That within minutes she'd be slung back into the frantic, high-pressure, achievement-driven life her whole family led. That once again her father—a man who likely would have preferred it if she weren't even there—was about to become the centre of her life.

If it weren't for the wilting white waxflower she cupped gently in her hand, she might have thought the past few days were all a dream.

CHAPTER TWELVE

A WEEK had gone by when Zach drove up to the imposing wrought-iron gates of the Kelly family's Ascot home.

A week with no clue as to what was happening in Meg's life bar what he read in every newspaper he could get his hands on, hoping he could trust what they said. A week spent living with the memory of her warm body wrapped around his as he slept in his now lonely bed. A week spent remembering that even while dealing with her worst nightmare Meg had still worried that Ruby might be upset about missing out on her peanut butter on white bread.

The gates of Kelly Manor opened as a florist's van trundled down the long, imposing driveway. Mounds of press lurked outside, but none of them pushed into the grounds, showing a measure of respect that surprised him.

He stared them down as they peered into his

car from a relatively safe distance. Him with his little girl in the back seat. His palms sweated so much he had to wipe them on his trousers.

He'd just have to get over it. The few months he was assured of having her all to himself he was no longer going to spend locking her away like some modern-day Rapunzel. The best thing he could do for her was to make sure she felt safe and loved, but also as if her future was one filled with boundless possibilities.

And while his little girl was blooming under his new philosophy, inside that huge house there was another woman in his life who was suffering. And he had no intention of abandoning either one.

He fixed the rearview mirror so he could catch Ruby's eye. 'Honey.'

'Yeah, Dad.'

'See all those people there? They're newspaper and TV reporters. They have cameras, and will get very close to the car. If you don't want your photo taken you can stick your head between your knees.'

'I don't mind.'

He turned to look over his shoulder. To look at his little girl. For a kid who had every reason to be as skittish as a newborn colt, she was one of the most gung-ho people he'd ever met. He could only hope that had a tiny bit to do with him.

'Okay, then,' he said, winking at her, 'here we go.'

He gunned the engine, turned into the driveway. Flash bulbs blinded him enough he had to drive with one hand over his eyes, but he made it through the gate and up the long curving drive in one piece.

'You all right, hon?' he asked Ruby once they were clear of the throng.

She nodded, her eyes wide, before she turned to peek through the tinted back window. 'Why did they want a photo of me?'

He smiled. 'Because you're just so adorable.'

She patted at the pink band around her head that Felicia had shown him how to slide into place in order to keep her long hair from her face. 'Can we ask them for a copy of the picture so I can take it to school? Clarissa won't believe me if I just tell her.'

Zach's smile turned to laughter. 'I'll see what I can do.'

Tracking down a paparazzo for a favour was one of the crazier things he'd ever agreed to.

Though when compared with the fortnight he'd had, maybe not.

He pulled his car in behind the red Jag that had taken Meg from him all those mornings ago. His hands gripped tight to the steering wheel as he remembered the haunted look in her eyes as she'd been driven away. He should have come sooner.

He was here now. He hoped that would be enough.

He held Ruby's hand as they walked up the steps towards the Georgian-style manor, passing two life-sized statues of Irish wolfhounds. He tilted his head at the dogs and poked a face. Ruby giggled. And he knew that he wasn't only here for himself—he was here for her.

Within seconds of his using the old-fashioned brass knocker, Meg's mother, Mary Kelly herself, opened the door. He saw Meg in her eyes, the shape of her chin, and the same inability to hide her true feelings from him behind her practised smile.

She was exhausted, she was anxious, but her husband was still very much alive.

Zach said, 'I'm so sorry to intrude, Mrs Kelly. My name is Zach Jones. I own the Juniper Falls Rainforest Retreat and was with Meg when she heard the news about your husband. I was hoping

I might be able to check how she and your husband were faring.'

'Of course, Zach, please come right in,' Mary said, welcoming him, a veritable stranger, into her home. This time he saw Meg in her natural warmth.

Ruby tucked in tight behind him so close she might as well have been sewn to his trousers. When Mary saw her, a spark lit her tired eyes. It was Meg all over again. He looked past her, wondering how close Meg might yet be.

Mary bent from the waist, placing her hands on her knees. 'And who might this gorgeous creature be?'

'This is Ruby,' he said. 'My daughter.'

Mary held out a hand and said, 'I'm very pleased to meet you, Ruby. As will my granddaughters be. Violet and Olivia are playing outside in the rear gardens now with their uncle Dylan. Would you like to come and say hello?'

Zach glanced past Mary again and wondered if everyone was playing outside with Uncle Dylan. Then he crouched down to her level and held her hands. 'Would you like to go outside and play? It's entirely up to you.'

Mary held out a hand. Ruby took it. Trusting. Sociable. Like her mother.

'James,' Mary said to a liveried man Zach hadn't even noticed standing by the entrance to what looked like a large sitting room, 'would you kindly take Mr Jones to Meg. I believe she's in the upstairs media room.'

'This way, sir,' James said before heading up the wide, carpeted stairs.

Family photographs lined the staircase wall. Dozens, dating back generations. He'd never had any photographs of his parents, and kept none of his childhood now. The Kelly wall of fame was thoroughly intimidating.

The closer they got to the top of the stairs, the more familiar faces became. Quinn and Mary sailing with two young boys scampering at their feet. The three boisterous-looking brothers, late teens, playing cricket in the backyard. And Meg at the beach, younger than Ruby was now, her bottom lip sticking out while her double scoop of ice cream melted on the ground at her feet.

And look at her now, he thought, his eyes resting on a much more recent picture of her walking down a city street, gorgeous in a silver party dress, pale pink high heels, hair flying as she grinned back at the camera. There was a measure of confidence in her eyes, secret confidence. He alone knew the hard work she'd done to feel as if she'd earned the right to hold her head high.

He reached out to wipe a smudge of dust from the picture.

'Sir, this way,' James said from the top of the stairs, his face discreetly averted.

Zach shoved his hands into his suit pockets and jogged the last few steps.

'Miss Meg is in the room at the end of the hall,' James said. 'Shall I announce you?'

Zach shook his head, gave James a slap on the arm, then headed towards the slightly ajar double doors. He pressed one open. It made no sound.

The large room was filled with overstuffed chairs in old-fashioned plaids and florals, which mixed incongruously with the discreet silver surround-sound speakers, the wall-to-wall built-in bookshelves stacked with DVDs, and the state-of-the-art cinema set-up.

And at the edge of the room, curled up on a tub chair, staring absently out of the open double windows leading to a small balcony, sat Meg.

His chest clenched at the sight of her in loose jeans, red winter socks and a long-sleeved cream-and-red T-shirt that clung to her curves. She wore not a lick of make-up and her hair had been scragged back into a low bun from which several long curls had escaped. She played absently with her lower lip while some movie he recognised as having not even been released at the cinema played out quietly on the massive projector screen behind her.

Now he was there he realised it was testimony of his years of obstinate will power that he'd managed to go without sight of her for a full week. And now he was there, now she was so close, he couldn't wait a second more.

He planted his feet and cleared his throat.

She glanced up. Dark circles ringed her deep blue eyes, making them look bruised. They took a moment to focus. Then she frowned. 'Zach?'

He nodded, suddenly not trusting his voice.

She dragged herself to her sock-clad feet and slowly walked to him as though she might be imagining him. He dug his fingernails into his palms to stop himself from taking the final steps and dragging her into his arms and kissing her for all he was worth.

'How's your father?' he asked.

She shook her head. Then nodded. 'He's had two more attacks this week. He's lucid, his blood pressure is stable, but he's fading and refusing to go to hospital no matter what any of us say.'

Her eyes flickered at that last part, and he wondered if she'd been one of the ones suggesting it, or if she'd stubbornly kept out of his way.

She waved a hand over her face as though swatting away a fly. 'What on earth are you doing here?'

'You left in such a hurry. You were so upset. I couldn't let you stay away without knowing…' *God, this was much harder than telling Ruby how much he cared.* 'Without knowing I've been thinking of you.'

Day and night. Night and day. He'd been sure he'd heard her laughter around the resort, caught her jasmine scent.

The sound of real laughter, children's laughter, spilled through the window and like a mother hen Meg upped and headed out through the French doors to check see. Zach followed.

From the small balcony he saw Ruby sitting on Mary's lap watching Meg's nieces, clad in fairy dresses and tiaras, running around the backyard flying kites. Below, sitting in matching white cane chairs and drinking iced tea, like something out of *The Great Gatsby*, a slew of other

Kellys—brothers, sisters, uncles, cousins, grand-parents—watched on.

'You brought Ruby *here*?' Meg asked, her voice thin, her hands gripping the concrete balustrade as if she were preparing to vault down onto the lawn and whisk Ruby away from the clutches of her family.

He understood why she'd resisted the idea of having children. But she was made to be a mum. She was a natural protector, an instinctive defender of those who couldn't defend themselves. As a child she might not have been able to fight back when she was pushed down, but now? Now she was a warrior.

As far as he saw it, the only thing standing in the way of her fighting for her own happiness with as much purpose as she did so for others was fear. A broken-down ego was a fragile thing. Not easily repaired. He just had to make her see how strong she had become.

He said, 'She overheard me explaining to Felicia that your dad was sick. She wouldn't let me visit without her, or we would have been here sooner. She wanted to make sure you were okay.'

'Me? Is she okay?' Meg asked, her eyes glued to Ruby. 'I mean, is this making her think too much about her mum being sick? I'd hate to be the one to bring all that back up again.'

'She's fine. She's curious. She's amazing, really. Tough when she needs to be, and soft when she can be.'

Just like you, he wanted to say, but he knew she wasn't ready to hear it. Yet.

Meg spun on him, a ghost of her usual spirit flashing in her eyes bringing colour back to her cheeks. She shoved a finger into his chest, backing him into the shadow of the doorway. 'Do you have *any* idea how many reporters are camped out on the other side of your gate?'

'I drove in that way,' he said calmly, 'so, yes.'

'They're not as dim as they look, Zach. They'll have seen you. They'll have seen Ruby. They'll know who you are. They'll figure out who she is. She's cute, and funny, and female and your sole heir. They'll eat her alive. Didn't you hear a word I said?'

He reached out and held her upper arms; she calmed instantly, blinking up at him as if she were really seeing him for the first time. Her energy coursed through him like a wildfire and he wanted to kiss her so badly he had to grind his teeth to distract himself.

'I'm fully aware of all that,' he said. 'But I'm done hiding. I'm not going to teach her that's the best way to live because it's not. We've decided that life can come at us from any angle now and we'll take it on together.'

Meg blinked at him. She felt so small, but so warm, beneath his hands. She was his match, his inspiration, someone he wanted to know everything about, someone he wanted right beside him as he leapt into the new chapters of his life.

As a five-year-old his happiness had been in the hands of strangers; as a thirty-five-year-old his happiness was his to reach out and grab.

'So in that same vein, here we are,' he said, emphasising each of the last three words.

At the last second he held back from adding, *And we're yours if you'll have us.* She'd work it out. She had to. All it had ever taken for them to understand one another was a look.

He lifted a hand to run the backs of his fingers gently down her beautiful cheek. And saw the moment she understood when a flare of awareness lit her dazzling blue eyes. The same flare ignited in his stomach.

He swept a curl from her eyes. Then another until his hands cupped the sides of her face. He could practically taste her, feel the soft fullness of that mouth against his.

Suddenly she twisted out of his grasp, turned her back on him, and walked back into the room.

'Has anyone offered you a drink? Would you like some lemonade? James has made bucket-loads and it's magic. Really. He could sell the stuff and retire rich and never have to open another door for any of us again.'

He took a step towards her, arm outstretched. She slid gracefully behind an ottoman.

'Meg.'

She breathed deep and sank down onto the ottoman, as though she was so tired of fighting she could no longer stand.

He moved towards her. She held out a hand using the international sign for *back off*, and it stopped him in his tracks.

Her voice came to him, husky and defeated, as she said, 'Last weekend my family had been trying to get through to me for half an hour but I'd turned off my phone. I was heading to be with you and Ruby and it was easier to pretend they didn't exist if I wanted to believe that I could have what you have—a clean, fresh, new start.' She looked up at him. 'But this is who I am. This is where I need to be.'

'That's nonsensical.'

'Excuse me? Now I'm *nonsensical*?' She turned on him with such rancour in her eyes he backed up a step.

'*You're* not nonsensical,' he shot back, not giving her a chance to break eye contact. 'You're a human dynamo. You're an inspiration. You care so much for other people I know you don't take near enough time to care for yourself. And you've been a small miracle in my life. But believing you deserve to suffer right along with your father is ridiculous. You're punishing yourself for his mistakes.'

She blinked at him, her lips thin, her eyes raging. But at least she was listening.

'You've given me enough words of wisdom—it's my turn. Family *isn't* a given. It wasn't for me, and in the end it's not for you. Family is a choice. Because deciding who to share your life with is a choice, and those you choose to spend your life with are your family. Love the Kellys you love. But just because they are a vital and somewhat Herculean force in your life needn't ever stop you from stepping away and creating your own family.'

'Zach, it's not that simple.'

He took a careful step her way. 'All that ever stopped me was me. Ruby came along. I chose to take her into my life. And look at me now. All that's stopping you is you.'

She swallowed hard, her chin tilting as he came closer. 'I'm not you.'

'And for that I'm eternally grateful. But I'm also not your father. Ruby's not you. Ruby's not your niece. And you're not your father either.'

He sank to a crouch close enough he could touch her if he just reached out his hand. But even though it killed to do so, he held back. 'Meg, sweetheart, I came here today because it has become all too clear to me this week that you are my family. I choose you.'

Her eyes softened. Hope sprang within them. Until she shook her head. 'Well, you can't have me. You don't want me anywhere near your daughter.'

Zach's jaw clenched. *Now* she was being nonsensical. 'Meg, I told you, I'm past that. You helped me get past that. And Ruby adores you—'

She shook her head harder. 'Zach, please. If she's anything like I was at sixteen you'll lose half a head of hair.'

'Let me worry about my hair.'

She spun on the ottoman so her knees faced

him square on. 'Then worry about this. I ditched school at sixteen. I went clubbing every night. I drank daiquiris like they were lemonade. They let me in because of who I was, because of who my father was. When I chipped this tooth on a champagne flute I was sitting up front at a comedy bar, already on my second three-hundred-dollar bottle. *Sixteen years old.* That same night I was pulled over for drunk-driving, driving without a licence, under age, and a bag of pot was found in my glove compartment. I had friends in the car with me. Friends I could have killed had I not been stopped. Friends who for some reason are still my friends today. That could have been the end of me, but somebody put pressure where it was needed and I was let off with a warning. Somebody paid off every paper in town so that none of it ever came to light.'

'Somebody,' he said, still trying to filter the rest. 'Somebody meaning your father.'

She breathed in deep, ragged breaths. Her hands began to shake. He placed a gentle hand over hers, but he wasn't sure she even knew he was there.

Her voice sounded so small as she said, 'My trust fund wasn't meant to be mine until I was twenty-five. It was signed over at eighteen. I figured it was his way of finally washing his hands of me. That same day I approached my first doctor. But even I, with my glorious name, and glorious money, and batting baby blues had to wait until I had undergone six months of intensive therapy before a doctor would agree to—'

Her words ended on a choke and that was when his confidence took its first tumble. 'Agree to what?' he asked, needing to know even though he knew he'd regret it when he did.

'I've had my tubes tied, Zach.' She looked up at him then, at the end of her rope. 'It's irreversible. I can never have kids.'

Holy hell.

If Quinn Kelly weren't on death's door Zach feared in that moment what he might have done to the man.

Meg stared at him as if she half expected him to shake her senseless. Or run as fast as his shoes would carry him. But all he wanted to do was to take her in his arms and hug her. To hold her until she absolved herself. Until he got his head around what it meant to him. Until he stopped thinking what might have happened had Isabel done such a thing and Ruby had never been born.

'Aren't you going to say something?' she said, her voice tight, angry, desolate.

Zach ran a hard, fast hand over his face. What the hell could he possibly say?

'Zach?'

He stood and paced in a tight circle. 'I need a minute.'

'I should never have told you.' She shook her head so hard he was sure her brain must have been knocking against her skull.

'Hang on now, Meg. You know you've just thrown me a hand grenade there and I get the feeling you're certain I'm about to run for cover. I'm not, but I still need a minute.'

She stood and paced on the other side of the ottoman. 'You didn't have to know any of it. Nobody ever did! But you had to appear in my life and be all unimpressed by it and make me like you. And then you had to add Ruby to the mix. And then more and more and more of you. There. Everywhere. Not letting me have a minute to think about what we were doing. So if this—' she waved a hand over her chest '—is too hard for you to take, it's your own fault!'

'Meg, you picked the wrong man to try to push away. I'm not running. Not any more.'

'But see now, that's the thing. You are still running. You just don't know it,' she said, her voice suddenly so calm he wondered if he'd ever been in control of the conversation, even for a single second.

Zach brought his back foot to rest beside his front, feeling as if he needed to be upright for what was coming. 'This ought to be good.'

'That morning, at your house, Ruby gave me the card she'd made me.'

'The card?' *Oh, hell, the card.*

'The pink card with the chocolate muffin picture and the fur and feathers and glitter.' She swallowed before saying, 'The one you wouldn't give me yourself.'

Zach stood rooted to the floor as the import of that one small choice sank in. At the time it had been a split-second decision. An insurance policy, protecting his daughter and himself, that one last, tiny little bit.

In the end it might have cost him everything.

When he said nothing, Meg continued, 'Last week was something crazy. Something amazing and wonderful and I'll never forget a second of it. But the card only proved what I already knew—that you're nowhere near ready to take on the likes of me.'

Zach shook his head. The both of them were so adept at talking themselves into whatever they wanted to believe, this was all about to go belly up on the back of circular conversation.

He shut down reason and went purely on instinct, knowing if there was ever a moment to trust in the man he'd become this had to be it.

'Watch me,' he said, then shoved the ottoman out of the way with a foot and gathered her into his arms. As though she'd been holding herself up by nothing more than will power she collapsed against him.

He kissed the top of her head. The edge of her ear. The lift at the edge of her lips.

With a sigh she tilted her head and kissed him back, her lips clinging so gently, so tenderly, so lovingly to his.

It took all of his strength not to lift her in his arms and carry her to the couch and prove to her in the most basic way that he was right and she was wrong.

Far too soon she pulled away, looking down so he couldn't see into her eyes. He snuck a finger beneath her chin and made her face him.

Her chest rose and fell. Her eyes were as wild

and blue as his lake amidst a summer storm. 'Why don't you hate me for what I did to myself?'

'Because I know why you did it.'

'Remind me, please. Right now I'm struggling to come up with a good excuse.'

'You made sure nobody could ever reject you again as fully as you rejected yourself.'

She swallowed and a big fat tear rolled down her cheek. He brushed her hair from her eyes and breathed through it lest he join her.

'God, you were eighteen,' he said, his voice rasping through his tight throat. 'You were still a kid. Those blasted doctors should be hung. But it would be impossible for me to ever hate *you*. How could I when I love you so very much?'

Her eyes glistened, flickering between his. He'd said it. He'd told her. He was her safe place to come home to.

He thought he had her. Until she held out her hands in supplication. He could see in the utter transparency of her expression how much it meant to her.

It just didn't matter.

He let her go as though his fingers had been burnt, rather than his heart. She wrapped her arms back about her body and headed back over to the French doors to watch the interplay below from a safe distance—the only family she thought she deserved, the kids she'd convinced herself she'd never have.

'Please stay as long as you want while Ruby's having such a good time,' she said, polite as could be. 'James will show you out.'

There was nothing more he could do or say. He did as she asked and walked away.

He'd spent his adult life protecting himself from just this situation, from blindly loving someone with no guarantee they'd love him back. But Meg had smashed through that wall with all the subtlety of a wrecking ball, convincing him he'd found someone worth the risk.

As he jogged numbly down the steps with generations of stubborn-chinned Kellys watching on he realised the one thing he hadn't considered was that for her the risk of loving him might yet be too great.

CHAPTER THIRTEEN

As the sun set Meg sat out on one of the white cane chairs looking over the now-empty back lawn, the divine sound of kids just being kids echoing in the back of her mind.

The rest of her felt like toast. Three-day-old burnt toast that had fallen butter-side down on the kitchen floor and been kicked into the dust-filled gap beneath the fridge.

Zach had come to her daunting family home and left his precious daughter playing outside with her nieces as though if they were her blood they could do no wrong. He'd looked more dashing and beautiful and terrified than she'd ever seen him look. He'd offered himself up to the press, he'd heard her last and most devastating of secrets, a secret that meant she could never give him the kind of family he was ready for, and he'd still told her he loved her.

There was nothing more he could have done to

prove himself as the man she'd known he could be. And still she'd sent him away.

'Sweetheart,' her mother said, a hand curving over her shoulder. 'Are you coming in for dinner?'

Meg smiled up at her mother and stretched until her tight muscles began to feel useable again. 'I'll be in in a minute.'

She felt her mum's hesitation. 'Your father's alone right now if you wanted to have a chat. I'd noticed you haven't been in to see him since you came home, and I thought, perhaps, now might be a good time.'

Meg stilled, then tucked her feet onto the chair and wrapped her arms about her knees. Her mum was right about one thing: there was no time like the present. 'Mum, can you sit for a minute?'

Mary sat, perched on the edge of the seat as though ready to take flight. It made it easier for Meg to say what she needed to say, as she was almost sure her mum knew what was coming.

'Mum, I don't much want to talk to him. And I think you know why.'

Mary clasped her hands together until the knuckles turned white. 'Darling, he's so sick, surely you can—'

'Mum,' she said gently, but it was enough for her mother to close her lips.

Meg leaned forward and took her mum's hands in hers. 'You know how he treated me when I was a kid.' Even using the endearing term 'Dad' felt wrong. It always had.

Mary said, 'He's exacting, and puts as much pressure on all of you as he always has on himself. His work was so much more stressful back then. The business was in its infancy. His father was hard on him too. And everything he did was for the betterment of the family.'

Meg nodded along. She'd heard it all before. 'Is that why the two of you had me? For the betterment of the family?' She swallowed. 'To keep the family from falling apart when Dad had an affair?'

Mary opened her mouth to deny everything, then something in her changed, relaxed, as though she didn't have the energy to keep up the pretence any longer. She took a hand and cupped it under Meg's chin. 'You always were the most sensitive child. You were a blessing at a time we needed one most. But you can't only blame your father. We both did things we shouldn't have done.'

'*You* had an affair?' Meg asked, sitting up so straight so fast her back cracked.

Mary nodded, her eyes filling with tears. 'It was short-lived. It was foolish. But in the end only good came of it as it proved to both of us that we were where we wanted to be after all. We chose to be a family again.' She reached out and tucked a curl behind Meg's ear. 'Having you after that was the best choice I've made in my life.'

A choice. Meg had always wondered if she'd been a stopgap measure, never looking at it from the angle that she'd been a purposeful *choice*. The massive delineation rang so loud in Meg's ears she almost couldn't think. But it was fighting hard against the clang of another. 'Am I his daughter?'

Mary's eyes grew wide with shock. 'Of course you are. Look at you. You have his eyes. You have his pluck. You certainly have his temper. Your sweet temperament and endless capacity to forgive are definitely from my side.'

Her mother leaned forward and kissed her cheek. 'Now that's the last we need to hear of that. Don't be long. Dinner's on soon. And your father is still up there alone.'

Meg nodded, but stayed put as her mother walked away.

Forgiveness.

Zach had forgiven his foster parents for their weaknesses for the sake of his own family. Her mother had forgiven her father for his trespasses for the sake of her family. Her father had never forgiven himself and self-condemnation left only bitterness in its stead.

Meg had to forgive herself the unhealthy choices she'd made at sixteen. The desperate one she'd made at eighteen. Only then could she fully embrace the many exceptional choices she'd made since then. The keeping of friends she'd had since school. Being an integral part of her family's success. For unreservedly giving to those far less fortunate than herself.

For falling in love with Zach.

That had to be just about the smartest thing she'd ever done in her whole life. He knew her. He understood her. He loved her. But even more importantly, he'd helped her to realise how far she'd come in knowing, understanding and loving herself.

Could he ever forgive her for abandoning him? Could she ever forgive herself? Before she had room to find out, there was one last person who needed to see how far she'd come too.

* * *

Late that night, after a typically long, noisy, combative Kelly family dinner populated by her mum, all her brothers and their significant others, a dog-tired Meg made her way back up the stairs, past the wall of beautifully framed, lovingly tended family pictures, and she slid into her father's room.

Flat against the wall she could hear his uneven breathing. Flat against the wall she wasn't going to be able to do anything. She walked to his bed, and sat carefully on the edge.

He looked old. Frail. His skin was like rice paper. Even his eyelids were wrinkled. Like this he seemed so harmless.

He flinched, then looked into her face with his fierce blue eyes and turned a not too happy shade of pink as he bellowed, 'Jeez, child, could you have snuck in here any more quietly?'

'Don't shout!' she shot back, moving hurriedly to sit farther down the edge of the huge bed. 'You'll pop something and I doubt I'm the one you'd want trying to plug it up.'

He tried to sit up, failed, swore to the high heavens, and then slumped gingerly back onto the huge mound of pillows. 'What on earth are you doing here, girl? I was informed you were whooping it up on holiday.'

'I've been back a few days now.'

'Not for my sake, I hope.'

'No. Of course not,' she said, her voice droll. 'The girls were one down on their backyard cricket side. I had to come back for the sisters.'

His eyes were entirely clear when he said, 'You've never been any good at cricket.'

'Mmm, so you've taken great delight in telling me on numerous occasions.'

Quinn scoffed. 'Would you prefer I butter you up? Resting on your laurels never helped anyone.'

'No,' she said. 'You've made well sure my laurels have never given me any rest.'

And there it was. Back to square one. The two of them watching each other cagily from opposite corners of the ring.

Meg flattened a sock-clad foot on the ground, preparing to get out of Dodge, when it hit her that heading out that door meant nothing would have changed.

Unless she could make the break from her past she'd end up playing the 'It-Girl' for ever. Brushing off her blonde wig every time she did the kind of work that really gave her satisfaction. Dating men who never challenged her. Trying to pretend that Zach Jones never existed. Trying to convince herself that sharing every piece of herself, her fears, her joys, her body, her soul with him had been nothing but a holiday romance.

Not good enough. Not any more.

'Dad.' She reached out and took his cool hand. It stiffened, but she didn't let go. 'It appears my Kelly blood runs deeper than I even knew. I do believe I'm going to miss you.'

'Gallivanting off again, are you?'

She almost laughed. Stubborn old fool. Instead she took his words at face value.

'I will, in fact. I'll be taking leave of my Kelly duties for a bit.'

She would? *Yeah*, she thought with an inner sigh of relief, *she would*.

He glared at her as though she'd said she was renouncing her name, her religion, and the old country just to be contrary. She raised both eyebrows and glared right on back.

'The thing is, Dad,' she said, 'I currently volunteer at the Valley Women's Shelter every week. Have been doing so for some time now. It's tough, it's terrifying and I love it madly. So much so I've decided my PR work for the family is going to have to slot in around that from now on rather than the other way around. In fact, I might even take a social work course, which would cut into that time even more.'

He opened his mouth, no doubt to cut her down twenty ways from Sunday. She held up a hand and said, 'Not this time. The decision's been made. And there's more. I'm in love, Dad, with an amazing man who knows everything about me—everything—and he loves me anyway. Can you believe it?'

She could hardly believe it herself, but saying the words out loud finally made it all utterly, beautifully, intensely real.

'I'm tired, child,' he said, turning away. 'Can't you have this conversation with your mother?'

'I will in good time. But I wanted to have it with you too. For *you* to know that I've reached a point in my life when I feel as though I might just be really, really happy.'

'And you need to tell me this now in case I don't wake up in the morning?'

She lifted an eyebrow. 'That's exactly why. So now you know. Your daughter has turned out just fine.'

He looked her in the eye, for the longest time she could ever remember him doing so. His eyes, so very like hers. His inability to forgive so far removed from hers. Then he settled deeper into his pillows and looked up at the fringing hanging off the canopy bed as though it held more interest than anything she'd had to say.

'Fine,' he said. 'Now I know.'

It wasn't congratulations. It wasn't an act of contrition. Yet Meg felt her oldest wounds beginning to mend.

A soft rap on the door was followed by James's face poking through the gap. James slipped into the room with a box of Krispy Kreme doughnuts.

She opened her mouth to rouse at James, then let it fall shut. She wasn't her father's keeper any more than he was hers. So without another word she just hopped off the bed and walked out, pretending she hadn't seen.

Feeling as if she were living a good inch higher off the ground than she had been her whole life, Meg floated into her old bedroom, grabbed her handbag, fixed her hair, swiped on some lip gloss, spritzed on some perfume and continued floating down the stairs.

She passed the library where the family had gathered for after-dinner drinks. Dylan called out, 'Get in here, kiddo. I want to run through next week's schedule. There's a dozen odd things I need you to do for me.'

Her shoes touched solid ground. Telling Dylan he'd have to find someone else next week would take all night.

She caught James the butler's eye as he eased silently into the room from another door. And seeing her escape, mouthed 'sorry' then said, 'Did you know James is feeding Dad dough-nuts?'

Brendan made to scold, but Cameron got in first, laughing his head off. And as their collec-tive attention was diverted Meg took her chance and escaped.

And then she was gone, jogging down the dark front steps of the manor two at a time, the rush of summer air blowing her hair off her face, making her skin tingle, making her lungs feel open and free.

Or maybe it was the thought of a man with dark chocolate eyes, adorable curls, warm, strong arms, enough chutzpah to put her in her place, and a capacity to love her despite knowing the worst she had to offer that had every sense feeling as if it was truly alive.

She hopped into her Jag and burned down the Kelly Manor driveway, spinning gravel in her wake.

Only when Meg hit the locked gates outside the Juniper Falls Rainforest Retreat did she realise she hadn't exactly mapped out any kind of plan.

She simply pressed the intercom. A sleepy voice answered. 'Juniper Falls Rainforest Retreat, how can I be of assistance?'

'Hi. Meg Kelly here. Can you, uh, by any chance, wake Zach Jones and tell him I'm here?'

After a pause the voice said, 'I sincerely wish I could, Ms Kelly, but you are not down on my sheet as being expected.'

'I know. And I'm sorry about that. But this is a surprise visit. Of sorts. A last-minute but long-overdue kind of thing. You see I'm here to…'

To what? Oh, to hell with it. Zach had laid himself bare for her, to her family, to the press, to his little girl. If she was ever going to prove to him she was right there with him, she had to do the same.

'I've come to tell him that I'm in love with him!'

The gates whirred open instantly. She crawled through to find two men grinning at her from their booth. One doffed his cap, the other blushed like mad.

'Take the route around the back of Waratah House past the garage,' one said, 'and keep on following the fence line. You'll practically drive straight into Mr Jones's private carport. Good luck!'

She gave them a jaunty salute and spun off, feeling high as a kite, and as terrified as if she were in the middle of one of those walking-down-the-middle-of-the-Queen-Street-Mall-naked dreams.

But there was no backing down now. Her secret love was out there for her father and all Zach's staff to know. There was nothing, *nothing*, stopping her but herself, and herself was pressing down hard on the accelerator.

Zach was waiting by the garage at the side of his house wearing nothing but thin, faded, cotton pyjama bottoms when Meg's noisy old car zoomed up, lights on high beam.

He hated to think what had brought her here, tonight, at such a time. He reached for her car door and opened it before she'd even come to a stop. 'Meg, don't tell me your dad—?'

She half stumbled out of the car. 'He's fine.

He's the same. But we talked. Well, I talked, he pretended not to listen. And it felt like letting out a sour, stale breath I'd been holding for almost thirty years. The next breath in was…ecstasy. I could never have done that without your encouragement. So first I have to thank you for that.'

He opened his mouth to try to slow her down, but she kept on going.

'I talked with my mum too. Boy, did so many things become clear. Even you'll be shocked. Or maybe not. I've probably used up your shock quota for the year by now. Or maybe I'd just been locked up inside all week and what I needed was fresh air and sunshine to see things clearly. You taught me that too. So thanks again.'

She looked up into the sky, arms outstretched, breathing deep, then seemed to realise the velvet black sky was littered with stars. She frowned.

Worried Meg might be about to spontaneously combust, Zach took her by the elbow and walked her to the octagonal pool house around the side of his property. Once inside the snug room he turned on a lamp, and placed her on a bamboo love seat.

Her entire, beautifully nubile body jiggled. He

clenched his hands at his sides and struggled to keep his eyes on her face. 'I hate to ask,' he said, 'but have you been drinking?'

She looked up at him, all big blue eyes and pink cheeks and red lips raw from being nibbled at. Or had she put on make-up since he'd last seen her? Lip gloss, rouge, mascara, perfume? Had she done that for him? His fingers un-clenched a very little.

'Coffee,' she said. 'Loads and loads of coffee from a couple of drive-through places on the way. I haven't slept much in the past few days and I needed to be awake for this. And since I wasn't actually sure that you had coffee on hand, or if you'd merely been using the promise of coffee as a lure all this time—'

She shook her head, seeming to realise she hadn't taken a breath. Then she gingerly reached out and took his hand and gently drew him down onto the seat next to her.

His fingers gripped hers and pleasure flooded through him. It seemed that even after she had put him through one of the most gruelling and sobering afternoons of his entire life, his body was not nearly as immune to her as his brain would have liked.

'Meg,' he said, his voice gravelly, 'it's after midnight.'

'It is?' she asked, looking around as if she only just realised where she was.

'I'm usually used to functioning at this hour, but it's been a very long day.'

'Tell me about it.' Her eyes swung back to his. Warm, inviting blue. Calm, settled blue. Vivid with a great purpose blue. A tiny ray of hope split the night. At least it felt like hope. Hope wasn't something he'd experienced all that much of in his life, but it felt good whatever it was.

Not sure he could stand to have it dashed twice in one day, he asked, 'Did you have a particular purpose in coming all the way out here?'

She turned his hand over and placed her palm against his. It was cool and small and light. He ached to pull it to his lips and kiss it for the longest time. But the purpose in her eyes was something he did not want to divert.

'I don't quite know where to start,' she said. 'I feel like I'm on daylight savings time. It all made such perfect sense about an hour and a half ago.'

He took a calming breath. 'What did?'

'That you came to the house today to tell me that

you loved me,' she said. 'And for some great daft muddle of a reason I tried to convince you that it wasn't the most glorious news I'd ever heard.'

Zach's heart lurched. Gloriously.

'You love me,' she said again, shuffling closer. 'You, Zach Jones, love me. You love me enough to give me the space I needed to confront my past so that finally I could see further than a designer-shoe-clad foot in front of my own face, which was as far as I'd dare look into the future for such a long time.'

He did. And he had. On the drive home he'd realised she needed more time. And that he'd wait for her as long as she needed. A half a day was as good as he could have hoped.

He did what he'd been aching to do since the moment she arrived and slid a hand around the back of her neck. 'I must be crazy, but I do truly love you.'

'You do?' Her voice was so soft and unsure, her eyes so big and bright, Zach did all he could do and laughed.

His heart felt like a rocket ready to take off. The countdown had begun inside him the moment she'd hopped out of the car and if she didn't reciprocate and soon he was going to explode. 'If you have any feelings for me whatsoever then you'll put me out of my misery and fast.'

Her blinking slowed and, as was her way, she looked him dead in the eye. At the same time she laid a gentle hand on his cheek and it was all he could do not to ravage her on the spot.

'I've lived with a debilitating fear of rejection my entire life. I combated it by being whatever I had to be to be loved by as many people as possible. You made me feel like I actually had to earn your respect. And when I did my opinion counted as much as yours, if not more because it was fresh and new. For those reasons and about a trillion others I do love you.'

She needn't have said another word for the rest of time. But being that she was who she was, she kept on giving.

'I love that you own a million health resorts, but have a thing for chocolate muffins. I love that you push my buttons leaving me nowhere to hide. I love your eyes, your arms, your bare feet, and the crease that appears in your right cheek only when you laugh. But most of all I love that you are ambitious, and hard-working and wilful, but it took less than half a second for you to change your entire life for the sake of one small girl. You are a unique specimen amongst men. And I love you so much my heart is full to bursting with it.'

The rocket inside him went off, filling the last of the empty places inside him with nothing but warmth. 'You have no idea what it feels like to hear you say that.'

'So tell me.'

He laid a matching hand on her cheek, her softness seeping into him, melting away the last of his sharp edges. 'After so many years spent not believing love was in store for me, I'm still halfway stunned that I actually believe you.'

She nodded. Glanced at his lips. Licked her own. Then swung her legs so they rested atop his. His soft cotton pants did nothing to hide the stirrings beneath.

'So what now?' she asked, her voice a husky whisper in the darkness.

'Are you kidding me? Do you want a play by play?'

She pulled back and gave him a look he feared he was going to be on the receiving end of for a very long time. 'I meant we aren't the only ones affected by this.'

'How about we keep the press release in the drawer for a few days yet?'

'Don't be smart. I meant Ruby and you know it.'

'She made me pancakes, but she never made me a card. I have the feeling you're going to be a big hit. And as for your other concerns, you have to remember she comes from tough stock.'

She raised an eyebrow. 'You think the Kellys aren't tough? They suck you in and there's no getting out. Dylan and Cameron are intractable and they've both managed to convince perfectly lovely women to be with them. And you took one look at me and you were gone. Kellys are competitive, ambitious, opinionated, defiant—'

'Sweetheart, they're you.'

'Me? I'm a marshmallow.'

'Nah. You just do it prettier.'

'Zach—'

'She'll be fine. Honestly. And at the first sign she isn't then we'll deal with that then. Okay?'

She thought about it a moment, then nodded.

'Though,' he said, 'there is one other way to fix any concern you might have over your family's influence over our girl.'

'How's that?'

He twirled her hair between his fingers. 'Don't be a Kelly any more.'

She shook her head so hard her hair fell in

messy waves over her shoulders. 'They may all be as mad as March hares, but I do love them too.'

'Of course you do. Anyone who stepped foot inside that behemoth of a house of yours would see that as a clan you're just about unbreakable. But that's not what I meant. I mean you wouldn't be a Kelly any more if you changed your last name to Jones.'

'Very funny,' she said, slapping him on his bare chest. He clutched her hand to him and her fingers curled against his bare skin. 'So is now a good time to admit you're not the first person I told?'

He waited for his offer to sink in, but she was obviously still too wired. 'That you love your family?'

'That I love you!'

'Dare I ask?'

'I kind of let it slip to the two security guards who let me in.'

Zach laughed. He laughed so hard the windows of the tiny thatched pool house shook. 'Then again,' he finally managed, 'what's the use of one more secret? Everyone's going to find out eventually.'

'They will?' she asked.

'Marry me and there's no stopping them.'

Her eyes grew as big as saucers and he knew this time she'd heard him.

'You can't just say something like that to a girl, especially one in my highly caffeinated state.'

'I can and I will.'

'You really want to marry me? Even knowing everything you know? Even though I can't…' She swallowed down an obvious lump in her throat. 'I can't give you any more kids.'

Zach knew better. He'd Googled like a madman the minute Ruby was asleep. The operation she'd had was irreversible. She couldn't conceive naturally. But it didn't rule out IVF. He knew she'd have no idea because she'd have been too terrified to check. But now wasn't the time for that. They'd get there when and if the time was right, as they seemed to get to everything else when they were good and ready. Only this time he'd make sure they'd get there together.

'Meg,' he said, running his thumb down the side of her face, 'I certainly don't want to marry anyone else.'

'Ah,' she said, her voice getting wobblier by the second. 'The last of the great romantics.'

'How's this for romantic?' He took her hand,

lifted it to his lips and left a gentle trail of kisses up each finger and across her palm. Her eyes fluttered closed and her mouth fell open. He took advantage, pulling her to him and kissing her for all he was worth.

She melted against him, warm and languid, and he had not a clue how much time passed before they fell apart.

She gripped his upper arms for support and her famous blue eyes fluttered open, looking into his as if she'd just had some kind of religious experience. God, he was going to love being with this woman.

He asked, 'Tell me that's a yes.'

She snuck her arms around his torso and hugged him tight, her chin resting on his shoulder, her words sliding against his ear. 'Yes.'

Yes! He mentally punched a fist in the air.

He said, 'We are never going to be able to live this down, are we?'

'What's that?'

'Meg Kelly, heiress, society princess, only daughter of the Ascot Kellys, the Kelly Investment Group Kellys, marries orphan-made-good Zach Jones.'

'Did you have any idea I could be so magnanimous?' she asked.

He laughed. Warm all over now, and only getting hotter every second, she wiggled her body further atop his.

'But first,' she said, running a finger in circles over his bare chest, 'before we go one step further, we need to get some things straight.'

'Honey,' he said, sliding a finger along the neckline of her stretch T-shirt. 'Believe it or not I'm worth double what you are. A pre-nup wouldn't be worth the paper it's signed on.'

Meg breathed out long and slow and finished with a smile that hovered halfway between beatific and a threat. 'Kellys don't do pre-nups. Kellys do for ever.'

Zach's next breath matched hers. *For ever*. Never ever did he think he'd see the day when he believed in for ever. But as he let his hand slide over her shoulder and more firmly down her back until she curled like a cat, he couldn't wait for for ever to start. 'So what do we have to get straight?'

Her eyes fluttered closed. 'I've jogged my last. I refuse to let wheat grass touch my lips ever again. And there is no way I'm getting up before the birds every day. Not even for you.'

'And chocolate, and coffee…'

Her voice was breathy as she said, 'Will for ever be a staple in my diet. You want me, you take my predilections.'

'Oh, I want you all right,' he said, stealing a kiss on her beautiful pale neck.

She shivered. 'And are you sure you really understand that you get my family too. They live over an hour away, but they aren't backwards about dropping in unannounced.'

'I actually liked your family, those I met anyway. Your mum was wonderful with Ruby. Truly. And your brothers are all sporty types, right?'

Her eyes opened in time for her to roll them. 'They'll see you as manna from heaven. Thank goodness for Rye and Tabby and my new sisters-in-law, all sensible indoor-type women.'

'Thank goodness for indoor-type women everywhere.' He reached out and switched off the lamp.

'Well, what just happened there?' she said into the darkness.

'Just in case,' he said. 'Guests have been known to come wandering to this part of the resort on occasion.'

'How impolite.'

'How indeed.'

Thankfully the moon was not obscured by a single cloud so he could still make out Meg's shape, her soft curves, her smile. He kissed the end of her nose. The corner of her lush mouth. The curve of her cheek. When he found the edge of her ear lobe her head lolled back on her neck as though her muscles had turned to liquid. 'You're too easy.'

'Try playing me at any board game on the planet and you'll be singing another tune, my friend.'

Instead he chose another indoor game, which left them both winners.

And afterwards, scads of coffee or no coffee, Meg fell asleep on the floor of the pool house, wrapped in his old, warm, soft, favourite, red, woollen blanket and in his arms. Her face peaceful, the dark rings beneath her eyes gone.

Content. Happy. Home.

EPILOGUE

Six weeks after making Juniper Falls her home, and a little over a month after Quinn Kelly's colossal and extremely moving state funeral—attended by no less than three foreign heads of state—Meg stood waiting at the gates of the Juniper Falls resort. Her high ponytail bounced about her shoulders as she hopped on the spot, and her hot-pink high heels kept getting stuck in the grass.

She glanced down at her brand-new engagement ring—a pink diamond solitaire as chosen by fashionista-in-the-making Ruby—glittering beautifully on her left hand and thought for about the hundredth time that her life couldn't feel any different than it had two months before.

Quite apart from becoming more at home with her spectacularly beautiful new digs, her new man, and the new little girl in her life, she was still attending sporadic events as Meg Kelly, the face of the Kelly family, ones she had hand-picked herself. She was still volunteering at least twice a week at the Valley Women's Shelter, only now she did so without any kind of disguise, internal or external, and the satisfaction it gave her had increased a hundredfold.

But this day, at the beginning of the next to last week of the summer school holidays, she was going to work for her new family's business.

A big white bus finally came through the Juniper Falls gates. It had barely pulled to a stop when what seemed like a thousand kids spilled out. Bedraggled urchins the lot of them. With dark eyes all but popping out of their pale faces as they took in elegant Waratah House and the lushly encroaching rainforest.

Meg clapped her hands loud enough for the group to quiet down. 'Okay, guys, I need you to do me a big favour and get yourself organised in one long line, alphabetical by first name.'

'What if two of us have the same name?' a big kid with a missing front tooth asked.

'Excellent question. Then the one with the longest big toe goes up top. Right?'

A couple of kids whipped off their shoes and holey socks, just in case.

Meg grinned. 'If you have it done in five minutes, there's ice cream waiting for you in the restaurant.'

The loudest whoop she'd ever heard had her holding her hands over her ears and running for the side of the bus as the kids frantically introduced themselves to one another, which was the actual point of the exercise.

After the bus driver, whom Meg waved up the hill towards food, Zach was the last to hop off the bus. He looked as raggedy and wide-eyed as the rest of them. After an hour's trip up the mountain with this lot she wasn't surprised.

She sidled up to him and wrapped her arm around his waist. 'There's my big, brave, manly man. You survived.'

He said, 'The week's not over yet.'

Together they watched the Juniper Falls ground crew, headed by Felicia—now the resort's official Children's Activities Coordinator as well as Ruby's some time babysitter—keeping the kids whipped into an eager frenzy.

'I never thought I'd say this, but thank goodness Ruby's a reader not a runner,' Zach said.

Meg bit her lip. She knew better. The first time she'd seen Ruby she'd been swinging up a storm, her clothes covered in evidence of further adventure. But that was another mystery her dad would never have to know about. Now there was an extra pair of eyes looking out for Ruby, eyes experienced in the ways of feisty young girls, those mysteries ought to become fewer and further between.

Meg laid a hand on Zach's chest. 'I've babysat Brendan's girls a thousand times. Believe me, let them run it out and they'll sleep where they fall come dark.'

'From your mouth to God's ears.'

They watched on in silence as the rowdy kids walked single file towards the restaurant.

'Can you believe they're really here?' she asked.

Zach shook his head.

An idea Zach had thrown out over dinner one night had become Meg's obsession. The whole week at the resort had been booked out for a hundred pre-teens, some treading water in the foster system, others from families who'd been through Meg's shelter.

Zach had put out word within the Olympic fraternity and several well-known athletes would run them ragged. The resort's staff would teach them things like how to resolve issues with words not fists. Rock-star mates of Meg's were to host a couple of dance parties, celebrity chefs to cook up healthy, fun food. And they'd be spoilt rotten.

But best of all, exposing these kids to Zach's story, and subsequent success, would broaden the horizons they dared to reach for. Exposing Meg to these kids had already broadened hers more than she'd thought possible.

She leaned her head on his shoulder as a mass squeal of delight echoed from the restaurant.

Zach said, 'I hate that Ruby's missing this.'

'She'll be back in a couple of days, so she won't miss much. I know I've said so a hundred times, but thanks for letting Mum have her. Ruby will be a brilliant influence on Brendan's girls, and having all three girls has been the highlight of Mum's month. She's promised not to mention croquet lessons, or Baroque appreciation classes or a course in *commedia dell'arte.*'

Zach nodded silently, his back ramrod straight.

'You've got used to having her home these holidays, haven't you?' she asked.

He slid a hand over her hair, tugging the end of her ponytail, and nodded.

'Yeah,' she said. 'Me too. We don't really have to send her back to school next week, do we?'

He kissed the top of her head. 'You're the one who came from the good family—how did you end up being the bad influence?'

'I'm Libran. I will do anything to make people love me.'

'Mmm, and there I was thinking people couldn't help loving you just because you're you. And all along it was the accident of your birth.'

'Happy accident?' she asked, looking up at him again.

He appeared to think about it for a moment. Then two.

Meg moved to pinch his arm, but he caught her hand in time and held it behind her back. Heat slid through her centre, the kind that still caught her off guard after all these weeks, the kind she didn't see herself ever getting used to.

And then he kissed her with the kind of sweet, sensitive, all-consuming passion she never planned on getting used to.

Eons later they pulled apart when the sound of big tyres crunching against the white gravel drive split the peaceful silence.

The next of the four remaining buses was pulling in, and Dylan's harrowed face was peering out the front window. Tabitha bouncing about next to him the likely reason.

Meg grabbed Zach's hand and pulled him inside the first bus. They jogged to the back bench seat and hunkered down with Meg atop Zach's lap, her arms about his neck so that they could watch from a covert vantage point as Tabitha, Dylan and his fiancée, Wynnie, attempted to corral their group.

'You should have let Rylie do a series on her TV show about what we're doing here this week, you know,' Meg said. 'The publicity would have been amazing.'

'It would have. If we wanted publicity.'

The public figure and the private benefactor in Meg both struggled to be given free rein. 'But think of the fundraising opportunity—'

'I have more than enough funds to do this any time I want.'

She sat up straight. 'As do I. But I wish the world knew what an amazing man you are.'

'So long as you know, and Ruby has a vague sense of it, and your family suspects, then the world can think whatever it wants.'

'You know what else?' Meg asked, curling closer. 'This way I get to keep you all to myself. And talking of having you to myself, how many sleeps till we head off to St Barts for the Grand Opening?'

'Ah, twelve.' He ran a finger down her nose before sliding it beneath her chin. 'We still have time for it to be a honeymoon instead, you know.'

Though the idea felt just as thrilling now as the first time he'd suggested it, she knew that she wanted her family, her whole extended family, to be a part of the happy day when it finally came.

'A quickie wedding?' she said. 'A four-day honeymoon? Sometimes I think you don't know me at all.'

The finger beneath her chin moved to slide behind her ear and she struggled not to purr.

'Fine. Then when we get back,' he said, his voice gentle, 'can we continue that talk from the other night?'

She nodded. Her next breath in shook. And then she smiled. 'We can do better than that. I made an appointment with a fertility specialist at Monash IVF in Melbourne for not long after we come home. They practically invented the procedure, so if we're going to start finding out the possibilities of maybe one day having another child, then that's where we start.'

Zach leaned in to plant a kiss on her lips. Talk about heart-warming. 'No matter what happens, always know I'll always love you.'

She kissed him back. 'Always know I'll always love you too.'

He nodded. Promise sealed. He moved in for another kiss, when Meg stayed him with a finger.

'I just had a horrible thought,' Meg said, biting back a grin.

Zach's eyes narrowed. 'Do I really want to know?'

'What if Ruby asks for *commedia dell'arte* classes?'

'I'm not going to be the one to say no.'

'Yeah, me neither. They were actually kind of fun. Oh, look.'

The next bus pulled up and Cameron and his wife, Rosie, stood at the front clapping madly and singing some travel song they'd forced on the poor kids in their bus.

'You know what else is fun?' Zach said, nuzzling against Meg's ear.

She turned back to face him. 'Do I really want to know?'

Zach slowly pressed Meg down against the

leather seat, waved at her the keys he'd used to lock the bus door, and grinned. 'Yeah, you really want to know.'

MILLS & BOON PUBLISH EIGHT LARGE PRINT TITLES A MONTH. THESE ARE THE EIGHT TITLES FOR AUGUST 2010.

THE ITALIAN DUKE'S VIRGIN MISTRESS
Penny Jordan

THE BILLIONAIRE'S HOUSEKEEPER MISTRESS
Emma Darcy

BROODING BILLIONAIRE, IMPOVERISHED PRINCESS
Robyn Donald

THE GREEK TYCOON'S ACHILLES HEEL
Lucy Gordon

ACCIDENTALLY THE SHEIKH'S WIFE
Barbara McMahon

MARRYING THE SCARRED SHEIKH
Barbara McMahon

MILLIONAIRE DAD'S SOS
Ally Blake

HER LONE COWBOY
Donna Alward

MILLS & BOON PUBLISH EIGHT LARGE PRINT TITLES A MONTH. THESE ARE THE EIGHT TITLES FOR SEPTEMBER 2010.

—————————— ❧ ——————————

VIRGIN ON HER WEDDING NIGHT
Lynne Graham

BLACKWOLF'S REDEMPTION
Sandra Marton

THE SHY BRIDE
Lucy Monroe

PENNILESS AND PURCHASED
Julia James

BEAUTY AND THE RECLUSIVE PRINCE
Raye Morgan

EXECUTIVE: EXPECTING TINY TWINS
Barbara Hannay

A WEDDING AT LEOPARD TREE LODGE
Liz Fielding

THREE TIMES A BRIDESMAID…
Nicola Marsh

POLLY

Freya North holds a Masters Degree in History of Art from the Courtauld Institute. She has worked for the National Art Collections Fund as well as for a commercial sculpture garden and has freelanced as a picture researcher. *Polly* follows her first two, highly acclaimed, novels *Sally* and *Chloë*.

FREYA NORTH

Polly

WILLIAM HEINEMANN : LONDON

Extracts on pages 3, 147 and 265 from 'Moonlight in Vermont' by Karl Suessdorf
and John Blackburn
Extracts on page 179 from: 'Tam O' Shanter' by Robert Burns; 'Pied Beauty' by
Gerald Manley Hopkins; 'Sonnet, Bright Star' by John Keats; 'Proverbial
Philosophy, 1st series. Of Discretion' by Martin Farquhar Tupper; 'Lead Kindly
Night' by John Henry Newman.

First published in the United Kingdom in 1998 by
William Heinemann

1 3 5 7 9 10 8 6 4 2

William Heinemann
Random House UK Limited
20 Vauxhall Bridge Road, London SW1V 2SA

Random House Australia (Pty) Limited
20 Alfred Street, Milsons Point, Sydney, New South Wales 2061, Australia

Random House New Zealand Limited
18 Poland Road, Glenfield
Auckland 10, New Zealand

Random House South Africa (Pty) Limited
Endulini, 5a Jubilee Road, Parktown 2193, South Africa

Random House UK Limited Reg. No. 954009

A CIP catalogue record for this book is available from the British Library

Papers used by Random House UK Limited are natural, recyclable products made
from wood grown in sustainable forests. The manufacturing processes conform to the
environmental regulations of the country of origin

Typeset by SX Composing DTP, Rayleigh, Essex
Printed and bound in the United Kingdom by
Redwood Books, Trowbridge, Wiltshire

ISBN 0 434 00392 1

With thanks to all at VA, SR, VT – especially MH

This book is for my friends and family in the United States.
See you soon.

MICHAELMAS

Pennies in a stream
Falling leaves of sycamore
Moonlight in Vermont

Karl Suessdorf & John Blackburn, *Moonlight in Vermont*

ONE

*I*f Polly Fenton had thought for one moment that a year in America was going to have serious ramifications for her accent *and* her relationship with Max Fyfield, she very probably would not be going. But the concept hasn't crossed her mind and so she is trading Belsize Park, London, for Hubbardtons Spring, Vermont, on a teachers' exchange programme.

Tomorrow.

Today, she must pack and prepare.

Currently, she is wrapping articles of clothing around bumper-sized jars of Marmite.

'Look, Buster, I've never been to America,' she explains to her oversized ginger tom-cat who regards her reproachfully. 'This is an *amazing* opportunity,' she clarifies, as much to herself as to Buster's withering yawn. 'Max said so,' she furthers, looking at a photograph of him, clasping it to her heart before swaddling it in pairs of knickers and placing it in the suitcase.

Apart from Buster, Polly actually has everyone's blessing. The offer of the exchange wasn't even put out to tender amongst the school staff and when Polly asked Max what he thought, he declared, 'Go West, young woman. Wow!'

Her friends have taken to talking to her in American accents, scattering twangy sentences with liberal dashings of 'sonava', 'goddam' and 'gee'. Such supportive reactions have enabled Polly to feel just on the verge of rather excited about her year away. And why shouldn't she be? Her life in London is safe and lovely and she knows it will greet her as such on her return. And yet, over the last week and particularly today, on packing, those quivers of excitement are masking tremors of fear.

She is twenty-seven years old, petite in stature but large in character. Her dead straight, rich brown hair hangs in a neat, fringed bob, the gloss and hue of dark, clear honey (though she wishes it were a more Marmitey shade and sheen, of course). Eyes that are mostly rich hazel turn khaki in times of extreme emotion. They invariably change colour on a daily basis when some fact or fantasy subsumes her.

Presently, with some trepidation, she is rifling through her bathroom cabinet deciding what to take.

'Do you know, I've never been away from home for more than a fortnight,' she says to herself, very quietly. 'I haven't been apart from Max for more than four days – and then only twice in our five years.'

She sits on the edge of the bath and her eyes well army-issue green. Her throat is tight. Here it comes. She cries sharply for a few seconds until her throat loosens.

'Oh dear,' she says, catching her breath and sniffing loudly, while a sorry smile etches its way across her lips. 'That's better. Much better,' she laughs, as the ablutionary effect of the sob settles in and her eyes shine hazel. 'Absolutely fine. Where was I?'

Though she taps her temples and scrunches her brow, she can't remember what she was to do in the bathroom so she returns to her bedroom and regards the open suitcase on the bed, gaping like a cavernous, ravenous mouth. She fears that once the lid is closed, the contents might be consumed. She giggles at her ludicrously active imagination developed, as a necessity, in childhood.

If you'd been brought up by an aunt who made Trappist monks seem fervent conversationalists, you too would turn to the most unlikely of objects for a chat.

Polly regards the suitcase, half tempted to take everything out and place it all back in her cupboard and drawers.

Do I really want to go? But, for a whole year?

Too late to back out now.

'Is that enough Marmite? Have I packed enough clothes?'

Polly weighs the merit of another jar of Marmite against another pair of jeans, looking from one to the other, chewing her lip and procrastinating.

I'm going to the home of the Blue Jean – bloody brilliant!

I'm going away from the home of Marmite – why would I want to do that?

The clothing loses, easily, and the jar of Marmite is wrapped in a T-shirt currently lying unproductive in the suitcase.

She returns to the bathroom. Dilemma. To pack a half-empty bottle of shampoo or buy new. Where? At the airport? Or over there, in America?

'Saved by the bell!' Polly cheers, straightening her brow and running away from the shampoo conundrum to answer the door.

'Lalalalala–America!'

It's Max. Singing. He has a lovely voice. Polly throws her arms about his neck and buries her face there while he wraps his arms about her waist and lifts her up. They waddle through the communal hallway back to her flat.

'Switch the light off, bitch!' comes the familiar tirade from Edith Dale, the old woman living on the top floor.

'Hullo, hullo? What is the noise please? Is it Sunday?' asks Miss Klee, the frail Swiss woman who lives on the floor above Polly.

'It's Monday, Miss Klee, the eighth of September,' a muffled Max informs, Polly still clasped on to him, while he flicks the hallway light back on.

Back in Polly's flat, Max sets her down. She goes over to

the French doors, sighs at her minute patio and then returns to him.

'I don't want to go, I don't want to go,' she whispers, drumming her fists lightly against his chest. 'Tell me I don't have to!' she pleads. 'Tell me to stay.'

Max holds her wrists and lays her hands either side of her face. 'Daft thing,' he says with affection, noting her eyes are currently a very sludgy green. 'Of course you're going. It's an amazing opportunity.'

'A-*maze*-ing,' Polly repeats ruefully. 'Will you miss me?' she implores, scanning Max's face which she knows off by heart, wondering how on earth she'll cope without easy access to it over the next year.

'Will you *miss* me?' she asks again, this time pouting becomingly.

'Just as much as you'll miss me,' Max assures, pressing his finger gently on the tip of her nose. Her eyes smart with tears but she swallows them away for the time being.

'Packed?' he asks, 'ready?'

'Yes,' says Polly in a small voice, 'and no.'

'Clothes as well as Marmite?'

'Yes,' Polly replies, 'and yes. The jars would crack otherwise, wouldn't they? Come and see.'

The lid on the suitcase had fallen closed and, as she lifted it, Polly wondered whether the contents would be entire, or half eaten.

'Absolutely fine,' she said, on close scrutiny.

'Hey?' said Max, casting his eyes away from the rattle of hangers in the cupboard, the hungry shelves.

'Oh, nothing,' Polly smiled.

'Come here, Button,' he said quietly. She went over to him and slid her fingers into the front pockets of his trousers.

'Why do you call me Button?' she asked for the thousandth time. Max replied with his thousandth shrug. They heaved the suitcase from the bed and curled up together in the impression it had left.

8

'Can't I pack you?' Polly asked, walking fingertips over his face.

'You'd have to forego a lot of Marmite,' Max qualified, taking her hand and kissing the palm.

'Do you know, I don't think I can live without either of you,' said Polly honestly, folding her fingers lightly over his nose.

Lazily, Max travelled his hand over her body, admiring, as ever he did, her petite frame. Max knelt up beside Polly and looked down upon her.

Polly Fenton. Like a figure '2', folded like that. Just us two, too. I must soak it all up. Commit it all to memory, although I don't doubt absence making my heart all the fonder. Strange, though.

Polly had placed an arm across Max's knees, her hand patting his stomach.

'I'm going to America,' she told him quietly, as if for the first time. 'Can't wait,' she said, eyes wide. 'Don't want to go,' she continued, eyes wider still, khaki flecking across them as he watched. Max laughed softly through his nose and bent low to kiss her forehead. Suddenly her arms were around his neck and, though it threatened to break his back, he let her kiss him as if she would never stop. Dozens of feathery lip pinches, like popcorn popping, one after another after another, small and involuntary noises accompanying them. It made him smile but still she continued, kissing his teeth now instead. He pulled away, cocked his head and observed her, returning his lips to hers and just pressing against them, no puckering, while privately asking himself 'Is she really going?'

Max placed his arms either side of Polly's head and straddled her. He dipped his upper body low, like a press-up, and kissed her nose. He continued these press-up lip-presses, alighting on her forehead, her cheek, her left eye, her chin, her nose, her right eye, her forehead again. As he neared her nose for the third time, she held his face gently and greeted his lips with hers. A long, soft kiss, soon enough a deeper

9

kiss; eyes open and so close that they blurred; passion and love legible regardless.

Up they sat and undressed themselves, like they always did. You touch me while I touch you, like we always do. Under the covers. Cuddle sweetly, kiss lightly. Kiss with tongues. Move closer and grind subconsciously. Fondle her breasts. Feel his cock. Finger her sex. Sidle down his torso and then suck him. Hear his breathing quicken. Good. Flip her over and lick her. Enough. Cover her. Enter her. Hold his buttocks. Kiss his neck. Squeeze her nipples. Kiss. Smile.

Moan. Move.
Swap places.
Move. Moan.
Swap again.
Silence.
Not any more.
Come.
Together.
Kissing and smiling.
Like they always did.

'Will you miss me?' she had asked.

'Just as much as you'll miss me,' he had replied, gently and with confidence. Max and Polly, Polly and Max. Maxanpolly had become a familiar descriptive term amongst those who knew them, one frequently employed to quantify the level of compatibility amongst others.

'No, I do like him – but we're not talking maxanpolly here.'
'They've become totally maxanpollified.'

Polly Fenton and Max Fyfield were the couple that other couples loved, envied and invariably aspired to; after all, they had maintained their relationship through their early twenties. It seemed there had always been Max and Polly. That there would always be Max and Polly was a fact undisputed and oft proclaimed by those who knew them, for it created a soft web of safety. What a lovely balance: thirty-year-old Max, the quiet, freelance draughtsman;

contemplative, generous, handsome in a boyish way with his fawn flop of hair, grey-blue eyes and open smile. Polly the English teacher, petite and pretty, a lively sparkle to Max's warm glow, an eager conversationalist to Max's well-chosen few words. She is as feminine as he is masculine; he's not hero-tall or model-macho but he appears strong and manly when he has Polly attached to him.

Max tips his head and maybe touches a shoulder when he greets people, while Polly hugs them liberally. Friends in need turn to Max for his measured, sober assistance. If they wish to celebrate or chat, they seek Polly because she will share their excitement and wear their emotions. Like salt and pepper, sugar and spice; they complement each other. Polly and Max fit. Polly will be greatly missed while she is away. But she'll be back. Of course she will. She's going away tomorrow but she'll be back, as she would say, 'in a jiff'.

Tomorrow is now today. Yesterday went far too quickly. Now tomorrow will see Polly wake up over the sea and far away because today Polly is leaving England for America. At four thirty. Tomorrow, Max won't have seen Polly since yesterday. Polly and Max have not said much so far today. Polly has been scurrying around her flat, double-checking things already triple-checked yesterday. She has left little notes dotted here and there to assist her American proxy with the ways and wills of the boiler, the cooker, Buster, and the patio doors. Polly knows little about her counterpart apart from her name (Jen Carter), her age (same as Polly) and her subject (English too, of course).

'Do you think The Jen Carter Person will be happy here?' Polly asks Max. 'Do you think she'll like my flat?'

'Yes. And yes,' Max assures, adding that a note explaining how the television worked was really not necessary. 'Maybe just warn her that here we have only five channels.'

'Radio?' Polly suggests, pen poised above a yellow Post-it note. Max shakes his head. He pulls Polly's hair through his hands into a pony tail, tugs it so her head comes back, and kisses her nose.

'A map to the launderette!' Polly exclaims, busying herself with red and blue pens.

'I'll start loading the car,' he says, turning away from her. It had seemed such a great idea, such a wonderful opportunity that she should go. Now Max feels ambivalent, wonders whether they should have discussed it in more depth, just talked more really.

'And I must warn her of Buster's food fads,' Polly says to herself.

'I'll load the car,' Max says.

Max opens the bonnet of his Beetle which is really the boot and smiles broadly at Polly's suitcase and the knowledge of all those jars of Marmite. He hates the stuff and yet had he not sneaked a jar from Polly yesterday? Just to keep. To have and to hold.

'You can have it back once you're home again,' he had said, holding the jar aloft while Polly jumped to reach it.

'Let me check the sell-by date. OK. But it must be this very jar – no substitute.'

A substitute? Ludicrous!

Max places her small rucksack on top of the suitcase and reads its bulges easily. Walkman. Water. Two paperbacks. One pair of thick socks. Bits and pieces from the bathroom.

Damn, I should have written a little note, or brought a little something to slip in as a surprise.

Too late, Max, because here she is. See her? Locking the door and resting her forehead lightly against it for a moment? Now walking down the steps. Walking towards you with a brave, manufactured smile aboard her small face. Isn't time strange? You've had five years together and suddenly it doesn't seem enough. Eight days ago she wasn't going until next week – ages away in the face of a whole week together. Then you had to think in terms of days. Yesterday it was tomorrow. This morning it was this

12

afternoon. Now, at noon, it is merely a case of less than a handful of hours.

'You ready? Shall we go?'
   'Yes and no.'
   'The sooner you go, the sooner you'll be back, hey?'
   'Can't wait to get rid of me, is it?'
   'You know what I mean.'
   'I do.'
   'Shall we?'
   'Sure thing, babe. Let's burn rubber, hon. Hit it.'
   'Polly Fenton! Don't you *dare* forsake your dulcet tones before you've even left our shores!'
   'Max, my lover, 'twas but a jest. My accent and I will sail through this year untainted and return to you unblemished, in one piece. Absolutely fine and in a jiff.'

At Heathrow, Max bought Polly two bottles of her favourite shampoo because there was space in her rucksack and time to do it. They sat over cups of coffee and small bottles of orange juice, not daring to finish them. They tried to do the *Guardian* crossword but found that the airport tannoy played havoc with the necessary lobe of the brain. They declared the airport clock fast, their watches must be slow, that *can't* be the time. Did you hear that? Yes, I did. Oh, that they were hard of hearing!
   'Did you hear that?'
   'Yes I did.'
   'What does "last call" actually mean, Max? Might there not be a "final" one we could wait for?'
   'Maybe.'

'Oh dear,' Polly says, 'they've called me by name. Should I go now?'
   'Yes.'
   'I know we said you wouldn't, but would you? Come all the way?'

13

'All the way?'

'To passport control at any rate?' she whispers, hiding the colour of her eyes from Max as she closes them to kiss him. Her lips are quivering too much for her to pucker them properly. Max doesn't mind; he knows her intention and echoes her sentiment with a clumsy bash of his lips against her cheek.

'Come on Polly, it's time.'

Silently, they try to pretend they have no idea where passport control is but there's no avoiding it, all paths seem to lead there and yet they cannot see beyond it; beyond the neon sign 'Departures', beyond the uniformed officials behind their melamine lecterns.

'Here we are.'

'Can't.'

'You have to.'

'Max. Can't.'

'Button, you can.'

'*Would passenger Polly Fenton, flying Virgin Atlantic to Boston, please make her way to the departure lounge.*'

'Oh dear. Bye bye.'

'Bye, sweet girl.'

'Hold me, Max.'

'*Would passenger Polly Fenton, flying Virgin Atlantic to Boston, please make her way to the departure lounge.*'

'You have to go.'

'I know. Hold me a moment longer.'

'*This is the final call for passenger Polly Fenton, flying Virgin Atlantic to Boston, make your way to the departure lounge immediately.*'

'Got everything?'

'Um, not sure, shall we check?'

'You have everything.'

'I do?'

'You do.'

'I do. OK.'

'Off you go.'

14

'Bye bye.'
'Bye bye.'
'Bye.'

Max watched her go away from him.

God, she can't.

'Polly!'

He ran towards her. Someone was examining her passport.

Wait!

'Polly!'

They were handing her passport back to her.

Oh bloody hell, what am I? – what the? – Jesusgod.

'Polly?'

Her tear-streaked face turned to him.

They regarded each other, Polly biting her lip in a futile
bid to keep tears at bay. She wanted to smile for Max. She
couldn't if she was clamping on to her lips. Tears and a
smile were much better than neither of either. She lavished
both on him. He cupped her face in his hands and pressed
his lips against her forehead. Then he held her at arm's
length and took hold of her wrists.

Jesusgod, I can't believe I—

'Marry me.'

There!

Pardon?

Polly was stunned and far too choked to speak her reply.
The passport officer cleared his throat and addressed her,
rather ominously, by name. Polly wiped her nose on Max's
shirt. He took her left hand and slipped something along her
fourth finger. The orange plastic neck-ring from the small
bottle of fruit juice. Scratchy and ridiculously oversized.
Exquisite.

'You'll have a proper one when you come home. Promise.'

TWO

*W*hen John Hubbardton died in 1906 at the age of eighty-nine, he had a minor river and, consequently, the small town along its banks named after him. That the town's school, which he had founded in 1878, should also be renamed in his honour was a foregone conclusion. Lower South River thus became Hubbardtons River, the town of Lower South was renamed Hubbardtons Spring and the Lower South School became The John Hubbardton Academy. The mountain, in whose embrace all three lay, was also given the man's name. By the 1920s, river, town, school and mountain were known universally as Hubbardtons. One lived in Hubbardtons, one's kids were at school at Hubbardtons; summers were spent canoeing Hubbardtons, winters skiing Hubbardtons. We'll discover the town and the river alongside Polly when she arrives, maybe the mountain too, if she learns to ski, but we can have a sneak preview of the school now, for Polly herself is re-reading her information pack. She is two hours into her journey.

The John Hubbardton Academy is a prep school. Not, you understand, in the British sense (small boys learning rugger and round vowels in preparation for Eton); Hubbardtons is a high-school, a boarding-school, *'proud to*

16

provide a rounded preparation for college', as proclaimed on page one of the glossy brochure.

'Here at the John Hubbardton Academy, we're one big family,' commences page two. There are 240 students and 45 full-time teachers. When John Hubbardton founded the school 118 years ago it was, by necessity, co-ed. The school went temporarily all-male in a perverted stance against the 1960s, but extended an apology and an invitation to females a decade later. Currently, two thirds of both students and teachers are male. But no one is complaining.

'We work and play, and we learn and live. Together. And we have 150 acres to do it in.'

It certainly looks picturesque from the brochure. Whether the buildings are genuinely old, or just old-style, is irrelevant; they are structurally pleasing and set attractively within grand grounds sympathetically landscaped. The superb backdrop of the Green Mountains completes the picture. Seemingly seamless; from the brochure photographs at least.

Polly slips the folder into the seat pouch in front of her, in between the safety instructions and the duty-free catalogue.

Poor old Jen Carter, whoever she may be. Do you know, I'm not sure that BGS is a fair trade for the JHA. I can't believe Max proposed!

In 1820, when Belsize Park sat just outside London, a thoroughly modern building was built for the purpose of overseeing the education of young ladies residing locally. The establishment was duly named Belsize Ladies' College. An insignia was designed (an open book with a lit candle propped, somewhat precariously, at its centre) and a motto was chosen (*Cherchez la femme*).

Until the turn of the century, sixty pupils were attended to by six teachers in this one building. 1900 saw the first expansion of the school with the purchase of the four-storey house next door, and similar shrewd acquisitions followed in the early decades. Now, there are 300 girls and twenty-

17

seven teachers squeezed into a coterie of old houses around the original school building; ingeniously interconnected by a series of corridors, covered walkways and iron staircases. No one is quite sure when the college for ladies became a school for girls but the institute is known now as Belsize Girls' School. The insignia and the motto remain.

The grounds at BGS comprise two concrete rectangles over which the layout of a pair of netball courts are super-imposed in red lines; two tennis courts, likewise, in blue. An oak tree, protected by an unquestioned ancient law, stands defiant, slap in the middle of the larger rectangle. It makes for interesting reinterpretations of the rules of netball and tennis. Winter and summer terms, the girls can choose to play hockey and cricket respectively on the manicured sports fields owned by the nearby public boys' school. Needless to say, the popularity of these two sports vastly outweigh tennis and netball. In the spring term, there is a choice between pottery classes in the cellar of the sixth-form house, or choral society at the boys' school. Unsurprisingly, you never heard so many fine voices.

Polly has taught English at Belsize Girls' School for five years. She landed the position the day after she had forlornly sent out her seventeenth job application, the morning of the day when Max first asked her out. Something divine was intervening and she welcomed it. She still feels truly blessed.

I hope this Jen Carter Person will be happy living my life for me – or at least a part of it – while I'm gone.

Polly wriggles her feet into the red socks that came free with the flight and places the complimentary 'snooze-mask' over her tired eyes as, indeed, the passengers either side of her have done. Three hours to go.

Oh, for Marmite on toast.

Think about Max. Marriage. Marmite. Mmm!

* * *

'Pollygirl set sail OK then?'

Dominic handed his brother a glass of his incomparable home-brew which he had poured on hearing Max's car return. Max nodded, made an affirmative noise in his throat and accepted the beer with unbridled gratitude, downing half the pint swiftly and with eyes closed as if it was some elixir. Or in the hope, at least, that the fast-working potency of the beverage might lead him to believe that Polly had not gone at all.

The brothers sat down on their sofa and supped in amiable silence. Both had kicked off their shoes and had their legs stretched out in front of them; ankles crossed on the coffee table built, quite obviously, for that precise purpose. Dominic flicked between television channels, finally choosing a cartoon and silencing the volume.

'So,' he said.

'Yes,' Max replied.

Dominic replenished their glasses and they continued to sit alongside each other, the occasional chuckle acknowledging that antics in animation are as entertaining without sound as with.

'So,' Max said eventually, as if concluding a lengthy soliloquy.

'Yup,' said Dominic, in utter understanding. Close friends often know what each other is about to say, they may even finish sentences for one another; but close friends who are also siblings can conduct entire conversations without saying a word. And so it is with Dominic and Max, five years separate them and nothing comes between them. They can have entire conversations in utter silence.

They shared a bedroom when they were young and, for the past seven years, Dominic has rented the second bedroom of his flat to his younger brother.

'It's in the wrong side of Hampstead,' he had warned Max.

'How on earth can there be a wrong side to Hampstead?' Max, then in Streatham, had marvelled, already heaping his belongings into black bin bags.

19

So the boys kept home together and never wavered from the four golden rules they had devised during that journey seven years ago from south to north London. Sitting-room to appear to be tidy, cleaning duties on alternate Saturdays, fridge always to contain milk and alcohol, and CD collection to be communal. The draughtsman and photographer, both freelance and with adjacent studios nearby, living and working alongside each other in peace and harmony. They never fight for the shower or the phone, they never argue about washing up, they invariably have the same taste in TV and radio programming. And their combined CD collection is not so much communal as duplicate.

Dominic Fyfield is five years older, two inches taller and a stone heavier than his brother. Like Max, Dominic is handsome in face and character. Where his features are not as fine as Max's (his hair is a touch coarser and his eyes a little plainer), Dominic's disposition is more effortlessly outgoing. Both brothers have winning smiles but Dominic shamelessly employs his to wholly libidinous ends. Dominic, however, respects Max's monogamy just as much as Max marvels at his brother's stamina and ability to chop and change, mix and match, when it comes to women. Max does, however, frequently call his brother a tart. Dominic, though, accepts it only as a profound compliment.

'Why thank you, good man. Praise indeed from one as staid and unadventurous as you, Maximilian.'

'Ah! But at least I know where my next metaphorical hot meal is coming from. Ever thought you might go hungry?'

'*Moi*? Pah!'

The Fyfield brothers are a lovely balance because they are different enough not to be competitive. Neither brother covets the other's life because they are content and settled and secure with their own patterns. Neither, therefore, passes judgement. They disagree frequently but they rarely argue. And though Dominic lavishes many a smile on Polly, it is with no intent other than his seal of approval, acknowledgement of his brother's good fortune.

20

On first meeting her, Dominic had put her to the test and discovered she came through with colours blazing. He regaled Max with his findings.

'Bit small?' Dominic suggested.

'But perfectly formed,' Max justified.

'Mmm,' conceded Dominic, 'nicely put together. Bright too.'

'As a button,' confirmed Max.

'Gregarious and outgoing,' said Dominic, throwing a cushion at his brother. 'Good balance for you, you fusty old fart.'

'I don't think you can talk about farts being fusty, Dom,' warned Max with a retaliation of cushions, 'it's the pot calling the kettle black.'

'Bastard! Flatulence is a serious medical matter. OK, OK. So this Polly Fenton is a teacher.'

'Yup, English.'

'Shame it's not PE but never mind. Remember that PE teacher I went out with?'

'Unforgettable,' cringed Max.

'Gave a whole new meaning to the term "games mistress", I can tell you.'

'I can hear her still,' Max groaned.

Dominic had a private reminisce, of which Max decided not to partake, before returning his attention to his brother's new girlfriend.

'Fenton. Do you know, she actually apologized to me for not being related to Roger. Now that's what I call impressive.'

'Who?'

'Maximus Cretinous! *Roh*-ger *Fen*-ton,' Dominic stressed as though spoken italics would assist, 'seminal nineteenth-century photographer? Crimean War?'

'Right, right,' hurried Max. 'She's not related to James either.'

'Who he?'

'*Jay*-ums *Fen*-ton, dickhead,' Max relished. 'Come on – landmark British poet, journalist, critic? *The Memory of War?*'

Dominic regarded his brother slyly. 'Swot!' he declared, with a friendly punch to the biceps.

'Back to Polly?' Max, ever the pacifist, suggested; so they chinked glasses and toasted her health and Max's very good fortune.

'Get you, Max!' mused Dominic. 'Is she tickling your fancy or melting your heart?'

'We're not talking marriage here,' Max had laughed, standing and stretching, and offering his brother a choice between a frozen lasagne ready-meal or beans on toast.

'She'll be half-way through her journey now,' Dominic remarks, listening to his watch, checking it against the time on the video and phoning the talking clock to make absolutely sure.

'Oh, and I asked her to marry me,' Max says to Dominic, as if informing him merely that he had invited Polly along to the cinema with them.

'Oh yes?' says Dominic, keeping a straight face but unable to do anything about the sparkle in his eyes.

'Yup,' says Max, 'just before she went through passport control.'

'Did she, er, accept graciously?' asked Dominic, all wide eyed and winsome.

'Not in so many words,' said Max slowly, 'what with all her sobbing and hugging me. And her nose all blocked up.' He proffered the crumpled section of his shirt as proof.

'Ah,' said Dominic, further convinced that all women were soft. And so, it now transpired, was his brother. 'Bet she made off with your diamond!'

'Actually,' said Max, burping lightly under his breath and passing his glass for another refill, 'it was all a bit spur-of-the-moment. The words sort of tumbled out. Anyway, she's having to make do with the plastic jigger from a small bottle of fruit juice. Until she comes home.'

* * *

With eyes shut and further concealed by the eye-mask; body wrapped, chin to knee, against the controlled chill of aeroplane air-conditioning by a thin, synthetic blanket, Polly concentrates on forgetting the whirr and smell of the plane, the words and pictures of the Hubbardtons brochure, to transport herself back to the then and there of her departure from Max. And his words. And their meaning.

Marry me.

Me?

Who else.

But I haven't really thought about it – not outside the context of a soft-focus day-dream. We've never spoken seriously about it – like we might be tempting fate if we did. But there again, who else would I marry?

She wriggles in her seat and retrieves the orange plastic neck-ring from the back pocket of her jeans. She places it on her finger, under the blanket, eyes scrunched shut even behind the eye-mask, desperate to recreate the sensation when Max did so. It is too large, of course. Somehow, its symbolism is almost too big for her to contemplate as well, thousands of feet up in the air, on her way to foreign climes. For a whole year. She'll think seriously on it anon of course, perhaps on the banks of some lonely stream, under the bough of some lofty maple, when she feels alone and a million miles away.

I'm bound to, frequently.

God, a whole year. And so far away.

The eye-mask forces her tears back against her eyes. The noise of the aircraft prevents anyone hearing her sniff. She returns the plastic neck-ring ring to the back pocket of her jeans. It's serrated.

Sharper than you'd think.

The glut of emotions enveloping her at Heathrow had been complex: the pain of parting from Max; the apprehension of leaving kin and country; a fear of flying; the love of the job she was leaving; concern for the position she was exchanging it for. Not to mention the bombard of emotion subsuming her when the man she loved proposed marriage. Out of the blue.

So spontaneous – very un-Max. Wonder if he thought about it, whether he really truly meant it?

'Oh dear,' she wails suddenly, out loud, tasting the blanket inadvertently, 'I didn't actually say "yes".'

The shock of it!

THREE

*P*olly was immensely excited to see Cape Cod from the aeroplane window.

'Do you know, it looks exactly the same as it does on a map!' she exclaimed to her neighbour who was still wearing the blindfold. 'Look!' Polly urged, with a gentle but insistent nudge, 'it's like an arm, a crook at the elbow, a hand cupping the sea against it. Look!'

Her fellow passenger did indeed look and then retreated back behind his eye-mask hoping sincerely that no other cartographical features would solicit his neighbour before they landed in Boston.

As Polly waited at the luggage carousel, she suddenly had absolutely no idea who would be meeting her. In the event, she would have made a bee-line for Kate Tracey anyway, whether or not she had been brandishing the enormous board emblazoned with Polly's name. Amongst the sea of faces and the barrage of name signs, Kate's easy smile reached out to Polly immediately. As she approached, she marvelled at the coincidence that the name on the sign was indeed her very own.

'Polly?' the woman mouthed, from some distance.

'Yes!' Polly mouthed back, nodding and grinning.

'Polly!' the woman declared when they were close to, 'hi there!'

'Hullo,' said Polly, a little breathless, 'how do you do?'

'I'm Kate Tracey, welcome,' the woman said, gripping the placard between her knees so she could shake Polly's hand heartily, 'how you doing?'

'Oh,' said Polly, 'absolutely fine, thank you.'

'Good! This is Bogey. Bogey say hi.'

Polly hadn't even seen the dog, having been preoccupied with Kate's glinting eyes behind red-rimmed owl-frame spectacles.

'Hullo Bogey!' Polly declared, flopping to her knees and encircling her arms about the oversized Airedale's neck while he slurped at her cheek. 'As in Humphrey?' she asked Kate.

'Sure thing,' Kate confirmed, trading the dog's lead for Polly's trolley.

'I'm Fenton as in Roger and James,' Polly explained, jigging to keep up with Kate who was slaloming effortlessly through the concourse towards the exit, 'although I'm related to neither. Unfortunately.'

'That's too bad,' rued Kate kindly, coming to a standstill, cocking her head and nodding at Polly, 'I'm kinda partial to British photographers *and* British poets.'

Polly was most impressed.

'I've had rampant affairs with *both* species,' confided Kate through the side of her mouth while she walked. 'Rampant!' she all but growled. 'In the sixties,' she said, by way of justification.

Polly laughed.

I like this woman!

What's she like then?

She's head of art at Hubbardtons. I suppose she must be in her early fifties, but she's quite trendy with her hair cut into a wonderful feathery crop and her face framed by these wacky specs. She has a round, sparkling face and chipmunk cheeks when she smiles. She's wearing a lovely old leather

*jacket – which has obviously known no other owner –
checked trousers and funky chunky boots. She walks incredibly fast and, oh how funny, she's just clicked and winked at
the newspaper-stand chap. He must be a hundred and
twenty. Ha! Here's her car and it's a real slice of America –
what they call a station-wagon, I think, with that faux
wooden panelling along the side?*

*Do you know, I'm actually here! I'm in America, in the car
park at Logan Airport. It's not frightening, it's fantastic.
Can't believe it. Wow!*

'All right! Here we go, luggage in the trunk, Bogey in the
back, Polly up front with me.'

'How long will the journey take?'

'About three and a half.'

'Bet that's just round the block for you – rather than
London to Liverpool for me. Is it scenic?'

'Round the what? I've been to Liverpool, you know, in the
sixties, of course. And yup, the route's pretty.'

'Fantastic! I've never been to America.'

'You're gonna have a lot of fun,' said Kate, nodding sagely
and tapping Polly lightly on the knee. 'You'll never want to
leave.' Polly tapped Kate back.

Oh yes I will. Everything I am is in the UK.

'I like your checked trousers,' she said instead.

Kate laughed, short and sharp. 'They're plaid pants over
here.'

The journey passed quickly, Kate talking nineteen to the
dozen while Polly's eyes, like her ears, worked overtime to
take in all she could.

School on Saturdays – nightmare!

Wooden houses. Big cars. Sidewalks. Very fat people.
Fantastically thin people.

So I'm to have a room at Kate's house for the first term.

Driving on the wrong side. Policemen with guns and cool
glasses.

*Term started last Thursday but the first weekly faculty
meeting is this Thursday evening.*

The most enormous trucks imaginable, huge radiator grilles quite menacing. Truck drivers up in the gods with baseball caps. Kids with baseball caps back to front.

There'll be no more than twelve in a class – that's phenomenal.

The Charles River. Sculling. Harvard round the bend and out of sight. Concord River. Connecticut River.

Kate, lovely Kate, stopping at a tiny bakery just across the state line, buying me a cinnamon bun and a double decaff coffee.

'We're gonna have a whole lot of fun. You're gonna just love school, you'll fit in a dream.'

Will I? Hope I live up to your expectations – you seem to have decided an awful lot about me.

It was dark when they reached Hubbardtons Spring but Polly was vaguely aware that the houses, for the most part, were white planked and that the dark, woolly masses looming in the background were the tree-covered hills.

'95 per cent of Vermont is tree covered,' Kate informed the squinting Polly. 'Hell, there's a nip in the air, come on in.'

The front door, it transpired, was never used. Kate explained it was for show and that the house would have looked kind of funny without one. Polly was led instead around the side of the house, up wooden steps to the wooden deck where three men drank beer from small bottles and, after brief 'hi's and 'hullo's all round, she led Polly into the house. Straight into the warm kitchen which smelt divine, passed a gargantuan fridge smothered with photos and various magnets, round a corner, up some stairs, along a corridor, down three steps and sharp left into an 'L' shaped room with a decisive chill to it.

'Been airing it for you. It's not really been used since Great Aunt Clara died.'

Polly looked horrified.

'Hey! That was ten years ago. And she was one helluva lady. You want to unpack? You want a beer?'

'Yes and no,' said Polly. 'I don't think I like beer.'

'Tell you what, I'll fetch you one that'll change your mind. And your *life*. I'll put money on it.'

With Kate disappeared, Polly shut the windows and closed the double curtains; lace first, chintz second. She absorbed the details of the room in an instant: painted white iron queen-size bed with a handmade patchwork quilt, an old rocker with two slats missing from the back, a chest of drawers warped sufficiently for none to be closed flush, a bookcase crammed full, framed prints of Van Gogh's bedroom, Monet's water-lily garden and Cézanne's gardener, and an exquisite watercolour of maple trees ablaze in the autumn.

'Fall,' corrected Kate, making Polly realize she must have been talking out loud. 'Here you go,' she sang, thrusting a cold bottle of life-changing beer into Polly's hands, 'I'll be out the back with the guys. You take your time. We'll have dinner in forty-five.'

Supper? Isn't it one in the morning?

Not for you Polly, it's only eight o'clock.

But Max'll be fast asleep. I can't call him.

It's already tomorrow for Max. He hasn't seen you since yesterday.

I haven't even said 'yes' yet.

'The guys' turned out to be Kate's husband Clinton ('As in Eastwood?' Polly had asked in awe. 'Sure!' he had responded. 'Or as in President. But we'll go for the former if you don't mind.'); another foreign exchange teacher who was Chinese and asked to be called Charles with a silent 's' though his real name sounded something like Bik-toy-ng, and finally another young teacher from Hubbardtons called Greg who informed Polly he taught 'Math'.

'Sss?' suggested Polly, imagining only one side on a triangle, one axis on a graph, no long division and absolutely no multiplication.

'Math-th!' Greg brandished, though it made him spit slightly.

'That's some bandanna,' praised Clinton gently as he heaped spaghetti on to her plate.

To her horror, Polly realized that the Virgin Atlantic complimentary eye-mask was still propped up on her forehead.

'You want to trade?' Kate asked. 'For another beer, say?'

'Yes,' mumbled crimson-cheeked Polly, biting her lip and digging her nails into the mask, 'and yes.'

Kate examined the snooze-mask carefully and then tucked it into her pocket triumphantly.

Concerned that the new arrival should vanquish jet-lag, the group ensured that Polly did not go to bed until a respectable half past ten though it meant, on waking the next morning, that she had little recollection of the latter part of the night before, could not remember what or if she'd eaten and had to be reintroduced to Greg from scratch later that morning.

After ten hours of thick, dreamless sleep, Polly felt eager to set her first full day in motion and to acquaint herself with her new town, her new job and as many new peers as her mind could possibly catalogue. There seemed to be no one around, a feeble 'Morning?' from the bedroom door brought no reply. After encountering two dead ends, Polly found her way back to the kitchen and occupied herself by introducing herself to the fridge door where she came across Kate through the decades alongside affable-looking people with great teeth. The magnets holding the photos in place were quite something: colonial houses, a host of Disney characters, a golden angel, various dogs, a Red Sox shirt, a variety of bagels and doughnuts – all in miniature and mostly chipped.

'I don't call it my kitsch-en for nothing!'

'Kate!'

'Good morning there! I'm going to have you fetch the bread and milk, that way you'll catch the layout of the town – and I can show you the short cut to school later.'

'Fine,' shrugged Polly, 'fire away.'

'Out the back door, over the lawn, through the passageway

between those two houses there – with me so far? Hang a left, cross the street, first right. The store is the first building on the left. Got that?'

'Aye, Cap'n Tracey.'

'Hey? Who?'

'You!' said Polly fondly.

It didn't come as much of a surprise that the store was called Hubbardtons. The proprietor told Polly that Great John himself had worked there as a young boy. And bought all his provisions there throughout his life.

'Kate's sent me for her daily bread,' Polly explained.

'Sure thing,' said the proprietor, who was really too old to be wearing a denim skirt and sneakers, 'and what'll I call you?'

'Oh, I'm Polly Fenton. From England. I've come to teach at the John Hubbardton Academy. English.'

'Uh-huh, Hubbardtons,' said the proprietor, whose hair was neatly held in place with a child's novelty hair grips, 'I'm pleased to meet you, my name's Marsha – but you write it Mar-see-a, OK? That's Mar-C.I.A. See?' Polly nodded vigorously, wondering when she'd ever need to write to the proprietor of Hubbardtons Grocery Store.

It did not take much scrutinizing for Polly to familiarize herself with the layout of Hubbardtons Spring, though she would need a map to find her way round the school grounds for the first week. The town was laid out neatly either side of Main Street with Hubbardtons River running parallel to it. Though shrouded from view by a thatch of pine and maple, the water chattered constantly and Polly was all ears. There was a small fire station at one end of Main Street, at the other a church; white, wooden and archetypal (Polly once had a New England calendar with one on every page), marking a fork in the road. One leg obviously skirted alongside Hubbardtons (the river), the other marched upwards towards Hubbardtons (the mountain). Along Main Street, small stores sat amicably with houses and most of the buildings had flags outside, brightly coloured silk designs alongside the ubiquitous Stars and Stripes waving to Polly.

Everywhere I look I'm being welcomed. And yet no one really knows me at all. Poor Jen Carter, I can't imagine a Belsize Park reception coming anywhere near as close.

Though she was keen to undertake a thorough exploration of Main Street and where it led, she was keener to taste the warm bread she was carrying. She returned to Pleasant Street, off by heart, back to Kate's home.

'Did you meet Marsha with the C.I.A?' joked Kate, tearing a hunk of bread and offering the loaf to Polly to do the same.

'Met Marsha,' Polly confirmed, wrestling with the lid of the Marmite and then offering it to Kate.

'Jelly?' traded Kate, with her mouth full.

'Please,' said Polly, accepting blueberry jam without raising her eyebrows.

A very different taste to good old Marmite. A rather pleasant surprise.

You have to try new things.

The next morning, with her body clock just about reset for Vermont, it was time for Polly to go to school. The John Hubbardton Academy was more impressive, more beautiful than either the brochure suggested or Polly had imagined. Neat pathways cut through well-tended swathes of lawn and led to the various buildings which made up the school. It was evident that they varied greatly in age, and therefore style, but the uniformity of the copper-red brick with creamy-grey stone windows and detailing gave the campus a homogeneity. Kate named each building and its resident faculty, and introduced Polly to practically everyone who passed by. Polly absorbed names such as Brentwood, Stuyvesant, Peter, Finnigan and Stewart though she forgot immediately which was architecture and which was human – and which was teacher and who was the pupil.

'This is me,' Kate said, clasping the pillar on the porch of a small but noble building, 'this is where art matters.'

'Where do I go?' Polly asked. 'Where's "me"?'

'See that place directly opposite,' asked Kate, pointing to a majestic three-storey building with a great furl of steps leading up to it, 'that's Hubbardton Hall. That's where the fundamentals are housed: English, Math, History – also the admin offices. Go up the stairs and knock on the first door to your left. They'll be waiting. They know you're here. They'll show you to your class. Enjoy!'

Dutifully, Polly crossed the lawn (via the path, of course), climbed the stairs (twelve) and knocked on the first door to her left.

'Enter!'

It was a woman's voice. Polly popped her head around the door.

'Hullo?'

The woman sat at a word processor and smiled broadly at Polly without taking her eyes from the screen.

'Hi there. He'll be right with you.'

Sure enough, whoever 'he' was appeared from a connecting door and bowled over to Polly with his hand outstretched; a substantial figure with dark curls and an opaque beard.

'Powers!' he boomed, shaking her hand with both of his clasped around it.

'Fenton!' Polly replied, loudly and hastily and as she thought she ought. They observed each other, both slightly puzzled. The man continued to shake her hand while he cocked his head, said 'hmm'.

'Come,' he said, 'you have a class to teach.'

He led her along the grand entrance hall, clad with portraits of Great J.H. and reverberating with the echo of footsteps and chatter. No one appeared to be looking at her and there were too many of them for her to focus on. It was just another day at school. And now she was part of it. She was the new girl. She had to fit in.

I have to fit in. People have expectations. I was chosen.

'Your first class, lit crit, are freshmen and sophomore together.'

'I see,' said Polly, clueless, 'what years are they?'

'Ninth and tenth grade.'

'I see,' said Polly, none the wiser, wondering how Jen Carter was fairing with Upper Third and Lower Fourth.

'Jackson!' Polly's chaperon called to a good-looking man with a goatee beard and John Lennon spectacles, 'come over here!'

'Hey Powers, how are you? Hi there,' he nodded to Polly, 'I'm Jackson Thomas, I teach English too.'

'Hullo,' responded Polly, trying to sound casual and look at ease, 'I'm Fenton, Polly.'

The men regarded her and, while Jackson Thomas still wore the perplexed look that had been Powers's previously, Powers suddenly burst out laughing, slapped Jackson on the back and patted Polly's shoulders liberally.

'What?' laughed Polly with a little discomfort.

'Hey?' enquired Jackson.

'Fenton!' Powers laughed.

'Yes?' said Polly.

Suddenly Jackson roared alongside him.

'Sorry?' asked Polly, now a little irritated and her eye colour saying so. The joke was on her but what on earth was it?

'My name,' said Powers, 'is Powers Mateland. This is my colleague, Jackson Thomas.'

'Mateland,' mused Polly, thinking it an odd Christian name, but there again, this *was* America.

'My *name*,' Powers repeated, slowly and theatrically, 'is Powers. And *his* name,' he chuckled, wagging his thumb at the bespectacled one, 'is Jackson. Your name, unless I'm very much mistaken, is Polly. We don't subscribe to the formality of using surnames here at Hubbardtons. I hope that's cool with you?'

Polly looked hard at her shoes and tried to shuffle in a nonchalant manner.

Idiot girl!

She looked up at the men.

Powers and Jackson.

'I see,' she said cautiously before warming to the unaffected smiles the men bestowed on her, 'I thought—'

'I know – kinda weird to meet people christened Jackson and Powers when you've lived your life in a country of Johns and Henrys?'

Polly looked at the men's shoes. Powers was wearing well-worn moccasins; Jackson had a pair of highly polished classic penny loafers. She looked up, shook her head and raised her eyebrows, obviously at herself.

'What a twit I am, please excuse me,' she said, while a delighted Powers mouthed '*twit?*' with twisted eyebrows at Jackson. 'May I cordially introduce myself? I am Polly Fenton and I am most pleased to make your acquaintance.'

Her voice came out more clipped than usual, but only she was aware of it.

Mind you, that's probably what they're expecting. I won't let them down. I'll play along.

They all shook hands anew and Jackson led Polly to her classroom.

'I have the class next to yours,' he reassured her, 'so if you need me, just holler.'

'Righty ho,' said Polly, though she'd never used the phrase before.

'You know how to holler, don't you?' growled Jackson with a wink.

FOUR

*I*t seems wise, at this point, to introduce Megan Reilly because no doubt we'll bear witness to much of Polly's experience through their correspondence by letter and phone. Megan, a fellow teacher at BGS, is Polly's closest friend. She is two years older than Polly but they started at BGS on the same day, five years ago. Megan teaches Maths. With an 's'. She is taller and more substantial than Polly, but that's not hard. Though her distant Irish roots have left no trace of an accent, Megan has the dark, twirling tresses and lough-blue eyes of her Reilly ancestors. She has a slick, biting sense of humour, and the tortoiseshell spectacles she wears serve to magnify the wicked glint to her eye. She's effortlessly glamorous without a scrape of make-up, her hair sometimes swirled on top of her head, sometimes cascading down her back and, while she merely nods at current trends, she always looks enviably stylish and expensive – in school as much as out.

'You have this intuitive flair for layering,' Louise Bray, head of History and a slave to fashion, told her begrudgingly as she fingered Megan's soft, burgundy cardigan over a peach silk waistcoat worn on top of a cream linen shirt; a white cotton T-shirt just visible beneath it all and a scarf with all the above colours draped about her shoulders.

'Regulation school colours,' Megan explained with a shrug.

A flair for layers – bum! I just threw on whatever was clean and to hand.

Megan lives in a maisonette on the good side of Kilburn and she only ever walks to school. It is, in fact, more of a march; she covers the side streets of West Hampstead in under ten minutes, invariably jay-walks the Finchley Road at Swiss Cottage and is at school, unswervingly, at 8.15 a.m. She is always home in time for *Neighbours* (an obsession about which she feels neither guilt nor embarrassment), apart from Wednesdays when she plays violin in the school orchestra.

It is 8.15 a.m. Megan makes coffee in the staff room. The other teachers mill around, some in conversation, some analysing their registers, others gazing down at the netball-court-cum-playground-cum-arboretum, deciding on today's tactics to keep their girls in order. To Megan, however, the staff room may as well have been empty. Polly's absence was all the more stark to her because none of the other teachers appeared to notice it. Despite her universal popularity, Megan felt utterly alone without Polly and she felt her exuberance being sapped. Megan was not used to not having Polly there. Not after five years in which they'd snatched whatever spare time the school day bestowed on them to natter and laugh and share their space together. Their conversations could span school scandals, the beef crisis, cinema and Marks & Spencer ready-meals, in great detail and all in an easy five minutes. Five minutes were ample. In retrospect, they had been so precious too and the bond between the women was strong. Invariably, the topic turned, at some point and on a daily basis, to the Fyfield brothers; usually over lunch-time or an evening's telephone call, when they could confer more leisurely. After all, Megan has borne witness to Polly's relationship with Max from the start. She adores Max. And she has also had her eye on Dominic for some time.

It is 8.20 a.m. Megan Reilly has been charged with showing Jen Carter around school and she awaits her arrival with some suspicion. Polly's replacement? She can't take Polly's place. There is no substitute. She is irreplaceable. And yet This Carter Woman has taken Polly's place in more ways than one because of course she's now ensconced at Polly's place – her flat – too. Megan had phoned the previous evening to welcome Jennifer Carter but was so perturbed to discover Polly's answering machine already boasting a new message in a transatlantic twang that she hung up and phoned Max in disgust (and dismay – having prayed hard for Dominic to answer the call).

'That Carter Woman's been tampering with Polly's phone!' she launched.

'Hullo Megan,' said Max, 'how are you? Polly did leave a little yellow Post-it on the answerphone with instructions. And her permission.'

Megan chewed her thumb and decided she'd overlook the situation. But log it, all the same. 'Has Polly phoned yet?' she asked, 'has she arrived, do you know?'

'She has arrived, Meg,' said Max pseudo-breezily, 'I phoned the airline to check. But no, I haven't heard from her and I don't really expect to tonight. Long journey and everything. Hopefully tomorrow. You haven't heard a peep, have you?'

'No, sadly, no.'

'You will.'

'Will what?'

'Hear from Polly, of course.'

'Oh yes. I'm not used *not* to speaking to her daily, on the blower.'

'She'll have lots to tell you. She already has.'

'Has what?'

'Lots to tell you.'

'Oh, undoubtedly.'

Both sighed.

'Max, do you feel, you know – easy – about This Carter Woman living in Polly's place? Cuddling Buster? Using the bubble bath? Fiddling about?'

'Well,' paused Max, 'Polly gave her blessing. And gave me "site management responsibilities" as it were, so I'll keep my eye on things. The Carter Woman has my number. And I have a set of keys.'

This appeased Megan.

'How's Dominic then? He OK?'

'Yes,' said Max, throwing a suggestive wink over to his brother, 'he's fine. Megan, we really oughtn't to call her The Carter Woman, not before we've even met her. She might be perfectly OK. She's probably very nice.'

'But she sure ain't Polly!' Megan declared in pure New York.

Max fell silent.

'Better go, Meg. Better keep the line free, just in case.'

8.30 a.m. Mrs Elms, headmistress of stereotypical St Trinian's proportions, marched into the staff room.

'Good morning, everybody,' she cried, her iron-coloured curls and dark burgundy lipstick fixed until home time. 'Here she is – *locum tenens* for Polly Fenton – Miss Jennifer Carter!' and she applauded extravagantly, nudging the stranger into centre stage.

'Actually,' the girl replied, shoulders square, 'it's Jen and it's Ms.'

'Nonsense!' cajoled Mrs Elms to Jen's unhidden horror. 'At BGS, if we're not Mrs we're Miss. Unless we're Mr, of course. Isn't that right, Bill?' she declared to the art teacher who nodded in a vague sort of way, as befitting his calling.

'Mr Hardy!' Mrs Elms proclaimed proudly, outstretching her hand to the man and thrusting Jen's into it. 'Mr Bill Hardy,' Mrs Elms continued, 'this is Miss Carter. *Jen*,' she enunciated, 'is that right, dear?'

'Uh huh,' said Jen, who looked tired and, Megan discerned with a tiny touch of sympathy, tearful.

Mrs Elms went through the entire staff body in the same manner, grabbing hands and thrusting Jen's into them. She came to Megan.

'And this, Miss Carter, this is Miss Megan Reilly. Hands, ladies. Super. There are no hands safer than Miss Reilly's, my dear. She'll deliver you to your class and show you the ropes. And the stairs and the corridors, ha!'

With that, Mrs Elms turned on her squat-heeled shoes and left on the double to prepare herself for assembly.

'She's not even fifty,' Megan whispered to Jen, 'isn't that frightening?'

'Sure is. Do I really have to be a *Miss*?'

'Well,' said Megan, thrusting an unrequested coffee into Jen's hands, 'that all depends on your pronunciation now, doesn't it!' She winked at Jen.

'Is this decaff?'

'Dat is right,' joked Megan, masking sudden irritation with a daft foreign accent, 'dis is de caff and dat is de tea!'

*　*　*

'Good morning, ladies and gentlemen, I am Polly Fenton and I'll be teaching English this year.'

Who? Us! Ladies and gentlemen – us? Cool!

Ten hands shot into the air and fresh, eager faces implored her to choose me, choose *me*.

This can't really be unadulterated enthusiasm, genuine politeness, can it? Surely it must be the start of some horrible jest?

You're at Hubbardtons now, Polly, you can shake off the wariness that the BGS girls have instilled in you.

The hands still soared heavenward.

'Er, yes?' said Polly, marvelling that the room was carpeted. 'Gentleman with the baseball cap?'

'Mrs, Miss or Ms, ma'am?'

His face was earnest. After all, he wasn't sure he'd even met a gentleman before, let alone been referred to as one.

'Miss,' confirmed Polly with a relieved smile; he was clearly enthusiastic and polite and not the practical joker type.

A class of ten? Do you know, that's less than the weekly detention crowd at BGS!

Polly looked about her, nine pairs of hands lay neatly on the tables in front of them. A tenth pair were hidden but heard, tapping away at a lap-top. Polly cleared her throat.

'You there? With the computer?'

'Yes, Ma'am?'

'Miss,' said Polly. 'What are you doing?'

'I'm just logging "Miss Polly Fenton" into my file, Ma'am.'

'Miss,' said Polly.

'Miss,' said the girl, closing the lid of the machine and giving Polly her undivided attention, prefixed by a shy smile and then a beaming, glinting grin displaying a mouth with more metal than enamel.

'Okey dokey,' said Polly, surprised at her choice of phrase, 'you now know me, but who on earth are you? Plural!'

The students delivered their names.

Oh that they could wear name badges too! How ever am I to distinguish between AJ and TC? Lauren and Laurel? And two Bens, would you believe, not to mention a Heidi, a Forrest and the two others whose names I've completely forgotten?

'Super!' Polly declared instead. 'And could you let me know which of you are the semaphores?'

The class laughed politely and AJ, who turned out to be the boy wearing the baseball cap, corrected her kindly and informed her that *he* was a sophomore and sixteen years of age, and that TC, Forrest, Lauren and Ed (ah, that was it, Ed!) were as well. Laurel, the girl with the lap-top, explained that she was a freshman and had just turned fifteen. Polly deduced that the remaining freshmen were both Bens, Heidi and the boy with no name, who was rather

41

overweight but wore the sweetest smile Polly had ever seen in a fifteen-year-old.

'Splendid,' said Polly and, as she did so, she observed ten pairs of eyes glaze slightly while the smiles stretched at her vocabulary. 'Let's crack on. What's so funny? Lauren?'

'It's just, like, your accent's so neat, I guess we're gonna have a bunch of fun learning English from an English lady.'

It was the first time Polly had ever been referred to as a lady so she chose to go easy on Lauren's command of the English language.

'Thank you, Lauren, but I'd rather you spoke of a *bunch* of flowers tied with a *neat* ribbon – and perhaps an *accent* that is, for example, jolly nice, and English *lessons* which, I assure you, are to be tremendous fun.'

The class gave her a swift round of applause; Polly bowed graciously, somewhat mystified by her unpremeditated plumminess and her employment of the forbidden adjective, *nice*.

'Now,' she said, rummaging in her large bag, 'now, have I a treat for you. Where the Dickens—? Ah, here we are. Pumblechook!' she declared suddenly, fixing a wild smile on Heidi and making her jump. Silence rapt the students. Polly left her table, on which she had been perched, and walked slowly around the semicircle of desks in front of her, distributing books. 'Snodgrass!' she whispered to TC; 'Sergeant Buzfuz!' she declared to Forrest. She walked behind Ben (*with the blond hair, must remember*) and cried 'Pecksniff!' above his head as she clasped his shoulders. The class were captivated, Lauren looked positively frightened as Miss Fenton approached her, held on to her eyes and uttered 'Uriah Heap!' in sombre tones. Miss Fenton placed both hands on Ed's desk and growled 'Chuzzlewit!', before going to AJ, removing his baseball cap and replacing it, backwards, while she cried 'Mr Tappertit!' The second Ben (*curly hair, snub nose; curly hair, snub nose*) she greeted with 'Bumble!' before singing 'Mrs Fezziwig!' to Laurel. Just the nameless boy. Polly stood in front of him and tipped her head, 'Dick Swiveller,' she declared, after some thought.

'No, Miss Fenton,' he said, slowly and ingenuously, 'I'm Dick Southwood Junior.'

Thank goodness for that.

'Miss?'

'Yes, AJ?'

'Who *are* these guys?'

'Dickens!' brandished Polly, 'Charles Dickens Esquire. Born the 7th of February 1812, died on June the 9th, 1870. With names as imaginative, as delicious to the tongue, as Snodgrass and Pumblechook, can you imagine how colourful and fantastic the characters are themselves? Do not such names bode well for marvellous stories?'

Somebody whistled in slow appreciation.

'Miss Fenton?'

'Yes Laurel Lap-top?'

'Was that 1812?'

'Yes, and you don't have to commit it to the silicon memory of that machine. Switch it off, if you please, and tune in to this: David Copperfield.'

With copies distributed to each member of the class, Polly said 'Chapter One' while her eyes sparkled olive at the students. They read in silence until the end of class.

* * *

'Ladies! Lay-*deez*! Upper Four – attention this instant! Lucy Howard, back to your place. *On* your chair, young lady – do *not* soil that desk with your derrière. Quiet. Angela, excuse me, *Angela*! How do you fancy detention tomorrow? You don't? Well then, shut it! Thank you. How gracious you all are. This is Miss Carter, who's taking Miss Fenton's place for a year. She'll be your form teacher as well as English teacher to some of you. Alison Setton, bring me that paper aeroplane. Now!'

'Miss Reilly thinks she's so cool when really she's naff.'

'I *am* cool, Alison, you just can't handle it – detention

tomorrow – you can sew position tags on to the new netball vests. This, as I said, is Miss Carter. You are all to be cordial, friendly and SILENT.'

Megan Reilly fixed the class with an uncompromising stare, patted Jen on the shoulder and whispered to her that she was hoarse already, bless the blighters.

'A word of advice,' she disclosed in quiet warning, 'don't smile until half term.'

She patted the new teacher again and left the room, remonstrating to Jesus, Mary *and* Joseph when she heard the decibel level soar just as soon as she'd closed the door.

Jen Carter stood behind her desk and in front of a blackboard. She'd never used a blackboard before. At Hubbardtons they had expanses of wipe-away white. And odourless, non-toxic coloured markers.

She'd never heard such a racket.

She'd never taught a class with more than twelve students to it.

She'd never taught only girls.

She'd never met blighters.

How in hell's name was she going to gain their respect, how ever was she even going to get their attention?

Don't smile.

How long was it till half term?

She turned to the blackboard and began to write her name in long, sloping letters. The din continued, subsiding only temporarily when the chalk grated at a particular point on the board. It was like the volume being switched off. And then switched on, twice as loud, immediately after. She turned back to the class.

'Quiet, please.'

Did she say something?

Dunno. Couldn't hear it if she did.

Bet those teeth are capped.

Yeah. And those boobs are definitely plastic.

'Ladies,' she tried, 'quiet?'

Ha! We've got her, she's cracking.

44

Come on, let's all hum.

Yeah! And sway slightly.

'Per-lease!'

Jen turned back to the blackboard and stared at her name. Amazingly, the volume was cranked up a further two notches. Brainwave. She took a deep breath and then dragged her fingernails across the blackboard (capped teeth were impermeable to the screech) before spinning on her heels. The class, still soothing their jaws with their hands, were silent; momentarily at least. Fixing her eyes on the clock at the back of the classroom, Jen spoke from the pit of her stomach in deep, curdling tones.

'Shut. The fuck. Up.'

8.40 a.m.

Respect!

'Don't you *ever, EVER* make me swear again,' she told thirty pairs of awestruck eyes.

FIVE

'Kate, please may I use the phone?' asked Polly.

'Sure,' said Kate and, disconcerted by Polly's sludge-green eyes, she placed a wand of raw spaghetti between the pages of her book and discreetly left the kitchen as if she had been just about to anyway.

'Hullo?'

'Dom?'

'Hullo, Pollygirl – how *are* you? How's it going? What am I saying! Hold on. Max? *Max*! Quick! I'll pass you over. You take care, Miss Fenton – them yankies can be wankies. Max? *Max*! He's in the frigging bath, Polly. Would you believe it? Call back in five mins, yes?'

''Kay.'

'Hullo?'

'Meg?'

'Po-lly!'

The women shrieked at each other nonsensically down the phone for a moment.

'Max is in the bath.'

'So I'm your second choice – charming!'

'Dear Miss Reilly,' soothed Polly, knowing Megan meant no mischief, 'I've just finished my first full day. It's the first chance I've had to use the phone. I can't be too long – just give Max enough time to dry.'

'How are you, girl? What's it like?' asked Megan while she located Polly on the school photograph and stroked her with her little finger. 'Is it incredible? Have you met Tom Cruise yet?'

'Yes,' said Polly, 'and no.'

'Anyone who looks remotely like him? Brad Pitt, at a scrape?'

'No,' said Polly, 'and no. Or not that I've met so far, I'm afraid. There might be, but I'm jet lagged beyond belief. Do you know, this place, Meg, is so, so beautiful. There's so much space for the children – in class and out. Guess how many I have in a class?'

'Can't! Tell!'

'No. More. Than. Twelve.'

'Jee—'

'And they're all impeccably behaved. They're even *quiet* before class!'

'—zus. No wonder That Carter Woman looks so shell-shocked.'

'Everything OK?'

'If you call Upper Four OK.'

'Say no more. What was for lunch today?'

'Lunch? Pie and mash, or mashed ratatouille and mash. And some clumpy pink mash for pud.'

'Do you know what I had? Ask me!'

'I say, Miss Fenton, what did you have for lunch?'

'I had Caesar Salad with a selection of cold cuts and a freshly baked roll.'

'Stop, stop – that's just not on.'

'Well, I could have had vegetable burritos, if that makes you feel any better.'

'No it bloody doesn't.'

'Or there again, chicken papardelle with tarragon cream. The Federal Government subsidizes the food while making guidelines about fat content and protein quotas.'

'I'm weeping.'

'That's not all, Meg. There were four different types of coffee to choose from, and as many teas. And that's not counting the decaffeinated or detanninized strains! All fresh, I hasten to add, and free. No plasticated liquid from vending machines here. And, do you know, we have those fantastic swirly machines with fresh juice churning around available to us. All. Day. Long.'

'I'm over there!'

'No you're not,' said Polly quietly, 'you're over *there* – over the sea and far, far away. I better go, Max'll be waiting. Will you write?'

'I have done already. Posted it at lunch-time,' Megan paused and continued forlornly, 'when I went to the newsagent for a chocolate fest in lieu of lousy lunch.'

'Polly? Polly? You there? That you?'

Speak some more. Let me listen.

'Polly?'

'Oh, Max.'

They hung on to their respective receivers with eyes closed and hearts bursting. They could hear each other breathe. How fantastic.

'I couldn't phone till now,' Polly explained, 'I've had every minute organized.'

'I know,' Max soothed, 'I'm sure. I imagined. What's it like? School and where you're staying?'

'Lovely – everywhere and everyone. So friendly and welcoming. The school is magnificent and the children are a dream – only I hope I don't wake up. I just talked shop with Megan so she'll fill you in, if you like. How's Buster?'

'Fine, I presume – I haven't heard anything to the contrary.'

'Will you phone The Jen Carter Person and just double-check everything's OK at the flat?'

''Course I will. Can I have your number there? Thanks.'

'God, you sound so close it's cruel.'

'You in your pyjamas, Polly?'

'No, silly, it's only six o'clock here. In fact, I'm in a frock because it's something called Formal Meal tonight.'

'Which knickers are you wearing?'

'Hold on a – let me check. The pair with the blue roses.'

'Divine.'

'Funny fellow.'

'I miss you madly, Polly.'

Oh my God, I haven't actively missed you yet Max, because I haven't actually had time to. That's terrible of me.

'Polly? You there? I was saying how I miss you.'

'Do you?' she said sweetly.

'I do,' Max confirmed softly, not registering Polly's pause.

'Oh dear! Do you know, I haven't said "I do" to you yet, have I!'

'No, actually, not in so many words. Do you still have your ring?'

'Maximilian, would I mislay something as precious as that?'

I must take it from the back pocket of my jeans and put it somewhere safe.

'You'd better go, Polly. Better not take advantage of your hosts.'

''Kay. Will you phone soon? Will you phone on Saturday?'

'Absolutely. Night night.'

'Night.'

Polly walked slowly to her room. She went to her jeans and slipped her hand into the back pockets. And then those at the front. She fell to her knees and walked a methodical circle with her hands around the chair over which her jeans lay. She looked under the bed. And in the bin. And in the pockets of her other jeans. And in her jacket pocket. She looked behind the bedside table. She went to the bathroom and searched through her toilet bag. She went back to the bedroom, bit her nails and her lip and muffled a strangled yelp by hurling herself on to the bed. Burying her face into the pillows she sobbed. She bit, she hit them. She cursed herself. She stabbed at the bed with her fist. She cursed Great Aunt Clara. She swore profusely. She all but wore herself out. Finally, she sat cross-legged on the bed, snorting through a heavy nose and rubbing hard at itching eyes.

I can't have lost it!

It seems you have.

I haven't even said yes, yet, I haven't said 'I do'.

It seems you haven't.

Max, who's been at the centre of my world, is offering me lifelong security, he's going to provide me with my own family at last. And I haven't even bloody accepted his offer. I can't tell anyone I'm engaged unless I've formally agreed to be. I can't tell people unless I have a ring to show them. As proof. And I can't tell Max that I'll marry him if I have to tell him that I've lost his ring.

You haven't even told Megan yet, either, have you? Wonder why. No time to think on it now. Wash your face and make haste for Formal Meal.

'Jennifer Carter speaking.'

'Oh, um, hullo, er, my name's Max Fyfield – I'm, er, Polly's—'

'Sure! Max, hi there, nice to speak to you.'

'I just thought I'd give you a bell to see if you've settled in OK? All all right with the flat?'

'Everything's cool here, thanks. Your Polly's left me these little notes every place. Feel like I know her.'

'And Buster? He's OK? Not terrorizing you? Just roar at him if he is – and ignore him if he replies.'

'Buster's adorable. He's on my lap right now.'

'Ah, super. Polly will be pleased. Have you met Megan Reilly yet?'

'Sure, she's shown me round the school and has been real sweet.'

50

God, how Megan'll cringe if she ever hears such terminology!

'Great, great. And how was school? Those girls can be a handful. An excess of intelligence and money, I fear.'

'I think,' said Jen, 'that we have arrived at an understanding.'

'Good, good,' stumbled Max, 'well, I just phoned to see that everything's tickety boo.'

'What's that? Tickety *boo*? Ha!'

'Yes, ha! I'm glad you seem to have settled. Do call if you need anything.'

'Sure. Many thanks, Max.'

'Bye then.'

'Bye now.'

Jen heaved Buster so that he stood on his hind legs on her lap.

'All I need,' she told him, 'to make my picture perfect, is one Chip Jonson.'

SIX

*I*f it had been Megan Reilly, and not Polly Fenton, who was at Hubbardtons, she would have swiftly traded ten Tom Cruises, and gladly forfeited the hope of Dominic Fyfield, for even a chance with Chip Jonson. But for Megan, who is in London, in the staff room, listening to Jen drone on about how wonderful her boyfriend Chip is, the man is merely a name. And a seemingly daft one at that.

Polly has not yet met him, for if an athletic trainer rarely has reason to venture from the gym complex, seldom does he need to cross right over the playing fields to the main school buildings. And four days into her stay, Polly would be unable to locate the gym or the drama building and has no need, as yet, to visit either. She has now met her junior and senior students and has begun to weave her infectious love of literature and language deep into the fabric of her classes. She's had no need to holler for Jackson Thomas, much to his chagrin. He hopes to grab her off duty, off her guard (just grab her, really), at the House Raising this coming Sunday. They'll be building a house for Jojo Baxter, who teaches journalism and hockey. Everyone's invited. Polly's been invited. She's looking forward to it very much.

'They'll build a whole house? In a day?' she said to Kate, incredulous.

'Yup,' Kate confirmed as if there was nothing untoward about the concept at all, 'I'm down to bake pies. You want to help?'

'Absolutely,' said Polly, 'I could make a bakewell tart.'

'I'm sure you do,' Kate replied ingenuously.

It was the first occasion, since the journey from Boston, that Kate and Polly were alone for any length of time. Formal Meal, the faculty meeting and Kate's involvement with the local flamenco club had occupied them and kept them apart. Yet a quick, wide wave from Polly across the quadrangle; a brief exchange over the salad bar at lunch; a note from Kate, magnetized to the fridge by Mickey Mouse, offering Polly unrestricted access to her bicycle, saw a burgeoning fondness develop between the two. Now, they're making pie. Apple. Cherry. Blueberry. No bakewell. Baked beautifully.

This is Vermont, not Derbyshire. When in Rome – and all that.

'Tell me about home, Polly, paint me a picture.'

'Home,' Polly explained, taking Kate at her word and drawing a disproportionate plan in the flour, 'is a small, rented flat with a patio and mad neighbours in leafy Belsize Park. That's in North London for your information.'

'Neat,' Kate enthused.

'Not very,' apologized Polly.

'How mad?' Kate asked, eyes alive above a huge smile.

'Absolutely bonkers,' Polly assured her.

'Bonkers!' Kate declared, having her first taste of the word and finding it delicious.

They made pastry in silence for a while.

'Home,' Polly started again, 'is really a fat tom-cat called Buster and a darling boy called Max.'

'Uh huh,' murmured Kate: an excellent phrase to elicit further details.

'Yes,' said Polly quietly, 'I've had them both for five years.

In fact —' she started before a small voice warned her against continuing.

You can't tell her. You've no proof, remember.

(More to the point, Polly, you haven't clarified the situation with Max, have you?)

'Uh huh,' Kate repeated as she pricked the top of the pies, 'that must be kinda tough. I'll bet you're missing them both.'

With a degree of guilt which she covered with a hasty 'Oh yes, of course', Polly realized that she had still been too busy to have actively missed Max. 'He said he'd phone on Saturday. That's tomorrow.'

Only I hope he calls before the Blues Brothers evening starts at Finnigan's. (That's Finnigan House – senior male dorm. Everyone invited.) I'm on duty, you see. Me and Charle(s) and Lorna – she's lovely, I met her at lunch today. She teaches drama and voice. I think we're about the same age.

'What does Max do?' Kate asked, genuinely interested.

Polly smiled. 'You'd love him,' she said, 'he's very artistic, very talented. Officially, he's a self-employed graphic designer, only he likes to be known as a freelance draughtsman.'

Kate nodded approvingly. 'He sounds special. That right?'

'Absolutely,' enthused Polly. 'He is,' she said. 'In fact —'

No.

Not yet.

Kate refrained from the uh-huh of encouragement that was on the tip of her tongue. Polly looked suddenly lost and lonely so she handed her the bowl of blueberries and changed the subject instead.

Saturday. School for Polly finished at two but she joined the other off-duty teachers and students to eat hot dogs while watching the senior boys in a football match. She had no idea what these extravagantly padded, already beefy boys were doing, but there seemed to be more rucks than rugger and much less fancy footwork than footie. The buttocks,

54

however, were incomparably pert and neat and made the game a pleasure to watch. Even more so, once Kate had explained the rules in under a minute, with ketchup on her chin. Soon, Polly was cheering with the best of them, much to Jackson's delight.

'So she *can* holler,' he mused through the side of his mouth and to no one, 'and boy, can she *holler.*'

Polly returned to Kate's alone, forgoing the post-match refreshments and post mortem so she could guard the phone and leap on it as soon as it rang.

I'm going to say yes, you see. I'm going to accept his proposal. Then I can finally tell everyone.

The house, however, remained silent until Kate, Charle(s) and Bogey returned an hour later. Kate scanned Polly's face hopefully, so Polly shook her head and shrugged her shoulders with hastily employed nonchalance, offering to make tea for the troops. The phone rang as soon as she left it; she tried not to jump on it but failed. It was Clinton for Kate. Polly tried not to register her disappointment. She failed.

It's half past bloody six. That's half eleven over there. Where is he?

After Polly had poured cranberry juice instead of milk into the tea, Kate suggested, very kindly, why didn't *she* make the call and beat *him* to it?

'Ain't nothing like making a man good and guilty,' she drawled like Mae West. 'They usually repent extravagantly! Go on, I'm going to take a shower.'

It was seven o'clock. The Blues Brothers evening at Finnigan's started in half an hour. It was midnight in Britain.

Actually, one minute past. It's tomorrow. And Max said he'd phone me yesterday.

A strange voice, male and Scottish, answered the phone in England. Polly presumed she had misdialled so she hung up and rang again, staring at the number pad and speaking them out loud as she dialled. The same voice.

God, I hope everything's OK.

'Er, hullo, is Max there? Max Fyfield.' There was

55

interference on the line. She tapped the receiver against her hand. It wasn't interference, it was background noise. Music, muffled. Voices, many.

'Hullo?' said the Scotsman.

'Max Fyfield?' stressed Polly, trying not to shout. It sounded like the receiver was dropped. 'Hullo?' she said. 'Hullo? Max?'

Click.

The line was dead.

She dialled again, distressed and a little angry. Who was that man? How dare he!

'Hullo?'

'Thank God,' said Polly, eyes to the heavens, 'Dom, it's me. Max there?'

'Hullo? Oh Polly! Hi! Hold on. *Max*! Hold on,' said Dom, disappearing with an unpromising clatter to locate his brother.

'Polly?'

'Max – hullo, I was er. You said you'd —'

Suddenly she wanted to cry.

Don't be so silly.

Why do you want to cry?

I don't know. I don't want to be here. I feel frightened. It all feels too fragile.

'Sorry,' Max rushed. 'Oh God, so sorry. I, er, well actually I forgot. Hey *you* – get the Osmonds *off* the turntable! *And* Slade. Kool and the Gang can stay. Polly? There you are – I was going to call you earlier but Dominic had me running errands and opening wine. Dom! *Dom!* The chilli – the coffee table. God that was close.'

'Max,' Polly asked, trying to control the shake in her voice, 'what's happening? What's going on?'

I feel lonely. I'm frightened.

What of?

'Dom has a few friends round,' Max explained lightly.

Precisely.

'Anyone I know?'

What's wrong with that? Why do I feel shaky?

'Er, don't think so.'

'Meg?'

I can hear a woman laughing. He's just covered the mouthpiece with his hand. Why? Why's he done that?

'Meg?' Polly repeated, staring around Kate's kitchen, the people on the fridge; realizing that she was, essentially, amongst strangers. Alone.

I'm alone. Over here. Over there. I just delude myself that I'm allowed into people's spheres, that they'll make me part of their world, their family.

'Megan was here earlier but she had to leave as she was meeting Jen Carter for a drink.'

I've been replaced. Oh, most wicked haste.

'Max – why didn't *you* phone *me*?' Polly consciously let slip into baby voice. 'Like you promised?'

'I'm sorry Button,' he said, his voice distant (*he sounds distant*), 'I forgot. I was busy.'

No!

Yes – anyway, Polly, who is it who's been too preoccupied even to think of him much, let alone miss him at all? Were you expecting life in London to be frozen in time until your return?

'Polly?'

'Yes,' she said in a small voice, 'I'm still here.'

'I'd better go now, this isn't the best time for a chat, is it? There's chilli on the carpet and Dominic's off his face. God, he's out on the balcony. Doing opera. I must go – I'll call you soon, promise. 'Kay?'

''Kay.'

What else could she say?

'Love you,' Max cooed.

Don't say that.

''Kay,' she said, chewing the inside of her cheek. She replaced the handset and stared blankly at the fridge of smiles.

*

'You OK?' asked Kate, understanding now the provenance of Polly's deepening eye colour.

'Yup,' said Polly, a little more croakily than she would have liked, 'absolutely fine.'

Kate offered Polly a cherry tomato. She bit it and winced as the delicious, tart juice caused a stab of sharpness to zip along her jaw. She swallowed. Hard.

'All set?' Kate asked.

'Do you know,' Polly replied, 'I think I'll give it a miss. Jet lag, you see. And building a house tomorrow – have to be strong, hey!'

'Well,' cautioned Kate, 'I don't think you can give it a miss. You're on duty, Polly. That's your job. That's what you're paid for. That's why you're here.'

Kate didn't tell her that it wouldn't be a problem for another teacher to stand in. She didn't tell her because she didn't want Polly not to go. She thought Polly ought not to be alone. Not on her first Saturday night in America. She hardly knew the girl, not properly. But she knew her well enough to see that loneliness was uncharted anathema to Polly Fenton. Kate cared.

So Miss Fenton went through the motions of being a teacher that night. She knew the film well, having seen it many times at university, and knew what to heckle and when to sing. But though she did so at all the opportune moments, gaining much admiration from the students in the process, there was no passion behind it and she felt no fun. She could have talked to Lorna, really she could. Really talked. She'd have liked that; Lorna too, hopefully. But she couldn't because it was so noisy. And she was on duty.

What is it, Polly? What, exactly, has unnerved you so?

It feels too far to be safe.

How do you mean?

It's new. I've never not been near him. We've rarely done things apart. 'While the cat's away', hey?

How about 'absence makes the heart grow fonder', surely?

More like 'out of sight, out of mind'. I must be losing mine.
I don't know, do you know I just feel – uneasy. All of a sud-
den. I suppose I just presumed all to be so secure. After five
years, you slip into an easy routine. Or is it complacency?
I'm not going to say 'yes'. I'd better not. Not for a while.

Power game?

Safety net.

Fighting sleep, Polly forced images of Max to assault her
instead. Max drunk. Max stoned. Max having a brilliant time
without her. Max necking someone, tall and blonde. Max's
mind being utterly devoid of Polly.

She'd never done this to herself before.

She'd never seen Max like that.

What are you doing, Fenton? That's not Max – not Max at
all.

Look what Sunday has brought – a breathtakingly beautiful
morning. Polly slept well, eventually, and her fears that
smiling would elude her entire stay have proven unfounded:
she grins broadly at the morning. Dew covers the lawn in a
sweeping kiss and the very tips of just one or two leaves on
each maple tree wink a crimson preview to Polly. New
England. Vermont. Fall. How lucky.

Trading Old for New.

'Just you wait,' says Kate, pushing a mug of erbal tea (most
definitely no 'h') into Polly's hands, 'another four weeks and
man, you'll weep!' They sip and sigh awhile.

'All set?' Kate asks.

'Won't I need a hammer?' asks Polly. Kate laughs and
gives her a quick, spontaneous hug.

'Nope!' she declares, 'that's for the guys. You know there
won't be one nail or screw used, just oak pegs?'

How could Polly know? She's never been to a house raising before.

Can a scent be deafening? Technically, probably not;
grammatically, debatable too. However, it occurs to Polly, as

59

she and Kate stride towards the site, that it is the most appropriate word to use.

The scent of pine is deafening.

Definitely; it is deafening and divine.

The pine, not yet seen, has been felled, planed and is ready to be made into a house.

From the right-hand fork at the end of Main Street, a small, well-maintained lane leads off it to the right. It continues severely up hill; over the petticoats and on to the very skirt of Mount Hubbardtons. Not that John Hubbardton was a cross-dresser, of course; it's merely the price he must pay for having a mountain previously known as Sister Mountain renamed in his honour. After half a mile, a dirt track leads off the lane and it is here that we catch up with Polly and Kate. Kate is telling her all about Jojo Baxter but Polly can hardly hear her for the scent of pine. She closes her eyes and breathes deeply. It's so heady. She stumbles as she goes. Kate links arms with her. For support.

'Are these my Queens of Tarts?'

'Hey Jojo!' Kate sang, loading all the tarts on to Polly's already laden arms so she could embrace Jojo. 'How's it going?'

'Good, good. You must be Polly? Hi there, I'm Jojo. I'm starving and we've hardly gotten started. Save my soul and send me to heaven: blueberry, cherry *and* apple? *Queens* of Tarts, queens!'

Polly fell for Jojo immediately and knew instinctively that they'd see eye to eye — not least because they were absolutely the same height.

There were people and pine everywhere. By the time Polly had laid the pies on one of three trestles set up in a rambling shack on the edge of the clearing, the population on Jojo's site seemed to have doubled. What a crowd! Adults and children and most ages represented therein. The site for the house had already been prepared in the form of a large, rectangular platform; children were scampering over it; women were pacing it, imagining the kitchen and my! what an awesome bedroom; men were analysing it with tape measures, spirit levels and the failsafe eye. There were three enormous wooden 'A' frames; one lay on the platform, the other two at either end. Nearby, stacks of pine in differing configurations were planked up in neat piles six foot high. A single sheet of white paper, tacked to one plank, had a list of ten, polite points. This was how you raised a house. As easy as apple pie.

This is America, thought Polly, venturing nearer to the platform and absorbing all surrounding her as she went, *not just the pine and the fact that folk build houses for their friends in a day. No; alongside the pies and pumpernickel, the accents and the stunning scenery, this enormous sense of spirit embodies America, surely.*

Wasn't all of this a film? Harrison Ford?

The house raising might well have been staged just for an English tourist. But just as Polly was neither ignored or stared at, nor was she over-welcomed. She felt at ease. She was not a tourist, she was not at the cinema. People allowed her to occupy a space amongst them. She fitted in just fine.

All America is here: wholesome kids, caring women, buddy-buddy men, Boston beans baking deep in that pit over there, the children's tree house with the Stars and Stripes. I hear terminology I wrongly thought would irritate me, I smell the gargantuan feast that will revive the pioneers mid-morning. I baked a pie. I smell pine. I'm part of this. I belong.

The first 'A' frame was aligned, hauled and coaxed into its place with little ado.

'Hold it right there, Ed.'

'Easy! Easy!'

'Up she goes. She's up.'

'Way to go, guys!'

While the children now played in the trees and by the stream, the women chatted and marvelled and ensured that beakers were overflowing with fruit juice. The builders were all voluntary – Clinton and Jackson and a couple of other

Hubbardton teachers amongst them. There were also Jojo's friends and family who had travelled across the state, some even down from Canada, to be a part of the day. There were Jude and Ed, her hillbilly-looking nephews whose sensitive and polite demeanour was utterly at odds with their thick necks and thatched hair, their calloused, stout hands and seam-stretching thighs. Nearby, a couple of elderly men in great shape (who actually didn't look silly in their checked shirts and worn jeans), spoke about e-mail and software while they flung ropes about like dab hands. A goofy teenager set up a plumb-line and cried 'Yo!' triumphantly while Clinton and Jackson rigged up a 'come-along' to secure the correct tautness between struts. A small army of men wore tool belts slung like holsters; whipping out hammers with a speed that would have done John Wayne proud, or twirling their tools with all the flair of a rock-and-roll drummer. Everyone had a job to do, everyone knew their place. Overseeing the entire operation was a small, wiry man, the architect and only paid member of the team, bearded strangely minus a moustache, who darted nimbly around the growing skeleton, heaping praise, advice and instructions with a softly spoken voice. All three 'A' frames were now in place and point four on the list had been reached.

Every strut, joist and plank had a home in either a notch, a wedge or a grip in a neighbouring plank, strut or joist. Corresponding holes in the wood allowed for oak pegs to further secure the bond. A jigsaw puzzle the size and shape of a house. The hillside rang with the song of chatter, of laughter and of knock, knock, knock on wood. Enter two carpenters, father and son: Bob and Mikey McCabe. Polly had a doughnut in one hand and a small offcut of pine in the other and she was intermittently sniffing the two when she first caught sight of Mikey. Tall and lithe in physique, his dark hair long. He had the most beautiful forearms, ditto his strong, muscled legs with their masculine smattering of dark hairs. His face was so handsome it could well be illegal.

62

Polly bit into the wood, hard, and thought to herself that English doughnuts were so much softer and more tasty and who on earth was that scrumptious man and he's taken his T-shirt off, oh my God.

She was utterly taken aback. She had no control over her eyes as they darted to and from this figure. Her heart pounded. She was horrified and exhilarated.

But I don't look twice at normal men.

Normal?

I mean, real-life blokes. Only Max. For the past five years. Apart from film stars – who don't count.

She let the doughnut fall to the ground as if it were an off-cut of pine, and she placed the offcut of pine, teethmarks and all, on to a plate of doughnuts.

Polly Fenton doesn't look twice. But I can't keep my eyes off him.

'Isn't this great!' squeezed Jojo, at her side.

'Super duper,' agreed Polly in fine style, half relieved to be led away from this apparent danger zone, half ruing the fact that stirring the beans prevented visual access to Mikey McCabe.

'He's out of sight,' she lamented softly to the great saucepan as she sat on her heels over the pit.

'Isn't he just!' colluded Kate cautiously but with a skew smile. 'Outa sight. Totally.'

'I meant,' fumbled Polly, immensely uncomfortable and almost lost for words, 'I meant – absolutely nothing. Nothing at all.'

Kate doffed her head and departed with a smile that was kind. And wise. And something else too.

Outa sight, Polly twanged to herself.

Max is out of her mind.

She is totally engrossed in the sensation of the present.

SEVEN

'*H*ey there,' he said, bowling over to her at lunch-time with an easy smile, 'I'm Mikey.'

A warm, firm handshake.

Look at his neck. His Adam's apple. Shoulders. Chest.

No don't.

'Hullo,' she responded, 'I'm Polly.' Desperate to be demure and disinterested. Failing.

Fight the smile.

Failing.

Am I blushing?

Yes.

'From England, hey?'

'Yes, from Old Blighty,' Polly enunciated. He nodded and smiled, displaying perfect white teeth behind full, deep red lips. The morning's exertion had had superb consequences for his appearance; his hair was damp and tousled and scraped hastily into a pony tail while sweat and sawdust gave a subtle glisten to his body and had made his eyes watery and dark. Polly tried not to stare and hoped sincerely that her pupils were not dilating visibly. If they were (they were), he was too well mannered to acknowledge it.

*

The house was all but finished by four o'clock. The roof was slatted and watertight. There were no side walls at the moment as Jojo, predictably, had run out of money. However, even in its skeletal state it was stunning. It was obvious what a gorgeous home it was going to be when complete; occupying this spectacular position in the lie of Hubbardtons, overlooking the main cluster of houses of Hubbardtons and just a twenty-minute walk for Jojo to her classes at Hubbardtons.

The little architect started a round of applause when the job was done, which was followed by liberal high-fiving and unabashed hugging. The men then jumped from the structure and stood back to look on it, nodding and congratulating each other and themselves. They finished the last of the beans and made another inroad into the batch of pies before disappearing to their pick-ups and returning with fiddles. They played until dusk. Polly counted seven violins as she tapped her toes with her mouth agape. There were two bonfires. She sat by Kate at the smaller. Mikey McCabe was playing his fiddle around the other; jigging and twisting, turning and stamping. He had jeans on. But Polly could clearly see his legs beneath them. She really couldn't take her eyes off him. She couldn't really. He was magnificent.

Polly ate little at supper for she was still full from lunch. She washed up diligently and made tea for Kate, Clinton and Charle(s).

'I have a slight headache,' she said, swiping her brow with the back of her hand so that she covered her eyes as she spoke, 'I think I'll take a stroll.'

'You want to wait till I've finished my tea?' offered Kate.

'I think I'll go right now if you don't mind,' Polly declined politely, 'I must nip it in the bud.'

A headache? A stroll? But Polly is positively stomping along Main Street, forking right, then right again. Springing through the petticoats then climbing up on to the skirts of Hubbardtons.

No moon. No need.

I must nip it in the bud.

Turn right.

The house, pale yellow-pink in night light, still smelling divine.

'Hey! You came.'

'Mikey.'

'You came.'

'I can't do this.'

'You're here.'

Mikey was leaning against one of the corner posts of the house. Polly climbed on to the platform and walked over to him. He was still in jeans and now wore a polarfleece top to ward off the chill of the September night. He had her locked into his eyes. She could not get away. Not even if she had tried.

'I,' Polly said, as Mikey straightened up and walked over to meet her, bang in the centre of the house, 'can't do this.'

'Do what?' he asked softly, his lips parted and damp. 'Do this?' he enquired as he stroked her hair and brought her hand to touch his. 'Or this?' he asked, pulling her closer and breathing a kiss on to her forehead. 'Or is it this,' he wondered aloud as he tipped up her chin and lowered his face over hers, 'that you can't do?' Their lips were less than an inch apart. She could feel his breath over her cheek. His eyes were so close, so dark and deep. She could hardly breathe. 'Is it this that you can't do,' he said, without the question mark, as he sank his lips against hers. He flicked his tongue. It was surprisingly cold against her top lip. She really could not breathe. As she gasped for air, he plunged his tongue deep into her mouth where it immediately leapt about, sweeping across the underside of her teeth, pressing at the roof of her mouth, searching out her tongue and pulling it into a frantic dance with his. Her arms were about his shoulders.

How did they get there?

She was kissing with a hunger that umpteen apple pies

could not diminish. Mikey pulled away and placed his hands on his hips.

'Well, girl, it sure looks like you *can*, indeed, do this.'

Polly could not speak, let alone protest, because her voice, it seemed, was only for gasping and her heart was in her mouth anyway. Simultaneously, it was also beating hard and fast between her legs. Mikey came close again, encircled one hand around Polly's waist and pushed the other up under her crotch. He pressed and rubbed and as he did so, the seam of her jeans massaged her clitoris. She could have fainted. Instead, she moaned and swayed, closed her eyes and tensed her thighs as he grazed her neck with his teeth. He took his hand away and cupped her right breast, suddenly pinching hard at the nipple. Now they weren't kissing. They weren't saying anything. They were breathing heavily, gorging on each other's faces.

'Christ,' Mikey said hoarsely, scooping Polly against himself, bucking his groin gently against her. Automatically, she travelled her hand down his body and felt his erection defiant through denim. She rubbed him and squeezed along the impressive length of his cock while they stared at each other. They ate at each other's mouths again.

A noise. Footsteps.

'Hallo?'

Jojo! Quick! Into the trees.

'Hallo?'

They watched as Jojo clambered aboard her new house and walked round it in a slow waltz of sorts.

'Hi there, little house!' they heard her repeat over and over as she circumnavigated her domain. She didn't stay long. They neither resented nor blamed her for coming. They'd have done the same, they agreed, if it was their house built on this beautiful plot of land. Jojo walked away, singing and skipping as she went. Mikey had his back to a tree and pulled Polly against him but facing away from him. She pushed her arms back so she could hold on to the belt loops of his jeans and steady herself. It caused her body to arch forward and gave unlimited access to Mikey's hands. He felt along her stomach, slipped his fingers down the front of her jeans as far as he could reach and then slid them under her knickers. He could not reach far enough, despite her wriggling, so he cupped and fondled both her breasts instead and then encircled her neck with his hands, squeezing, quite tightly. It felt dangerous. It was. Wasn't it?

The ground was unbelievably soft. Mikey had laid her down on it, removed her boots and jeans and placed his fleece and his shirt under her body. He was stepping out of his jeans, looming over her in white jockey shorts, his erection holding out the fabric like the mast of a marquee. He straddled her, kissed her and then set to work on each of her nipples in turn, while she tried to reach his cock which was tantalizingly beyond her stretch. God she wanted him. All of him. Inside her. She bucked her body up and sat with her face against his stomach, his cock stiff between her breasts. She had a hand on each buttock and started, teasingly slowly, to inch his underpants down. The shaft of his penis sprang out of the fabric, his balls still concealed.

'Polly,' he murmured, 'God, you're something else.' Slowly she lowered her mouth over his cock, making sure he could feel her hot breath over it before her lips touched down.

'Polly,' his voice was rising with his excitement. She kissed the very tip of him with the lightest of lips. Then she gulped down as much of him as would reasonably fit.

'Polly.'

Gosh, his voice was high. What power!

'Polly!'

Hang on, that's not his voice at all. That's Kate's.

Kate?

What's going on?

Where's Mikey gone?

'Come on sleepy head, it's school time.'

If fantasy is fiction, does it preclude reality entirely? Dreams may not be real but they are genuine; truth often contained therein.

Was the reality really only that Mikey had merely done no more than greet her, introduce himself and ask if she was from England, and all briefly at lunch-time? Was that really all he had done?

Polly felt quite sick. Sick with dismay that it had only been a damn dream, sick with worry that she should be thus dismayed and sick at herself for her perceived infidelity. That she had had the dream at all deeply distressed her and yet she was also troubled by her disappointment at being woken. She worried that she had been writhing as Kate tried to wake her. Had she said anything revealing in her sleep? Why had she never dreamt about Max in such a way? Had he ever dreamt so explicitly about her? About anyone else? But it made her feel sick that he might have done; about someone else. And yet how could she have done this? To Max? Would she even have noticed Mikey had she not felt so uneasy about the phone call with Max?

I haven't fantasized like this at all. Haven't ever needed to. Hang on, it wasn't a fantasy at all – it was but a dream. Phew! I can't determine what I dream. I'm innocent.

She lay in bed, her hand resting gently over her pubis. The hair there was damp. She tunnelled between the lips of her sex; she oozed wetness. With an ear peeled and eyes clamped to the slightly ajar door, she masturbated. She didn't think of Max. She didn't think of Mikey. She thought instead of a film star and closed her eyes as she came.

* * *

Dominic's party was OK, Max supposes, as he settles at his drawing board and leafs through the briefs clipped at the top.

Quite good, actually. Except for being lumbered with the clearing up because Dom's hangover rendered him

*immobile all day. Shame that Polly phoned. I can't believe I
forgot, that's not like me.*

Max must work on the design for a media agency's
Christmas party invitation, and comes up with an idea to
manipulate the text into the shape of a wine glass. Because
he must perfect the design first, he ignores the precise wording the client has ordered. A letter to Polly will provide the
perfect practice vehicle. He doodles wine-glass shapes
quickly and then commences.

> *Darling Pollygirl Button Fenton, It's*
> *Monday morning and you've been gone*
> *a week. Almost. It's excruciating to*
> *remember that this time last week I still*
> *had you for a few hours. I think of you*
> *there, over in the land of hamburgers and*
> *bad spelling. 'O-U-R', I can hear you*
> *cry as the students insist on the*
> *flavor of a poem and its colorful*
> *imagery. Is your accent in-*
> *tact? I suppose I just*
> *dread you coming*
> *home changed*
> *in any way*
> *at all.*
> *Polly.*
> *Polly.*
> *Polly.*
> *Button.*
> *Let's write a letter*
> *a week and let's send*
> *them Swiftair too. Will you*
> *be back for Christmas? Love you. Max. x.*

It's a good design, Max is pleased with it. He can't show
the client this particular one, of course, not least because
he's going to send it to Polly straight away. After lunch, he'll

re-do it and insert the commissioned wording. Somehow, he feels closer to Polly just writing to her than he did when speaking to her by phone but he'll call her at midnight because he must, because no doubt she'll be waiting. That's in twelve hours' time. Currently, Mikey McCabe is laying her down under the trees. Max isn't to know, though. How can he know what Polly is dreaming?

Polly beat Max to it. She skipped dinner easily because she hadn't been able to eat all day anyway. She felt wretched, believing herself to have been unfaithful. She also felt sick with worry that she was far from Max's mind anyway, that she was perhaps slipping from his heart. Why else would he have forgotten to call her? Why else would he be so preoccupied with some stupid party of Dominic's? Adrenalin surged as she dialled.

'Hullo?'

Bloody Dominic.

'Dominic, it's Polly. Max, please.'

I don't like you any more.

'Hey Polly!'

Party animal, bad influence.

'Max, please.'

'Sure,' said Dominic, unaware of his crime and presuming Polly merely being frugal with the transatlantic call. 'Take care, girl, speak to you soon.'

Hopefully not.

'Polly?'

He sounds tired.

'Hullo.'

She sounds low.

'I,' stumbled Max, 'I wrote to you today. Posted it Swiftair.'

'Thank you,' Polly responded, having still not received his first letter.

Well, have you written to him?

I've almost finished a very long letter, actually, that I

started before I even left England and continued on the flight.

'Saturday?' she started, feeling low and little and at last forgetting all about Mikey.

'God, I'm so sorry about all of that,' Max said, 'I felt terrible.'

'So did I,' Polly said carefully. She could envisage Max so clearly, most probably sat on the kitchen table, socked feet on a chair. Maybe in his Norwegian fisherman jumper. No, it's still mild; probably a polo shirt on top of a T-shirt.

'Polly?' said Max, leaving the kitchen table and pressing his forehead against the fridge, 'still there?'

'Yes,' she affirmed quietly.

'I don't like this,' Max said sadly.

'What?' responded the tiny voice over an ocean and a continent away, 'what's "this"?'

'Speaking to you,' he explained, 'on the phone. It seems only to magnify the physical distance between us.'

Polly was quiet. Max continued, 'I find it painful. I can't say enough. I can't say it right. As you said, the telephone is cruel, Button, it gives you false hope of intimacy. You sound so clear. You sound just like you. You sound so bloody near. But you're not. I could turn around, positive that you're just beside me. See, but you're not. Do you see?'

'I do,' answered Polly, searching for Max in Kate's kitchen and not finding him. He had shed light on a situation she previously could not fathom and she felt relieved and settled for it. 'Do you know, you're quite right, Max. I think if I hadn't actually phoned on Saturday – just heard about the evening in a sentence in a letter some time later instead – I wouldn't have felt so —' Words eluded her.

Max, Max, I do love you. I know that I do.

'Polly? You wouldn't have felt so – what?'

'Um,' she pondered, 'isolated?'

'Ah.'

'So open to wild suggestion.'

On my part as much as yours. Bloody Mikey McCabe – as if!

72

They fell silent and listened to each other breathe. If Max closed his eyes, he could almost feel the top of her head by his lips. Polly shut her eyes and conjured Max standing right beside her.

'Max,' she said, without opening her eyes so that he'd remain there for a few moments longer, 'what are you wearing?'

'My navy polo shirt and a red T-shirt, why?'

'Just wondered,' Polly replied with a smile. 'I thought you were, you see. In your socks?'

'Indeed. Bet you're wearing your floaty brown skirt and your cream Aran knit?'

'Spot on, boyo!' said Polly in her black jeans and her new, grey, Hubbardtons Academy sweatshirt.

But I love him. White lies are a lover's duty. His happiness is my charge.

'See,' Max announced, 'we don't need the phone at all, do we? I think I feel closer to you without it – do you agree?'

'Yes,' said Polly, crying silently, wishing she was in her brown skirt and Aran knit, 'it's true. The distance is spelt out so heartlessly by the phone.'

'So, shall we telepathize instead of telephone? See how it goes?'

'Let's,' Polly agreed, 'and write. Often.'

'Weekly,' Max assured her.

'At the very least.'

'Swiftair,' Max stressed.

''Kay,' said Polly.

Polly slept superbly that night. She dreamt Max had appeared at Hubbardtons in his Beetle. When she had asked him what on earth he was doing there (her feet off the floor, her arms clamped about his neck and his answer initially swamped by her kisses) he said his studio was around the corner, like it always was, silly old thing.

Max slept fitfully. He knew he'd made a sensible suggestion, done the right thing (as was his wont), but it currently served only to acknowledge unequivocally that Polly was far away and for a long time too. It made him sad. Confused a little. How could he not want to speak to her directly? In his dream, he went to Polly's flat expecting her to be there. Why wouldn't she be? America? Where's that then? Only Polly wasn't there at all. The woman who answered the door had never heard of her. Come on in, please, she invited Max. They sat on the sofa that the woman assured him belonged to no Polly Fenton. She made him tea. She looked like a supermodel and she gave him a terrific blow job.

Max wrenched himself awake in a sweat.

'No!'

He'd messed the sheets.

'God, no.'

He went to the kitchen, drank water and made himself cocoa. It was half four in the morning. It was still yesterday in Vermont.

Shall I call her? Just quickly?

He resisted.

He felt awful.

I don't care if it was a dream. I can't believe I did that to Polly.

He slept the rest of the night on the sofa.

EIGHT

*T*he first month crawled along for Max but for Polly, it passed at more of a scamper. She had little time to herself but as that was something she had never craved, she did not really notice. She was happy to be so occupied; if there wasn't an evening meeting, a study hour to supervise, lessons to prepare or essays to mark, Polly was easily persuaded to join a group of teachers for a drink at the picturesque village of Grafton, or a movie in the nondescript town of Normansbury in lieu of a sensible early night. Her advisees also took much of her spare time but she gave it to them willingly – each teacher was Adviser for up to six students; on call for advice, comfort and any etcetera that the advisee might require. Polly's full clutch of six turned to her often; partly because it meant they could leave the school grounds and have cookies at Kate's, partly because Miss Fenton was 'cool', 'so, so nice' and 'just the best' anyway.

Most of the male freshmen and seniors are in love with her. The sophomores and juniors in between simply adore her. She thinks of them as her seraphims and Junos. English lessons have swiftly become favourite; the homework prompt and pleasing. Powers Mateland is delighted. She's had no need to holler for Jackson Thomas, nor has he succeeded in asking her for a date. She's always busy, that Polly Fenton, skipping about smiling, eyes alive; chatting away to students, teachers, herself and who knows what.

Excluding the house raising, Polly has had only four days off and she has willingly filled every moment of these. She went to a lunch-time concert with Kate at the Isabella Stewart Gardner Museum in Boston, taking the seven-hour round trip in her stride like a native. She's driven a laden minibus up to Hanover in New Hampshire to watch an Ivy League football game between Dartmouth College and Princeton, and she has spent the past two Sundays with Lorna, who she likes very much. Last week they browsed around Keene and found a lovely bistro for lunch where they whiled away the hours until it was suddenly time to order supper. Yesterday, Lorna and Polly took a trip to Manchester where they had an exhilarating day over-spending in the factory outlets, buying things they really didn't need but at prices so good they'd have been mad not to. The notion that they'd probably like each other has been proven, and a friendship between the two has developed effortlessly.

Lorna now knows all about Max. She has a boyfriend back home in Ohio and it's good to talk about the trials of long-distance love with one who knows. With one as fun as Polly. Polly has even called her Megan, absent-mindedly, once or twice, though she looks nothing like her, but Lorna was more than flattered.

'Will you guys get married?' she asked, having told Polly that she and Tom plan to. Sometime.

'Maybe,' guards Polly for the time being, 'probably.'

Why am I being guarded?

Just because I haven't found the neck-ring ring?

Or because maybe, for the first time, it's nice to be known – and liked – just as Polly. You know, without the Maxand bit.

For his part, Max doesn't really mind that she hasn't said 'yes' formally, officially. He doesn't need to hear it because he doesn't doubt her feelings towards him, he has no need to.

It's just her scatty, emotional disposition. Plus, she probably wants to say 'yes' to my face, with a deluge of kisses. Anyway, she has so much on her plate. She probably thinks she's actually accepted already.

Because when you're that committed, that sure, there's no need to rush, isn't that right, Max?

* * *

'Miss Fenton, if it's not Mountain Day today, can you coach us soccer?'

Though it had nothing to do with Hardy, the class had worked well through the double period and Polly was happy to ease off in these last ten minutes.

'Hold on, Heidi – what's Mountain Day?'

'Mountain Day? Miss Fenton, it's the best – the bell, like, sounds four times, everybody meets on the hockey field and we all, like, hit the mountains for the day – it's just the best. Mr Jonson organizes it. No one knows when it'll be – not even Mr Mateland. It's so cool.'

Polly absorbed the detail, ignored the repetitious element of Heidi's explanation, and nodded. 'OK,' she said, 'but why footie?'

'Hey?'

'Soccer.'

'You're from England, right!' Heidi announced as if Miss Fenton had lost her mind.

'The home of the game?' stressed AJ, perturbed by Miss Fenton's blank expression.

Laurel's hand shot up as she closed the lid of her lap-top.

'Laurel?'

'Bet you were born with your boots on!'

How ever am I going to let them down gently?

'Yo!' called curly-hair-snub-nose-Ben, his arm stretched, '*Up the Arsenal!* Is that right?' he quickly added, with sincerity.

'*Come on you reds!*' chanted TC.

'Scumming home, scumming home, football's scumming home,' sang TC, who presumed that to scum for home was particularly fancy footwork all players should aspire to.

'You gonna coach us or what?' asked Dick, slapping podgy hands down on the desk and fixing Miss Fenton with a look of hope mixed with exasperation.

'I'm frightfully sorry to disappoint you,' Polly said, wondering where on earth the adverb had come from, 'but I've never kicked a football in my life.'

The class stared at her in disbelief. A further, conclusive shrug from Miss Fenton saw hurt and disappointment criss-cross the ten faces.

'How about netball?'

Begrudgingly, the class said they'd meet her in the main gym at lunch-time, if there was a free court.

The main gym at lunch-time. It was free and Polly's jaw dropped.

Look at it! And this is only the main gym – there's another one too, and a weights room and a stretch studio as well.

Looking around at the superbly maintained hall, Polly couldn't wait to describe it all to Megan. Suddenly, she had an overwhelming surge of sympathy for The Jen Carter Person as she recalled the BGS gym; its frayed ropes, plastic-covered mats that clung cruelly to sweaty legs, and the floor with the varnish chipped into tessellations by squadrons of nimble-fingered games-wary girls. And the ceiling that served to amplify their squawks and protestations. She also realized with some guilt that she had quite a lot to recount to Megan, having been most uncharacteristically lax in her correspondence.

'Righty ho!' called Polly, positioning her class and some bystanders who wanted to join in, into some semblance of two netball teams. 'Blast, no bibs!' Hastily, she scribbled capital letters on to paper and safety-pinned them to the students' shirts.

'What's "ga"?' asked blond-hair-Ben suspiciously.

'Goal Attack,' Polly explained, pinning a large 'C' to Laurel and deciding that Dick would be safest as 'GD'. ('Cool,' he said, to her relief.)

The game lasted twelve and a half minutes before the players went on strike.

'*What?*' Heidi exclaimed, squinting at Miss Fenton to make double sure it was English she was speaking, 'you can't *run*? With the *ball*? You gotta *stop* and pass it on?'

Whistles of incredulity and snorts of disbelief ricochetted around the hall.

'Hey Miss Fenton,' Lauren called to save the day, 'how about we teach *you* basketball?'

'It'll be the best twelve and a half minutes of your life,' AJ assured her, flipping his cap round back to front.

'Yes, siree,' confirmed Forrest.

'Game on!' TC chanted and clapped.

After quarter of an hour, Polly had to admit that basketball was a 'far superior' game to netball ('Does that mean she likes it?' asked Lauren quietly. 'I guess so,' said Ed). 'However,' she continued, 'my leg is killing me – so I shall bow out gracefully and watch from the sidelines.'

'I sure am sorry 'bout that,' said AJ, who had collided with her at high speed and, being big for his age, had come off scot-free. Polly brushed away his apology while he shook his head gravely.

'Stiff upper lip and all that!' she explained, wondering how to make hers rigid because the pain from her leg was causing it to quiver.

'Go see Mr Jonson,' Heidi suggested. 'That's what he's, like, here for – his office is off of the weights room through there.'

You can't be Mr Jonson, the athletic trainer. You're a film star, surely?

'Mr Jonson?'

'Yes?'

You are *Mr Jonson? Wait till I tell Meg!*

'Um, I'm Polly Fenton.'

'Hey,' Mr Jonson smiled, beach-blond and brawny, and looking fantastic in his jogging pants and cosy sweatshirt, 'I'm Chip.'

'Chip?' Polly repeated, wondering, but only as an aside, if he had actually been christened that way, 'I've never met anyone called Chip. I'm Polly.'

'Ditto Polly,' Chip laughed, walking towards her and shaking her hand. 'Aren't you the chick who puts the kettle on?'

Polly put her hands on her hips and smiled wryly.

'Ah yes,' she countered slowly, 'I remember you, you're Fish-and!'

Chip held his hands up in surrender and nodded.

She is cute. I had no idea. It's a whole month into term and I had no idea.

'Pardon?' said Polly.

'I was thinking, you must have been here a month and I had no idea,' he shrugged.

''Bout what?' Polly asked.

''Bout who's standing in for Jen Carter,' Chip explained. 'I guess I just don't have much cause to go to the main buildings, being the Athletic Trainer. Hell, Stuyvesant House could burn down and I'd probably not know. I'm kinda out of the way here.'

'What does an athletic trainer do exactly?' Polly asked, perusing the walls of Chip's office. 'We don't have such things in our school, in England full stop, I don't think,' she continued, admiring the array of photos depicting him excelling in a variety of sports. A cabinet full of medals and trophies too. What a hero!

'Well,' said Chip, 'I'm on call if there's a sports-related injury. Or if a kid's training, I'll devise a programme. If they have a bad back, or whatever, I see to it. I administer physio, rehab, hydrotherapy – you know?'

'Really!' Polly gasped in awe, pitying poor Miss Henry who looked like a man but preferred women and was head of P.E. at BGS. '*Hydro*therapy?'

'Sure,' shrugged Chip. 'We have a couple of whirlpools,' he explained, as if they should be no more eye-opening than a couple of table-tennis tables. 'So what can I do for you? Or did you just come by to say hi?'

'Hi, hullo. Actually, it's my *leg*,' Polly stressed. 'Young AJ and I collided.'

'Not on some fine detail of Shakespeare, surely – I know the kid's opinionated but hey!'

'No no!' Polly laughed, warming to Chip's wit and smile. 'Basketball. And anyway, it's Hardy at the mo'.'

'Kiss me?' asked Chip, turning his head and looking at Polly through slanted eyes.

'Pardonwhat?' Polly reacted whilst struggling against being swallowed whole by his gaze.

'*Kiss me Hardy?*' Chip illumined, the picture of innocence.

Look at that picture of him finishing the Boston Marathon. How can anyone look that composed and, um, pleasing, after twenty-six miles?

'And 385 yards,' said Chip, reading her mind.

'*Thomas,*' she stressed, leaping back on to safer ground, 'Hardy. Thomas Hardy.'

'I gathered,' Chip said, motioning Polly to a chair while he drew another up close.

'*Far from the Madding Crowd,*' Polly continued vaguely, wondering if Chip's tan was genuine.

'Yup,' said Chip, 'as I said, I'm pretty cut off out here. Now, let's take a look at this leg. You want to take your pants down?'

What!

No!

Yes?

'Your trousers?' he spelt out with a 'w' and a 'z'.

Yes!

No?

Polly rolled down her leggings, suddenly horribly aware of her bikini-line fuzz, pale thighs and rather bristly lower legs. Chip placed cool hands around her calf and lifted her leg on to his lap, admiring her smooth milky skin to himself.

'Play much?' he asked, pressing gently. 'This hurt?'

'No and yes!' Polly all but yelled. Chip winced for her, holding her leg steady. And tenderly. And for longer than was probably necessary, not that Polly would have known. He hovered his hand above it; kept it there, suspended. Polly could feel a cushion of heat. Odd. It was soothing. It gave her a strange feeling.

'That's one helluva whack you've gotten yourself, lady!'

'*Dialect words*,' she quoted, in a bid to belittle the blush she knew she wore. '*Those terrible marks of the beast to the truly genteel.*'

'Hey?' asked Chip.

'Hardy,' Polly nodded, adding 'Thomas' quickly before Chip could quote Nelson again.

'You calling me an animal?' he laughed, hovering a fist above her throbbing shin.

'No, no, no. I'm far too genteel,' Polly heard herself say.

Chip sent her on her way with some arnica, a cool pack, and his assurance that there was no damage done.

A very private, quiet side of Polly wasn't so sure.

Nor, Chip realized, removing the photograph of Jen from his desk and relegating it to the bottom drawer, was he.

* * *

Max was shopping at Budgens in Belsize Park because he couldn't face the one-way system encircling Sainsbury's in Camden Town; he didn't like Safeway because the television adverts irritated him supremely, and Waitrose in Swiss Cottage was far too extravagant midweek (which made the Rosslyn Delicatessen in Hampstead a luxury completely out of the question). Yet he loathed Budgens intensely. He only needed a few basics, few of which the store had anyway, but there he was, he realized, mainly because it was Polly's stamping ground and therefore offered some connection, some comfort in lieu of the real thing. In lieu of an overdue letter.

He bought half a basketful of provisions and was about to make a swift exit when the Lottery machine and the passport-photo machine suggested he do otherwise.

I'll buy a ticket for Polly!

I'll pose for some daft passport photos to send with it!

He procrastinated for some time over which numbers to pick before marking off six boxes.

27 for her age, 30 for mine, 5 for the years we've been together (and the weeks we've now been apart), 19 for the date in December when she'll be home for Christmas. Damn, two more. 13 because I'm not suspicious, I mean superstitious, and because it equals 'M' in the alphabet. 16, likewise, for 'P'.

'How will I know if she's won?' he asked the sales assistant who regarded him most warily, not imagining that there was anyone in the UK who had never before bought a Lottery ticket.

'It flashes up half-way through *Blind Date*,' she informed him as if he was a halfwit.

'On the television?' Max asked, to her stupefied look. 'When's it on? *Blind Date*?' he pressed, thinking the girl's grimace of exasperation was merely some unfortunate facial mishap.

'Sa-Urday nigh-,' she said, dropping her 't's in mystification, ''bou- eigh-.'

Max thanked her and asked her what coins he needed for the passport-photo machine.

While waiting for the snaps to develop, a sickening lurch hit his stomach.

Oh bloody hell, the ice-cream!

He'd treated himself to a comfort-size tub of Häagen-Dazs 'Cookie Dough Dynamo' which he had no intention of sharing with Dominic, no matter how starving his brother might be, how hard he might plead, how temptingly he might bribe. Currently, the tub was at the bottom of the plastic bag;

Max could feel it because he was holding the bag next to him as he waited by the whirring passport machine. He looked at his watch and then at the store's clock and estimated he had been faffing around, gambling and posing, for at least fifteen minutes since paying for his goods. He added on another ten minutes since he had plucked the ice-cream from the freezer cabinet and placed it with relish in the then empty basket.

Still the machine rumbled and clicked and though he looked up the chute he could see nothing. He sat down, alongside a cackle of old ladies, on the orange chairs provided by the store.

Nothing for it, I'll have to salvage what I can.

He took the ice-cream tub from the bag and gave it a gentle squeeze. It yielded ominously quickly to his touch. He eased the lid off easily and pulled back the film cover, licking it meticulously. Slowly, he licked at the goopy surface of the ice-cream. Actually, it hadn't melted much at all. But enough, all the same, to warrant him lapping at the softer parts.

'Like the cutest puppy,' Jen Carter, bearing witness to the whole episode while she waited in the queue, said to herself.

As Max was waiting for the machine to blow-dry the photos which had finally appeared, a blonde woman, lean and too tanned for this time of year, approached him.

'Looks like you could use one of these,' she said in an American accent, offering him a Maryland cookie. He looked at her bewildered.

How can biscuits help with drying photos?

'Sorry?' he said, a quick glance at the machine to see that the blow-drying was still in operation.

Come on, machine.

'For your ice-cream?' said the woman, tapping the tub with the biscuit packet. 'Like, in place of a *spoon*.'

'Right, right!' Max responded, a little embarrassed, glaring at the machine to hurry up. He'd recently read an article about supermarkets being hotbeds for '*singles in search of sex*' and was increasingly worried that there were ulterior motives for this woman and her cookies. The machine was silent. Thank God.

My hands are full; bugger and damn!

'Here, let me,' the woman offered.

'No, no,' rushed Max, 'honestly.'

Too late.

She had the photos. Though she pretended not to look, she'd have seen the one of him pulling his monkey face. And the one below of his wide-eyed theatrical pout. In a glance.

'Er,' Max stumbled, 'thanks, right, yes, thank you. Fine. They're for my girlfriend. She's in America.'

'My home, my country,' sighed the woman, clasping hands (and the photos) to her breast and smiling.

'Yes,' said Max, inadvertently clapping eyes on her breast, 'Vermont.'

The woman's smile fixed itself and then dropped. She scoured Max's face and he found himself rooted by a pair of very blue eyes.

'Vermont?' she gasped, 'you wouldn't be—?' She let the sentence hang. England sure was small – but not that small, surely.

Max's eyes alighted on cat biscuits, tinned salmon and condensed milk visible in the woman's plastic bag.

Buster.

'You're not—' he stopped. They stared at each other, searching for some further clue.

'I'm Jen Carter,' she laughed, eyes dancing while her brow twitched becomingly.

'Good Lord!' Max chuckled, shaking his head and grinning back, 'I'm Polly's Max.'

'You don't say.'

'I do,' he assured her, 'I am.'

They shook their heads and then shook hands.

'Well well,' Max said, handing Jen the ice-cream while he restored order to his shopping bag.

'Can I tempt you,' Jen asked, 'with Polly's spoons? You

want to eat up your ice-cream back at the apartment? Check the place over? Say hi to Buster?'

What an offer. Of course he did.

Aha. Is autumn to be a season of trysts? A helluva fruity mess? A little bit of harmless swinging? Mixing if not matching? Musical affairs? Bed jumping and wife swapping? But no one's married here. Yet. Does that make it any less significant? Easier? Does that make it right? Or just not as wrong?

Hold on, I thought these four characters were besotted with their true partners? Fenton and Fyfield. Miss American Pie and her hunk of Chip. It might be an interesting notion in terms of our tale's plot – but what of the potential chaos in our characters' lives? We know these people. The thought wouldn't enter their minds, would it? Or if it did, if it crept in, it would be banished at once, of course. Or, if not quite *at once*, it would be considered carefully – and then rejected defiantly. Surely.

NINE

*W*hile Jen cursed autumn for dressing the pavements in a lethal cloak of sodden leaves and for giving her a stuffy cold, Polly praised the fall frequently each day for its stunning blaze of cool fire. She was rarely without a smile or a spring to her step and her delight and her energy were infectious. Trudging across Hampstead Heath in its October livery of russets and browns was one thing, but jogging or cycling or sitting – just living – in Vermont, in a landscape which boasted every possible hue of red, orange and yellow was something else entirely.

'Forget Keats!' Polly told her senior class, ' "Season of mists and mellow fruitfulness"? I hardly think so. Don't take any notice of him – he never came to Vermont, you see. But if he had, class, how do you think he would have described it? Anyone? Don?'

'Er, "season of pumpkin and palette of fire"?'

'Good! Laura?'

' "Trees clad the colour of passion; sun slumbering till spring"?'

'Super! Kevin?'

' "Fall: the sweep of flame that is the swansong of the maple." '

'Terrific! Gosh, look at it out there – come on, let's spend the remainder of the lesson outside composing odes.'

The Bench, Hockey Pitch
19th October

Darling Max,
My class are composing odes to the fall so I thought I'd do the same but in letter form to you. I've told the seniors to forget Keats – do you think that very wicked? But most of them are eighteen years old, so I'm sure they can handle such an order! I won't tell the juniors to do so as they're far too impressionable, and I can't instruct the freshers and sofs because I doubt they know who Keats is. I think the seniors feel liberated, relieved in some way – given carte blanche *to shake off the spectre of hallowed literature, to praise nature in whatever terms they choose. They're pick-ing some excellent ones too.*

As you know, I don't believe in God, but I have to credit and thank some thing; *whoever, whatever. As the fall has taken hold, it is as if some divine, huge power is laying their hand over the land in a slow, magical sweeping. Initially, just the fingertips of some of the leaves on a few of the trees were touched with crimson. Within a week, every tree had a flourish of copper or brass amongst the remaining green – as if a whole branchful had been given a celestial handshake. Now the maples are cloaked in incredible swathes of colours from the highest yellow to the deepest maroon; so vivid and bright that I don't know whether to weep or wear sunglasses. No mists, no mellow fruitfulness; instead an amazing clarity, crystal-clean light and a clear breeze. This land is rich indeed, for the leaves are made of gold, of rubies, of garnets. Ho! Sorry to prattle on in such syrupy terms, but I really have fallen under the spell of this place.*

The only drawback is the Rodin Syndrome. Now that I have experienced the fall in Vermont, I fear any other autumn anywhere else will surely seem second-rate and mediocre. Rather like all other sculpture once the work of Rodin is known.

God, I wish you were here. It is absolutely beautiful but it would be even better if I could share it. I mean, I go jogging with Lorna and cycling with Clinton (I'm quite fit now – you'd love my tight butt) (that's American for firm bum) but what I crave is a long, loping walk with you.

Damn – time and paper run out on me – and my juniors are about to have the surprise of their lives: they're about to meet Chaucer and, while they adore my dulcet tones, I'm not sure what they'll make of my Middle English accent.

I love you, Max-i-mine. My own 'verray parfit gentil knight', I miss you. Write soon,

Polly.

PS. pls send more Marmite – Kate's gone crazy for it and is using it in everything – Bogey's food included.

'Yeah, hello?'

'Chip?'

'Jen! How are you? Hey, it's great to hear from you. I was going to call you only there's a hockey tournament soon and suddenly the whole team have gotten aches and sprains.'

'Hey, that's OK, I've been pretty busy too.'

'So how's it going?'

'Good, good – how's Hubbardtons?'

'Pretty much the same. I think tomorrow'll be Mountain Day.'

'Hey – isn't that classified information? Wish I could be there.'

'You don't have some day similar, in London England?'

'Nope. Nothing that comes close. Something called Mufti when the kids can wear their own clothes – but that's only the last day of term.'

'Some way off.'

'Sure is. You know, it's kinda weird living in someone

else's apartment. There're these crazy women above me – one is old, Swiss and nutty as hell, the other's an out-and-out psycho. I haven't managed to come in without one or other noticing – so I'm either sworn at or asked the date, time and year and the whereabouts of some guy called Franz.'

'Sounds entertaining?'

'I guess. I think I prefer being Dorm Mother to ten girls though. So, have you met Polly Fenton?'

'Er, Polly Fenton. No, no, I haven't as yet.'

'Oh?'

'No, I've been real busy.'

'Sure. She's pretty.'

'How do you know?'

'I met her boyfriend and he showed me photos.'

'She has a boyfriend?'

'Yes. Chip?'

'Yeah?'

'You there?'

'Sure.'

'You went kinda distant.'

'I was miles away, I was just – you know. I don't know, I'm bushed.'

'Sure.'

'So what's he like?'

'Who?'

'This boyfriend guy.'

'Oh, he's really sweet and helpful – the boiler here's a little temperamental so he's going to have someone come fix it. He and his brother are making dinner for me and Megan this weekend.'

'Great.'

'Yeah. You want to know who Megan is?'

'I'd love to but I gotta go – I have a kid for hydrotherapy in five.'

'Sure. I love you, Chip.'

'Love you too, Jen.'

*

Hullo Button,

Lovely to receive your letters – two arrived this morning though you sent them a week apart. Royal Mail – 1, USA Post – 0. You wrote beautifully about the fall and I wish so much I could share it with you. Maybe another year we could take our holiday there.

London is sludgy and slippery, and strolling over the Heath becomes a maudlin trudge without you, kicking the leaves, all rosy-cheeked and alive. There have been some great films on at the Everyman but all Dominic will be coaxed to see is Die Very Hard 27 *and* Star Trek 43. *Plebeian.*

Work has been going well; some new commissions as well as potboilers from the faithful. I enclose photos and a Lottery ticket – the acquisition of both being highly traumatic so I hope you'll be grateful.

You'll never guess who I bumped into.

Jen Carter!

At Budgens.

You'll be pleased to hear that Buster is living the life to which he is accustomed: her shopping consisted of little else than tinned salmon and condensed milk. I popped back to the flat and, rest assured, all is neat and tidy, with Post-it notes still in place. I thought it would be friendly to invite her over for supper, along with Megan – such an evening will provide Jen with some company, Megan with some hope, and Dominic with a choice!

I'll report back with Technicolor detail!

Love and miss you intensely,

Max.

Pollyanna Fentonio,
You have written me but one letter.
A plague of itching upon you.
Yours sincerely,
Megan Reilly
PS. Affliction can be lifted for the price of a phone call.
A long one. Soon.

'Hullo?'
'I'm sorry. Sorry. Very. Please forgive me.'
'Are you itching, Fenton?'
'Yes. Oh yes. Terribly. I beg of you, lift the curse!'
'How long do you intend this call to last?'
'Ooh, ten mins?'
'Then you can itch away at your leisure.'
'Fifteen?'
'Done.'
Polly and Megan dissolved into a fit of giggles.
'How's Kate?' Megan asked. 'And the Japanese chap – Henry without the "y"?'
'Kate is lovely,' Polly assured her, 'Charle(s) is Chinese. And I've met a Megan, only she's called Lorna Hendry.'
'Huh?'
'A surrogate. For you. She teaches drama.'
'Then she's only *acting* as your friend, you poor deluded soul.'
'Charming.'
'Aren't I just!' Megan chuckled and sighed Polly's name before filling her in on BGS gossip with no pause for breath.
'How's Jen Carter shaping up?'
'Surprisingly well – she's determined not to smile till half term but she's already having the last laugh as she's foisted e e cummings on to your A level group.'
'Wow – they had trouble enough with Gerard Manley Hopkins!'

'Talking of men,' Megan reasoned, in a very sober voice, 'still no sight of Tom Cruise?'

Suddenly, a wave of excitement engulfed Polly; she didn't see it coming and wasn't sure quite how to ride it now it was here.

'Not. As. Such,' she said, the sparkle to her voice loud and clear, an image of Chip filling her mind's eye. Megan whooped with expectant delight.

'It was Mountain Day yesterday,' Polly continued, voice high and fast, 'we were just settling down to some Oscar Wilde in earnest when the bell sounded four times.'

'Ding a ling ling!' drawled Megan as she settled herself into the waft of cushions on her sofa.

'It was all organized by the Athletic Trainer bloke – a day's outing in the mountains. The seniors go for a strenuous stomp to the peak of Hubbardtons, the juniors have a bracing walk half-way up, and the other years have more of a nature trek in the lower slopes.'

'You?'

'I was a bracing walker – it was a totally awesome day, believe me.'

'*Totally awesome* – what kind of language is that, dear Fenton?'

'*Touché*,' Polly mumbled a little embarrassed because it had actually felt rather nice to the tongue. '*Utterly wonderful* – that better? Anyway, it was the most perfect day for it – the colours here, Megan – God!'

'God? You're a non-believer!'

'I mean, God-the-colours-are-so-incredible.'

'Totally awesome?'

'Totally.'

'And where does Tom Cruise fit in, might I ask?' Megan chastened. 'Did you find him up a tree making syrup?'

'Silly,' Polly laughed, 'you don't tap for sap till March.'

'OK,' Megan reasoned slowly, 'you came across him chopping wood – all divine forearms and moppable brow?'

'Meg-an!'

'Well then, where is he? And who?'

'He's the Athletic Trainer,' Polly explained openly.

'Tom Cruise?'

'Meg, you're a sick woman. Not Tom Cruise but On A Par With.'

'A-ha!' Megan declared, hamming up her ignorance for Polly's pleasure.

'He's amazing and gorgeous.'

What did Polly just say?

'What? How?' Megan asked sternly, a little confused. 'Quantify, please?'

'Well, I suppose he's an easy six foot and devastatingly brawny because of all the sport – you know the type: wide shoulders, tapered waist and neat bum?'

'I know *of* the sort,' qualified Megan ruefully, 'but I've never had the precise pleasure.'

'Well, he has a very handsome face – aesthetically chiselled with pool-deep eyes, neat ears and expert lips.'

'How on earth do *you* know if they're expert!' Megan snorted. *You're far too Maxanpollified to comment on the kissability of any other male.*

'I'm guessing,' said Polly with a shrug that Megan, to her relief, could hear.

'What's his hair like?'

'Light brown, short and cropped.'

'Yuk – US Marine style?'

'No.'

'Brad Pitt style?'

'Yes?' said Polly tentatively, trying quickly to recall Mr Pitt's diverse coiffure without frustrating Megan further. Megan, however, was already groaning her approval.

'Has he a name?' she asked breathlessly. 'This On-A-Par-With?'

'Chip,' Polly answered, 'Chip Jonson.'

Megan was struck speechless and felt uneasy at once.

What? Who?

Jen's Chip?

Doesn't Polly know? Who's keeping what from whom?

'I know his name's, er, odd,' Polly continued, misreading the pause, 'but it's a very, very minor glitch, I assure you. Do you know, when you know him, you see that it actually rather suits him. Hullo? Meg? Have you fainted from some sort of Tantric orgasm already?'

'No, no,' Meg said quietly, catching a drift of danger but unsure who the victim was, 'almost.'

'You'd love him,' Polly declared, feeling rather proud.

'Sounds like you're rather taken with him yourself!' Megan said as lightly as she could. 'Sure there's room for me?'

'*What?*' Polly laughed in amazement.

'All this praise,' Megan reasoned, 'and superlatives. Sure you haven't fallen for him? Wouldn't rather have him for yourself?'

'Me?' Polly declared, 'don't be daft!'

The thought hadn't entered Polly's head. Megan, however – and however inadvertently – had placed it there. And there it lingered. In a far, dark corner. Half hidden.

* * *

Dominic and Max are putting the finishing touches to a sizeable lasagne. Dominic is enveloped in the scent of Calvin Klein aftershave. Max, who has tomato paste smeared on his denim shirt, grates Parmesan over the surface of the pasta.

'Now smell your hands,' Dominic says gleefully. Max takes them to his nose.

'That's never cheese!' he groans, wrinkling his nose at the sourness and scrubbing his hands energetically. Dominic passes him a bottle of sun lotion which is in the cutlery drawer and is the closest thing the Fyfields have to hand cream. Max inadvertently squirts out too great a quantity and offers his palm to Dominic that he might take some. His brother refuses, saying it would produce an olfactory clash with the Calvin Klein.

95

'Vain dick,' says Max, adding the excess hand cream to the tomato paste on his shirt, taking it off and bundling it into the washing machine. Dominic flicks his hand through his hair and holds his head haughtily.

'I got it,' he says with a shrug, 'I flaunt it!'

The doorbell rings. Max rifles through a pile of still-to-be-ironed laundry for the least crumpled shirt. It belongs to his brother whose permission is neither sought nor needed. The doorbell sounds again. Dominic rubs his hands, a lascivious smile inching its way across his lips.

'So I'm having the choice of a blonde or a brunette – that right?'

'Dominic,' Max declares, putting on the shirt, buttoning it up out of sync but not noticing, 'you're incorrigible. Both girls are invited for each other's safety.'

He goes to answer the door while Dominic checks his reflection and gives himself an approving wink.

The meal was a resounding success. Everybody laughed at Dominic's jokes and he dispensed his great smile freely and equally to Megan and Jen. Jen opened up after a mouthful or two of lasagne and amused them with tales of Hubbardtons: school, town, river and mountain. She and Megan then regaled the boys with the antics of the BGS girls over the past weeks. Megan asked Dominic to show them his recent work and the gasps of admiration that his photographs received from the girls were soon bestowed on Max's creme brulée. Polly was mentioned in passing. Chip wasn't mentioned at all. There was too much else to talk about, in Hampstead, in the here and now. Furtive smiles and glances criss-crossed the table. People that perhaps shouldn't have seen, saw; the actual subjects, for the most part, were oblivious.

'Well,' said Max later, washing while Dominic wiped, 'which is it to be, blonde or brunette?'

Dominic wound the tea towel around his hand and flicked it at his brother, sharply, while he pondered. At the beginning of the evening, he might have chosen the blonde. But there again, that could jeopardize the future ambitions he had for Miss Reilly. Anyway, he'd observed the American, once or twice, cast her gaze in his brother's direction. Not that he'd be telling Max. Not fair on Polly. No point anyway.

'Very, very nice,' Dominic mused, returning the tea towel to its more usual function.

'Which?'

'Both. But Megan's my girl – she lives round the corner.'

'I think you'll find Belsize Park's nearer than Kilburn,' Max reasoned.

'Lower West Hampstead, according to Meg,' Dominic cautioned. 'Furthermore, Megan won't be buggering off back to the States.'

'True,' said Max, 'plus the fact that Jen already has a boyfriend back home.'

'Does she?' Dominic asked, putting away the last of the plates.

Doesn't act like it.

'Yes,' Max confirmed, pulling the plug and rinsing around the sink, 'she told Megan.'

But she hasn't told you, mused Dominic.

TEN

*A*n excess of physical perfection can be a hazardous thing. The possessor, becoming accustomed to the myopic flattery of admirers, inevitably considers himself worthy of such regard. Those wishing to be possessed by him heedlessly presume that a beautiful soul is in accordance with such a seemly exterior; even if all evidence is to the contrary.

Physical perfection can pose a trap for all concerned. It is laid by the possessor – unintentionally initially, soon enough consciously – and it can lure even the seemingly resilient. Once the possessor sees how effective his snare can be, setting it can become quite addictive. Avoiding it – even for those utterly aware of its existence, its whereabouts, its repercussions – becomes impossible. Consenting prey. Willing captive.

'Hey Kate.'
  'Hey Chip.'
  'Polly about?'
  'Sure – I'll just go call her. Po-lly!'
  'Oh, hullo Chip.'
  'Hey Polly. Want to take a walk? It's a beautiful evening.'

'A walk? Um. OK. Why not?'

Why not indeed.

They invited Kate too, but she declined. They asked Charle(s), who sat at the kitchen table writing to his wife and daughter, and he accepted. A pang of disappointment hit Polly but she reprimanded herself instantly.

Of course Charle(s) is welcome. It's a walk, for heaven's sake.

Chip was not so much disappointed as annoyed at Charle(s)'s acceptance. Had he not fixed him a twitch of his mouth and a darkening of his eyes in warning while he asked? Didn't gesture and expression transcend language barriers? Obviously not.

And Charle(s)? Charle(s) himself is innocent. He'd love to go for a walk on a beautiful night. Furthermore, he felt it a duty to his knowledge of Max and Jen's existence to accompany Polly and Chip. He could finish his letter later; in fact, a paragraph describing the night sky in America might be a very good addition. His wife would like that.

In the event, the walk was genial and innocent. All three admired the stars and pointed out the constellations they knew. Polly breathed deeply, standing still every now and then to implore the men to agree that it was a perfect night – wasn't the air pure, didn't the sound of tumbling Hubbardtons provide a super soundtrack, didn't the mountains look velvety? Chip asked pertinent questions about how Charle(s) felt to be in America, how it compared with China, what did he miss and what did he now feel he could not live without. Charle(s) said 'Hershey bars' and they all laughed. By the time they arrived back, an hour later, Chip had Charle(s)'s seal of approval and when Chip visited a few nights later, and a couple of times thereafter, Charle(s) felt fine about declining the invitation for a stroll. In Chip's hands, Charle(s) decided, Polly was safe to revere her surroundings and wax lyrical about nature. He was not needed.

Chip Jonson had ulterior motives, of course he did. He

wanted the thrill of the chaste. The longer the phase lasted, the more delicious the result. The carefully contrived innocent edge to his flirting flattered Polly. She looked forward to his visits, and she felt and liked the lift that a nod from across the hockey pitch could give her during her day.

'He's such a nice bloke,' she said to Lorna, who bore witness to one such greeting, 'don't you think?'

'Jen Carter seems to think so,' Lorna advised for safety's sake.

'*My* Jen Carter?' Polly asked, wondering what her replacement had to do with the merits of Chip's character.

'Sure – they've been going together since last spring.'

'Really?' Polly asked, elongating the word.

Why had her heartbeat picked up?

Why do I feel slightly embarrassed? Straighten my brow. Why should it wrinkle?

'Sure,' Lorna shrugged easily.

Actually, thought Polly later on as she propped herself up in Great Aunt Clara's bed, pen poised over a pad which had read 'Darling Max' for two days, *it makes me feel rather safe. Poor chap must be lonely too.*

Which chap?

Chip chap. He's obviously comforted that I have a love over the sea and far away as well.

Does he know about Max, then?

Doesn't he?

Have you told him?

Do you know, I don't think I have! We're going to go for a drink in Grafton tomorrow. A group of us, you know. I'll tell him then, so everything can be out in the open and we can get on with being good friends.

Just good friends.

Of course.

It wasn't a question, Polly. It's a cliché.

The group for Grafton dwindled to just two and you can guess who they were. Chip hadn't actually asked anyone else, so when Polly attempted to confirm their company she was met with apologies and excuses.

Shame, she thought, *but never mind.*

You're relieved. You're excited.

No, no. OK then, but I mean why shouldn't I be? It really doesn't matter if it's one or many – these are my friends, my new community.

'Hey Charle(s).'

'Chip, a good evening.'

'Want to join us for a drink?'

'Thank you kindly but accept my apologies, I am tired tonight and, as you see, my students' homework is plentiful.'

'Sure,' said Chip, flicking through sheaves of Physics as if they were a lifestyle magazine, 'another time.'

'Certainly,' said Charle(s).

'Looks like it's just you and me, Fenton,' Chip shrugged to Polly. 'Want to take a rain check?'

Oh. Doesn't he want to go? I like it that he's taken to calling me Fenton. He drops the 't', like he does for 'mountain'. It sounds nice. Fen'un. Doesn't he want to go for a drink then?

'I'm easy,' Polly shrugged back, dipping her finger into Marmite and dabbing it on to her tongue. She offered the jar for Chip to try. He contorted his face and did strange things with his lips while groaning. Polly laughed. So did Charle(s). Kate said, 'Hey, go easy there, we're waiting on a shipment.'

'That stuff is gross,' Chip said hoarsely. 'But hey, No Weakness, I always say.' With that, he dabbed his finger into the jar and then sucked on it hard. He performed a similar sequence of facial gymnastics, this time accompanied by appreciative humming. 'Actually, it's kinda OK, an acquired taste, I guess. Anyways, something you've never experienced before always takes a little getting used to.'

'Yes,' said Polly, screwing the top firmly on the jar, 'I suppose it does.'

101

Polly, don't you dare start reading great significance behind the fact that Max can't abide Marmite but Chip has already trained himself to like it.

The old coaching inn at Grafton provided Chip and Polly with dark-green leather armchairs, a roaring fire and discreet staff.

'Does this remind you of back home?' asked Chip, motioning to the surroundings with two glasses of Jack Daniels in his hands.

'Actually, not really,' Polly confided, a clear image of the Holly Bush pub, all smoky, noisy and cramped, in her mind's eye.

I'll just quickly tell him about back home.

Why's he looking at me like that? Have I something on my nose?

She checked. She didn't.

'Where will you be for Christmas?' she asked, sipping her whiskey, wishing it didn't have an 'e' or ice.

'Back home, I guess,' said Chip, taking a sonorous glug at his glass.

'North Carolina?' Polly reminded herself.

'Yip,' said Chip, 'and you?'

'Oh, I'll be going back to England. For a fortnight,' Polly said.

'Where do your family live?' Chip asked.

'Oh,' said Polly with an open face and straight voice, 'heaven.'

'Jeez man, I'm sorry,' Chip fumbled, laying his hand over Polly's wrist in a sweet gesture.

''Sokay,' Polly assured him, patting his hand and chancing upon his elegant, tanned fingers, 'I never really knew them.'

'Little Orphan Polly,' mused Chip. 'How Dickensian.'

Polly laughed breezily, bolstered by Chip's concern. 'My aunt, who brought me up, is also not around,' she explained.

'Oh? Where's she?'

102

'Same place as my parents.'

'Can I get my damned foot further in it, I wonder?' Chip groaned, holding his head in his hands and lowering it until it neared the table. Polly poked him gently on the arm. He looked up at her.

'Silly billy,' she said, delighted at the phrase and its immediate effect on Chip.

I must have something on my nose.

'So,' said Chip, wrenching his eyes away from hers to ponder into the crook of his finger, 'it must be Christmas at the orphanage for Li'l Miss Fen'un.'

Polly played along, pulling as bedraggled a face as she could; turning soon enough into a smile of prodigious proportions.

'Nope,' she said, holding on to Chip's gaze, 'just me and my boyf and his bruv.'

'Your who and his what?'

'Max and Dominic – my boyfriend and his brother respectively.'

Chip raised a glass to their names, respectfully. Supposedly. He went quiet. Then he went to the bar to refill their glasses. Polly's eyes followed him.

He is completely gorgeous. Objectively speaking. I wish Megan were here to see this!

And Max?

Look, he's just a really nice bloke – very friendly and great company. And he has a girlfriend, so that makes everything cosy.

So why did he just wink at you from the bar?

He's just friendly. Probably has something in his eye.

'Do you know,' Polly started, thanking Chip for the lack of ice, 'my Max met your Jen!'

See? There's no issue here.

'Who?' he said, the picture of innocence.

'Um, Jen Carter,' Polly elaborated, keeping her eyes steady, 'from Hubbardtons. She's in my flat. I thought you were, you know, an item?'

'Oh,' Chip said, tipping his head and his hands this way and that, 'kinda.'

That's good enough. That'll do.

Polly, pleased that all was out in the open and above board, was happy for Chip to move on to other subjects.

'Wasn't Mountain Day just the best?'

'Smashing!' Polly enthused, 'I can't believe it was a month ago.'

'Have you still held on to all those leaves and twigs and stuff you were collecting?'

'Oh yes,' said Polly, 'I want to make a scrap book of my stay, you see. And anyway, I just like to collect twigs and leaves.'

'And stuff.'

'Stuff too. They're nice to have.'

'Well,' Chip says, leaning towards her, 'the snow'll be here soon and it'll be just white white white.'

'Will it be white,' laughed Polly, 'when the snow comes?'

'Very,' Chip assured her. 'You ski?'

'Actually, no.'

'Want me to teach you?'

Polly regarded him slyly. 'Well, can you ski, Mr Jonson?'

Chip tapped his chest and raised his chin. 'Gold medal. Class of '89.'

'You'll do,' Polly said, raising her glass while concentrating on the fire.

So will you, Chip decided, chinking her glass. 'Bottoms up!' he announced in a poor accent but with commendable aplomb. Polly raised her eyebrows. And then smiled.

With the Jack Daniels lubricating their vocal chords and the glow of the fire increasing the warmth between them, it was easy to talk through the evening and on into the night.

Polly thinks very hard about Max later that night. She concentrates. About marriage too. About herself.

I love Max with all my heart. I've never imagined, let alone desired, being with anybody else.

The only man I would ever want to marry.
But . . .

do I really want to?

She weeps as silently as she can.

I'm just crying because Max is my darling boy and I love him so deeply. I'm crying because he has asked me to marry him. I'm crying because I don't really know what marriage is, having never really known one. Am I mad? How can a poor little orphan even consider jeopardizing the security, the anchor, that the man who wants to marry her provides?

She sits up in bed and turns on the bedside lamp. A warm glow is cast. This is her room. It was Great Aunt Clara's but it's Polly's now. Her space. It harbours her thoughts and she feels safe here. For Polly, this room consolidates all that Vermont means in general; nobody in her pre-America life knows exactly where she is, precisely what she is doing at any given moment, what it all really looks like. Here, in her room in Vermont, USA, she is Polly Fenton and she is strong. She is all by herself but not lonely.

So why does she weep?

There is no connection with back home.

Is that why she cries?

She is absolutely on her own.

Is that the reason?

This very fact is at once frightening and thoroughly liberating. Polly feels closer to herself than ever she has because, in reality, there is only Polly. Here. Now.

She can describe her surroundings in minute detail, and she does so in her letters, but Megan and Max can't really know what it's like, they can only imagine. She can relate events to them such as Mountain Day, the house raising, Hallowe'en, Thanksgiving, but they have to call up images according to Polly's description. Max has never been in Kate's home, let alone with Polly in Great Aunt Clara's bed. Megan has never taken a class at Hubbardtons. It is no discredit to Polly's power of portrayal, but the houses and the mountains and the people that Max and Megan conjure look little like they actually do. For Megan, Chip Jonson is Tom Cruise with a Brad Pitt haircut. For Max, Great Aunt Clara's bedroom is smaller and more English-cottage than lofty New England colonial. For Megan and Max, the face they put to Kate is not hers at all. In their minds, they make Polly's students in the mould of American kids they know from films and television sitcoms.

No one from Polly's England has ever had brunch at the Sunnyside Diner, nor eaten grits. Polly will never eat grits again but that's because she's tried them. She can't describe the taste sensation of grits convincingly though she has tried painstakingly by letter, but she's pretty sure that Megan wouldn't care for it and that Max would hate it. Polly knows, however, that imagining is often not enough; sometimes one actually has to try things before one can make a decision on their merit.

See Polly sitting up in bed, crying silently behind her hands? She is resigned to the similarity between grits and Chip Jonson.

I'm crying because I know I'll have to try it. Even though I think I know it'll be a taste I won't much like.

She steps down from the bed and gazes at Cézanne's portrait of the gardener.

Oh to step within the safety of the picture. To snuggle on his lap, to have him say not a lot, just to understand.

She wishes she were at Giverny, amongst Monet's water-lilies, and she stares at the print until form and space are even more blurred than the artist intended.

Van Gogh's bedroom. Simple and bright. Not unlike Great Aunt Clara's. Close my eyes. Open.

The watercolour of the maples blazing in the fall.

And where I am.

She remembers Mountain Day, over a month ago. Trick or treating well over a fortnight ago. Thanksgiving dinner the day before yesterday, perhaps her favourite day so far. All the waifs and strays from Hubbardtons, for whom home was just too far to travel, converged on Kate's. Never had Polly felt so much part of a family as she did amongst all these temporarily orphaned folk whose families were celebrating in distant states without them. Twenty-eight of them in all, for whom Kate's party, despite mountains of cranberries, two overweight turkeys and her inimitable hospitality, was still second best to spending the holiday at home. Polly, however, praised the vastness of the United States for providing her, that night, with an extended family with whom to celebrate. She gave thanks for them. Something new and something to be cherished. She wished she'd had many Thanksgivings. She wished she could have this again, same time every year. She wanted to have that very first taste of buttery pumpkin pie again and again. She resolved to observe Thanksgiving from hereon after. The last Thursday of every November, she would invite everyone she knew, convert them all to the warmth of this American festival of family and home.

Time was passing. How soon she had felt settled. How quickly term had rolled by. Soon she'll leave and go home. For a while. But she's here, for a while longer.

Back in bed again, Polly is hugging her knees and breathing into the comforter which is not doing the job its name implies. She has stopped crying. She sits very still, it is very quiet. She can hear herself think. There is no distraction in the silent clasp of the night.

I can't help but be attracted to Chip. I don't know what to do about it. This is new and it is terrifying and exciting. Maybe just a kiss will do it. A tiny one, I won't need more. Just a kiss to waylay this hunger, to remind and prove to me that Max, and a life with him, is all I really want.

She closes her eyes. Max. Chip. They merge. Chip is back. Remember his eyes, his lingering gaze earlier this evening? You were happy to look directly at them – easy, open and the most pool-deep blue. Not Max blue. A new blue. But which is the true blue?

God. What am I even thinking? No. Please let me get

home, to my Max, so I can heed the feeling and not feel the
need.

'I smell danger,' Polly murmurs as she sidles down deep into bed, 'but it is laced with an intoxicating aroma.'

ELEVEN

Slowly, he unbuttoned Polly's shirt and brushed it away gently from her shoulders. A plain white bra promised the most perfect breasts behind, but for the time being he was happy to feast his gaze on the flesh currently available. He pushed her against the wall, pressed against her and took her mouth with his. A flap of curtain fell across her shoulder and down one side; her eyes were closed, her lips parted, her neck taut and twisted, just like a Klimt painting. As she stretched her arms up and about his neck, her slim frame elongated and allowed him to slip his hands down the waistband of her skirt and circumnavigate. Her flesh was initially warm and smooth yet seemed to prickle damp instantly under his touch. He left one hand down the back of her skirt where his fingers rested on the cleft of her buttocks. His other hand he took back up to her throat before letting it flow down her torso to her thigh. He grabbed at her, she gasped and kissed him deeper. He sidled his hand up the skirt, tracing lightly the front of her thigh and inching his way upwards, excruciatingly slowly. Her legs were closed tightly but yielded to his feathery touch immediately. Suddenly he cupped his hand forcefully against the mound of her sex. Warm cotton hid it from direct touch but the moistness he excited from her soon filtered its way through to greet his probing fingers.

He took his hands away and clasped her head instead; as he did so, she felt an unwelcome coldness filter over her back and continue between her legs. He watched her eyes burn khaki as disappointment mixed with desire coursed across them. It pleased him. She ground against him for warmth, for more. He clasped the tops of her arms and brought her away from the wall, away from the half-masked safety of the curtain and into the middle of the room, centre stage. Her blouse undone. Her bra peeping through. Her short, floaty skirt twisted. He was still fully clothed. He was still holding her arms. Tightly. Almost painfully. He hadn't said a word. She hadn't wanted him to. He sat her down on the sofa whilst he knelt between her legs, pushed her shirt right away and deftly unclasped her bra. And there they were, those gorgeous, perfect breasts; exquisite pink and pert, previously demure behind a white cotton bra, positively brazen now they were out in the open. He kissed from one to the other, just above the nipple, then returned his mouth a little lower; his hot, desirous breath whispering over them, lips encircling and then taking them greedily. Bite. Taste. Tease.

He felt her breathing quicken through the rise, fall and flutter of her chest. Her hands swept through his hair. Up he stood, his groin at her eye level. She unbuckled his belt, unbuttoned his jeans and pushed them away. His erection had forced the fly of his boxer shorts agape and she buried her nose in the opening. She could smell a close, warm saltiness, the prelude to sex, and she breathed it in deeply so the scent became a taste. His pubic hair tickled her, his cock was just out of reach and view; it was torturous and thrilled her. He yanked down his boxers and she gasped at the sight of him; stiff, proud and powerful. She pressed her lips gently against his balls and felt them tighten in anticipation. She inched her mouth along the length of his erection, the glans beyond her stretch though she bent her neck commendably.

110

He grasped his cock and levered it down a little, she opened her mouth and encircled it obligingly. He bucked gently as she sucked. It was difficult to breathe. She was light-headed. Her hand was over his hand over his cock. His other hand travelled from her neck to her nipple to her lips, where he pressed so he could determine his pride in her mouth.

Suddenly, he pulled out, panting. They watched as his cock leapt and danced in dry ecstasy.

'Quick.' He sounded hoarse.

She wriggled free of her knickers. The skirt could stay, it was small and flimsy and wouldn't get in the way. Its presence also made her seem all the more naked. She lay back, opened her legs and closed her eyes, anticipating the long overdue sensation. There. She could feel the head of his prick poke gently at her before easing its way in a little. Here.

God, it's been so long. It feels like it won't fit.

She felt tight but it served only to increase the exquisite intensity. She wondered if he was all the way in. He pushed.

Ah, not quite.

He thrust.

Oh God, there.

He held the top of her head while she wrapped her arms around his waist, grabbing her wrists securely. Their bodies were intertwined and absolutely glued. They humped into and against each other, grinding down, bucking up. He was so hard she swore she could feel his prick right in her stomach. She felt so tight and dark that he was sure he was within her for good. What a place to be! His head pushed into her neck, her lips at his shoulder. Their breathing was tense and audible and further increased the eroticism. As she came, she bit into him and cried out. It triggered his climax and his cock seemed to thrust itself even deeper, plunge even higher in its final drive.

It looked as if their bodies were to be eternally in spasm; the pleasure was so intense they wouldn't have cared if they were. They could see themselves in the mirror, in the reflection of the television too, in the panes of the glazed door and they watched awhile, marvelling. It was as if their bodies had been frozen in their final, orgasmic buck. They regarded themselves joined at the groin, heads locked together, mouths merged; space between their stomachs and torsos, legs all over the place.

'Polly Polly,' he said, 'welcome home.'

Polly opened her eyes. For an instant he did not know them, nor, it appeared, did they know him. Only for a moment, though; soon enough they melted into a rich olive green. Quick enough for him to discredit that second when they were strange and he was a stranger.

'Hey Max,' she said.

'He's missed you so, so much,' said Megan, spooning mounds of cappuccino foam into her mouth, 'I think it's quite taken him by surprise – you know, the intensity of his longing.'

'Bless,' sighed Polly gently, wondering which end of the chocolate éclair looked the most appetizing.

'Want to go halves?' Megan asked hopefully, proffering the towering *mille-feuille* for Polly to assess.

'Sure,' said Polly, her eyes sparkling. The éclair was far easier to divide than the *mille-feuille* so they devoured it swiftly before launching into Megan's plate with forks and fingers nimble.

''Sgood to be back,' said Polly quietly, looking around the West Hampstead coffee shop, their old haunt; smiling at the waitress, accepting a welcome-back wink from the owner.

'It's probably what's kept you going out there,' Megan reasoned, 'imagining how sweet the reunion would be. Was it dreamy?' she asked, bringing her head close, her eyes soft and hopeful. Polly nodded and then motioned to the waitress for a third round of cappuccinos. Megan retrieved her pocket diary, put on her glasses and ruffled through the pages; twiddling a biro in her lips, 'so how long do you have?'

'A fortnight,' Polly told her, taking the diary and starting from the back, 'I go back on January the 4th. Here.'

'Next year!' Megan proclaimed. 'There – makes it sound an age away.'

Polly nodded but Megan found the gesture illegible.

I've never seen her so quiet. Can't still be jet lag?

'Tell me about school,' said Polly, eager for a change of topic. She settled into the chair, took a sip of coffee and gazed at the passers-by scuttling along West End Lane under umbrellas. God it was dreary.

Where are the mountains? The colour? The vastness? The energy?

'School,' pondered Megan, 'is pretty much as you left it. They revarnished the floor at the beginning of term but sixty assemblies later it's sufficiently chipped and dinted to warrant redoing already.' Polly smiled as a clear picture of Lucy Howard's fingers ploughing the floor during prayers came to mind. Megan continued, telling her which teachers had been reduced to tears by Upper Four, how many detentions she had dished out and how many C-minuses she'd given in the end of term reports. 'I gave Fanny Balcombe a D bracket-plus which was by far the most pleasurable thing I've done in ages, and I had to give Jenny Newman an A minus which was rather galling – she may be the most mischievous student in the school but her work is faultless. How about your young yankee doodles?'

Images of AJ and the two Bens, of Heidi and Forrest, of the Keats-weary seniors, the Dickens-wary Junos, the slang-ready seraphims, the angelic freshers, embraced Polly.

How can I begin to tell her?

'Hey?' Megan asked, taking her finger to the rim of the cup, scooping at the stubborn froth.

'They're something else,' said Polly dreamily, shaking her head and smiling in a distant sort of way.

'And The Lorna Woman?'

'We've gotten quite close,' Polly declared.

'You've *what*!' Megan exclaimed. Polly looked shocked and reached her hand to her friend.

'God, it doesn't belittle our friendship,' she stressed.

'That's not what I meant,' Megan clarified, 'it's what you *said.*'

'What did I say?' Polly asked, racking her brains.

'That word – you know – an American one!'

'Huh?'

'Not that one – though you're overusing that too, I might add – no, you said "gotten". Gracious, Polly Fenton, scrub out that gob!'

Polly laughed. 'I like it,' she justified. 'Anyway, its origins are Old English so there. I'm talking fourteenth century.'

Funny how over there I'm all BBC World Service – and yet back here, I'm pure Yankee Doodle Dandy.

Megan conceded defeat graciously but shot a worried glance at Polly that went unnoticed.

Quietly, she knew she could not continue to blame jet lag for Polly's distance. So what was causing it?

'Anyway,' Megan continued brightly, 'Max missed you to bits. I've spoken to him once a week on average.'

'Buster hasn't,' rued Polly. 'He asked me to marry him,' she suddenly announced. 'He proposed just before I left.'

'Buster?'

'Max.'

'Jesus, Mary, Joseph and *all* the Disciples!' Megan exclaimed, standing up and then sitting back down, 'why ever did you not tell me till now!' She was beaming and her eyes watered. Polly smiled from one corner of her mouth.

'It made me feel too far away whenever I thought about it,' Polly replied truthfully. Megan considered this and then nodded. 'So I am to be your bridesmaid, yes? Let's see, I'd rather like shot silk in burgundy. A column of it – cut for maximum cleavage exposure. And I'll wear my hair down and all gypsified. And I'll carry a single ivory rose – I'm not really the posy type. Let's go to Paris for your hen night. I'll come to John Lewis and help you choose your wedding list – loads of Le Creuset and fine Egyptian cotton. Oh Polly! Polly Fentonfyfield!'

'Perhaps,' said Polly. Megan pulled Polly's hair and pinched her on the arm.

'*Perhaps*, she says! My arse!'

'I have to accept first,' Polly explained, 'I have to say "yes" to Max.'

'What! You haven't said "yes"? When did he ask? Why haven't you, you dizzy cow!'

'I am a dizzy cow,' said Polly forlornly. Suddenly she looked small, confused and sad. Weary too. It upset Megan, who was still flabbergasted that Polly hadn't yet snapped the boy up with a million 'yes please's.

'You OK?' she asked quietly instead. Polly nodded and blinked away tears quickly, but not quick enough for Megan not to have noticed.

'I'm just tired,' Polly said. 'Must be the jet lag.'

Max and Dominic are in Waitrose. Extravagant, maybe, but Christmas three days away is reason enough. They cut a nice pair in this woman-dominant environment and housewives nudge each other as their trolleys pass.

He could pick my fruit! He could stuff my basket! I'd like to take him down an aisle or two! I wouldn't mind packing him! Bet he could deliver the goods!

The boys are oblivious: there is a job in hand and they've forgotten their list though it took most of the previous evening to compile. Consequently, they are making slow progress up and down the aisles. They cannot distinguish between goods that they need and those which merely tickle their fancy. Thus a packet of Cape gooseberries, taste unknown, is chosen because Dominic, who is slightly dyslexic, misreads them as 'syphilis' and thinks them a hoot. They also fill a large section of the trolley with 'something for Justin'. They often shop for Justin: just-in-case essentials, such as frozen pizzas, ready-made garlic bread, jars of Korma and Madras sauces and boil-in-the-bag rice.

'Gotta hava boxa Bud,' Dominic chants, disappearing down an aisle and out of sight, while Max stands in awe of the herb and spice selection. Max journeys on, choosing the darkest, cold-pressed olive oil because he's well informed that it is worth the extra four pounds. And its colour reminds him of Polly's eyes when she's particularly tired. Or sad. Or angry. Or worried. He has also read his Delia Smith, has our Max, and the realization that cooking may not be as complicated as he previously thought is very pleasing. He'll be cooking up a feast while Polly's home, veritable banquets fit for his queen.

Dominic returns, laden with a bumper-size carton of Budweiser beer. Max shoots him a withering look in jest and goes in search of Semillon-Chardonnay. When he returns, Dominic can hardly wait to show him the chocolate Rice Krispie cake he came across.

'Remember these? Joy of holy joys. Polly coming Christmas Eve and Boxing Day too?' he asks. Max nods. Dominic adds three more Rice Krispie cakes to the trolley for good measure and in spite of his brother's raised eyebrow.

'Are we agreed on wild mushroom risotto for Christmas Eve, duck on Christmas Day and, er, frozen pizzas and garlic bread on Boxing Day?' he asks Dominic.

'Agreed,' his brother confirms.

'I thought I'd try trifle,' Max continues, 'with this mascarpone stuff.'

'Use whatever you like — just as long as it's boozy,' Dominic nods. 'Where's Polly today?'

'With Megan. She's meeting us at the flat for lunch.'

'Megan too?'

'Don't think so.'

'The luscious Ms Reilly,' Dominic muses, 'will she be around over the festive period? Might this be my chance to wield my mistletoe with gay abandon in her direction? In her nether region? Might this be my chance just to take her out for a drink at any rate?'

'I do believe she's captured your heart,' Max commented nonchalantly.

116

'No,' Dominic dismissed him, rather too breezily, whilst taking great interest in the Schwartz spices, 'just my imagination.'

'Well,' Max said, 'I'm afraid she's going home to Limerick.'

'*There was a young lad called Max,*' Dominic begins, holding up a packet of iced buns for his brother's approval, 'what rhymes with Max?'

'Fax,' suggests Max, nodding vigorously at the cakes, 'wax, tax, thorax.'

'Hmm,' Dominic muses. '*There was a fine cad called Dom – who, da da da da –* help.'

'Aplomb,' proposes Max, taking a packet of frozen spinach, removing the bag of fresh from the trolley and surreptitiously placing it amongst the sliced bread, '*who seduced with panache and aplomb.*'

'*He —*' Dominic stumbles, 'go on?'

'*He thought with his dick.*'

'Hey?'

'*Which soon made the girls sick.*'

'What?'

'*So they'd turn for their pleasure to Tom.*'

'Who the hell is Tom?'

'I don't know,' says Max, 'but he rhymes.'

The Fyfields are at the check-out being checked out by the cashiers and customers alike.

'*There was a young girl called Polly,*' Dominic starts in a whisper, '*Who at Christmas wore nothing but holly.*' Max chuckles as he unloads the trolley. '*A sprig or two there,*' Dominic continues, '*was all that she'd wear.*'

'*She'd make your eyes water, by golly!*' Max concludes. It was so easy to imagine Polly decorated with the festive shrub, Max finishes the packing with a wry smile and a faraway gaze. Dominic prods him in the direction of the lift to the basement car park.

'Not a lot rhymes with Megan or Meg,' rues Dominic, bleeping the central-locking system of his Peugeot into life.

'Just as well, really,' says Max, loading the shopping into the boot.

When the brothers arrived home, Polly had been and gone. She left a note apologizing for breaking their lunch invitation but explained that she was full of cake and all talked out. She'd gone back home for a rest, she wrote, and would return later. Dominic could sense Max's disappointment. Historically, Polly would gladly await the return of the Fyfields from the supermarket because unpacking shopping was an activity she loved and they loathed.

'Jet lag,' he said to Max with a wise nod.

'Yes,' said Max quietly, holding the olive oil up to the light.

As he unpacked the shopping, he reprimanded himself for his melancholia.

It took a lot of bottle for her to go to the States in the first place. She was homesick at first, wasn't she? She spent the rest of term working hard on acclimatizing and she succeeded – I know because her letters became so much more narrative and factual than the very early ones of scumbled emotions. And now she's home, back where she started, back where she wants to be, but only for a fortnight.

He made room in the freezer for the Justins.

If I know Polly, she's probably just sad and worried that she'll have to leave again so soon.

He reorganized the spice rack, then he squeezed gently at the existing tomatoes and discarded any that wrinkled.

She was so emotional to be back. Strange squeaks was all I could make out as she came hurtling through Customs to cling on to me, her face buried in my neck. 'Can't look at you,' she pipped, 'don't know what to say.'

He regarded three open cartons of milk, sniffed at each and poured two away.

It was a funny journey back. She'd gabble nineteen to the dozen and then fall silent for ages. When we arrived at her flat, she walked very quietly around each room. It was as

118

she'd left it – good old Jennifer C. When Buster sauntered in, she regarded him in utter silence; it was only when he turned on his tail witheringly that she fell on her knees, scooped him up and squeezed him until he yowled.

He took down his copy of Delia Smith and checked off the shopping against her lists of ingredients.

And then we made love. On the settee. And then at last she looked at me and said my name. She's still tired and, OK, a little distant – I know that. But I reckon, of all people, I can tell between jet lag and some underlying issue. Polly's exhausted and disorientated, that's all.

He put Delia Smith back on the shelf, between the lava lamp and Dominic's litre tankard from Germany.

We need more cookery books.

TWELVE

*P*olly was indeed exhausted but jet lag was no longer accountable. It was the deluge of confused emotion threatening to consume her which she found so depleting. She felt shy of Max, that if she let him look into her eyes for any length of time he would surely see her contemplated infidelity written there. She tried not to give too much thinking time to Chip, but he popped up regularly in her mind's eye and she was slow to send him away. Nothing of consequence had passed between the two of them by the end of term, the smiles and walks and easy conversation continued in much the same way. Chip had not yet set his trap, for he esteemed timing and location greatly – and neither the one nor the other had been hitherto compliant. For her part, Polly felt safe being alternately appalled and titillated by her lust in utter privacy, and did not speak aloud of it, not even to herself.

Now, back in London, she would imagine Chip to be by her side as she walked or pottered about, and she spun elaborate fantasies; romantic films in miniature, complete with close-ups and score. And yet the one night she spent alone since her return, she thought only of Max and sobbed for him well into the early hours.

He's all I have.

The next day she clung to him; turning up at his flat at breakfast-time, begging him to let her sit quietly in his office and give her small errands to run; resting her head against his back with her arms about his waist as he did the washing up, snuggling up to him in the bath, on the sofa, in bed. Saying very little, looking very small.

The truth of it was that Polly felt totally disorientated being back in England and the emotion was new and utterly bewildering.

But I'm meant to love England without even thinking about it. Born and bred here, to live, love and die here – surely? Why's the place irritating me then? Why is it all so dull and dreary? Is my country to be my life?

Strangely, after comparatively so short a time, America seemed somehow preferable and Polly could convince herself quite easily that she was eminently more suited to life over there, a life far away from London and those who knew her.

But wasn't the Polly Fenton we first met proud to carry the Union Jack over the Atlantic in a breeze of floral cotton and a blaze of beautifully enunciated jolly goods, frightfullies, and super-dupers? Wasn't she the one so utterly committed to the life she was temporarily leaving? Didn't she positively thrive on the love and company of her friends, her surrogate family after all? Didn't she want for nothing but the security of her friendships and the certainty of Max, the love she felt and received? Wasn't being the life and soul a core part of her happiness and proof of her sense of belonging?

It continued to be, but somehow a secret part of her wished to trade communities. In England she now felt swamped and wary; in America she had felt capable, independent and vibrant. It took but a term to learn that not only could she survive all by herself in a foreign country and among strangers, but that she could actually have a rather wonderful time doing it. Suddenly, she found it a burden to be Polly Fenton amongst her established crowd in England, for she understood how they were utterly dependent on her being bright and breezy, chatty and open and, of course, unconditionally in love with Max Fyfield. As she'd always been; as, surely, she could only ever continue to be.

It seems there's so little about me that is sacred and private – admittedly, that's my own fault for loving my friends as deeply as I do and wanting to involve them in all aspects of my life and psyche. I mean, they're my family in all but flesh and blood. And yet, do you know, all of a sudden it's making me crave privacy. It's making me hold back.

Surrounded by those who adored her, Polly realized with horror that she dared not confide in any of them. Thus she felt more alone, here back home, than ever she had all the way over there. She knew that she was withdrawn and enormously tired, and was acutely aware and appalled that the combination created an unwelcome petulance about her.

'Everyone's so pleased to see me,' she explained to the craved-for silence of her flat, 'they're so happy to have me home yet I'm sullen, ungracious and distracted. Everyone's so interested in what I've been doing, who I've met, what it's like – and yet I curse them to myself and wish they'd shut up and leave me alone.'

How can they? When has Polly Fenton ever wanted to be alone and without attention?

'But they fuss over me, brandishing maps and "gee, honey"s and preconceptions, misconceptions and "*Ooh! tell us all about It*".'

Defining 'it' and adapting her replies to suit the enquirer, was demanding. At a gathering organized by the Fyfields in her honour three nights ago, Polly steered right away from even mentioning her companions at Hubbardtons, in favour of informed treatises on the Vermont weather, financial analysis of the cost of comparable things, and detailed portraits of the school, landscape and environs. Everyone kept informing her how glad she must be to be back home, with Max, with them.

Like I'm incomplete without them. There's more to me,

there is, I know it. I'm not just Max's girl, I'm not just their friend the teacher. I wish they wouldn't pressurize me so. I won't be the open book they take me for. An open book need not necessarily be a closed story.

Do you know, I think what I crave now is a secret of whose existence only I am aware. Like something hugely precious hidden in a drawer that only I know about, that I can literally take out, admire and enjoy, without anyone knowing about it, hurting no one. A private talisman, something of my very own that I can call on to give me pleasure and strength, to remind me of my success of being myself. A kiss from Chip would do. Undoubtedly.

Being back seemed only to make more of a muddle of it all. Yet how easily she could have opened up to Megan over the *mille-feuille* that morning. Instead, she had filled her mouth with cake and cappuccino to stop herself saying 'Help me Meg, what should I do? I'm in a quandary; suddenly the man that I love is not the same as the one I desire.'

How would Megan respond, Polly wonders this afternoon, in the safety of being alone in her living-room. In her mind, she makes her confidante offer a whole host of supportive suggestions.

a) Compassion (a sympathetic hand on Polly's arm): *God, how awful for you. I don't know what to say. Just tread carefully. Be utterly sure that you can handle it. I don't want you to end up hurt. What a dilemma.*

b) Excitement (a lively smile and a friendly pinch): *Ooh! Tell me again what he looks like – define his level of gorgeousness. Describe his hands again, and his eyes. Tell me once more how you felt – and where – when he walked you to the covered bridge that night.*

c) Conspiracy (heads locked together, eyes burning and alive): *You wicked wench, you! Just a kiss? With a real-life Brad Cruise? Who are you trying to kid! I'd go for full-blown sex, if I were you. Get it out of your system, girl – do it now, before you commit to Max for good.*

d) Sensible (a tender squeeze and a rub to her back): *The thing is, Polly, you'll probably regret it if you don't – which could have far more serious consequences than if you do. You'll be able to forget all about it once you have. If it's just a taste that you want, then stick out that tongue. One kiss can't hurt. It can't hurt if you're sure that just the one will suffice.*

There is point (e), of course, but Polly studiously ignores it because she has no control over it. She hasn't made that one up. It exists without her. Of course it does. I hardly need to disclose it.

e) Disgust: Megan's face criss-crossed with horror and utter bewilderment transcending the need for her to say *Are you completely mad, Polly? Could you really do that to Max? Jeopardize all that you have? You? Don't even think about it. Don't you dare.*

Buster stomped into the room and Polly changed the subject, quickly. The cat wound his body around her legs and then slumped down at her feet, cleaning his anus meticulously. Polly sat alongside him and scratched his neck, causing him to change target and lick at her hand as if it was part of his own anatomy. She thanked him and called him charming.

'Oh, cat,' she sighed, 'I can't think what to do – about the here and now or about the there and soon.'

Buster regarded her sternly and then sauntered away to sit on the window-sill and concentrate on the rain outside.

'It's not that I feel caught between two countries,' she said as she walked to the kitchen and put two slices of bread in the toaster, 'or even two men. It's almost as if I am swaying between two notions of myself and am unable to determine in which one lies reality. Polly the known, dependable, lively, friendly teacher and gregarious appendage to Max Fyfield? Or a young woman, turning twenty-eight, a little confused but acutely aware that her strength, independence and self-awareness are to be discovered, treasured.'

She shivered and held her face close to the toaster until

her eyes smarted and her nose tingled. At the back of her mind, Mick Jagger was singing '*You can't always get what you want*'.

'I know,' she told him, 'but you also said that perhaps if I try, I might get what I need.'

Damn. What is it that I need? A kiss from Chip? Can such a thing really be that weighty? Or do I need clarification that I do indeed want to journey into the sunset of my life alongside Max Fyfield?

Jim Morrison suddenly appeared to remind her that wishful was sinful.

'Hypocrite!' she accused him. 'If I told you someone's gone and lit my fire, you'd tell me to neither hesitate nor wallow.'

Now Mr Jagger was back, colluding with Mr Morrison, trying to gain her sympathy, to tempt her with their backlist of hits. Luckily, the toast popped up and came to her emotional rescue before she could break on through to the other side.

Marmite. Lots.

Have some toast with your Marmite, Max would tease. Polly could hear him so clearly.

'Ssh!' she protested, shaking her head to banish the image. She took the plate into her living-room and ran into Bob Dylan.

'Go away!' she shouted at him before he'd even opened his mouth, but not before he'd struck a chord.

'I need to update my record collection,' said Polly very loudly and with contrived breeziness, flicking the television on and then off again, having a quick sob with toast stuck in her throat.

THIRTEEN

'Keep still, stop bloody fidgeting!'

Dominic stepped in front of his tripod and regarded Polly with an expression so exasperated that she immediately begged forgiveness and promised not to move an inch. Polly frequently modelled for Dominic; never the main subject of his work, but as an accessory, a prop, for a variety of projects. Invariably, he required only parts of her and these she was willing to give because she loved his work and was flattered that he should want to use her body so creatively and with such an interesting use of focus and scale. Her knees had featured strongly in his last assignment, her earlobes and the nape of her neck in the one before that.

'Better,' he said from behind the lens to a drum roll of clicks, 'good.' He reappeared to rearrange her pose and she let him fiddle with her fingers and the lighting.

'It's a series for my next show,' he had explained to her, 'called "Time Pieces". I want to do imaginative things with watches and clock faces and the human hand and eye. Time passing, life passing, faces and eyes as indicators of it all.'

'And the fingers?' Polly enquired.

'Because, quite simply, they're incredibly photogenic

126

things. Just humour my bullshit-waffle – I make good photos in spite of it!'

Currently, Polly had an antique watch with a butter-soft leather strap twisted around her fingers.

'OK,' said Dominic, 'now pop it into the palm of your hand, close your fingers and then unfold them – just slightly – for a little peep. Look, watch me; like this. Excellent. Bugger,' he grumbled, 'can't see the hands.'

'Hey?' said Polly in disbelief, the camera appearing to focus on nothing else.

'Of the watch,' Dominic explained, 'can you move them so they read ten past one? Yes! Oh yes, lovely. Hold it. Great. That's it.'

They broke for a cup of tea and a softening digestive biscuit from a long since opened packet.

'Time's passing, Pollygirl.'

'Isn't it just,' Polly agreed.

'When's the big day, then?' Dominic asked with a little nudge.

'Day after the day after tomorrow,' Polly told him with a fleeting but telling sparkle.

Dominic fell silent and regarded her reproachfully. 'I meant,' he said, 'when are you going to marry my brother, not leave him?'

'I'm not leaving him!' Polly rushed, reddening. There was a perceptiveness to Dominic's tone for which she would never have credited him previously, and it unnerved her.

'So, then, when?'

'We haven't picked a date precisely,' she told him truthfully, and as breezily as she could.

'Oh.'

'Once I'm home for good,' Polly continued carefully, taking another digestive, bending it without eating it, smiling very widely for Dominic.

'So, you're leaving on Friday,' he responded through a slight shower of crumbs.

'Suppose,' she said, looking away quickly but not before a

mixture of grief and excitement scumbled across her face and settled as sludge in her eyes. She could not prevent it, she could not hide it; the blatancy was there for Dominic to witness. Consciously, Dominic let an edgy silence hang a moment longer. Polly wiped her hands on her skirt methodically and raised her eyebrows. 'Back to work?'

'My muse!' he proclaimed, letting her off the hook and banishing the unsettling image. 'Better take advantage of you while I can, eh?' He had no idea what to do with the inkling that something might be amiss.

Come on, take stock. I mean, this is Pollygirl Fenton we're talking.

'Now I'm going to zoom in on your eyes,' he told her, 'and then, later, transpose famous clock faces over your irises.'

Pity it won't be in colour – just get a load of that khaki hue.

Suddenly, the clock tower at Hubbardtons, between the main hall and the dining-room, flitted across Polly's mind and at once transported her back to Vermont. She could even smell morning grass. She shut her eyes and felt the fresh air against her skin.

Behind closed eyelids, Polly shifted her focus just slightly, over to the right, a little more – there! Petersfield House; colonial, wooden and pretty, her new home for her new responsibility as Dorm Mother to twelve girls. Sweep round 45 degrees, beyond the bike porch, to the hockey field. Beyond it, the sports hall, the gym, the Athletic Trainer's surgery. Behind it all, lofty Hubbardtons wearing the velvet mauve of its early winter plumage while awaiting its annual cloak of snow to swathe away its contours until spring.

Faintly, now louder: voices.

'Hey there, Polly, welcome back, honey.'

'Hi Polly, hold up!'

'Yo, Miss Fenton, good to see you.'

'Hey Fen'un, looking good. How's it going?'

Hullo Kate, hey Lorna, morning AJ, hullo Chip. It's nice to

128

be back. It's good to see you too. It's going fine. It's going to be fine.

'Oy!'

Who?

Polly opens her eyes.

Dominic.

Hampstead.

'I can't superimpose Big Ben or the Selfridges clock over closed eyelids!'

'I was miles away,' Polly apologized, still miles away and finding it difficult to get back.

A photographer's skill is his heightened sense of looking. Just then, Polly's vivid reel of Hubbardtons continued to run across her opened eyes. In an instant, Dominic saw.

She's gone already.

It explained so much.

Her distance. The change in her.

He walked towards her, the intensity of his gaze rendering her powerless to close her eyes again though she was desperate to, just to look away, even to blink.

She's hardly here at all. She wants to leave. She'd rather be over there. Something's happening to her. Something's happened. No. How can it? She's only Polly.

'What is it, Polly?' he asked, uncomfortably close to her face, his tone accusatory and unsettling. 'What's going on? Something's wrong, isn't it?'

'What?' she said with an edged laugh, Dominic's eyes still locked on to hers though she flitted her gaze desperately. 'Nothing's wrong.'

It won't be wrong. It's going to make things right.

'It bloody is,' Dominic countered. 'You've been,' he stumbled, 'you've been – you just haven't been you.'

'Dominic!' Polly protested, shivering as if she was as naked as she felt. 'What on earth are you going on about?'

'I don't know, Polly,' Dominic replied measuredly, backing away from her and regarding her through slanted eyes, 'you tell me. I just don't know. You've been distant and moody and that's not like you. In fact, *furtive* is the best word. Not pleasant, at any rate.'

'I'm just tired,' she pleaded in weak defence.

'Well,' said Dominic, dismantling his equipment, 'I don't want to photograph your eyes.'

'Dom!'

'No, Polly,' he said sternly, hands on hips, 'you won't do. I don't like what I see.'

'Hullo?'

'Megan?'

'Yes?'

'Dominic here. Fyfield. As in Maxanpolly.'

'Hullo there!'

There is only one Dominic. He needs neither introduction nor genealogical clarification. And he's on the end of my phone.

'Hi.'

'Hi.'

'I was wondering if you'd, er, if I could, um. I mean, it's Polly's last night, as you know, and she and Max are going to do something suitably romantic and private – you know, lots of candles, syrupy music and soft focus. So I was wondering if you'd like to go out for dinner. Or something.'

Sweet baby Jesus and his lovely mother Mary! Is Dominic Fyfield asking me out on a date?

'Um,' hesitated Megan for good effect and with a monstrous smile she was relieved Dominic could not see, 'well, actually, yes I would. That sounds lovely. Thanks. Great. See you later then.'

'Suitably romantic and private', hey Mr Fyfield? Better not be outdone by baby brother! Must phone Polly.

'Polly?'

'Meg!'

'You OK? Still on for tea and cake at three?'

'Yes. And yes. You?'

'Oh yes. But maybe not a whole pastry. Maybe we should *share*.'

'Oh?'

'Oh yes, I wouldn't want to spoil my *dinner* now, would I?'

'No?'

'Ho! Dinner *date*. I have one too!'

'Yes?'

'Indeed I do. The Fyfield Boy's just phoned.'

'Max? You joining us?'

'Dominic, you idiot woman.'

'Yo!'

'Pardon?'

'I'm sealing my approval with an expression of excitement!'

'Ah ha. See you at three then?'

'Later, dude.'

'Enough, Fenton. I know you're trying gently to ease yourself back into the swing of all things American, but just let me hear you say "Jolly good, tea at three".'

'Jolly good, tea at three.'

The girls shared a mountainous portion of pavlova. As it happened, Polly couldn't have managed a portion to herself anyway. The glut of emotions weighed heavy on her stomach. Dominic's intuition had surprised and unnerved her. She felt unsettled. She felt disorientated. She couldn't possibly leave England. She wasn't ready. Her trip home had passed so quickly. She didn't want to go back to America. She wasn't ready. What could she have been thinking? She wished she'd never gone out there in the first place. She regretted coming home to England for Christmas.

'You ready to go back?' Megan asked gently, right on cue. 'Packed?'

'No,' Polly replied, 'and no.' How she wanted to open up, to let Megan in; confide, seek advice, approval, disapproval

– whatever – just so she did not feel so alone and so solely responsible for any action she might take. Instead, she bit her cheek and held back, though she lacked the courage and the voice to speak anyway.

'What's in store for you, next term?' Megan asked, using her index finger as a spatula against the plate.

Don't ask.

'Pardon?'

'Well,' said Polly quickly, 'I'm moving from Kate's to Petersfield House to be a Dorm Mom—'

'Does that have capitals? Is it on your job description?' interrupted Megan.

'Yes and yes,' Polly smiled and nodded, 'and in class, we're going for manners and wit with a dose of Austen and Wilde.'

'They'll love that,' said Megan, etching dreamy expressions across the imagined faces of Polly's anglophile students.

'How about you?' asked Polly; desperate to be distracted, needing an anchor with England, keen to divert the focus away from herself.

'Mocks,' groaned Megan to Polly's say-no-more expression.

'And *you*,' Polly stressed, 'yourself?'

Megan's eyes glinted as she spun a lock of her hair through her fingers, a sly smile broadening across her lips. She arranged sugar cubes into the letter 'D' and then took one out, sucking on it luxuriously.

'I'm going to have a Dalliance with Dominic.'

'Just a dalliance,' Polly responded. It was not a question.

Now that Dominic had Megan all to himself and out of context, he was delighted to discover anew just how gorgeous she was. Previously, that she was Polly's close friend had somehow diminished her stand-alone merits. He had often flirted with her but elaborately and artificially because the very presence of Max and Polly had encouraged it. Tonight, there was no connection other than Max and Polly being absent and thus enabling this situation to have arisen. Dominic, aware and repentant that he had invariably acted up when in the presence of his brother, his brother's girl-friend and her soul-mate, now made a conscious effort to be himself. Megan, who had already pinched herself a number of times to verify the actuality of the evening, relaxed. To her delight, she discovered that Dominic was not merely a gor-geous playboy to whom she would have surrendered herself willingly anyway; he was also attentive, intelligent and witty. And all the more attractive because of it.

'Are you busy Saturday?' Dominic asked as coffee came and went and came again at his instigation.

'Saturday, Saturday,' Megan mulled, though a clear pic-ture of her even clearer diary came into view, 'yes, I think I am. I'll have to double-check, though.'

'Well, if you are free,' said Dominic, hoping sincerely that she would be, 'we could go to the flicks.'

'Have you seen the new Bruce Willis?' Megan asked, her eyes sparkling.

'No,' said Dominic, with his devastating grin, 'Max won't come and see it with me. Might you, then?'

'Will I!' Megan enthused, 'I love Brucie-boy. If I'm free.'

'Of course,' said Dominic, asking for the bill and winking, very quickly, but straight at Megan.

FOURTEEN

Max thought Polly looked quite the most beautiful he had ever seen her, standing there in her stockinged feet, her hand held by frail Miss Klee while they weathered a diatribe from an incensed Mrs Dale. Polly was wearing a softly tailored shift dress the colour of blackberry and her hair, recently trimmed to just below her jawline, her fringe skimming her neat eyebrows, gleamed like mahogany, framing her face and accentuating the shine of her eyes. A lick of mascara emphasized her eyes, a swipe of lipstick made her already kissable lips even more so. Slender, milky arms, gorgeous knees, shapely calves and dainty ankles; what a package! Max congratulated himself and thrust his hands deep into the pockets of his chinos to conceal his burgeoning erection.

'Good evening, Miss Klee,' he said, tipping his head in her direction, but with his eyes locked on to Polly.

'Good evening,' Miss Klee said to him with absolutely no recognition, 'is it evening?'

'It is,' said Max kindly, taking her hand from Polly's and leading her up the stairs to her flat, 'half past seven, already.'

'Mrs Dale,' he replied calmly over his shoulder, to a torrent of abuse, on his way back down, 'there is neither point nor merit in speaking like that. You will cause yourself an injury with all that rage. I shall turn the communal light off just as soon as we're safely inside Miss Fenton's flat.'

He performed this simple action as promised and closed Polly's door behind him, heaving out a theatrical sigh, 'Women!'

'Darling Max,' marvelled Polly, trailing her fingertips over his cheek and down the side of his neck, 'such a gentleman.' Max responded to the compliment with a flourish of a bow. Polly nestled against him, lost in her confusion but comforted by the sanctuary of his heartbeat.

'Do you love me?' he muffled into the top of her head. 'Will you miss me?'

'Yes,' said Polly, 'and yes.'

'You hungry?' he murmured. 'Shall we go?'

'Yes,' said Polly, 'and yes.'

Hampstead Heath was inky dark as they walked to their favourite restaurant in South End Green. It was like stepping into somewhere Mediterranean: pastel-washed walls, sunny waiters, fresh, colourful food, animated chatter; a perfect antidote to the damp chill of January in north London. The staff, uniformly camp and lavish with compliments, sashayed around the tables seeing to the diners' every need and pampering them for the duration of their visit. The quality of the dishes and the showmanship of the staff kept Max and Polly entertained. Their waiter hyperbolized on Polly's eyes and paid such attention to the details of Max's outfit that Max wondered whether he should just take the shirt from his back and leave it as part of the tip. When each dish was brought to the table, their waiter placed it down with such care and attention that Max and Polly felt almost guilty for disturbing the platter's design and eating the contents.

'You'll think back on this,' said Max, gazing with ardour at his zest-speckled chocolate orange terrine, 'when you're facing yet another muffin at that funny diner you told me about.'

At once, tears filmed Polly's eyes, stinging.

'Sweetie,' whispered Max, alarmed, reaching for her wrist.

'I'd almost forgotten that I have to leave tomorrow,' Polly explained in an extremely small voice.

'Are you not happy?'

'Not happy?' she gasped, bewildered.

'*There?*' stressed Max.

Polly smiled bravely but could not answer directly.

Neither Here Nor There – hey, Mr Bryson?

'It's OK,' she qualified, concentrating on a spoonful of creme brulée. 'I'm all right.'

'You'll be fine, Button,' Max said warmly, squeezing her wrist, 'Easter hols aren't so far away. You'll be back before you know it.'

Will I?

Polly mouthed 'I know', fighting against her tightening throat to keep her composure and finish her pudding.

It was nearing midnight when they arrived home, but it felt too early, too ominous to go to bed because they both knew that they would make love and then fall asleep, and that when they awoke it would suddenly be tomorrow and time for Polly to go. So, they made strong coffee and thought of things to talk about. They played three rounds of backgammon, they perused old photograph albums, they chose LPs over CDs for nostalgia's sake, and sang along.

'Not The Doors,' pleaded Polly, having already warned Max away from the Rolling Stones.

'Dylan?' he suggested. Polly puckered her eyebrows and shook her head.

'What, then?' Max laughed. 'Your record collection, though sizeable, is somewhat limited.'

'Something soft and mellow,' Polly said.

'So I suppose that's a "no" to – bloody hell, Frankie Goes to Hollywood?' exclaimed Max while Polly shrank on the settee, hiding her eyes in shame.

136

'Polly Goes to Vermont,' she then said forlornly, taking her hands from her face and regarding Max with sadness and affection.

'Relax,' he said.

'Don't do it?'

'How about Fleetwood Mac?' Max recommended, on the verge of exasperation, record sleeves fanned on the floor about him. 'Haven't heard them in ages.'

'Done,' said Polly.

'*Rumours*?' Max said.

'What? What do you mean?'

'*Rumours* or *Tusk*?'

'Oh,' said Polly, '*Rumours*, yes.'

The old vinyl crackled into life and Stevie Nicks's incomparably husky, corncracked voice provided great ambience for Polly and Max to fold into one another on the settee. Max was in her arms, resting his face against her breasts and it felt good, affirming for both; she kissed the top of his head again and again and tightened her clasp about him.

I love you so much. I know that I do. I don't want to hurt you.

Music filled the room and the lyrics confronted Polly's soul. Was she to make Max cry? To decimate his notion of love?

Shut up Stevie. Please. Don't. It isn't over now. It doesn't have to be.

Doesn't it? Will you be able to pick up the pieces and move forward?

I won't break anything. I promise. I'll be careful, so careful.

'Well, my own precious Gold Dust Woman,' yawned Max, raising a bleary face from Polly's embrace, 'I'm shagged – but not too shagged to shag. Bed? Come on, then.'

'Max,' said Polly, holding on to Max's trouser leg as he rose.

'What?' he said, stretching and blinking tired eyes.

She looked at him, all of him. 'Nothing,' she replied, allowing Max to pull her to her feet and lead her to her last night in England.

*

Polly hardly slept last night. Now, in the early hours of the day when once more she shall leave England, she gazes across at Max who has been coming more clearly into focus as the soft-silver light of dawn filters through the gap between curtains. She takes her finger lightly to his side-burn and follows it down to the start of his earlobe. She places the back of her hand under his nose and feels his warm, rhythmic breathing. She touches his bottom lip very gently but he twitches and gruffles and turns away from her. She lies in the half light and lets hot, oily tears scorch their way out to splash, dangerously loudly, on her pillow. She feels resigned, as if there is an inevitability about which she can now do very little. She doesn't want to go back to America but she doesn't really want to stay in England either. She oughtn't to have anything to do with Chip Jonson but she's looking forward to seeing him again. She loves only Max but knows that she cannot go forward with him just yet.

Didn't Tennessee Williams say something about a time for departure even when there's no certain place to go?

What if it was?

She cuddles up to Max.

'I love you,' she says with eyes closed and her cheek pressed against his shoulder blades, 'I. Really. Really. Do.'

'Loveyoutoo,' Max responds sleepily, patting her thigh, 'goback sleep.' She stays as she is, wishing she could be locked into the here and now forever. She can see the alarm clock. They have to rise in an hour. They have to leave in three. Her plane departs in six. This time tomorrow she'll still be fast asleep during the first night in her new accom-modation, in her new role. When she wakes, she won't have seen Max since yesterday; it will feel ages ago. So far away.

Polly did not scamper and dart as she had the morning of her September departure. Instead, she was methodical about preparing her flat for Jen Carter's return.

'What's she like?' she asked Max yet again. 'What does she look like?'

'Nice,' he shrugged, 'and nice.'

Carefully, Polly grafted the given image of Jen next to one of Chip.

Out of bounds. Out of order. See? Chip and Jen. Max and me.

'Anyway,' Max concluded, glancing at Polly's case and then looking away, 'Jen's paying your rent and being an excellent surrogate to Buster.'

'And I'm indebted,' said Polly, writing a brief note to the woman and Sellotaping it to the television; the best place, she presumed, for an American to find it.

Hang on – how much TV do I watch in the States? Hardly any – but more than Kate, that's for sure. Lorna doesn't even have one in her room. My students speak more of sports heroes and rock stars.

She removed the note and relocated it near to Buster's food supply in the kitchen.

'You ready?' asked Max.

'No,' said Polly, going to him and kissing him on the side of his lips.

'Shall we go?' he asked.

'No,' she replied, holding the door open for him and double locking it behind them.

Polly's calmness has been swept away by the rush and clutch of Heathrow. She panics that she is in the wrong queue, that her seat might be too far back, that the in-flight film will be the same as a fortnight ago, that she left the bathroom light on, that no one will meet her at Logan Airport. Max keeps a steadying hand on her shoulder and kisses her forehead at regular intervals. It serves only to tighten the knot in her stomach and harden the lump in her throat, but he is not to know and Polly doesn't tell him. She doesn't want to talk; she doesn't feel like it, she doesn't trust her voice, she doesn't know where to look. She holds on to his hand tightly, dropping contact only once or twice: when she has to go beyond a white line to check in, and at the very doorway of the ladies' toilet.

'You've a while yet,' says Max when she emerges. 'They haven't even called the flight. Coffee?'

Polly realizes how tired Max looks.

'Did you not sleep?' she asks him.

'Yes?' he answers, puzzled.

But he looks tired. And pale.

And you wonder why?

They don't say very much. Max musters interesting, detached topics for discussion but Polly obviously doesn't feel like answering in any detail, even less so when he tries to engage her to talk about the coming term at Hubbardtons. They end up sitting close and sipping in near silence – if there is such a thing at Heathrow.

'Do you want to be on your own?' he asks, not looking at her.

'No!' she jumps, horrified. 'What do you mean?'

'Here, silly,' he clarifies, 'while you wait for your flight.'

'No, no,' she shakes her head and reaches for his hand. He kisses hers. She kisses his back. 'Please wait,' she asks.

'OK,' he says.

The departure board flashes up that the flight has a two-hour delay.

'Go if you want,' she says, 'don't feel you have to wait.'

'Maybe,' Max says, 'would you mind?' Polly shakes her head and looks away. 'I've a backlog of work now – you bloody distraction, you!'

'Go if you want,' she says forlornly.

'Do you want me to go or something?' Max laughs.

'No!' Polly exclaims, horrified that she is so easy to read.

'Airports are unsettling,' Max defines, 'I don't know, there's a sort of finality – different to seeing someone off from a station or a doorstep.'

'Taking to the skies?' Polly suggests.

'Yes,' Max says, 'flying off into the sunset. Flying away.'

'Do you want to go?'

'I'll go, then.'

'If you want to.'

'You'll be all right?'

'I'll be fine.'

'Have a mooch around Duty Free?'

'I'll be fine.'

As Max is about to leave, Polly wants to renege her consent but she can't and she doesn't.

'I'll just go to the loo,' she says, 'will you wait?'

'Well, I'm going too – so we'll meet back here then.'

Sitting in the cubicle, Polly weeps sharply. She doesn't want Max to leave, but she knows she's no company for him to want to stay. She splashes cold water on her face, her cheeks burning, her eyes red; she can hardly look at herself but a glance is all that's needed.

What am I doing? What is all this? Where have I gone? Mad, I've gone mad. What can I be thinking? Risk all of this? Madness.

She can't stay in the toilets forever. It's hardly the place to take deep breaths. Consequently, when she emerges and sees Max waiting there, she breaks down.

'Sorry sorry sorry,' she pleads into his chest.

'Button, hey,' he soothes, 'sorry for what?'

'It's gone so quickly,' she sobs, looking at him briefly, 'my trip home. I haven't done enough. I haven't been – nice.'

'Silly,' Max chides lovingly, 'what are you talking about?'

'I've been – distant. Tired.'

'Well,' Max ponders kindly, 'I haven't taken anything by it.'

But you should have, you should have! You shouldn't have stood for it! You're too good. You're an accessory. I love you so very much – far more than I like myself.

'Hey, come on now,' he says in a sensible voice, searching for a tissue and blotting her tears with his thumb in the meantime, 'it kills me to see you like this. Upping sticks to another country is an emotional as well as physical upheaval. You must have just about felt settled over there, when you had to return home and pick up where you left off in September. It can't have been easy for you; I know that, I know you.'

No you don't. Don't let me off the hook! Tell me off. Threaten me.

Polly bit her lip and sniffed, clutching at Max's arms to steady her, to keep him with her.

Please don't go. Please say I don't have to go.

'Come on, Button mine,' he hugs her hard, 'no more tears. It makes me so sad – and the image lingers. I need your smile to take away with me, to see me through till Easter.'

Polly looks as if she is about to cry afresh.

'Go on,' Max nudges her, 'a tiny one. Go on. Just for a mo'. A millisecond, then.' Max photographs her from every angle with an invisible camera, saying 'Cor, what a stunner!' in Cockney. Polly can't help but smile and laugh.

'You OK?' he asks, once his imaginary film has been used twice over.

'Fine,' Polly affirms, 'I'm fine.'

'I'm going to go,' Max nods, scouring her face with concern and love. 'The sooner I've gone, the sooner it will be that I'm with you again. I think. If you see what I mean.'

Polly smiles in understanding.

'Oh – kay,' he lingers.

''Kay,' says Polly, standing on tip toes to kiss him good-bye.

He has walked away from her. He is walking towards the sign for the car parks. She closes her eyes and opens them again, the split second of detachment serving to allow her to see him afresh: a figure, a man, attractive and masculine, nicely dressed, a lovely walk. He is being stopped by two ladies dressed in saris the shades of the sun. They are asking him something, probably because he looks so approachable and kind, knowledgable; one who might help. He is listening carefully, looking about him, craning his neck, scouring

142

the departure hall. He points for them but they're short women. Polly watches as he takes control of their trolley and leads them through the throng. She loses sight of him and walks towards where he stood. She locates him some way away; the women are thanking him profusely but he is holding his hands up in a don't-mention-it way.

He's so lovely.

He leaves them. He doesn't see Polly. Two small children are charging about, heading in his direction; he weaves and dips to keep out of their way. One collides with his leg and takes a tumble. Max sets the child straight. The child runs off.

He's so special.

Max walks on. Polly is watching all the time. He goes to a news stand and emerges with the *Guardian* and a carton of Ribena. He's looking up at the sign for the car parks. He's walking with conviction. He's gone. Polly can no longer see him.

He's gone.

Yes.

My God, no!

She dodges the crowds and heads in the direction he took.

What on earth have I been thinking. It's him. Only him. Only ever him. For ever.

'Max!'

Can't you see? No one could love me more.

He's in sight but he can't hear her. He's fiddling with change and token at the ticket machine.

'Max!'

He's pressing all sorts of buttons. He's scratching his head and laughing with other bemused drivers. Polly runs towards him, something hard in her small rucksack digs into her back.

So what?

'Max?' she's out of breath but with him. He looks amazed, his eyebrows are doing a funny, lovely dance.

'Max?'

'What are you doing here?' He guides her away from the

whirring machine to a nearby corner but it smells of urine so he steers her away, backtracking towards the departure hall.

'Sweetie,' he soothes, kissing her cheek while he closes a hand behind her neck, 'silly thing.'

'No,' she says, clearly and rather loudly.

'Not silly?' he asks.

'No,' she is wide-eyed and adorably serious.

'OK,' he says slowly. He looks at his prepaid ticket to the car park. 'Darling, I have to go – these things are only active for eight minutes – then the cars spontaneously combust. And I'm arrested. I think.'

Polly nods vigorously. Her heart is thundering though she is no longer out of breath.

'Bye bye?' he asks.

'Max!' she all but shouts.

He regards her and cocks his head, 'Yes?'

'I will,' she declares, 'I will. I will, I do, I shall, yes. Yes, yes.'

'Crikey!' he marvels at her enthusiasm. 'Wow.' He tips his head the other way, 'you will *what*, exactly?'

'Marry you!' Polly announces, triumphantly, 'you bloody bet your bottom bloody dollar I'll marry you.'

Max bursts out laughing. 'Haven't you said yes to me already, then?'

LENT

Icy finger wave
Ski trails on a mountain side
Snowlight in Vermont

Karl Suessdorf & John Blackburn, *Moonlight in Vermont*

FIFTEEN

*A*n exposure to too much altitude, combined with the crossing of too many time zones and the slightest change in culture or landscape, can all play havoc with the mind, the heart and the most resolute of souls. Polly Fenton, well aware of this, was determined that it would not be so with her. Fortuitously, the mundanity, the back-to-work and down-to-earthness which met her, were a far cry from the stylized emotional reunions she'd conjured and half-anticipated, direct from a lot at Universal Studios. In reality, she seemed to settle back into her routine much more easily than she had in London. This in itself was affirming.

Seductive even.

And then there was the snow.

Polly hadn't expected snow, but a recent dusting greeted her on arrival in Boston (Kate was there to meet her, of course she was) and had enveloped the town of Hubbardtons with a cosy sound-proofing by the time they arrived back. It was all so picturesque, so bewitching. With the start of Lent Term still a few days off, Hubbardtons Academy was blissfully quiet too. Even Mount Hubbardton seemed somewhat diminished by its gentle powdering of young snow. Only Hubbardtons the river and Hubbardtons the General Store bustled as usual.

'Polly Fenton,' Kate declared, stamping snow from her shoes, regarding Polly greeting all the familiar faces on the fridge of smiles, 'you've had a haircut and you've gotten thinner – and you look tired and pale.'

'Gosh, do I?' Polly responded, twisting her hair between finger and thumb and checking her reflection in the window. Amused at the return of her clean vowels and choice vocabulary, she asked, 'Was I awfully fat before?'

'Hell no!' chided Kate, 'you just look a little – well, *little*.'

It was lovely to hear the word pronounced with a click and roll of the tongue, without concession to one 't', let alone two. Polly made a note to practise her pronunciation a li'le la'er.

'You go on some kinda diet?'

'Gracious no!'

'You forget to eat?'

'Honestly, I ate plenty.'

'That guy of yours some lousy cook?'

'On the contrary,' remonstrated Polly, 'I do declare!'

'Well,' said Kate, gouging a huge wedge from something brown and gooey, 'wrap your lips around this and tell me all about your trip home.'

The snow, the brownies, Kate's affection – Polly felt she was being wooed.

But now, I can be seduced without falling prey.

'I'm going to marry Max,' said Polly with a full mouth some minutes later, chocolate chips wedging themselves to her teeth while globs of marshmallow threatened to glue her jaws together.

See!

She masticated and hummed while Kate beamed her approval and congratulated her heartily.

'That's so so *nice*,' Kate clapped, 'Polly's getting wed. You must bring Max over here some time.'

'Certainly,' said Polly, contemplating aside how she would have said 'you bet' if she was still back in London.

Wondering, quietly, why she and Max had not arranged such a visit.

It's not the right time. I'm working. Later, maybe.

'You want to stay here tonight?' Kate asked. 'Move into Petersfield tomorrow?'

Polly accepted another monstrous portion of Kate's heavenly concoction and thought hard while she licked and chewed.

'Do you know,' she said at length, smacking her lips and attempting to dislodge debris from her teeth with her finger and tongue, 'if I stayed tonight, not only would I not leave tomorrow, I very probably would not leave at all.'

'I'm cool with that,' Kate smiled.

'And so, no doubt, would my future Dorm Daughters be,' Polly laughed.

'Jeez,' said Kate, holding her head in her hands, 'can you only imagine! No problem, we'll move you this afternoon – only come for dinner tonight, hey? You've already gotten a sneak preview of dessert.'

Petersfield House was a traditional, planked Vermont dwelling of three principal floors and a further floor converted from the attic. It was painted white; the window frames and bannister around the porch, blue-grey. The ground floor was taken by the McLellan family: Rick McLellan who taught science, Martha McLellan who taught computing and their toddlers Billy and Kevin who, in their infancy, had taught many a fascinated student how to change a diaper and make a lullaby effective. Up a floor to five bedrooms, three of them doubles, for the students; onwards to the second floor with the Dorm Mother's apartment, the 'easy' room and the bathrooms; finally the top floor, divided into four single bedrooms of quirky dimensions and slanted ceilings, most usually given to seniors.

Polly had been shown her apartment at Petersfield House towards the end of the previous term but now, whitewashed (more of a lemon-vanilla wash) and sparkling, she felt she was viewing it anew. An 'L' shaped sitting-room with a tiny kitchenette and a picture-perfect view to Mount Hubbardtons led to a small double bedroom with a rather luxurious and large bathroom *en suite*. Polly loved it at once and went about unpacking, singing *My My Hey Hey* in a very passable Neil Young accent. She sang *Sugar Mountain* all the way through in honour of Mount Hubbardtons' icing-sugar sprinkling while she arranged her books and cassettes on the shelves in the sitting-room. Unfortunately, she was humming *Only Love Can Break Your Heart* when she came across her framed photograph of Max but changed her tune at once to *Heart of Gold*, singing it melodiously while she placed the photograph by the bed and gazed on it a while.

With Marmite in my cupboards and my boy by my bed, this place is now home indeed.

Polly went to check the view from the bedroom window. It looked out across the hockey pitch to the gyms. And the athletic trainer's surgery. She noticed in passing, that's all.

I wonder who else'll notice my haircut.

Term started with a great spewing of bag-laden children from an army of station wagons and Cherokee Jeeps.

'Parents!' Polly marvelled to herself, skipping downstairs. 'Do you know, it didn't really occur to me that my kids have *parents*. I thought of them as, I don't know, *autonomous* – because we all live here together and don't go home at night. But here they are with their other families, their life that stretches pre- and post-Hubbardtons Academy.'

As she went to meet and greet, she thought how much smaller and younger the students appeared when seen alongside the adults who bred them.

'Hey Miss Fenton, great hairstyle! Will you come meet my folks?'

'Of course, AJ, it'll be a pleasure.'

When AJ introduced her to his portly father and rather glamorous mother, Polly realized she had absolutely no idea of their surname. When she thought a little deeper, she found she didn't even know what the A or the J stood for. Luckily, the indigenous geniality for which Americans are famed, and often unfairly derided, bowled in to the rescue.

'Steve Harvey,' AJ's father boomed, brandishing a smile of an inordinate number of teeth, shaking Polly's hand and squeezing her arm warmly, 'An-th-ony has told us so much about you. This is my wife, Jenny.'

'Jenny Harvey,' smiled the wife, repeating the warmth of the greeting with just as many pearly teeth, and taking Polly's free hand in both of hers, 'An-th-ony's nose has been buried in books the whole vacation.' She whistled slowly in appreciation. AJ blushed and shuffled.

'Jolly good!' Polly declared, obviously to Steve and Jenny's delight as they tightened their hold on her hands. 'He's a pleasure to teach and should do really well.'

'Miss Fenton,' AJ muffled once his parents had gone to shake Lorna's hands, 'please don't call me An-th-ony, OK? I like being AJ.'

'OK,' said Polly slowly, 'but I'll seal my promise if you'll tell me what the "J" stands for.'

'Gawd, do I got to?'

'You mean, "Dear Lord, must I?" And for that aberration, yes you must!'

'Jerome. It's Jerome.'

'Jerome, OK, Jerome – but that's a terrific name, couldn't I call you by it?'

'Please don't. Just AJ?'

'Want to know my middle name?'

'Sure.'

'Elizabeth.'

'Wow! Like the Queen?'

'One and the same.'

'Cool.'

'Yeah, so I guess on the whole they're a good bunch – but, as I say, keep a watch on Beth and Johanna.' Rick McLellan was advising Polly on her Dorm Daughters.

'Beth who was caught smoking drugs,' Polly reminded herself out loud.

'That's right, she's on a S.A.P.,' Rick confirmed.

'S.A.P.,' spelt Polly, closing her eyes and murmuring 'Student Assistance Programme' for confirmation. 'And S.A.T.s,' she continued, somewhat triumphantly, tossing her hair, eyes now open, 'are Scholastic Aptitude Tests.'

'You got it,' Rick clicked his tongue, 'but don't ask me what G.C.S.E stands for – or why your private schools are public! Anyhow, back to Beth and the S.A.P. Drugs mean final probation status, straight up. She had to sign a contract with the S.A.P. and if she violates that – in any way – she's out. She'll continue to be randomly tested and evaluated by an outside counsellor.'

'For a year,' said Polly.

'Yup, a year. Pretty pricey – random testing's forty bucks a pop. Anyhow, she's half-way through and she's a good kid. She just made one emotionally and financially expensive slip-up.'

'And Johanna?' asked Polly, thinking that no doubt half the fifth and sixth forms at BGS would be on S.A.P.s if their extra-curricular activities were researched.

'Johanna,' Rick said carefully, 'kinda likes the guys.'

'Say no more,' Polly laughed, accepting Rick's invitation to join his family for coffee, and to teach his sons an English nursery rhyme.

There were twelve girls in her sitting-room, most taller than her. Polly recognized them all but knew by name only the five who were in her English classes. She had yet to put faces to the infamous Johanna and Beth but found she had guessed correctly once each girl had introduced herself.

'Super,' said Polly, asking Beth to pass the Coke around. 'Well, as you know, I'm Miss Fenton – and I like to think that, as a teacher, I'm reasonable, fun and young. And I take absolutely no nonsense whatsoever, however inventive the excuse. Respect me and I'll respect you. Cross the line, or ignore it – and I'll have your guts for garters.'

The girls were stunned into a fear-drenched silence.

'Our what for what?' Jodie whispered, trying to see through Miss Fenton's floaty skirt for hideous proof.

'Exactly,' Polly whispered back, drumming her fingers against her thighs. It was only when she winked, still straight-faced, that a hushed cycle of relief was exhaled. Polly smiled broadly. 'Tell you what, once your rooms are shipshape, you can show me around and we can have a good one-to-one.'

The idea was met with approval and Polly noticed the girls looking around her apartment.

'You can tell a lot about a person by the way they organize a room – and their belongings therein, of course.'

'Yeah right!' laughed Zoe, brandishing a clutch of Polly's cassettes, 'Fleetwood Mac – yes siree!'

Soon enough, all twelve girls were analysing Polly's musical tastes and finding much amusement in the process; even greater entertainment in the results.

'OK, OK,' Polly said, 'I'm unashamedly old and square.'

The girls observed her with sympathy. Most of them thought her quite stylish, in a quaintly English way, with her neat figure set off by her floaty skirt and black, skinny rib polo neck, her sweet face framed by her glossy, straight bob.

'But,' Polly continued, letting the silence hang until the girls' attention was restored, 'I am both teacher and Dorm Mum – and, for both, it is a *prerequisite* to be old and square. So, listen up while I run a few rules by you – OK?'

The girls gathered loosely around her while she discoursed about tidiness (brushing down her jumper for emphasis), study hours (nodding towards her old brass alarm clock), telephone permission (grabbing her own handset and holding it aloft) and exit passes (reading the rules verbatim from the guidelines issued by Powers Mateland).

'Girls,' Polly warned, 'just remember your guts and my garters.'

All twelve observed her before nodding and saying 'Sure, Miss Fenton', practically in unison.

'Lorna!'

'Polly!'

Having seen each other at various distances during the day, this was the first opportunity they had had for a few minutes together so they grabbed each other and hugged in reunion. Lorna ruffled Polly's hair, which she straightened immediately.

'How was Christmas?' Polly asked. 'And the lovely Tom?'

'Pretty cool,' Lorna nodded, 'both of them. And Max?'

'Darling Boy,' Polly proclaimed, 'I've loads to tell you.'

'Me too,' said Lorna.

'Why don't you come up to my rooms during study hour?' Polly suggested.

'Just you try and keep me away!' Lorna drawled. 'Hey Chip!'

Where?

Oh yes.

'Hey guys,' said Chip, looking only at Polly, 'how's it going?'

'Fine,' Polly sang, disappointed that she'd noticed anew just how handsome the man was.

Merely an objective observation, come on now. And how come he hasn't objectively acknowledged my new haircut?

'Pretty good,' said Lorna.

'Cool,' said Chip. 'Great bangs, Polly.'

'What? Did you?' Polly retorted, at once flustered. Chip looked imploringly at her and then made a strange motion across his forehead. However, it took Lorna to tweak Polly's fringe before she could make the translation.

He noticed!

'How was your Christmas?' Polly asked, eager to establish a casual and ordinary atmosphere to serve as a footing thereafter.

156

'It was a lot of fun,' Chip acknowledged. 'How was it for you? In the orphanage?'

Polly punched him lightly on the arm and said her Christmas had been brilliant.

Chip looked up at the sky.

'It's gonna be one helluva season,' he said to Lorna. 'We gotta get Fen'un up on skis.'

'Absolutely,' Lorna agreed.

'I'm game,' chirped Polly, delighted to be called by her surname, especially with its 't' being dropped. She accepted Chip's slow, penetrating smile at face value only.

'Hey, I gotta split,' he said, 'check you later.'

'Later,' Lorna replied.

'Cheerio,' said Polly.

'*Check you later* – gee, that guy,' said Lorna as she and Polly marvelled at the sight of him jogging across the hockey pitch. Lorna looked to Polly as if she was expecting some sort of answer.

'Yes,' Polly said.

'Yes?' Lorna queried.

'Yes, he's a nice bloke.'

'He's a danger,' said Lorna with a light but knowing look. 'Beware. Be wary.'

'Me?' Polly snorted.

'Yes you,' Lorna said, 'it's you he'd like to "check later". I know what he's like. And I know what he likes. And I know, too, that he always gets what he wants.'

'*You can't always —*' Polly began to sing. Lorna hummed alongside her and then they both devolved into giggles, la-la-ing away.

'Anyway,' said Polly, 'aren't you forgetting Jen Carter?'

'*I'm* not – but don't put it past him to.'

'Look,' said Polly, 'thank you for your concern. Chip Jonson is a really lovely chap and fiendishly good-looking too. But I have Max Fyfield. And I'm afraid poor Mr Jonson pales into insignificance in comparison. You really have nothing to worry about me. I'm sorted.'

157

'That's good,' Lorna all but warned, 'I'm pleased to hear it.'

'You'll be even more pleased,' Polly said, 'to hear that I'm going to marry him.'

'Max?'

'Max.'

SIXTEEN

*W*hen Polly had been back in England for Christmas, it had been easy to recall and denounce America a dangerous place fraught with emotional pressure, to blame it for her inner turmoil. It was only on returning that Polly realized the accusation could be more fairly levelled at her home country. Life in Vermont had slipped smoothly into a prosaic routine; though her days were fantastically full, they were relatively free of stress. Indeed, the most taxing thing to have befallen her so far was a return to Manchester with Lorna on their one free day off. The dilemma, over which she expended much energy and deliberation, was whether or not to buy the microfibre body from the DKNY outlet. She decided to be abstemious, and was resolutely so – until two miles out of town when she made a screeching U-turn, paid cash and said not to bother with a bag.

Of course, Polly fully empathized with the plight of her senior students studying for their S.A.T.s, consequently giving over much of her free time to extra lessons on Charles Dickens or the vagaries of punctuation. Similarly, she was accommodating to any of the Petersfield girls who required her advice, her English copy of *Elle* magazine, or merely her company. Often they came to her with a variety of problems which she found, to her pride and their relief, she could quite easily unravel for them. She had hated being at boarding-school when she was the pupil; it was thus heartening now to see how such an institution could really function, to contribute actively to its success, to be an essential stitch in its fabric.

A lovely, colourful American quilt.

Being Dorm Mother was long, hard work but rewarding too. Polly was on duty from eight in the morning until lights out at ten thirty at night, thirteen days out of fourteen. She enjoyed the company, she liked the daily routine at Hubbardtons, she loved eating in the dining-room surrounded by the din of animated chatter. She was a part of this special community. With its beautiful buildings ergonomically laid out, it was like living in a safe, hermetic village where the worries of rent and bills, neighbours and landlords, had no place. Most of all, Polly loved her students indiscriminately; those who shone academically, those who were the clowns of the class, those who tried so hard, those who just bumbled along. She was not prejudiced.

I am a teacher – how could I be? I love my students – I am a teacher, how could I not? They are my clutch, my brood.

Polly just about found time alone for long enough to write brief letters home. She had written to Max at length when she first arrived back but as soon as school was in session, she quite literally had to cut corners: for her second letter, she took scissors to the page and created a heart shape which she filled with sweet nothings because there was very little to recount anyway. This term, however, Polly felt no guilt about the briefness of her notes back to Max; though incredibly busy, she made the time to think of him, to repeat to herself that they would always be together. Her one letter to Megan merely compared and contrasted S.A.T.s with A levels, with a *'P.S. Say hullo to Dominic'*. Usually, she sent a message to him via her letters to Max, but she now felt shy and wary, fearing that if Max relayed her regards it might provoke Dominic to confide his doubts.

Dominic, Dominic – you had it all wrong. There was only ever your brother for me. No question of it, no question at all. Not any more. Not now.

And Chip? Chip Jonson continues to be, as Polly herself says, a very nice chap – she has taste and discernment and the determination not to be fooled by appearances alone. They have waved at each other from afar and Chip has been up to visit her on a few occasions. Though she has never been on her own, he has stayed long enough to enjoy a glass of Coke and light conversation with the goggle-eyed students and their glance-avoiding teacher. However, it is the fact that Polly is dodging eye contact, however subconsciously or conscientiously, that heartens Chip the most. He is now presented with more of a challenge than he would have anticipated, considering the state of affairs at the end of last term, but he doesn't mind. He rather relishes the ingenuity he must now effect in setting his trap.

Chip Jonson might not subscribe to monogamy or fidelity, but is it not merely opinion and society which extol and validate these principles as virtues, and condemn those who refute them as immoral? As sinners?

Can't certain sins be fun too?

And, ultimately, edifying?

Chip means no harm, he simply loves sport.

'It's like fishing,' he muses to himself, having bandaged the last limb for the afternoon, 'I'm just the guy who lays the bait – the decision whether or not to take it is out of my hands. Women get hooked – and I reckon they enjoy the exhilaration of the reeling in and all. Being admired. Finally, being released.'

He looks out of the window and observes the third-floor bedroom window at Petersfield House. In the corner of his surgery, his beloved fishing rod is propped. Near to it, a picture of him; in shorts, bare-chested, hair tousled, lips in a broad smile and biceps taut as he holds aloft a twelve-pound salmon for the camera and posterity.

'I always release what I catch,' he says quietly as he ventures to the photograph to scrutinize the precise details. 'When I let that fish go, it just hung around in the shallows, quite happily, before making for home.'

Ah, but if you saw a most beautiful salmon swim so near to your bait, circle it even, but then decide to swim away, would you not cast your line again? And again?

Christ, that would be some fish – sure I would!

Polly came across Zoe who was in tears and utterly inconsolable. She had popped back to Petersfield in the lunch hour and, from her bathroom, heard the sound of crying from the floor above.

'Zoe,' she said gently on discovery, 'poppet, what ever is it?'

'Leave. Me. Please,' the girl stammered through her sobs.

'Hey,' Polly soothed before continuing carefully, 'you simply can't weep all by yourself – what a dreadfully lonely thing to do.'

This raised the corners of Zoe's mouth slightly but Polly's warm smile in return served only to replenish the tears.

'Come, come,' she said, kneeling in front of the girl, 'I can't have my Dorm Daughter so forlorn.'

Polly laid her hands softly on the heaving shoulders and the gesture, combined with her persistent tenderness, caused Zoe to sink into her embrace and really let go. Polly encouraged the girl to cry, comforting her with a host of soothing, maternal locutions until the sobbing subsided and the child was still.

'I'm sorry,' Zoe sniffed, 'I, like, trashed your shirt.'

'Blimey, don't worry about this old rag,' Polly exclaimed, regarding the sodden patch on her shirt before lying, 'I've had it yonks.'

'You're so funny,' Zoe smiled through the blur of her tears.

'That's better,' Polly praised. 'Now, share your problem and I promise you, though it may not be solved, it will certainly be halved.'

'I don't know,' Zoe faltered.

'I *do*,' Polly stressed.

'I guess,' Zoe responded, regarding Polly warily as if to make absolutely sure. Polly shuffled on her knees around the girl and then sat beside her, their backs against a wall adorned with photographs of Zoe's pets.

'I say,' said Polly, nodding towards the opposite wall which was smothered with posters of the leering, posturing Guns & Roses and other motley crews, 'if we're going to snuggle down to a heart to heart, I'd rather our backs were to *that* wall. They're deliciously frightening. They're making me feel rather faint!'

'They're the only men in my life,' rued Zoe bitterly.

'Fine,' Polly announced, 'we'll stay put and try not to be distracted.'

'*They're* the only men in *my* life,' Zoe repeated, imploringly. Polly took it as her cue.

'Boyfriend trouble?'

Zoe nodded.

'You know I've been, like, seeing Jim? Broad?'

'Is he?'

'Jim *Broad*, Miss Fenton.'

'God, yes of course, my Thursday morning set.'

'Anyhow, I found out that he was – you know – like, going with Tammy over the vacation?'

'Where to?'

'No. You know – like, making *out*?'

'Out. Oh. I see. Hang on, *Tammy*? Scott? She's in my Wednesday juniors?'

'Yeah. Slut.'

'Hey!'

'Well she is.'

'Go on—'

Zoe continued rapidly, with the inflection typical of American teenagers – raising the tone at the end of almost every sentence into a question of sorts. 'Jim says to me it was just, like, a *thing* – you know? A one off? He swears it meant nothing? Before, during or after? Crying and all? I go, so how come you did it then? He goes, I dunno? It just kinda happened. I say, so what now? He goes, I love you? And all that shit—'

'I beg your pardon.'

'Excuse me. So he says, like, how he feels for me? And that he doesn't want anything to change? He goes, she didn't mean shit to him? Excuse me. But, you know? Do I believe him? Like, can I? How can I ever forget?'

'How do you feel, you yourself?'

'I don't know, you know?'

'Rejected?'

'Sure.'

'Cross?'

'Ma'am, I'm *mad*.'

'Insecure?'

'You bet.'

'Untrusting?'

'Yeah. But, you know, most of all: hurt? I'm hurting so goddam much it's making me throw up.'

'You poor, poor bunny.'

It was all Polly could reasonably say. She hugged the child, stroked her hair and kissed the top of her head while making soothing noises; staring over to bare-chested Bon Jovi and thanking whoever that she'd nipped whatever it was, or could have been, in the bud.

'Hullo, Chip,' says Polly, returning to Petersfield from coffee with Kate. It is ten to eight at night, study hour starts in ten minutes.

'Hey Fen'un,' says Chip.

Snow has been falling for most of the afternoon and is deliciously crunchy underfoot. Now, at night, it casts a silver luminescence while wrapping silence around the land like a duvet.

'Man, you're one busy woman,' he exclaims.

'Tell me about it,' Polly responds kindly, deciding to forgo an analysis of Chip's hermaphroditic allusions. She looks at her watch. 'I'd better rush,' she says, waving her thumb in the direction of the front door, 'study hour and all that.'

'Your watch must be fast,' says Chip, looking at his, 'it's not yet five of eight.'

'I'd invite you up,' Polly says, 'but I've a heap of marking, plus Jane Laskey is coming up for a blitz on Dickens' characters as victims of circumstance.'

'Sounds like a bunch of fun,' Chip nods, wedging the toe of his boot into the snow.

'Oh,' Polly responds ingenuously, 'it's more than fun, it's wonderful.'

'You should see Hubbardtons at this time of year, at night, when there's snow.'

'Which?' Polly laughs, 'mountain, river, town or general store?'

'The river,' Chip laughs back, 'I know this place, about a mile off? It'll be looking so pretty. You want to go some time?'

'I'd love to,' Polly says.

Maybe Lorna would like to come along too.

'Cool,' Chip responds.

'Only I doubt that I have some time – I hardly have *any* time!' Surreptitiously, Polly gathers a fistful of snow from the gate behind her.

Poor bloke. Now that I'm holding the reins, I feel a little sorry for him and his futile wooing. Maybe I'll make a snowball and lighten the tone.

Chip shrugs and smiles and pulls out his trump card, 'Listen, I've not had the chance to tell you, but I have some news.'

'Oh yes?' Polly says, furious that her heart has picked up its beat a little.

'Yup,' Chip confirms, thrusting his hands into the pockets of his jeans.

He does look great in jeans – it's an objective observation, I'm allowed to notice, that's all.

That's all? Yes, Polly. No doubt he's sure to look even greater without them, judging by that comely faded patch down one side of his flies.

Oh, drop it.

'Go on,' Polly says, 'tell me. Wait – you're getting married!'

'Married?' Chip protests, looking utterly horrified. 'Hell no. I'm *leaving*.'

'Leaving who?' Polly asks, livid at her heartbeat.

'Who? *Where*, more like. Here,' Chip explains, 'Hubbardtons.'

'Hubbardtons?' Polly gasps, drawing on the 'h' as if she is about to choke.

'School, town, river, moun'ain, general store – yes siree.'

'Crikey,' says Polly who doesn't really know what to say or think or feel.

'I'm going to Chicago.'

'Crikey.'

'Athletic Trainer for one of the major colleges.'

'Wow. When?'

'Next term,' Chip announces. 'That makes this my last term after six glorious years at the John Hubbardton Academy.'

'Crumbs,' says Polly, making a strong effort to conjure an effortless-looking smile to mask any signs that her brain is doing overtime.

'Hey,' says Chip, nodding towards the house, 'it's eight. You'd better go.'

'God, yes,' says Polly.

'I'll catch you later, hey?'

Polly nods. Chip turns and saunters away.

'I say,' Polly calls after him just before he's out of earshot, 'congratulations!'

166

He holds up a hand and walks backwards for a few steps, the moonlight and the silvering from the snow catching his features and making him look truly godly. He turns and walks on. Polly lets her snowball drop to the ground. She treads it in as she turns for the house. She's freezing. Her fingers ache. Here's Beth.

'You're late,' Polly all but barks, 'study hour started five minutes ago.'

SEVENTEEN

'*G*od,' Polly whispered, alone at last in her apartment, 'bugger.' She went to the fridge and looked at the contents, closed the door, opened it and looked inside again. She slammed it shut. 'Shit.' An unopened envelope next to the phone caught her eye. 'Fuck.' It was a letter from Max. It had arrived that morning and she'd been saving it for the precious, private minutes which precede switching the light off on the day. She took the envelope and regarded it close to. She knew that hand-writing so well; confident, sloping and regular.

Like his walk.

Open it, then.

'I can't bloody open you,' she murmured to the envelope, 'not tonight. Not now. Bugger.'

'Miss Fenton?'

Polly jumped.

'Christ, Zoe!'

'Sorry. I just wanted to say, like, you know, thank you? For today? I appreciate it.'

'Don't mention it.'

'Well, thank you.'

'It's a pleasure.'

168

'Night, then.'

'Night.'

Poor Zoe. Poor poor girl. What are you thanking me for? I'm going to let you down so badly. Shit.

Sleep didn't do much good. By the next morning, Max's letter remained unopened and the light of the new day was certainly not clear: fresh snow was falling and swept a blanket of greyness over everything. Polly, still incapable of much speech other than monosyllabic fulminations, set her classes to read in silence while she gazed out of the window and swore to herself.

Shit.

But surely this is precisely what you wanted – temptation to quite literally vanish?

Fuck.

Where's the Polly who was so resolute about what she wanted and what she was and was *not* going to do?

Fuck.

Precisely.

Shit.

Maxmaxmaxmaxmaxmaxmaxmaxmaxmax – remember?

* * *

'Hey, Fen'un!'

Wank.

'Hullo, Chip.'

'You free tonight?'

'Actually, yes I am.'

'Go for a walk? See the river?'

Bugger.

'Lovely.'

Fuck.

'Say eight?'

'Eight.'

Oh God.

* * *

Lorna was building a snowman, assisted by a posse of focused freshmen and the McLellan toddlers.

'Hi there,' she said as Polly trudged over to her.

'And I thought I was incognito,' Polly responded, her face partially swallowed by a swathe of black wool, her figure camouflaged by the umpteen layers of clothing that the weather decreed.

'How's it going?' Lorna asked, patting a clump of snow between her mittened hands and handing it to Polly to put where she liked.

'Fine, fine, yup,' said Polly, adding the snow to the belly of the snowman.

'Really?' Lorna pushed. Polly's silence was disconcerting. Lorna regarded her looking away, looking wretched.

'OK you guys,' she said to the sculptors, not daring to take her eyes from Polly, 'I'm putting Bob in control, let's give this guy a head now, hey? I can see you all. All the time. I'm just going to talk through some business with Miss Fenton.'

There's nothing to talk through. It's none of your business.

'Hey honeychild, what's up?'

'Nothing.'

'Bull shit.'

Polly regarded Lorna. Lorna's face exuded concern.

For me.

'Spanner in the works,' said Polly with a shy smile.

'What in hell's name does that mean?' Lorna pressed, hugging her arms about herself and sniffing through her reddened nose.

'Chip's leaving,' Polly said expressionless, standing very still. She took her arms out to the side and then let them drop back down. She looked away.

'I know,' Lorna shrugged while her eyebrows danced and she scoured Polly's face. Lorna knew of Chip's thinly veiled

170

overtures to Polly, but she had no reason to even touch on the thought that Polly might have been beguiled.

Hey hey, imagination, whoah! Come on! I know all about Max. And Polly's like me. Even more so – she's engaged.

'But,' Polly started afresh, 'I mean. Fuck it. Nothing.'

'Fenton!' she exclaimed, having never heard the girl swear and finding that it did not become her. Polly shook her head, stamped in the snow and looked way out beyond Lorna's field of vision. Her eyes smarted and blazed khaki.

'So what that he's leaving?' Lorna continued lightly. 'You can learn to ski before he goes?'

'Cos that's why you're upset, right?

'Skiing, yes yes,' Polly said, forcing a smile.

I can't tell you. I can't do this to you. Nor to your Tom. Nonsense. I'm being greedy and weak. What I mean is, if I told you, no doubt you'd rightly admonish and reject me. But friends are my family, always have been and always will, so I can't afford not to have you all in my life.

'I can teach you to ski,' Lorna shrugged, glancing at the snowman and pleased with the proportion of his developing head.

'I'm just being daft,' Polly said quickly. 'I have a letter from Max.'

'Everything OK?' Lorna asked, suddenly alarmed and slightly embarrassed that she had touched on inaccurate conclusions.

'I haven't read it yet,' Polly said.

'You haven't?'

'Haven't had time.'

'A-ha! You want me to take your study hour, Polly? Free up some time for you tonight?'

Polly smiled back. 'I'm off duty tonight, as it goes.'

'Cool,' said Lorna, 'you want come over?'

Polly declined.

Lorna understood.

No she doesn't.

Lorna returned to her snowman and gave him her scarf.

171

Polly burrowed her face deeply into hers.
Can't talk to Lorna. Shit.

Polly was to meet Chip at the church which marked the fork
in the road at the end of Main Street. She met Kate on her
way, swaddled from recognition if it hadn't been for the
faithful Bogey by her side.

'Polly, hey there,' said Kate, shifting her brown paper sack
of Hubbardtons groceries. They greeted each other in what
they presumed to be the middle of the road, though snow's
unifying blanket blurred the distinction between street and
sidewalk. In the still, freezing air, the smell of fresh bread
was vivid and told Polly in no uncertain terms that she had
not eaten since lunch.

'You OK?' Kate asked, observing Polly's look of hunger
and confusion.

'Yup.'

'You coming or going?'

'Going,' said Polly, looking towards the church, 'for a
walk.'

'It's a beautiful evening,' Kate said in agreement, 'you
warm enough?'

'Yup.'

'You want company?'

'I have company,' said Polly slowly, looking again
towards the church; looking hungry and confused again.

'I can't guess who,' said Kate with a twinkle to the eye.
Polly regarded her with a disconcerted jerk. 'You OK?' Kate
repeated. Polly slumped her stiffened shoulders and shook
her head. 'What's up? You want to talk?' Polly let her eyes
close briefly while she nodded and then shook her head
vehemently instead. Kate took a bite from the French stick
and motioned for Polly to do the same. She did so gladly and
praised the respite it provided for her to chew instead of
talk.

'So?' Kate prompted.

'He's leaving,' Polly said, looking Kate straight in the eye.

'Yeah, I heard,' said Kate, 'that's just too bad.'

'Do you know, if he had been staying, I'd have been OK. I'd have been safe,' Polly announced. Kate tilted her head to ask for more. 'If he was staying,' Polly elaborated slowly, looking again towards the church, 'I could remain resolute. And strong. From necessity.' Kate tipped her head the other way, nodding slightly. 'But he's going,' Polly reiterated, 'and I'll never see him again. And that's a bloody dangerous notion.'

'You bet,' said Kate, grasping Polly's sentiment and taking hold of her arm as she did so.

'He's going,' Polly announced, regarding Kate full on, 'for good. And that very fact provides one huge safety net.'

Kate agreed by humming, softening her gaze but not leaving Polly's eyes.

'You see, whatever happens,' Polly continued, 'between now and then – he'll go.'

'Make hay while the sun shines?' Kate asked through the corner of her mouth and then smiling benevolently.

'Make out while the snow falls,' Polly retorted with an air of resignation and a passable American accent, regarding Kate watchfully, 'more like.'

Hang on, she's not judging me? Why not? How is it that I feel calm and lucid though I am confessing my intentions out loud? Excuse me, but how did she even know that we're talking about Chip when we've not mentioned names.

'Kate?'

'Polly?'

'Chip?' said Polly as a slight question. 'Yes?'

Kate winked and clicked her tongue approvingly.

'How did you know?' Polly marvelled. 'Did you guess? Was that difficult? Am I wicked? Or just transparent? Are you disappointed?'

'Whoah,' Kate laughed, chewing on more bread, 'I'll say just this – if I was you: young and gorgeous, miles away from home and on the threshold of lifelong commitment – and a guy like Chip showed me even an ounce of the attention he's been loading on you – I'd go for it. I'd think twice – as you have – but I'd go for it.'

'You would?'

'I would,' said Kate, pulling Bogey's ear through her fingers and shifting the shopping. 'I would because I *did*.'

'Did?' Polly questioned, 'did what?'

'What you're about to do.'

'Who? You?'

'Me.'

'With? Chip?'

Kate roared with laughter. 'One of his great-ancestors, more like! Listen up, kiddo, every woman is entitled to a Chip just once in her life. My Chip was called Dave.'

'Dave,' Polly repeated in awe.

'Let's say,' said Kate, tracing an arc with her foot, 'he was my genie of the lamp – he sure lit my fire and, after some pretty intense rubbing, he kinda made my wish come true too, I guess.'

Polly gave a short giggle, simultaneously horrified and delighted and heartened by Kate's revelation. 'What wish was that then?'

'That I wouldn't be making a mistake with Clinton.'

Polly gasped in relief and reverence. 'Ex*act*ly,' she proclaimed, crouching down and embracing Bogey, 'that's *exactly* how I feel.' She stood up and put her hands on her hips, 'But is it wicked?'

'Probably,' Kate cautioned. 'Like, how would you feel if Max was going through this? Confronted by the emotions you're feeling? Horny for some cute Chipette?' Polly shuddered. 'Exactly,' Kate said. 'But I'll tell you this and you listen up. Don't ever, *ever* let on. This is your secret and it's a guilty, precious, sacred one that you must take to your grave. Don't ever tell Max. This is something that you've gotta do – almost in honour of him, I guess, in some perverse way. But don't you tell him. Not in revenge. Not in the height of a fight. Not in years to come. Not ever, Polly, what*ever* the circumstance. OK? You hear?'

Polly nodded. 'Are you disappointed in me?' she asked.

Kate smiled. 'Disappointed? No. Disapproving? Yes. But I didn't approve of myself back then. Any road, right now I'm a woman who's been happily married twenty-eight years. But,' she said, holding her head high and nodding soberly at Polly, 'I do *understand* – and I guess that's what you need, someone who just understands and won't judge.'

'Just what I need,' mused Polly, laying her head gently against Kate's shoulder in intense gratitude.

'This is *not* my seal of approval,' Kate furthered sternly. 'I'm not going to be an accomplice, or some kinda accessory to the crime – and it *is* a crime. I'm not giving you the all clear or the go ahead, but I will provide you with my shoulder and with my ear. When you want. If you need.'

'I'll try and get through it without burdening you,' said Polly gravely before sighing heavily.

'Hey,' Kate laughed, pinching Polly playfully, 'lighten up here – we're talking rampant sex, remember. *Enjoy* – or there really will have been no point!'

Polly nodded and then looked alarmed. 'Rampant sex? No no, just a kiss. That'll do,' she rushed with no notion of how deluded she appeared.

'Whatever,' Kate said with a sly, knowing smile that made Polly plead 'No *really*'. 'Come Bogey, home.'

Kate left, with a stamping walk to combat slipping.

'Thanks, Kate,' Polly called after her.

Kate turned. Main Street was utterly quiet. The snow provided both sound-proofing as well as amplification for a mere whisper.

'Polly,' Kate's voice travelled, 'it's healthier to do and denounce, than not to and forever to wonder.'

'Beautiful night, huh?'
Just a kiss. God, you're gorgeous.
'Gorgeous.'
'You warm?'
I'm hot.

'I'm fine.'

'Cool.'

By the time Polly had watched Kate disappear and had made careful progress along Main Street, she had been fashionably late for Chip. As she had approached the church, she made out a shadowy figure leaning against the wall. Chip. It could only be. Only Chip could look so aesthetically, athletically rugged under layers of polar fleece and a voluminous ski jacket which served to accentuate the shapely musculature of his denim-clad legs beneath. His face, peeping above a fleece scarf and below a fleece cap, was sculptural, clean and perfectly framed. When he had smiled in welcome, his teeth outshone the snow and his glinting eyes outsparkled the stars; Polly was only too aware of the fatuous comparison, of the clichés, but she had fallen for them wholeheartedly.

It was heavy going, walking on the road, as the night-time drop in temperature had glazed the surface with a treacherous film of ice. If they ventured over to either side, it was a ponderous trudge through deeper snow. Polly didn't mind where they walked; either allowed for their bodies to bump and jostle and her occasional skid on the ice was rewarded with a helping hand from Chip.

'Easy there!'

'Thanks.'

The night air was searingly clear, absolutely freezing and, consequently, invigorating. Polly felt she could walk for miles. Good job – as it appeared they were going to.

'Ssh!' said Chip, stopping still and cocking his head, a finger to his ear, a hand on Polly's forearm. Polly listened hard. She heard silence and the oily tinkle of the river. She presumed that was Chip's point, so she smiled, hoping that the moonlight was catching her features and spinning silver over them as it was over Chip. His gaze and a slight parting of his lips told her she was, indeed, as attractive as she felt.

'OK,' he said, walking on, 'just near here – if I can find it under all this snow.'

He was now ahead of Polly; his capable, fit body making light of the going. She was subsumed by desire for him; he was seemingly so perfect that he was almost unreal.

If he isn't real, what's the harm?

She slowed her pace.

All this is just fantasy. Just playing. Acting. In fact, I'm going to pretend to fall, so he can rescue me and revive me with a purely medicinal kiss. Two, three, now!

With the skill of a stuntman, she choreographed a gracious slither to the ground with a beseeching yelp.

'Hey hey,' Chip soothed, coming to her rescue, 'you OK?'

'Yes,' Polly assured him, holding out her hand, 'clumsy clot that I am.'

'Clumsy clot,' Chip repeated with pleasure, taking her hand and helping her to her feet, his steadying grasp lingering for longer than necessary, 'I like that!' He brushed her jacket down and pulled her collar up. 'All set?'

Polly replied with a sizeable grin that masked disappointment laced with humiliation.

But you were meant to kiss me. Damn, it didn't work.

On they trudged.

'Here we go,' said Chip, cutting across the road and steadying himself with a tree. He held out his hand for Polly. 'Easy now.'

They scrambled and slid down the bank, appearing to make more noise than the river below them. 'Don't look behind you,' Chip warned at the base, 'not yet. Not till I say. OK?'

'Aye aye, cap'n,' Polly replied. Chip regarded her quizzically, shook his head and walked on. Polly thrust her hands into her pockets to curb a sudden urge to grab a handful of Chip's incomparable buttocks.

They skirted the edge of the river and made for an old stone bridge a few yards away. The ravages of time had provided a most conveniently placed bench low down on the bridge, where some of the rocks used in its construction had fallen away. Gallantly, Chip swept the snow off and motioned for Polly to take her seat. 'Look at me!' he warned her, 'don't look downstream till I say. OK?'

'Okey dokey,' said Polly, delighted to be ordered to gaze upon him. He sat down beside her. She held on tight to his eyes and found she could hardly breathe.

Kiss me. Now. Yes! It's going to happen.

'Oh-kay, doh-kay,' Chip mimicked in a murmur, 'you can look – now!'

Temporarily disappointed that the errant kiss was obviously on hold again, Polly swung her gaze reluctantly from suitor to stream and gasped. The scene was stunning. Moonlight was funnelled between the hills on either side, further deflected by the dense forestry in the lower reaches so that it illuminated only the stretch of river, revealing diamonds in the water and turning the wet boulders into platinum. The lowest trees either side were dark indigo, cloaked progressively with more snow as they climbed further up the bank. The water was like a wavering sheet of liquid silk, like mercury rolling and dripping, forever moving as a whole.

'Hey?' said Chip having given her some time to soak it up. He nudged her gently. Polly sighed and shook her head, turning to him and fully intending to hold his gaze. When she caught his eyes full on, she diverted hers immediately, shocked at the power and impact the sight of him had on her.

'Stunning,' she said to the river.

'Sure,' said Chip.

They sat alongside each other, comfortable on the bench furrowed from the base of the bridge, enjoying the scene and the serenity.

No one knows where I am, Polly marvelled, *at this precise moment. Only me. And if no one knows where I am, then no one can possibly know what I'm doing. Ignorance is bliss. Once done, no one can ever know what passed. I want to be kissed, actually I have to be. Right, I shall turn my head on the count of three and offer my lips for the taking.*

One

        Two

                Three

Chip's eyes, however, are closed. He appears to be in deep appreciation of Mother Nature and Hubbardtons River. A pang courses through Polly that maybe kissing isn't on his itinerary at all; just a devout contemplation of nature instead, of its gifts instilling harmony to the soul and clarity to the mind. She feels suddenly uncouth and so she stares hard about her, dragging unconnected stanzas of poetry to laud the scene that surrounds her.

Like the snow falls in the river,
A moment white then melts forever;

   Glory be to God for dappled things.

Bright star, would I were steadfast as thou art –

   Well-timed silence hath more eloquence than speech

The night is dark, and I am far from home

'Hey.' Chip nudges Polly gently from her thoughts and quotations. She smiles shyly and gazes again downstream. 'You want to go?'

'No,' she says quickly, 'a few more minutes.'

'Cool,' he says and settles back into the bridge bench. From the corner of her eye she can see his fabulous legs and her sex quivers at the notion of his knees.

Oh to rub against them.

She can feel his gaze burning on her face. She knows exactly where he is looking.

My cheek. My earlobe. Across to the corner of my mouth. Up to the tip of my nose. My eyes. Don't dare blink. My forehead. Sweeping up and over my hair, back to my lips. Down to my chin. I'll blink slowly. There, he saw. I'm going to lick my lips subconsciously; accidentally on purpose. There, he saw. Good. I'll turn slowly to him, just a half-turn of my head, my lips will be glistening. And then we'll kiss.

179

Polly turns her face, a half-turn, dragging her eyes around last from the magnificent pine on which they have gazed. Too slow. Chip is now looking over to Peter Mountain, shrouded ghostly pale in the moonlight.

Damn.

Polly returns her attention to the great pine. Some moments later she turns again to Chip. She encounters him staring at her full on and her gaze is commanded by his at once. He raises his hand slowly and she is sure that her heart can be seen beating hard at the base of her throat. In an excruciatingly slow, measured gesture, Chip takes his very fingertips to the side of Polly's mouth where they hover for a suspended moment. While watching their journey and still unsure of their final destination, though subsumed by lustful anticipation, Polly feels in control. She can sense her pupils dilating, her nipples must have hardened and she can feel her clitoris twitching in excitement against the seam of her jeans.

Come fingers, come. Touch me.

However, when Chip's fingers alight on the side of her mouth, warm and strong and determined, Polly leaps to her feet.

Her reaction horrifies her.

What the fuck did I do that for?

Do what, exactly?

Why have I jumped up? Sit down, idiot woman.

Chip, however, is returning his hand to the pocket of his ski jacket.

No no no! I didn't mean it. Sorry sorry. Quick! You can kiss me here, right now – press me against this stone bridge and take my mouth.

'Excuse me,' Chip is saying, slowly straightening himself and smiling kindly at Polly, 'I'm sorry,' he is shrugging, 'I guess we ought to head back.'

Polly is distraught, livid with herself, embarrassed. She says hardly a word, merely an awkward laugh or a 'yes' or a 'really' at Chip's polite conversation. Chip reads her silence as detachment. He is disappointed. Polly feels he is now distant from her, that he must be regarding her as some inexperienced kid; she feels small, wretched. It is not so much a missed opportunity but one that she actively fluffed and ruined. She doubts that there'll be another one.

And I should be glad of it.

Instead, she feels a failure and kicks herself – once or twice, quite literally. Chip thinks she is tripping because of the snow, but he refrains from offering her assistance, which depresses her more.

'I'm fine,' Polly smiles bravely as they reach the entrance to McCarther House where Chip is Dorm Parent this term, 'you go on in. I'll be fine.'

'You sure?'

'Sure I'm sure,' says Polly.

'I had a great evening,' he assures her, while Polly works hard on keeping her smarting eyes darting away from his gaze.

'Me too,' she says, turning and walking away. She goes directly to bed and begs sleep to take her quickly. She refuses to think of Chip. She still has not opened Max's letter.

EIGHTEEN

*I*t was at least a week before Chip and Polly met again. She'd spied him at a distance, once or twice, but had turned away from the sight of him in the hope that she had not been noticed. School started an hour and a half earlier in the Lent term to accommodate the skiers and though it thus ended an hour and a half earlier too, it remained mercifully a Chip-free zone for invariably he was the last to leave the slopes and inevitably he had a queue of the wounded awaiting his return and attention.

Polly hadn't exactly given up hope, she just had yet to decide what to do next. She believed the onus was now on her and it was onerous. Polly was indebted to her sizeable workload, took on the assistant directorship for the school revue, visited her advisees regularly and was a conscientious Dorm Mother. She synchronized two subsequent free evenings with Lorna and organized an ice-skating excursion to Keene on her day off. She finally read Max's letter. It was short and ever so sweet but she read it only the once, swiftly, and then mislaid it accidentally on purpose. She has yet to reply.

As much as she tried to avoid Chip, Polly also kept her distance from Kate because, in some way, she felt she had let her down. She dreaded Kate enquiring after the state of affairs; to admit that nothing had happened because she had actively prevented it would be far too humiliating. Polly told herself that to dull the twinkle in Kate's eye with the truth of the matter was an unbearable notion. Polly told herself that as Kate wanted to live again through Polly, how could she disappoint her so? Polly did not tell herself that she dreaded hearing the far more likely 'Probably just as well, hon' from Kate.

The bell had already rung for third period and Polly made her way to the classroom. She'd never been late and wondered why she was, and more importantly, why she wasn't actually that bothered. From the hush of the rooms she passed, save for the voice of an adult, she knew that other lessons were already under way. She could detect animated chatter coming from the end room, her class, but knew it was hoping too much that the focus might already be on Dickens. She had faith in her students, though, and knew that as soon as she appeared they would listen up and apply themselves.

If you are even under a minute late at BGS, you've lost the entire class for the duration of the lesson – and very probably the subsequent two or three as well.

As Polly passed Jackson Thomas's class, the door opened. It often did, so she kept on walking, as she always did, anticipating Jackson's whispered insinuations and futile offers. In her left arm, she held a clutch of books to her breast so she held up her right hand in a preventative gesture as she went.

'Thanks but no thanks,' she said lightly, looking straight ahead and continuing on her way, 'neither the time, the inclination, nor the money. Sorry!'

'Hey?'

That's not Jackson.

'Wait up!'

Chip!

Polly ground to a halt, still facing her direction of travel, then slowly turned around. Winter sunshine flooded down from the skylights and clung to Chip in a cloak of gossamer brilliance. Polly was rendered immobile and utterly silent by his steady, penetrating gaze. It was a moment of celluloid resonance, if ever there was one; no doubt a camera would have zoomed in for a stunning close-up of Chip's bone structure, before panning round to the startled delight in Polly's eyes. Indeed she even peeled her ears, fully expecting rousing background music, but all was silent save muffled teachers' voices and the low din coming from her class.

But this was neither film nor fiction. It was the here and now, or, rather, the there and then. Slowly Chip came towards Polly. Her left cheek was burning from a direct hit of sunlight that also rendered her partly blind. She held her breath, just waiting for someone to appear from a classroom. And yet she felt no fear of being caught, but dreaded instead that this electrifying moment and its possible consequences might be ruined. Chip came closer, he neither spoke, nor was he smiling; he was utterly focused and deadly serious, his eyes locked on to hers. His body now blocked the sun. She could see him clearly. His penetrative gaze made her head swim and caused a throbbing between her legs that she was sure was visible, it was so pronounced. And yet she remained oblivious to the fact that it was actually *her* eyes that were drawing *him* towards her like a magnet. The sound of the lessons surrounding them had reduced down to a distant hum. As Chip neared, Polly began to back up until the wall supported her. Her hair whisked against her jaw. She tossed her head like a filly and watched Chip's lips part, glistening, as if he was about to speak. He said nothing, he kept advancing. Polly's lips parted in anticipation of being kissed.

Come on.

Here? In the corridor? With staff and pupils but yards away and liable to appear at any moment?

Chip was but inches away. Closer than that. So close. Suddenly, Polly had no conception that she was in a corridor of a school in Vermont with a classload of children yards away in a room with the door wide open. She ceased to be Polly Fenton with a flat in Belsize Park and a cat called Buster. Max was an abbreviation, right? Not a name.

Suddenly, it really didn't matter who she, or who *he* was. It was enough that such a glorious specimen of virility was visibly attracted to her and coming to get her. Right now. Polly could have been anywhere and, at that precise moment, with the proximity of the anticipated, desired kiss so tantalizingly close, she wouldn't have cared who came across her.

It was hard to tell who initiated it, but suddenly Polly found her arms about Chip's neck, his tongue leaping about inside her mouth. He had one hand enmeshed in her hair while the other latched on to her breast, grasping on tight as if to open the door to a world of physical bliss. She was pushed against the wall, hard. Her books had slithered down her torso and were now caught precariously between their two bodies; sheaves of paper had already flown free to lie in a scatter around them.

Though their faces had seemed to hover and hesitate excruciatingly close, ultimately their lips had hardly touched before they were tonguing each other with abandon, greedily exploring the inside of each other's mouths and gobbling up the new taste. Their eyes were wide open and feasted on the sight of each other. Polly could hardly breathe but in order to kiss on, she had to; so she panted lightly when she could and held her breath at other times, which itself served to increase the light-headed sensation. Chip was making deep, desirous noises in his throat which sounded dangerously loud to Polly, yet the very volume, the sound of him, turned her on all the more.

Chip swapped hands deftly, cupping her head and her sex; her books secured, for the time being at least, under his elbow. Simultaneously, he pulled her hair and rubbed swiftly against the mound of her sex. She moaned involuntarily and he bit her lip to silence her. She pulled her head

185

away, in shock and pain, but on seeing his broad, dimpled, dazzling smile she melted again and enjoyed the fact that both sets of her lips now throbbed. Poking her tongue out to one side of her mouth, furling her eyelashes, cocking her head and regarding him lasciviously, Polly travelled her hand from his neck down his body, observing that it was at the point just above his navel when he closed his eyes and swayed a little. She left her hand still for a moment and then took it away.

'I have a class to teach,' she announced in a voice that was too husky to be hers, surely. 'I have a class to teach,' she repeated, clearing her throat but finding that the tone remained. Chip licked his lips and then held his hands up in mock surrender. As he did so, her books tumbled free and fell to the floor with a noisy clatter.

'Everything OK?' asked Jackson Thomas, suddenly in the doorway of his class room and seemingly more interested in the proximity of Chip to Polly than in her fallen books.

'Hey Miss Fenton, you need help?' called AJ from the other end of the corridor.

'I'm fine,' Polly told everyone with a separate nod, Chip included.

'She's fine,' Chip repeated to the audience, 'I think she was dazzled so she dropped her books.'

Dazzled indeed! Polly exerted an inordinate amount of self control not to laugh or show even an ounce of reaction.

'I'll be there in a mo', AJ, thanks.'

'OK,' said Jackson unconvinced, having noted the bulge in Chip's trousers and praying that Polly had nothing to do with it, nor even knew of its existence, 'OK.' He swayed against his door frame for a moment, said 'OK' a third time and then returned to his class, drawing the door ajar and then closing it cautiously some moments later.

The corridor was quiet again. Polly did not look at Chip.

'I have a class to teach,' she said, biting away at the blush of exhilaration which she knew criss-crossed her face while it coursed rapidly through her veins.

'I have an announcement to make,' Chip explained, 'I've done Mr Thomas's class and your guys, Miss Fenton, are next. All set?'

In her class room, Polly did not know where to look. She was suddenly sure that if she regarded Chip for too long, their connection would be clearly legible.

There again, won't it look suspicious if I don't regard him at all?

Consequently, and conscientiously, she looked to each of her pupils in turn, interspersing a non-committal glance at Chip after every other student. He was there to announce the ski teams and his news was accompanied by the appropriate cheers or groans.

'Heidi?' Polly asked, responding to the girl's politely up-stretched arm.

'You ski, Miss Fenton? Do you have mountains in England?'

'No and yes,' Polly informed, thinking that they really ought to be turning their attention to Dickens.

'We'll have your teacher up on skis, hey guys?' Chip encouraged, 'slaloming with the best of you!'

A raucous chorus of approval erupted, and much laughter too.

'Quiet!' Polly cried in consternation, the noise level anomalously close to that of a BGS class, 'Mr Jonson, if that is all, Estelle has something to say to Pip.'

Chip bowed his head and thanked her, apologizing to the class (with a wink that went unnoticed by Polly) for taking up too much of their lesson. In the doorway, just before he left, he simulated a parallel turn, smiled broadly at all asunder, letting it linger daringly on Polly. He shut the door behind him. Polly went over to it and pushed the weight of her body against it.

'Pip pip pip,' she uttered absent-mindedly, not knowing where to look or what to teach. 'Tell you what, chaps, how about you all pen a few paragraphs describing the sensation of skiing. If you don't ski, imagine what it might be like. If you hate skiing, tell me why – but curb any gruesome details, I don't want to be put off – there's a challenge, remember!'

Polly was on a high all day. She walked with a swagger that matched her mood and reminded her, with the friction of every stride, that her knickers were triumphantly damp. She ruffled Lorna's hair as she passed by in the dining hall and gave both Bens a high five, much to their amusement. She invited all her dorm daughters up for tea and biscuits and a further analysis of her musical tastes, though most of them brought their own offerings of Nirvana and asked for cookies and Coke instead.

It was at precisely nine minutes to eleven that night, when Polly was finally alone for the first time that day, that she was overcome with horror and a churning nausea. She paced from room to room, a hand at her mouth, soon both hands at her head, then hugging herself, soon hitting herself. Finally, she curled up in a corner of the bathroom and focused on her knees because all around her the tiles presented her with her own distorted reflection.

Distorted indeed.

At last, Polly, what a relief. Finally you feel guilt and remorse. You're pining for Max and cursing yourself for all that idiocy, this foray into infidelity. Yes?

No.

No?

Yes, fear and loathing have struck her deep. But, what is it that ails the very core of Polly's being? Guilt? Shame? Regret? Surely a combination of all three? No, that would be far too simple – and far too easy to purge and cure. Far too neat and tidy – we still have half a book remaining.

No. Our dishonest, floundering heroine feels wretched because of an outright lack of guilt, of shame and of regret. It is the very fact that she feels not one ounce of any of the aforementioned which terrifies her so, because new limits have been thereby set.

I thought one kiss would do. I thought it would be sufficient to rid my system of that troublesome notion.

And it wasn't?

It was a superb kiss.

And it wasn't enough?

It might have been if untold suffering and remorse succeeded the pleasure of the moment.

But it didn't?

Nope. I feel feisty and horny and hungry for more.

How much more?

Who knows?

I can't believe you're smiling, Polly. Thought you felt lousy?

I did. I know I should. But I simply don't.

NINETEEN

*P*olly felt ridiculous in salopettes. They belonged to Lorna who had assured her that it didn't matter that she was four inches taller and at least a stone heavier than Polly.

'Heck, they'll do their job.'

'They're very, well, *pink*,' was all Polly could muster in gratitude.

She tried them on very late, when she could be sure that no one would intrude. She hoped unrealistically that they'd suit her but on closer inspection of the cut and colour she doubted whether they would, had they even been made to measure. The suit consisted of a pair of dungarees in a restrictive, dense, rubbery material which flared out extravagantly beneath the knees. Polly knew this was to accommodate bulky ski boots but, standing there in horror in front of her mirror, she decided the boots would have to be enormous if they were to streamline the effect in the slightest. The upper part of the dungarees was a sickly baby-pink, the flared parts a fan of panelled sections in progressively virulent shades of the colour. The jacket was predominantly cerise, with stripes on the sleeves in a shade close to candy floss, a triangular panel down the back the colour of early

1980s lipstick and a strip either side of the zip at the front which could only be described as well-chewed bubblegum.

'God,' Polly wailed at the site of herself, 'I look absolutely hideous.' Her cheeks burned in humiliation, clashing loudly with the jacket. 'And my hair! But there's no way I'm even trying on the matching hat. Anyway, it's not just the colour scheme,' she whined, 'look how big it all is. I look like the Michelin Man slowly deflating.'

Polly performed a forlorn twirl and gasped at the exaggerated proportions of her usually trim bottom.

'Couldn't I just wear my jeans?'

She fiddled with the straps and zips in search of a better fit.

'Better – but still awful.'

She slumped down on to the sofa and regarded her baggy pink knees.

'Maybe I just won't go.'

When she awoke, the clarity and dazzle of the morning made light of the gloom with which she had met sleep.

After all, I'll be with Chip – and I haven't seen him for days, almost a week, what with the rewrites for the revue, Zoe's continuing problems in love and Forrest's inability to comprehend The Importance of Being Earnest.

Because she still dreaded her appearance in Lorna's ski suit, Polly decided to dress impeccably until school finished and the mountain beckoned. She put on a delicate floral skirt, which floated just above the knee and was totally unsuitable for the time of year, teaming it with a soft chenille polo neck and a pair of thick black woollen tights. And the padded snow boots it had been recently necessary to purchase. However, she also took a pair of suede pumps under her arm and changed into these as soon as she was safely inside the main hall. The unexpected sight of Chip coming out of Powers Mateland's office met her.

There's fate for you.

'Yo!'

'Good morning, Mr Jonson.'

'All set for the slopes?'

'As ready as ever I'll be, I suppose, but you have to promise not to laugh at me. Or at my costume. Especially at my costume.'

'How about I promise I'll *try*.'

'Nope. Not good enough.'

'All right. I promise.'

Chip held his hand to his heart to seal his oath and Polly touched his fingers lightly. He encircled hers quickly, fleetingly, tightly.

'Thank you,' she said and left for her class.

Chip didn't laugh. He was well used to the vagaries of ski fashion and found his full attention commanded by Polly's expression of stern concentration and burgeoning terror. The just-detectable jelly quiver of the ski suit told him she must be positively quaking underneath it all.

'You OK?' he asked gently. 'Feel good about this?'

'No,' Polly muttered, convinced that two hours' tuition had not been anywhere near enough, 'and no.'

'You'll be fine,' Chip nudged her amiably as the two Bens whizzed by at breakneck speed.

'Just remember what we've been learning, about keeping your tips together,' Chip said.

'My *what*?' Polly exclaimed.

'Your tips,' said Chip, 'with a "p". All set?'

Polly gave a non-committal nod, her eyes focused on the end of the nursery slope just a few yards away. A small group of students had gathered there in support (and curiosity) and Polly took heart from their muffled encouragement and mittened waves.

'All set,' she said, unconvincingly, to Chip. 'Are you absolutely sure I'm ready?'

'Gotta start somewhere,' Chip said kindly. 'Away you go — race you to the bottom. Hey, joke, man — it was a joke.'

'Count of three, please,' Polly quaked, trying to estimate

192

the gradient of the lower reaches of the nursery slope.

'One.'

God I feel sick.

'Two.'

Would I make much more of a fool of myself if I just bottled out?

'Three.'

Oh my God! Oh wow! I'm skiing! Do you know, I'm actually doing it. Wheeee! Fantastic! I love it. Oh no, I'm down already.

Chip told Polly that her first snowplough was 'commendable'; Polly herself thought it perfectly executed. Her audience, who had formed themselves hastily into a corps of well-padded cheerleaders, were chanting her name and dancing about in delight.

'I did it!' was all she could say, tears streaming down her face and a smile so wide it threatened to leap right off her face. Chip was right behind her.

'Lightning!' he praised.

'I did it!' she hugged him liberally, totally in keeping with the triumph of the situation and no one batted an eye. Apart from Forrest, who thought he'd have a hug too.

'You want to try a little way up?'

'I did it!'

'Go on, Miss Fenton, go up to that marker.'

'Can I do it?'

'Sure you can.'

'Yee hah! Let's go!'

What she gained in speed for her second snowplough, she lost in style; arriving at the bottom of the slope without brakes but with an exultant grin and slap bang into AJ's arms.

'Whoah, there, Miss F.'

'Again!' Polly cried, looking beseechingly from drag-lift to Chip while overlooking apology or thanks to AJ. Chip, however, was strict and responsible, which delighted Polly who only pretended that she really minded repeating the baby snowplough over and over. Finally, Chip allowed her to take a break. In fact, he had to force her as she'd have been utterly content keeping her tips together all day. The students were given a free half-hour before the last training spurt and disappeared in a cloud of excitable yelps and bright colours.

'You star!' Chip proclaimed, leading her towards the club hut. Her cheeks were crisply flushed, her eyes were darting a watery dance, her nose was endearingly red. She was breathing quickly, giving little dragon-like puffs in the cold, thin air of midwinter. Wisps of her hair peeped out from her fleece hat; one was caught at the corner of her mouth, on the lip balm she'd been applying liberally. *Must look after my lips.*

'A star,' Polly sparkled. 'Aren't I just?' He propped their skis and poles against the hut and held out his hand, having first scrutinized the slope for spies and eagle eyes. The sun was now hazed over but its warmth filtered through and fixed the bloom on Polly's cheeks.

'Come,' said Chip, 'you have a Bravery Award awaiting you.'

'Goody,' Polly sang, clumping and trudging alongside him. Chip took her some yards away to a thatch of maples, their boughs laden with swathes of white velvet.

'I know we're a little early,' Chip said theatrically to a tree, 'but it's one special day and if you could oblige we'd be real happy.' He placed his ear against the tree and his facial gesticulations suggested he was listening hard to the tree's reply. 'I think we're in luck,' he said to Polly, who giggled and brought her gloved hands together in muffled applause though she had no idea what a talking tree had to do with a Bravery Award. Chip caressed the bark and slipped his hand down the trunk a little until it rested on a small, metal protuberance. He gave a little tap, a little twist, and Polly saw a thin, delicate liquid seep out and trickle to the snow. She ventured closer and looked down. Chip crouched, took his glove off and picked a small, pale amber-coloured nugget from the snow.

'Here.'

Polly took off her glove and placed the little jewel in the

palm of her hand, holding it up to the light to admire it closely.

'Thank you,' she marvelled, 'it's gorgeous.'

'You eat it, you clutz,' Chip explained affectionately, 'Sugar On Snow.'

Polly did as she was told and closed her eyes as the mellow nuttiness filled her mouth. Chip's lips pressed lightly against hers and though her highly cherished, very important Bravery Award was still in her mouth, she was more than happy to share. She opened her lips and drew Chip in. They passed the fast disappearing lozenge between them until it was all gone. Their tongues lapped away at the pervasive taste of it in each other's mouths until their own unique flavours were discovered again and they feasted upon them.

Polly has taken to skiing on Tuesday and Thursday afternoons.

Because I rather think I have a natural aptitude for the sport.

You mean you fancy Chip and find all the attention, and legal physical contact, addictive.

No, shut up, don't be so ridiculous. I like the skiing – it's a fantastic way to keep fit. And it's exciting and new.

Yes, Polly, it's all exciting and new, but it doesn't mean that you're not deluding yourself. Look at all your marking you've had to relocate.

I'm gladly giving over free time for it so I can take to the slopes.

Yes? And the notion of Chip's Bravery Awards awaiting your progress has nothing to do with anything? They don't spur you on in some small way? Didn't you tell Chip yesterday that you were happy to forgo Sugar On Snow and go straight to the kiss?

You have to have an incentive.

Polly!

*

'I do hope you don't think me inconsiderate,' she had said beseechingly when they were once again in and amongst the maples in secret.

'Bravery Awards come in many guises,' Chip had assured her, wedging his knee up between her legs and sucking on her cold, crisp earlobe.

Inevitably, Polly became too big for her boots. At the end of her third week as self-titled Snow Queen, she turned up in a beautifully proportioned ski suit in dark red and navy, as flattering as it is possible for such an outfit to be, which she had bought with Lorna on a whim and a rare free Sunday. She was met by a chorus of approving whistling from the students, and a furtive pat on the rump from Chip.

'Listen, you mind practising your stem turns for a while? We have a race at the weekend and I need to spend time with the downhill team.'

'Mr Jonson,' Miss Fenton replied, as Laurel and Lauren appeared within earshot, 'I'll be fine. But promise me if I perfect them today, we can go on to parallel turns on Thursday?'

'We'll see,' was all Chip said.

'Jolly good,' Polly replied.

'We'll help,' said Laurel while Lauren nodded.

Polly did all the things her rational conscience was yelling at her not to do. She ran before she could walk and did not bother to look before she leapt. After an hour on the upper reaches of the nursery slope, she assured the two 'L's that she no longer needed baby-sitting, that she was in the nursery after all. The girls disappeared with snow boards, gratefully. Polly took the drag-lift higher than she'd hitherto ventured.

How difficult could a parallel turn be? She'd watched hundreds and decided that they must be as effortless as they looked. It was all about confidence, right? And keeping the skis, well, parallel. And doing something with your bottom and something with your knees, a sort of twisting thrust.

Lean into the mountain, remember. Bend the knees. Easy. Just watch.

Chip was some way up the slopes when he spied a hurtle of blue and red heading for the trees. All he could do was observe the inevitable while amusement churned with horror. The more she lost control, the less control she could recapture. She was leaning and lurching backwards precariously, picking up speed, and had obviously lost all sight of the path she should have been making. As she became dangerously close to the trees, self-preservation kicked in and she made what she thought would be a parallel turn. Only it wasn't exactly parallel. Mercifully, she missed the trees; unfortunately, she managed only 90 degrees and hurtled straight down the uneven reaches of the slope. A lone mogul, camouflaged to the uninitiated, halted her descent but sent her flying at a peculiar angle. Ultimately, Polly landed face down, her legs splayed but suspended with the skis wedged down into the snow; one pole digging into her solar plexus, the other lost, along with her left glove, her hat and her nerve.

Polly queued for the athletic trainer with four others. While they waited, they discussed their war wounds.

'I think I've done something gross to my knee,' said Tanya, the sophomore trampolinist.

'I've, like, totally screwed my shoulder?' said Zoe, who was in the gymnastics team.

'My ankle's gone again,' rued a squash-playing junior called Paul who Polly had never seen.

'My lower back,' grumbled Sam, a senior swimmer. 'How 'bout you, Ma'am?'

Polly sighed. 'I think I've cricked my neck and wrenched my inner thigh.' The students awarded her injuries the greatest 'wow'.

'OK,' said Chip when he arrived, his cheeks glowing gloriously. He walked along the line and made rapid assessments about severity and priority. 'I reckon we start at the bottom and work our way up, hey? Ankle, knee, back, shoulder, neck – Paul, Tanya, Sam, Zoe, Miss Fenton.'

'Shouldn't Miss Fenton go first?' Paul asked gallantly, 'I mean, she kinda has two injuries, you know?'

'Exactly,' Chip explained, looking only at Paul, 'I'll probably need to spend more time with her.'

When the four students had been sufficiently manipulated, bandaged and banished, it was nearing dinner-time.

'You hungry?' Chip asked Polly. She tried to shake her head but winced. 'You mind skipping dinner?' Chip continued, 'I reckon you need fixing before feeding.' Polly agreed with an impassioned humming sound. 'You done something to your jaw?' Chip asked. Again, Polly tried to shake her head. 'You can't speak?'

'I can speak,' she whispered, 'I just don't know what to say.'

Chip grinned at her and brought his lips to her forehead.

'It was pretty spectacular,' he chuckled into the top of her head.

'Please,' Polly pleaded, 'I'm so embarrassed.'

'Don't be.'

'I'm such a bloody idiot.'

'True. But it was kinda funny to watch.'

'Well,' Polly said, 'it's not remotely amusing to *feel*, I assure you.'

Chip took the back of her head gently in his hands before slipping them down until they encircled her neck. He then took one hand to her shoulder blade and his other round to the front, half covering her breast, murmuring encouraging '*uh-huh*'s all the while. 'OK,' he said, wiping his hands on his trousers for some reason, 'come lie here.' He helped Polly on to the examination table, unbuckled the bib of her dungarees and helped ease off her thermal polo neck.

'Cute,' he said, bending low to nuzzle her broderie anglaise bra.

'My neck,' she remonstrated, wanting Chip to fix it immediately so she could enjoy what was currently physiologically painful but psychologically tantalizing.

'Lie back,' she was told. Chip rested her head in his hands and moved his fingers in a gentle rhythm at the base of her skull.

'You might hear a snap,' he warned while a sickening, hollow crack rang out before Polly had a chance to panic.

'Wow,' she said, sitting bolt upright, her adrenalin pumping. She rolled her head very carefully and bestowed upon Chip a smile of immense gratitude and prodigious proportions. 'Let me see your hands,' she implored, sitting sideways on the table, her legs over the edge. Chip held out his palms for her to inspect. She scrutinized them closely and then kissed each in turn, accompanied by a titillating dab of her tongue tip. 'Healing hands,' she proclaimed, looking up at Chip, 'golden touch.' She held his wrists and brought his hands to her breasts, holding them against herself though she could feel that Chip needed no assistance.

'Polly,' he said throatily, 'man, I could lay you down and make love to you right now.'

'I can see that,' said Polly extremely sweetly, eyeing desirously the poking protuberance in his tracksuit bottoms. She gave an inviting heave of her breasts and licked her lips enticingly.

'But,' said Chip, with much clearing of his throat, 'there's the question of your inner thigh.' He peeled down her salopettes and ran his index finger along the waistband of her matching broderie anglaise knickers, pressing his little finger into her bellybutton. He whistled very low and very slowly. 'Man, I'm gonna have to send you to Nurse. I don't know if I can deal with this! I'm kinda, like, *totally* distracted.'

'Don't send me to Nurse,' Polly implored, pouting beseechingly.

I'm so wet it would be embarrassing!

Chip exhaled a few 'phew's, went to the sink and doused himself with cold water.

'OK, Miss Fenton,' he said, avoiding eye contact, 'your inner thigh please.'

TWENTY

*M*iss Fenton would definitely benefit from hydrotherapy. Mr Jonson was not sure how many sessions, but he estimated half a dozen. The damage to her adductor was not critical but he feared that any tightening, stiffening or reduction in mobility could well have consequences for the hip, possibly referred pain elsewhere.

'You OK with that?' Powers Mateland asked him. 'You want to send her to County?'

'She'll be fine,' said Chip, 'I have a treatment schedule mapped out.'

'She'll be in good hands,' praised Powers. 'The best – we're going to miss you, Chip. Know what? I'm sure gonna make your last three weeks full – anyone has even the slightest twinge, they're coming to you direct!'

'I'm flattered,' Chip acquiesced, 'and I'm going to miss Hubbardtons – majorly.'

'You got to go forward,' Powers conceded.

'Sure,' said Chip, 'it was a big decision but I feel good.'

'How about Jen? We gonna lose her too? She gonna follow in your footsteps?'

'We broke up,' said Chip.

200

'I'm sorry to hear that,' Powers said, privately unsurprised.

'It's recent,' said Chip, 'and, you know, like, quiet?'

Powers pulled an imaginary zip across his lips, slapped Chip between the shoulders and sent him on his way to fix Miss Fenton.

'I hope Belsize School for Girls is reaping as much from Jen as we at Hubbardtons are from Polly Fenton,' Powers mused. 'Isn't she just great?'

'She sure is,' Chip agreed openly, 'I'd better get going so she can make the revue rehearsal.'

Chip entered the hydrotherapy pool first and told Polly to sit herself carefully on the edge.

'Ooh, isn't it warm!' she marvelled, dangling her feet into the water. 'Do you like my cossie?'

'Your what?' asked Chip.

'This,' Polly explained, running her hands suggestively over her torso.

'It's real nice,' said Chip, who had hardly been able to keep his eyes off her figure. Clad in a flatteringly cut swimming costume, black piped in white, the contours of her figure were more sinuous than he had envisaged. She had looked thoroughly gorgeous in her cotton underwear, but in her swimsuit, she looked positively sexy.

Polly eased herself into the pool, Chip's hands gently on her waist.

'This is lovely,' she cooed, immersing herself to her jaw. She had pulled her hair into a pony tail perched high on her crown. Her bob was barely long enough and splayed out spikily from the band with escaped tendrils now wet and clinging to her neck in little silken trails. 'It's really just a glorified jacuzzi, isn't it?'

'It's a hydrotherapy pool,' Chip remonstrated, propelling himself behind her, the hardness in his shorts brushing her back as he did so. He looped his arms under Polly's and clasped his hands together just above her breast bone.

'Just relax,' he told her. She had no voice with which to answer. Her heart raced but her limbs were loose, her mind was clear and her conscience calm. Chip eased her around the water and congratulated her on the fine recovery of her neck, placing a round of kisses in the appropriate region. She turned herself to face him and they kissed, their wet limbs gliding around each other.

'Let's work on that thigh,' Chip said huskily, pushing her away, holding her from behind as before. He then turned the water jets off and sat Polly on the submerged ledge that ran round half the pool. The sensation of the bubbles evanescing into a tickle of fizz against the skin was gorgeous; the silence once the motors had stopped, and the serenity of the stilled water, were hypnotic.

I'll do whatever he says.

I bet you will.

'Let your legs just relax and slide them apart a little. Great. A little more. Great.'

Polly did as she was told. Chip took hold of each of her ankles. 'Hold on to the bars beside you. Good.'

God, see how it makes her tits jut? I gotta think adductor – I can't disrupt the programme but Jeez, I'm desperate to suck those nipples.

He gave just perceptible tugs to each leg in turn, rotating them subtly this way and that, praising Polly all the while; concentrating hard, aware that her eyes were scorching his face yet knowing he could not afford to catch her gaze.

Not yet. I got my job to do, man. Gotta stick to the programme. Gotta fix her adductor.

He slid his hands up until they rested behind her knees, gave further little pulls and rotated some more. Almost involuntarily, Polly let go of the bars and took her hands to his. They clasped each other tightly and Chip thrust his face to her right breast, biting at the nipple through the wet fabric.

'Stop,' he said hoarsely, launching himself to the opposite side of the pool, 'you gotta hold on to the bars, Polly. You gotta get fixed.'

202

They remained at either side of the pool, staring hard at each other, panting, like two boxers in a watery ring.

'C'mon, Polly, let me at your thigh.'

Anytime, Chip, come on over.

Once more, he took his hands to the backs of her knees and manipulated her legs for a few more minutes. Then he ran his hands up the fronts of her thighs, quite firmly, informing her he was searching out any tightness, tenderness or knots in the muscle. He took her right thigh and rolled it between his hands as if he were shaping dough. He did the same to her left leg but she caught her breath sharply.

'Easy there,' he soothed, 'did that hurt, huh? Can you take more?'

'Yes and yes,' said Polly bravely, while Chip began a sensitive massage of her left thigh. He rolled it again. 'Better?' he asked.

'Much,' Polly smiled.

'OK, now spread them wide for me,' he said in as normal a voice as such a request permitted. Polly obliged and Chip ran his hands up the entire length of her inner thighs firmly and very fast, sweeping round to the front of the leg when his thumbs were just about to touch the gusset of her swimsuit.

'Wider?' he implored. Polly opened her mind and her legs a couple more inches. 'Good girl.'

No I'm not.

This time, Chip's progress up her inner thighs was much slower, the pressure from his hands alternately light and then firm. His eyes were closed.

'Your eyes are closed,' Polly whispered, wishing she was allowed to let go of the bars.

'I can feel so much more intensely,' he explained, his eyes shut.

'Oh,' said Polly. Chip's hands whispered their way up and down her thighs, up and down, again and again, lightly, firmly, up and down. 'Oh,' Polly murmured. 'Oh,' she gasped.

'Whose eyes are closed now?' said Chip, kissing the tip of her nose and then letting his lips fall to hers fleetingly. 'Nearly finished.'

'Really?' protested a disappointed Polly. 'You sure?'

'Let me just work on this area,' Chip said, massaging the tops of her thighs. Occasionally, he let a knuckle brush against her crotch but she could not anticipate when exactly and, by the time she moved her groin against the friction, his hand had gone again.

Still he rubbed at her thighs, trailing his hands back towards her knees and working there awhile. He tiptoed his fingers up her legs in a drunken walk of sorts, lessening the pressure the higher he reached. Neither of them had their eyes shut as Chip walked his fingers straight along the centre of the gusset of her swimsuit; they were gorging themselves on the sight of each other. He pushed the palm of his hand against her sex and kissed her deeply. He took gentle bites at the length of her arm, licked her armpit and then sucked her chin.

'You can let your hands go,' he said. Polly released them from the bars at once and encircled Chip just as soon as she had. She drew him against her, in between her legs; his erection, compressed within his trunks, grazed enticingly against her sex. He swept his hands up and down her torso; first slipping them under the arm-straps of her costume to fondle her breasts, then taking them down and burrowing behind the gusset to tangle with her pubic hair and search out the secret pocket of wet warmth. He inserted a finger deep within her and kept it very still, turned on by the way she bore down on his hand, the sound of her moan as she increased the pleasure by herself. Suddenly, he made his finger dance; as it moved, so the seam of her costume caught against her clitoris and, with a gasp and a thrust, she climaxed and laughed.

Chip submerged himself underwater, his hands soon appearing above the surface like Excalibur. He pulled at her swimsuit and she wriggled free, mesmerized by his disappearing hands and her own sudden nudity. He came up for breath, sucked each nipple in turn and then disappeared again under the water. Soon he was tugging at her swimsuit, suddenly it was propelled from the water to land just behind her head. Polly grabbed on the bars when Chip started licking at her sex, and closed her legs around his neck in her bid to weld her crotch to his face. As soon as Chip surfaced for breath, he penetrated her in one long, luxurious, effortless plunge, dipping his head alternately to each nipple in rhythm with his thrusts.

Polly's mind was empty and her conscience was clear, I'm afraid. Unbelievably, she was thinking of nothing, just languishing in the untold physical pleasure of the event, of the here and now. The then and the soon were irrelevant, at least to Polly they were. She was totally preoccupied by Chip's knowledge of the human anatomy, what he was expecting her body to do, the limits to which it could be bent and twisted. He was fine tuning her awareness of her own body, his consummate exploration intensifying the sensations she was experiencing. Chip's cock was rock hard, his fitness and athleticism was obviously transferable to this ragingly hard extra limb of his, and he was able to bestow on it supreme gymnastic talent. Polly grabbed on to his biceps, her wet fingers digging deep, the pinks of her nails turning quite white.

The strength of his back allowed him to withdraw his cock just until the tip threatened to spring right out from Polly. Then, with expert control, he plunged it back inside her, fast and deep. She soon learned just how much of an angle to thrust her pelvis forward so that she could meet the dive of his cock and feel him welded within her. Bliss. She could hardly keep her mouth closed or her eyes open. Her second orgasm, just as exquisite as her first, was synchronized perfectly with Chip's climax.

'Oh yeah, oh baby.'

That's me he's gasping about!

Amazingly, just a few seconds later, his right hand disappeared down into the water and then surfaced brandishing a condom with a knot in the neck.

'My goodness,' Polly marvelled, 'whenever — I mean — however? I mean, wow.'

Hadn't thought of that. Thank God he had.

'I'm pretty cool at holding my breath,' Chip informed her proudly, tossing the condom out of the pool to land on Polly's crumpled swimsuit.

Polly had two more hydrotherapy sessions. One a week, with no contact, let alone physiotherapy, in between. The last session was on the penultimate day of term, just a few hours before the final performance of the school revue. When she took her bow at the end of the show, Polly spied Chip in the second row of the enthralled audience. He was alternately clapping high above his head and then taking his fingers to his mouth and whistling through them. He was smiling directly at her, broadly. She grinned back, triumphant and happy.

The next morning, there was no time for a private farewell. They were both busy, Polly especially so, as she was taking an early flight home to England. They spared each other a few moments, diplomatically meeting midway across the hockey pitch. Bye bye. So long. It's been lovely knowing you. It was great having you. Look after yourself. You take care, you hear. Keep in touch. You too.

Yes, yes.

As if.

Needless to say, Polly Fenton and Chip Jonson would never meet again.

TWENTY-ONE

January 24th   *Darling Girl,*
You think you're   *very clever, don't*
you – cutting your paper into a heart shape
and then filling it with your chat, but look at me and
my clever computer! Polly: 1 – Max: 2. Glad to hear
you're settling back OK, although by the time you read
this, no doubt term'll be almost a month old. By the way,
you'll be pleased to know that I managed to escape the air-
port car park with some very nifty and probably highly ille-
gal driving, and less than a minute to spare. But what I
think will interest you more, if you don't already know, is
that Dom and Meg's date was so successful that they
organized another. And another. And another.
In the three weeks since you've been gone,
they've averaged bi-weekly meet-
ings and quite a few phone
calls in between. 'Is
this the start of
something
beautiful?'
I asked
Dom.

The   boy   mumbled
something incoherent   and blushed, can you
believe? For her part, Megan has been looking
at me most shyly, making polite if banal conversation.
Ah, the first flush of love – I remember it well, don't you!
Talking of love and its associated activities, I wonder if
you'll learn to ski this term, as you hope? If you take to it,
how about winter nuptials – and a honeymoon on the
slopes? Think about it. Well, I'll close now – just writing
brings you to the forefront of my mind – not that you're ever
absent. But, with such a clear picture of how you looked
on our last night together, I find myself somewhat horny
and I reckon I'll be able to manage a fast, furtive
tug and catch the post! The latter is a priority
but unfortunately, the former is a necessity (i.e. I can't nip to the postbox
with a raging hard-on, can
I?) Oh Polly my sweet –
that you were here
to assist. That
you   were
j u s t
h e r e.
Max.
X
X
X
X
X
X
X
X
X
X
X
X
X

Staff dining room
Lunchtime
4th Feb

Hiya Polly,

Just thought I'd drop you a quick line to thank you for your analysis of the US education system, which arrived this morning. I think I'll stick with G.C.S.E.s and A levels. I wonder if you'll be home before you learn how well your students perform in those S.A.T.s?

Suffice it to say, BGS is BGS and I've been dishing out detentions like they're going out of fashion. Lynn Drewe has been suspended for snogging her boyfriend bang outside the main school entrance. At lunch-time. She wasn't wearing her blazer but was sporting his school tie in her hair. Two days later, we expelled Clare Allinson – she'd notched up a fine trade selling single Marlboro Lights to the first and second years. Business as usual, you could say.

School, I hasten to add – and right at the end of the letter to cajole you into responding immediately – is merely how I fill my days. My nights, my dearest friend, I am filling with one Dominic Fyfield. Or shall we say one Dominic Fyfield is filling me at night?

Want to know more?

Then beg!

Love you, child,

Megan

February 13th

Darling Button,

> I don't
> mean to alarm you but I
> fear there's something amiss
> with the post as it's been just over
> three weeks since I wrote to you. Shall
> we go back to using Swiftair? What we're
> saving on phone calls we may as well put
> into postage! Well, hopefully St Valentine
> will be kind and prompt tomorrow. I sent
> Cupid the Courier on a transatlantic drop
> last week. Let me know if he fails to
> deliver – I'll go directly to Piccadilly
> Circus and break his legs! On
> Monday night Dominic
> didn't come home

AT ALL

> and this morning
> (Thursday) Megan suddenly
> appeared while I was eating my
> Sugar Puffs. She was wearing my
> brother's sweatshirt and had yester-
> day's mascara smeared under her
> eyes. Love is in the air, Polly – and I send
> you a great deluge of the stuff along with
> this regrettably short note. It is, I hope
> you notice, in the shape of Infinity.
> Sort of. In an upside-down, turned-
> on-its-head sort of way. Write
> again, sweetie – remember
> postcodes and stuff.
> Max

Feb
18th
P o l l y ,
T h a n k s
for   your
V a l e n t i n e
note (I'm not
having   a   dig)
(OK, yes I am) –
very   trusting   to
send it ordinary mail
but it arrived safely
(second post, day before
yesterday, two days after
Valentine's   Day)   so   I'm
replying directly to encourage
more – and longer, please.
Sounds like you've taken a lot on,
this term. The revue sounds fun,
how many performances? I'm glad to
hear that you're enjoying skiing and
I'm sure you look perfectly gorgeous in
your friend's salopettes. Why don't you
treat yourself to a set of your own – then
you'll have to have a snowy honeymoon to
justify the purchase. I still have mine, up in the
attic somewhere – but there again, so is my skate-
board, my Raleigh Chopper bicycle and that funny
pole with the tennis ball hanging off it. Dominic has
asked me to tell you that he's decided not to use those
photos he took of you for his Timepieces show. Don't
know why – probably not happy with the chiaroscuro or
the focus or something, you know these artist types! By the
way, I've had loads of commissions recently, thank you for
asking (not), and I have a deadline for a sizeable project the
day after tomorrow. Forgive me, therefore, for writing no
more. I will soon, promise. Love you – I really do.   MF

Feb 21st

Polly Fenton,

If I'd have held my breath waiting for your reply – well, this letter would have been my death notice. Luckily, I'm so engrossed in nightly enactments of the Kama Sutra *with your boyfriend's brother, that I only realized yesterday that it's been a letterless month from you to me. Write soon – or I'll send Anna Powell from Upper Five over (she collided with Jeanette Butcher in netball and knocked poor Susie Waldren out cold in hockey). You've been warned.*

M Reilly (Miss)

5th March

Dear Polly,

'I'm so busy' isn't much of an excuse, I'm afraid. I don't care if you only have one day off every fourteen, or if taking on the school revue has eaten into your free periods in which you feel you must now mark homework. I'm cer-tainly not sympathetic to the fact that skiing now appears to be your priority. I'm your best friend and unless I'm treated as such, I shall sever all contact immediately – and sever your right hand when I see you at Easter (less than a month, I might add) – only then will you have a worthy excuse not to write.

Cow.

Bitch.

I hate you.

Megan

PS. Not really. But please write soon.
PPS. Everything OK?
PPPS. I thought I'd put the above into small writing, just in case.

5th
March
Button,
Thanks   for
your appallingly
short   letter.   Mind
you, I suppose writing
poetically and at length is the
last thing I'd feel like doing if I'd
had a fall skiing. You sure you're OK? It
sounds horrible. Does that mean you don't
want a honeymoon on the slopes? Glad that you're
having physio. What an advantage that the school
has an Athletic Trainer on site and on standby. Well, I
wish you a full and speedy recovery – I simply can't
allow your inner thigh to be tender and stiff on your
return (just over a fortnight – and counting). Tell the
Athletic Trainer to have you shipshape for me –
impress on her/him the importance of the mobility
of the inner thigh to this transatlantic relation-
ship and its long-awaited reunion. I've made
extensive plans, my lover, and I assure
you, your eyes will truly water.
Max

March 18th

Dear Polly,
Thanks for your line.
Here's one from me:
Let me know which day and which flight when you
finally decide – and if you want me to meet you at
Heathrow.
Max

TWENTY-TWO

*P*olly left New England before Max's last letter arrived. She was returning to England feeling cleansed and healthy and a day early. As a surprise. She was eager to fling her arms around him and beam a very literal and heartfelt 'I'm back!' to his gorgeous, flabbergasted, well-known and much-loved face.

How it'll make up for my appalling lack of correspondence. Looking back, it feels an incredibly long time since I last saw him. And yet this last term galloped by. Was there really time to write? I didn't put it off. There was just so much to do. Never mind. Just wait till he sees me!

It was Friday afternoon, three o'clock, Logan Airport. Polly was gazing at the planes lumbering along the runways, a pot of unseasonal but delicious frozen yoghurt to hand to last the two-hour wait before her departure.

I must try Jen Carter again – and if it's the answerphone once more, I'll just have to leave a message. I know she's not due to leave until tomorrow and I can't really turn up unannounced, even if it is my flat. There's such a thing as manners, as decorum.

'Hi, this is Jen. I can't take your call right now. Leave a message after the tone. Thanks.'

214

'Oh, yes, hullo Jen Carter, it's Polly Fenton here. Hope you're well and Buster's looking after you. Um, I hope it's OK with you – only I'm taking an early flight – God I hate these machines. What I want to say is, I arrive at Heathrow at about four in the morning, would you believe, and I wonder if you'd mind me sneaking in and crashing on the settee? I hope that's OK. I want to surprise Max, you see – he thinks I'm not due till Sunday afternoon. I really hope you don't mind, I'll be as quiet as a mouse – maybe we could have breakfast together and finally meet and swap stories! Hope all of this is OK. I'll see you at some point tomorrow. Thanks a lot. Yup, bye. OK. Thanks, Jen. Oh! Just in case you speak to Max or Megan or anyone, please don't let on, as I want it to be a surprise. I think I've already said that. Brilliant. Many thanks. See you tomorrow.'

Wedged into the window seat by a very large couple on honeymoon, Polly tried to watch the in-flight movie. She couldn't concentrate. She tried to sleep. She wasn't tired. She tried to read but couldn't settle into her book, though she was already half-way through it. She felt too fidgety. With nerves, with exhilaration. She was going to see Max so soon. She'd had such a brilliant time. Her fling, so often reasoned to herself, had served only to rekindle her love for Max.

Chip's gone. Spring's almost summer. The snow's melting. That was then.

Now she felt truly ready. Things wouldn't be the same, oh no, they'd be far better.

Kate said so, didn't she? Every woman deserved a Chip once in her life.

She also warned you that it was a heavy, guilty secret.

No, no. I won't feel guilty – that's stupid. Destructive. What would be the point?

I'm not going to tell you. And I'm not going to tell you how you should feel.

Do you know, I remember what she said by heart actually: 'It's healthier to do and denounce, than not to and forever to wonder.'

She also told you, in no uncertain terms, that it's a crime of which she does not approve.

Sod Kate, it's nothing to do with her anyway.

Glad to hear you say it.

It was just a fling. With a purpose. Much good will come of it. No remorse. No guilt. Otherwise, what was the point?

Polly, are you deluded or just immoral?

Leave me to look at the duty free.

There's always a price on duty.

How very odd to emerge at Belsize Park underground station at 5.45 in the morning. It should feel like elevenses time but a sleepless flight has meant that, in mind and body, Polly is happy to subscribe to English time immediately and feels sufficiently tired and disorientated.

Doesn't everything look sleepy and grey!

You do, too.

Look! That café, which used to be an opticians, is now a flower shop.

Life goes on without you, despite you presuming England to be somehow on hold while you're away. Months have passed, Polly. For them as well as you. Turn left. Left again.

Buster!

Polly's cat was sitting on somebody's garden wall, licking his paw and his chops. When he registered Polly, he yawned, scumbled down the wall, walked in the opposite direction and then turned back, swaggering along half the distance that separated them before sitting down in the middle of the pavement.

'You knew!' Polly exclaimed in a broken whisper, dumping her rucksack in the middle of the pavement and skipping over to him. 'You knew I was coming home, didn't you?'

The cat wriggled free from her bear hug, fled away a few yards and then turned and sauntered back to her.

'Buster, you've been fighting,' Polly chided as she heaved on her rucksack, scooped up Buster and carried him like a babe in arms, much to his clearly visible horror.

'Here we are,' Polly smiled, her key in the lock of the front door.

Surprise, surprise – no bloody lights on. I'm back, Mrs Dale! I'm switching the hall light on and you'll not know who it was when you wake up in a couple of hours. Edith Dale 0 – Polly Fenton 1!

'Buster!' she hissed as the cat scampered up the stairs towards the other flats, claws dragging surely too loudly on the poor carpet. However, as Buster loathed Mrs Dale as much as Polly feared her, he was soon down again, purring clangorously at his own front door.

'Ssh,' Polly whispered, easing her key and slipping into her flat. She had to swallow hard to suppress the urge to sing out 'I'm home!' to all asunder. She closed the door soundlessly and peeled her ears at the base of the five steps which led up to her bedroom and her bathroom. Silence.

Sleeping like a baby, good old Jen Carter. Sleep on, sleep tight, see you in the morning proper.

Polly went into her sitting-room, through to her tiny kitchen and drank down a glass of water without pausing for breath.

Yeuch! Thames Water – I'd forgotten how strongly it tastes and smells, but what can one expect? It's been filtered through six other people. In Vermont, our water is fresh from the mountains.

This *is* your water, Polly, don't lose sight of that. You'd better reacquire a taste for it.

She didn't dare boil the kettle though the notion of a cup of Earl Grey was all that had kept her from screaming on the flight. She opened the fridge, looked inside and assessed those contents which established a connection with Jen Carter, and those which presented utter disparity. She closed the fridge door. She had a headache.

Sitting on her settee, she gazed out to her small patio and was pleased to see, though now withered, a crowd of daffodils whose bulbs the squirrels had not pillaged. She yawned and realized that she was too exhausted to draw the curtains, to leave the settee into which she was now welded. She knew she was too tired for dawn to intrude on her slumber and so she curled up, smiled in welcome at her Picasso print, and fell asleep deeply. Somewhere, in a fugged corner of a nondescript dream, she heard someone laugh and gasp. And then she saw and heard nothing until the sound of the floorboards creaking above roused her. It was half past nine.

I'm awake. Wide. I am. I'm back. Here comes Jen. No? Not yet? She's gone into the bathroom. Wake up, Polly, stay awake!

Here comes Jen.

Polly sat neatly on the settee, clasping her hands and then unclasping them, taking a book to her lap and then putting it aside, while she counted the five stairs being descended.

Here comes Jen.

Jen jumped out of her skin.

'Hullo, at last,' Polly smiled.

'Who are you?' gasped a horrified Jen Carter. 'You Polly?'

''Course I'm Polly,' she laughed, holding out her hand, taking Jen's and shaking it warmly.

'What you doing here?' Jen continued, her eyebrows so furrowed that they had all but merged into one.

'I *live* here,' said Polly cautiously, tipping her head and wondering why the girl looked so appalled.

Aha! That's why.

Both girls turned their heads in the vague direction of the bathroom above. Someone was having a shower.

Hussy! Woman after my own heart! Put it there.

Polly held out her hand once more. Jen held on to it, somewhat distractedly. 'What you doing here?' she repeated.

Polly swivelled her head to regard the answering machine. It was flashing.

'I left you a message,' she explained, 'from Logan. Yesterday. Evening. For you. Did you not receive it?'

Frowning hard at the answering machine, Jen walked over to it and pressed 'play'. Nothing happened.

'Guard,' Jen said, over and over; Polly finally realizing it was to the good Lord whom she petitioned, not some hitherto unknown function of her answering machine.

'Volume,' Jen shrugged in apology to Polly, turning it back up so that the last drifts of Polly's message could be heard.

'I'm sorry,' Polly said, though for what she was unsure.

'No problem,' Jen said distractedly, her head pulled as if by some imaginary magnet in the approximate direction of the stairs. Polly watched Jen gulp as they heard the footfalls descend the short flight.

'I won't tell,' Polly smiled in what she hoped was a conniving and sisterly way.

Serves you right, Chip!

'Look—' Jen starts.

'Ssh!' Polly dismisses amicably.

'Breakfa—' says Max, entering the room, wearing boxer shorts and nothing else.

Serves you right, Polly.

TWENTY-THREE

*N*ow hold on a minute. Wait up. Hang about a bit. Steady on. What on earth? Whoah!

Leave the three of them suspended in their agony. Catch up on the events in England. We've hardly seen Max these past weeks. We've been too caught up with Polly. Did we really stop and wonder whether she'd written much, to Max, to anyone? Weren't we rather caught up in the tumble and sport that constituted Polly's spring term? We thought of Max in passing. We wondered what on earth Polly was doing. But we were also compelled to bear close witness to all that she was to do. Even if it meant we too pushed Max just out of our field of vision for a while. It's not just Polly who's been turning a blind eye. Unashamedly – regrettably.

Back track. Rewind.

* * *

'Polly get off OK?' Dominic asked Max when he returned from the airport.

'Fine,' Max smiled wistfully. 'She said "yes".'

'Yes?' puzzled Dominic. 'Want a beer?'

'Yes,' said Max.

'She said "yes" to a beer?'

Max gave his brother a withering look of profound pity and affection. 'To *marry*ing me, twat.'

'Hadn't she said "yes" already?' Dominic questioned with an air of suspicion.

'Just what I thought,' Max laughed. 'Anyway, it's all official and sealed and just waiting to be signed now. Perhaps some time in the autumn.'

'Feathering her bed, no doubt,' Dominic said very quietly and not to Max, who heard nevertheless.

'What did you say?'

'Nothing.'

'No, Dominic,' Max persisted defensively, 'what do you mean?'

'Nothing. Honestly.'

'Honesty? Well, tell me what you said then – I mean, I know what you *said*, but what are you implying?'

'Look,' said Dominic, trying to appear nonchalant and rifling somewhat pointlessly through the contents of their fridge to increase this impression, 'I don't know. It's just – I don't bloody know – but you're my brother and, if she marries you, she'd better treat you a damn sight better than she has this last fortnight.'

'What are you on about?' Max asked, backing away slightly, feeling at once humiliated and also angry. 'And how about your behaviour towards her? I don't think I heard you ask about Vermont at all.'

'You're my brother,' Dominic stressed, seeing the bait but tactfully swerving from it, 'my younger brother. It's my duty and my pleasure to look out for you.'

'And?'

'As I say, I just feel that Polly was distant. Uncharacteristically so.'

'You know she has her little quiet periods,' Max said impatiently, 'it would be impossible to sustain her level of effervescence constantly.'

'I'm just saying that she seemed distant, Max – aloof. Different.'

'You don't know what you're talking about,' Max warned.

Dominic shrugged.

'Fuck you, Dom.'

Dominic shrugged again.

Over the next month, the more Dominic fell for Megan, and the less often Polly wrote – and the less she wrote when she did – the more Dominic's suspicions seemed well grounded, the less he liked Polly, and the more he wished to protect his seemingly unsuspecting brother.

'I know what you mean,' rued Megan reluctantly, running her fingers through Dominic's hair. 'Her last letter to me was basically a carbon copy of that which she wrote to Max, not that I let on – he seemed delighted with it. A couple of paragraphs about the school revue and pink salopettes.'

'Don't you think it a little suspect?' Dominic asked, taking Megan's hand from his head and kissing each finger in turn.

'Pink salopettes and Polly is a notion more frightening than suspicious,' Megan laughed, wishing to lighten the tone, close the conversation and get down to some steamy sex.

Dominic couldn't resist. What was Polly worth anyway? Certainly not coming between him and the untold pleasures and wiles of Megan's gorgeous body.

'The trouble with Polly,' Megan pondered later, while sharing a post-coital bowl of cornflakes with Dominic at midnight, 'is that she does so adore people. She's so tactile and trusting. She loves to be loved – I feel it's what she lives for.'

'But can we trust her?' Dominic asked, placing a single cornflake on Megan's collar bone and then dabbing it off with his tongue. Megan swooned at his gesture and then pulled away to consider his words.

'I really can't believe that we couldn't. Not after all this time. Not Polly Fenton.'

Whenever specks of doubt and flickers of unease touched

down on Max, he swept them away as if they were dust on his shoulder. Furthermore, he reprimanded himself for being stupid, told himself to get a grip and threw himself into his work. He took on more commissions than he could handle in a working day, often staying in his studio until nine at night. This had a threefold function: it kept him utterly occupied and focused, his bank balance breathed a sigh of relief, and it kept Dominic at bay and off his back.

Max had always looked up to his older brother; previously he had been easily swayed by him. Swapping bicycles for skateboards. Having a flat-top haircut. Drinking a yard of ale. Supporting Spurs over the Gunners. Dropping acid on Primrose Hill. Going on the Waltzer at Hampstead Heath fair. Going for the vindaloo. However, when it came to the opposite sex, Max had never sought Dominic's advice, never subscribed to his methods, or been remotely envious of his brother's ability to maintain a ready selection of keen, separate and secret participants. He was thus insulted that his brother should insinuate that Polly was anything other than Max knew and loved her to be.

I mean, what would Dom know? Meg's the first woman who's proving more than a flirtation whereas Polly and I have been together for five years. I think I'm entitled to know best what she wants in life and I know that she wants for nothing in me.

At weekends, Max socialized with friends and assured them that Polly was fine, having a super time and yes, let's all do something when she's home in six weeks. What was the point in taking on board any of Dominic's misgivings? Max was sure to talk breezily about Polly in front of his brother. There was nothing wrong, nothing remotely amiss, anyway. Was there?

There's not a lot to say, really – certainly nothing to confide. Yes, she writes infrequently. Yes, her letters are becoming shorter and less, well, personalized. But I'm happy to credit distance with her distance – and acknowledge that her distance is most probably her means of survival. Anyway, the girl does want to spend her life with me after all. Doesn't she?

When no Valentine's card arrived, however, Max was somewhat unnerved. Not because he was taken in by all the commercialized panoply of the day, but because Polly was traditionally ridiculously slushy on February 14th. Last year she had cut the bread into heart-shapes before she toasted it. The year before, she left a trail of love-heart sweets from her front door to her bedroom, with an agonizing detour to the patio doors. The year before that, she'd hidden champagne and plastic cups in a bag under a thatch of shrubs on Golders Hill Park. This year, it was a hasty note which arrived two days late.

On Valentine's Day itself however, Max wondered, very quietly, if perhaps he was making excuses for her. Almost immediately, he told himself to shut up.

School revue, remember, on top of essays and dorm responsibilities.

He knew Polly; he loved her; there was nothing to worry about. Why should her termly absence cause any change to his life?

The nub of the matter was that he feared that the fact he doubted her somehow implied he was having doubts himself. Previously, he'd never really thought twice about the longevity of his relationship – once Polly was on the scene, he'd never touched upon the thought of her not being there. Of her not wanting him. Of him not wanting her.

'Hullo. Is that Jen?'

'Yeah?'

'Hullo there, this is Dominic Fyfield.'

What am I doing?

'Hi Dom, how you doing?'

'I'm very well, thanks – you?'

'Cool!'

'I was – we were, Max and I – wondering if you'd like to come over tomorrow night?'

Not that I've mentioned it to him just yet.

'A Tuesday night?'

'Not just any old Tuesday – it's Shrove Tuesday and we're going to have a pancake fest.'

'Hey, that sounds fun.'

'Edible fun, I hasten to add.'

'I'm there. I'll see you guys later.'

'Er, no – tomorrow?'

'Yeah – sure. That's what I said, hey?'

'Super.'

'Bye for now.'

I just want to observe, Dominic decided as he gazed at the telephone, *I just want to see if those signs are still there. I want to see if she sparkles at Max again. He deserves to be sparkled at.*

Jen sparkled. Dominic smiled. Megan licked her lips. Max enjoyed himself very much.

Max won the Highest Toss Grand Prix. Megan continued to lick her lips. Dominic was victorious in the Most Pancakes Consumed Competition. Jen brought maple syrup for which her English friends developed an instant and highly dangerous penchant.

'If it was snowing, we could have Sugar on Snow,' Jen explained. Max prayed out loud for snow. Everyone rushed over to the window to check and then collapsed on the sofa laughing.

'I'm going to have to repaint the kitchen ceiling,' Max moaned.

'That's some small price to pay for being Highest Toss Supreme Champion,' Jen justified.

'I don't want to think about pancakes,' Megan protested, patting her stomach and looking doe-eyed at Dominic for reassurance. His wink more than sufficed.

Ready? he mouthed.

Megan's wink more than answered.

'Right,' said Dominic, 'we're off.'

'Brilliant evening,' said Megan, 'see you at school, Jen.'

'Later, guys,' said Jen without looking at either of them.

'See you,' said Max.

'Do you think that's OK?' Megan wonders. 'To leave them? Unchaperoned?'

'Why shouldn't it be?' Dominic replies. 'What's the harm and where's the temptation?'

'True,' says Megan, her mind now meandering on to all the tempting things she could do to Dominic once they'd walked off the pancakes.

Jen and Max sat and watched the ten o'clock news.

'Hey, I gotta get going,' Jen said, when the news came to a feature on public utilities privatization, 'it's a school night, after all.'

'You can't go now,' Max remonstrated, 'we have to wait for *And Finally*.'

'And finally,' said Trevor MacDonald, right on cue, 'don't turn your nose up at mould. Thomas Wilson, a mechanic from Seaton in Devon, has found that it can form the basis of a fabric close to cashmere. Jenny Logan reports.'

Max and Jen regarded each other, wrinkled their noses and shook their heads.

'I'll walk you back,' said Max.

'No problem,' said Jen with a nonchalant shrug.

'I insist – anyway, I have a gut full of pancakes to walk off.'

'Heck – and I thought you were just being gentlemanly.'

'Did you take Jen home?' Dominic asks the next evening, juggling hot baked potatoes from oven to plate.

It's an innocent question.

'Yup. We walked,' Max replies, with no aside.

'Nice girl,' Dominic says. *Come on mate, respond.*

Max nods behind his hand, fanning the scalding potato which fills his mouth and makes speech impossible.

226

'Why don't we all go to the films on Saturday?' Dominic proposes lightly.

It's an innocent suggestion.

'That'd be fun,' says Max slightly breathlessly, having downed a pint-glass of water in one.

Quite the cosy little foursome.

TWENTY-FOUR

*W*ho is Jen Carter? This Jen Carter Person who slept with Max behind our backs? Or rather when we were preoccupied watching other things. Who is the person behind the tall and good-looking exterior: straight, tanned figure, straight white teeth and straight blonde hair? You'll find a good teacher, a great athlete and a friendly personality but you won't find much more. There's little to dislike about Jen but there's not much to go wild for either; she's amicable without being enchanting, she's easygoing but not dull. *Nice* is the most appropriate word because, like Jen, it is rather ordinary, a little unimaginative, not hugely expressive and oughtn't to surface too often.

She's a deceptive strawberry, is Jen Carter. You'd pick her from the punnet, with her promising exterior, but a bite reveals a taste that is merely pleasant. Often the smaller fruit, even that with a touch of greenness around the outer edge, will offer such sweetness to make your jaw sting. Sometimes, though, that's just too much; sometimes a non-committal taste is all that is desired. At least you know where you stand with *nice*.

And Chip?

They've been together since summer term last year.

That *long*?

Is she really Mr Jonson's type?

Jen Carter was indeed easy prey. But, you see, she is also a fabulous lay. Once he had her, Chip didn't have to try very hard to keep her; she wouldn't be going anywhere, why should she? She felt that. He knew that. Like mint-choc-chip ice-cream – if you like it, why bother to taste a different flavour? Stick with MCC. Like Nike Air trainers – if the fit is good, why change to Reebok? Like teaching English at Hubbardtons Academy – if you enjoy the job, why should you want to look for another elsewhere? Jen is not apathetic, she's simply nice and uncomplicated and that's how she likes her life to be too. She's always veered away from complications in favour of what's known.

Why meddle if it ain't broken, hey?

Say they're out of mint-choc-chip ice-cream?

Never gonna happen.

Say your feet change and Nike are no longer comfortable.

My feet won't change – they're my feet for Chrissake.

Say your contract at Hubbardtons Academy is not renewed.

Why wouldn't it be? Everything's cool.

That's probably the problem – a little too cool. And yet she sparkled at Max Fyfield, she made a bee-line for him in Budgen's. Ask her why and she'll just shrug and say he's a nice guy, he's cute.

Even Megan, initially keen to find fault in this girl proposing to masquerade for a year as Polly, found nothing to dislike apart from elements of pronunciation and these were more of an irritant anyway. Megan was pleased for Jen to join her, Dominic and Max for Sunday strolls, Monday movies and sometimes supper on Saturdays. She was happy to share her space in the staff room with her and was grateful for the education in low-fat matters and conversion to decaffeinated coffee.

'What's coffee without caffeine?' Max queried with visible

229

horror which he hoped was not impolite but which he could not help anyway.

Like a log-effect gas fire. Or skimmed milk. Or strawberry flavouring.

Now, Chip might be the epitome of Cute, but how Good he is, is a matter of some debate. He told Powers Mateland that he and Jen had broken up long before he informed Jen of the fact, but just before he jumped into the hydrotherapy pool with Polly (or, rather, jumped Polly in the jacuzzi). When Jen phoned him a week before the end of term to give him her flight details, he decided that now was as good a time as any. First, though, he would tell her about his new job in Chicago. He congratulated himself, thinking this very diplomatic, believing the one substantiated the other and would therefore lessen the blow each might have on Jen.

'I'm going to Chicago.'

'You can't meet me at Logan?'

'Sure, I can meet you – but I'm going to Chicago. I got a great job there. I think we should break up.'

'Hullo?' said Megan into her telephone receiver. 'Hullo?'

'Who is it?' Dominic whispered, sidling up to her on the sofa, wondering what should crease Megan's lovely forehead so. Megan shrugged and smiled. 'Hullo?' she said again. She heard scuffling and a gasp. 'Look,' she barked, 'if this is some heavy-breathing effort, it's pathetic and it isn't working – you sound more like a snivelling child.'

'Do you want me to—?' asked Dominic, gesturing the cutting of a throat. Megan shook her head but held the receiver out a little so he could hear for himself.

'Megan?'

'Hullo?'

'It's Jen.'

'God, I thought you were a heavy-breathing snivelling kid.'

'I'm snivellin' all right. I got no heating and no boyfriend.'

Megan listened patiently to a round of heaving, shivering sobs.

'Do you want to come over?' she asked gently, surprising herself that actually she wouldn't mind.

'No,' Jen sniffed.

'Would you like me to come over to you?' Megan prodded, realizing that she did feel for the girl.

'No,' Jen wailed.

'Would you like Max to come and fix your heating?' asked Dominic, taking the phone.

'Yes,' sobbed Jen, 'I'm so damned cold.'

Megan went to put the pasta on while Dominic dialled Max's studio.

Chump – or whatever his name is – chucks Jen. Polly's not been heard from for three weeks. Polly and Chunk are in the same place. Max the Forgotten and Jennifer the Jilted are in the same place too.

Nah!

Too corny to be credible.

'Max?'

I shouldn't encourage. It's none of my business.

'Dom.'

'Heating's down in Polly's flat.'

Go and make Jen feel warm. It'll do you good too.

'Shit. Did you tell her to tap the boiler to the rhythm of *Another One Bites The Dust*?'

'No – I couldn't remember which Queen tune it was – I was going to suggest *We Will Rock You*.'

'Wouldn't work – I went through their entire backlist until I struck success. OK, I'll go and give the boiler a whack.'

'Cheers.'

'You home later?'

'Depends.'

'On what?'

'On what Megan has to offer for pudding.'

Max had the boiler working and his idiosyncratic technique

soon had Jen smiling. Max regarded her; eyes red and hair hanging limply, smile worn on the exterior of her face alone. She looked vulnerable and tired and he felt compelled to stay; just a while. It was nine o'clock. A quiet chord chimed somewhere at the back of his mind.

'You OK?'

'Sure,' said Jen, turning away.

'Sure?' Max pressed.

'I got chucked,' Jen explained, holding aloft a jar of coffee and raising her eyebrows at Max. He could see that it was decaffeinated but he accepted with a gracious nod, knowing that Jen was offering the beverage in return for an understanding ear. 'You know?' she said. 'Ditched. Chip finished with me. He's going to Chicago.'

'I'm so sorry,' Max said kindly, hoping that lots of milk would make up for the lack of caffeine. 'Was it out of the blue?'

'I guess,' said Jen, 'I mean, he's been a little distant – hardly phones, doesn't write much. But, like, he swore things were cool. And, heck, I believed him – had no reason not to.'

Max wondered whether the milky coffee was the cause of his sudden queasiness. He usually took it black. Caffeinated. Real and strong.

'If it's any consolation,' he said quietly, 'Polly's been a little, um, *off* too, recently.'

'Yeah, but is she moving to Chicago?'

'Er, no.'

'And has she finished with you?'

'Well, no.'

Jen shrugged and rested her case, resting her head in her hands. Max wanted to reach to her, to offer some comfort but stopped himself in favour of decorum and a hopefully soothing, 'Poor you – it obviously wasn't meant to be.'

'I don't want to go home,' Jen rued, 'can you believe that?'

Max considered this and then nodded. 'I can understand – because, I suppose, it's where the reality of your life is indisputable. And that very fact is probably what most frightens you – am I right?'

Though Jen's smile was still small, it ran a little deeper. She took her hand to Max and he placed his other over the top of hers in comfort and support.

'Thanks Max,' said Jen, a slight sparkle temporarily lifting the dullness of her eyes.

*　*　*

Max Fyfield is the hero of our story. At this stage, Polly is merely our female lead for there is little heroic to commend her or elevate her status.

Max had no idea that, four days after holding Jen's hand over Polly's pine table, he would be having sex with her. And on the pine table too. He had no idea because he had no premeditated desire to, he had hatched no plan, no notion tickled his fancy. That's Max all over, honourable and trusting, fancying only Polly and hanging on patiently until he can tickle her fancy again. There is no ounce of scheming within him, not a bad bone in his body apart from his collar bone which he has broken twice in rugby. Perhaps it is because Max is so trusting that those around him trust him so, that he is revered and adored and gravitated towards. Max is so strong, isn't he? That's why those close to him know they can turn to him in their hours of need. Max doesn't have hours of need, does he? Doesn't need them. He's far too capable, mature and steady. Good job, really, because it would be absolutely devastating to see him otherwise. It would be like seeing your father cry. It would be like a king saying he couldn't cope. It would be like a fireman announcing he had lost his nerve. It would be unthinkable. Max is dependable, all who know him depend on it.

Now Polly we know to be inherently good, we know her potential to flow with love and passion, but she needs to shape up, she needs to be shown the error of her ways, she needs to feel utterly wretched; moreover, she deserves to.

233

And yet, because it is Polly who has come across Max *in fla-grante*, ironically – and perhaps unfairly – it is Max who will initially suffer sickening guilt. He will torment himself: how could he do this to her? He will chastise himself: what has she done to deserve it? He will feel utterly wretched. That Max will suffer is patently unfair, but the knowledge of his pain should hasten Polly's recovery, her restoration.

Would it appease his guilt if Polly was to admit to her crime? Or should she heed Kate's caution at all costs? What should she do? What are they going to do? What's going to happen? What do we want to happen? Wait. First, Max's interlude with Jen must be given appropriate lineage. We owe it to Max. He has every right to have his sexual prowess chronicled. From Polly's passion for Chip, one might very well wonder if Max's bedroom manners are somehow lacking. This is certainly not the case. Just ask Jen.

'Thanks a bunch, Max,' said Jen as she saw Max to the door; the flat and her spirit now sufficiently warmed.

'No problem,' Max responded. He smiled benevolently. 'You look after yourself – just call if you need anything, honestly. I'm a good listener *and* a good plumber.'

'Hug?'

'Sorry?'

Jen shrugged and cocked her head, 'I could sure use a hug,' she repeated, turning the palms of her hands for emphasis. *Hug* was a word Polly never used, she favoured *cuddle*, invariably requested in suitably babyish tones. Max was taken aback – not so much at the concept but at the sudden fact that a hug with Jen was actually very appealing and cuddles with Polly were at once dismissed.

Jen and Max hugged tenderly for a moment before Max made to pull away, presuming the action to be as short as the word, certainly a single gesture. However, the slightest pressure at the back of his neck from Jen's wrists invited and decided him to stay put a while longer. He closed his eyes and made an involuntary murmur in his throat which, to his relief, also sounded deceptively like platonic comfort. He stroked Jen's back in a consoling kind of way, while subconsciously logging the feel of her for future contemplation.

'You hug good,' said Jen with gratitude.

'Just add it to my aforementioned qualifications,' Max smiled.

Max walked back up Haverstock Hill pleasantly baffled.

Odd. Very odd. It's been ages since I felt another woman's body. I mean, I embrace my female friends, but I suppose I do so without actually feeling them, an easily executed gesture that I don't really think about. My hands and arms don't really log any interesting information. But Jen, she made my cock stir, damn and praise her. I didn't get hard – more of what I term a lob-on. When I made to go – but when she invited me to hold her a little longer – that's when. I wonder if she could tell. Why do I half hope that she could?

It felt different, a change. She's tall, she's slim and athletic. I mean, Polly's slim but in a soft way – hers is a body you want to scoop up, cradle. Jen? Lithe and sexy and she's, I don't know, I haven't really thought of her – certainly not in a compare and contrast with Polly. I won't dwell on it, though. It was just a hug, wasn't it? An Americanized platonic gesture. Any more would be dangerous, wouldn't it? I don't want any more anyway, do I? I don't really want to think about it any more. It could be dangerous. I shouldn't.

However, when the doormat was still letterless two mornings later, the answering machine silent, Max decided that now he too could do with a hug.

I don't know what time Polly arrives home the day after tomorrow because she has not contacted me to tell me. Polly has not been in touch for almost a month. I wonder. I do not want to wonder why. I want a hug and not a cuddle and I do not want to wonder why.

'Jen?'

Shit, I should hang up.

'Max, hi there.'

'How's the heating?'
That's good, keep it nice and neutral.
'Feeling hot.'
'Great. Um. I just.'
Come on, fool.
'You want to come for a bite to eat?'
Oh.
'Love to. When? Tonight?'
'Well, you ain't got much choice – I fly tomorrow after-noon. I'll see you at seven, hey?'
Oh.
'You will.'
Oh.

'Megan's coming over tonight,' said Dominic, warily regard-ing his brother who was staring hard at a totally uninspiring corner of their sitting-room.
Where's he gone?
'Oh yes?' Max mustered.
'Do you want to stay in and play the gooseberry from hell who ultimately meets an untimely and hideous death?' Dominic asked. 'Or will you play golden boy and bog off, thus earning an extravagant position in my will and my favour?'
'I'm going out,' Max said distractedly and left the room before his brother had a chance to ask where, when and with whom.
'Change of plan,' Dominic called outside the bathroom door half an hour later, 'I'm going round to Megan's. You *have* been invited, I might add; cordially by her, begrudg-ingly by me.'
Or are you still going out, dark horse?
'I'm going out,' filtered Max's reply through the door before the noise of the power-shower made further commu-nication impossible.
'Have fun, bro,' said Dominic quietly as he closed the front door.

Have a good time.

As Max was unzipping Jen's little black dress, he did wonder what on earth he was doing, what in God's name he was about to do and how the hell did he get to this stage anyway.

Not that this is hell.

Jen *had* welcomed him with a fine hug and a lingering kiss to each cheek which just grazed the corners of his mouth; she *had* toyed suggestively with an asparagus spear during dinner and then spoon-fed him the remainder of her Häagen Dazs once he had finished his own portion. She *had* touched his arm, his shoulder, at regular intervals to add unnecessary emphasis to their conversation.

As Max slipped his hand inside the back of her dress, stroked up her spine, over her shoulder, he wondered if he *had*, in any way, given her a come-on let alone the go-ahead?

But there again, Max *did* make a clearly nonchalant shrug in answer to Jen's enquiry of Polly's arrival times. He *did* touch Jen's arm twice, her knee once, during the meal, and didn't he allow his body to brush by hers as they did the washing up? Although it was utterly out of context, he *did* reiterate the fact that Polly's correspondence was sporadic and perfunctory and he *had* brushed away Jen's ensuing sympathy in a most blasé fashion. Most telling, though, he had allowed himself to be kissed and he willingly kissed back – without any hastily drawn justification regarding the clever prevention of decaffeinated coffee. Now, deftly, he was unhooking this woman's bra, grazing the side of her neck with his mouth, pushing the dress away and cupping her breasts, her bra hanging loosely over his hands. The pine table ceased to be Polly's as he and Jen gravitated towards it whilst they stripped each other of their clothing. And Polly ceased to exist when Max kissed his way down Jen's torso, spread her legs and licked at her sex.

Because they were not in love with each other, they took their pleasure greedily. They didn't bother with gentle kisses and hair stroking, meaningful looks and soothing caresses. They had one shared purpose: to feel good about

237

themselves and to reassert their worth. Max's virility was redefined and Jen's desirability reconfirmed.

'Chip must be mad,' Max panted, thrusting up inside Jen and pushing himself up on to his arms so he could peruse her fabulous figure.

'Polly should take care not to lose you,' Jen marvelled as she ran her index finger up the length of Max's cock, pouted her lips and sucked him straight into her mouth.

'Bite me,' Jen gasped, grabbing Max's buttocks and humping her groin; her sex sucking up his cock. Max bit her lower lip and neck and chewed on her nipples until she winced and begged him not to stop. They concentrated hard and at length on the sight of Max penetrating Jen.

'That's some cock,' Jen praised as Max drew it out and then plunged back into her.

Dream on, Chip.

'God, you've got great tits,' said Max as he rubbed the palm of his hands over her nipples and gorged himself on the sight and commendable size of them.

Bad luck, Polly.

Max and Jen regularly reached the point of orgasm but instinctively backed off. They were in no hurry. This was a night to remember. They interspersed penetrative sex with bouts of oral and aural sex. No woman had ever said 'Fuck me' to Max and the very sound of the words turned him on greatly. He was rough and assertive because she was begging for it. Jen was exhilarated to actually see a man being so actively turned on by her; Max's eyes were everywhere and the more he feasted on the sight of her, the harder he screwed her.

Look what I'm doing.

Yeah, look what I'm doing.

With their bodies wet with sweat, with saliva and with their juices, they peeled apart and caught their breath. Max sat on the farmhouse chair and Jen squatted over him, his hands just under her breasts as he levered her up and down. She sat right on him and let her body flow back while Max's

238

arms supported her. His cock shouldn't be able to bend in such an extreme way but, obviously, it could and it felt awesome. Jen wriggled up a little so that his cock sprang free and practically hit against his stomach. She sucked him again in two long movements and then she turned away from him, holding on tight to the table, her rump facing Max invitingly. He took her from behind and made her yell. He grabbed her hair and twisted her head, eating at her mouth while he bore down on her. Max held on to her waist and propelled himself into her, alternately slowing and then quickening the pace of his thrusts in response to her moaning. As they came, they regarded each other in the mirror on the wall to the right of them. They smiled triumphantly, at themselves, at each other.

Boy, you sure give Chip a run for his money.

Christ that was good.

Silently, they congratulated each other and themselves. Later, they slept without their bodies touching and dreamed independently of each other.

TWENTY-FIVE

Am I in Polly's bed?
         Oh Jesus.
                 It's in the past.
                         It's gone.
                                 I need a cold shower.
                                         That's better.
                                 I ought to have breakfast.
         I ought to seal it all with polite dignity.
     Yes.
Breakfast then.

TWENTY-SIX

*P*olly ran, an apple in one hand, her keys in the other. She was aware, when she bolted through the sitting-room, that Jen was nowhere and that Max stood with his back to the sofa, his head to one side, looking out at the patio. In his boxer shorts.

Good, he can't see me.

She grabbed her jacket and flew from her flat. Dashed along the communal hallway and blasted out into the street. She charged along, turned a corner and was sick.

Good, he didn't see me.

She rested against a lamppost and regarded the apple. She smelt it. Granny Smith.

I don't even have a Granny.

She hurled it in a strong, low shot. It bounced once, skittled along the tarmac and than came to rest. She jogged over to it, took it carefully in her hands as if it was a road-kill bird and she wept for it.

Look what I have the ability to do.

Funereally, she returned to the pavement and gently laid the apple to rest in somebody's front garden. She stood, in stillness and in silence, for a moment but found no peace. Her body needed to move as fast as her mind, to race alongside her heart. On she hurtled. To Swiss Cottage. All the way, in the gutter.

She ran on. By the time she reached Megan's street, Polly's breathing sounded like the asthmatic rasping of her childhood. She could barely see from the sweat which filmed over her eyes.

Megan's door.

It opened and Dominic appeared, stretching his arms above his head before closing the door.

Max's brother.

'Polly?'

She couldn't speak but hung on to him not for comfort but from necessity. Suddenly she felt very dizzy. She slid her grasp down his arms and crumpled her body to the pavement. He sat on his heels beside her.

'Polly?'

Gently, he pushed her head between her knees and kept a hand to the back of her drenched head. The heaving of her body eventually lessened. Dominic inched her backwards until she sat with her back to Megan's garden wall. Her head was still between her knees but Dominic's hand was gone. The breeze of a late March morning licked at her neck and she began to cool.

'Polly?'

'I'm early,' she said.

'Early?'

'I saw Jen,' she said.

'Jen?'

'And Max,' she said.

'*Max?*'

'In my flat, together,' she said.

'To-*geth*-er?'

'Yes.'

'Did you deserve this?' Dominic asks, holding her face roughly.

'Yes,' Polly replies, without flinching, before looking away.

Five minutes later, Polly rang Megan's bell.

'Pol! *Ly?*'

With an arm tenderly around Polly's shoulders, Megan guided her through into her flat. She eased Polly's jacket away, prised open her right hand to reveal deep purple scores from the pressure of her finger nails, prised open her left hand to find a sticky brown mush which, after a cautious sniff, turned out to be apple. She took her through to the kitchen and ran the tap, holding Polly's wrists and guiding her hands under the water. Then she dried them and switched on the kettle, her arm back around Polly's shoulders. Megan had seen her face only on opening the door. A glimpse had been enough. Now, she was careful to avoid eye contact for she perceived Polly to be as edgy as a fawn ready to bolt.

Megan wrapped Polly's hands around a mug of heavily sweetened tea and took her through to the sitting-room, to the comfortable settee, to the comfort of her bosom into which Polly cried. And cried and cried. Megan hummed *Oh Danny Boy* but the plaintive tune and Megan's melodious voice replenished Polly's tears so Megan fell silent while wondering what on earth was going on. Eventually, after clearing her nose directly into Megan's T-shirt, Polly took a deep, faltering breath and spoke.

'That's better,' she said. She turned to Megan and her brow crumpled. 'I'm early,' she explained. 'I left a message on my answering machine to say I'd be early. As a surprise. Not the message, but my early arrival.'

Megan nodded.

'I met Jen,' said Polly. Megan smiled. 'Max was there,' Polly continued.

'Not the boiler again?' Megan questioned, 'it's been playing up quite a lot recently.'

So have I, thought Polly.

'He's been round a few times to fix it.'

Chip came a few times and fixed me, thought Polly, rubbing her left thigh subconsciously.

'The boiler?' Megan asked again.

'Not the boiler. Max and Jen were – you know, together.'

'For the love of Jesus!' Megan exclaimed, crossing herself and dropping her head to her hands. '*Max?*' Polly nodded. 'You sure they were – they had – that it *wasn't* the boiler?'

Polly nodded.

'Bastard,' Megan spat. 'Bitch,' she hissed.

Shit, are we responsible in some way? Did we encourage Max? Jen? I mean, I never meant this to happen, of course.

'No,' said Polly in a quiet, hollow voice.

'No?' Megan jerked, 'hey?'

'It's my fault.'

'Don't you go blaming yourself,' Megan chided, poking Polly on the arm while quoting silently the dictum that had helped her through her early twenties: *all men are bastards.*

Polly smiled resignedly. 'It *is* my fault,' she said, with conviction. 'I was feathering my bed – but really I was making it and now I must lie in it.'

Megan had no idea to what she was alluding but she didn't ponder Polly's words for long; she was too busy thinking of the ways in which she could wring Max's neck and punish that Bloody Carter Woman. It would appease her own guilt.

Maxanpolly. Oh God, I don't want there to be no Maxanpolly. Mine is not to judge but to comfort. She needs to be soothed.

'Polly,' Megan said in a voice which suggested her friend had it all wrong, 'not Max?'

'It bloody was,' Polly retorted, crossing her arms and frowning.

'I mean,' Megan pondered, taking Polly's hands quite insistently, stroking them rhythmically, 'it's not Max's *style.* You know what I think? I think he was probably thinking of his age and his future – you know, with you. Well, I think he acted on the huge notion of both – but especially the forever-and-ever-amen business.'

'He needed to have a little taste just to convince himself he wouldn't like it?' Polly suggested.

'Precisely,' said Megan.

'He needed to visit America to satisfy himself that England is his home?'

'As it were,' said Megan.

Polly smiled at the irony to which her friend was blissfully ignorant. 'The smell of danger is an aroma most intoxicating.'

'Exactly,' said Megan, stroking Polly's thigh and tapping her knee cap.

Polly shook her head and laughed through her nose. She could hear Megan breathing. Louder still, though, she could hear Kate's words.

'Oh Megan,' said Polly forlornly, taking her friend's hand and holding it against her own cheek, 'I must go.'

As fast as Polly had quit Belsize Park, she walked back very slowly indeed. Megan had told her it would be safe to return, that Jen was taking an afternoon flight.

We should have crossed in mid air. In fact, our paths shouldn't have crossed at all.

Polly went into a newsagents in Swiss Cottage and bought two packets of crisps and a bumper-size bag of Maltesers. She stuffed her face. In public. Against school rules. So what. She felt sick but still she felt hungry. Her mind was as full as her stomach seemed empty. Both appeared to be whirring.

What did Jen and Max do exactly? And me? Me too? What does all this mean? Is there really a possibility that Max and I might not end up together? If we were to – would we have done all this?

When Dominic returned home, Max was there even though it was Saturday and he had latterly taken to working weekends.

'Hey.'

'Hey.'

'You OK?'

'I've fucked up, Dom, big time.'

'I just saw her – Polly – going to Meg's.'

'She tell you?'

Dominic nodded.

Tell me you did it because you wanted to – that I didn't push you into it. If I sowed the seed in your mind, Max, it only germinated because the bed was fertile.

'What have I done?'

'No Max,' Dominic said quite sternly, 'ask yourself the reason why you did it.'

Actually, Dominic felt proud of Max, for having asserted himself, for thinking with his prick but also for his prick having a conscience. And yet Dominic felt proud of Polly too, for he saw how she knew her suffering to be of her own making. Living and learning and tasting the bitterness of one's own fuck-up.

There's a fair bit of me in Polly – how many times have I been there, done that? But, unlike Polly, I've never had the same done to me. Perhaps I should've. But the thought of it makes me shudder. The irony is, she needed it to see the error of her ways, I wanted her to be taught a lesson – but her hurt and panic is god-awful. Max caused it – but while I'm satisfied that he has now regained his dignity, which I felt Polly was abusing over Christmas, he is suffering too, and I can't stand that. And what about poor Jen? She's the true innocent here, just some pawn who's on the board temporarily. I think it's temporarily. It's all a bit of a mess, really. What if it's all fucked up for good – and I've played a part?

If Dominic told Max of the state Polly was in, it would merely increase Max's turmoil. And yet he knew he had no right to inform his brother that Polly had basically confirmed his suspicions. That would pain Max even more. He had privileged information but under the restriction of secrecy.

I feel a little like, well, Puck. Or, more specifically, some mythical overseer, a Greek chorus of one. But I must not interfere. There is a limit to the extent to which I may guide, that I may assist. It is not for me to restore amends.

I know how I'd like the story to end – but it's up to the hero and the heroine to provide the conclusion that will be. Maybe it won't correspond with that which I have in mind. That would be a pity. But it's up to them.

TWENTY-SEVEN

*P*olly? Where are you? How are you?

I'm here. In my bedroom. Trying not to sob or feel quite so sick. I'm watching cars, trying to focus. I'll just wait for three consecutive red cars to come down the street and then I might go downstairs. Do something.

Are you just waiting for cars?

Where's Max?

Are you waiting for Max?

Is he coming? Do you know, I know a Beetle's engine off by heart. I keep imagining I can hear one.

You OK?

Polly?

Answer?

Leave me alone. I can't stand this silence. I want to whistle but I can't pucker my lips. They only tremble if I try. I can hum but I can't seem to do so in tune, it sounds ugly. Maybe silence is better. Somehow, though, it's deafening. But there again, maybe I'd rather not hear myself think.

Polly?

You OK?

Hey?

Leave me alone. I'm going to hum 'So Lonely' by the Police. Appropriate.

Polly?

You at a loose end?

Been sitting there for almost two days?

Not quite sure what to do?

I don't want to think about it. Go away.

Max?

Where are you?

Trying to work, don't distract me.

It's Sunday.

So?

'Hey.'

'Oh. Dom. I'm trying to work, don't distract me.'

'Sorry, but I'm going to. It's my job.'

'No, your job is as a photographer – go click your camera and coo "Give me sexy" or "Watch the birdy" to some dim model. Say cheese. Leave me alone. Fuck off. Please.'

Dominic observed his brother who, in just two days, looked visibly thinner and immensely tired; deflated, somehow. While Dominic made a quiet tour of his studio, he observed his brother focusing hard on the infuriating blank whiteness of his drawing board. He could see that Max's concentration was not directed at what to draw, but on blanking Dominic, stonily ignoring his existence, pressurizing him to go.

'You working?' Dominic asked as he neared Max, as if he had not heard a word of Max's diatribe or felt the vibes of hostility.

'Trying to.'

'Want me to piss off?'

'Yes.'

Dominic laid a hand on Max's shoulder and gave a short, strong squeeze. 'Sure,' he said and headed for the door.

'How could I have done such a thing?' Max suddenly

249

heard his own voice call after his brother. Dominic took his hand from the door knob and retraced his steps measuredly. Max was turned away from him, sitting quite still, head in his hands. Dominic pulled up a stool and faced his brother. Max's eyes were smarting. It unnerved Dominic, who never cried and was not prepared to see or accept his brother doing so. He hadn't seen Max cry since he didn't make the Colts Fifteen when he was twelve. It was something you grew out of. It wasn't necessary. Weakness. Get a grip.

'How could I?' Max repeated, imploringly; blinking hard and twitching his cheek muscles.

'Wait,' said Dominic carefully, relieved that his brother had successfully sucked and swallowed back the tears, 'can we talk hypothetically?'

Because breaking down means you've lost it. I must make you reason and think.

'What's the point?' Max said in a hollow voice, his throat tight and aching as it had not done since he didn't make the Colts when he was twelve.

'Well,' Dominic explained, 'nothing can undo what's done, but concerted analysis might help you fathom how you *should* be feeling, what you're entitled to feel – and the best course of action for you now to take.'

Max shrugged.

'Firstly,' Dominic started, 'did you enjoy yourself?'

In Max's silence, an image of Jen's breasts solicited him, unbeknown to Dominic.

'Was it good?' Dominic pressed.

Max stared at him blankly. He remembered the feeling of his climax, he saw an image of his groin wedged up against Jennifer's arse. Slowly he nodded.

'Yeah,' he said, a wry smile slipping out involuntarily.

'It was good?' Dominic prompted.

'Mindblowing,' Max confirmed, regarding his brother squarely.

'Do you want more?'

'No,' Max said decisively, his stare unflinching.

'Would you have wanted more if Polly hadn't found out?'

Max thought a moment but the answer was easy. 'No,' he said, 'I knew exactly what I was doing. It was equal footing for both. It would not have happened again.'

Dominic doffed his head and said *Perfect sex, lucky sod* to himself. 'Secondly,' he continued out loud, 'would you be feeling like this if Polly *hadn't* come across you?'

Max snorted, tossed his head. He shrugged. Dominic did not mind that Max had not answered specifically. 'Thirdly,' he picked up, 'have you wondered *why*?'

Max started and regarded him warily.

'Why what?'

'Why you did it?'

It would take a while for Max to grasp Dominic's point and Dominic knew instinctively it was time for him to leave his brother to his thoughts. Max would know now that his brother had only his best interests at heart. If he needed Dominic, he'd come — the notion was comforting for them both. Dominic rose to leave; gently he kissed the top of his brother's head.

I don't think I've ever done that.

He's never done that before.

Max didn't mind if his rolling tear was seen.

'Phone!' Polly sings, scrambling from her bed, 'Max! Phone.' She flies down the five steps and dives for the phone, holding it to her breast as she catches her breath and collects herself. 'Please please please. Darling boy,' she whispers. Closing her eyes, she takes the handset to her ear.

'Hullo?'

'Hey sweetie.'

Polly cannot answer.

'You OK? Was it OK for me to call? I couldn't *not*, if you see what I mean. Polly?'

Polly clears her throat, bites her cheek and swallows a sob.

'Hullo Megan.'

'You OK?'

'I think I should keep the line clear.'

'OK – I'm here for you, whatever the time and whenever you need.'

'Thanks,' Polly says, 'I'd better go.'

She replaces the handset slowly, dreading the silence and solitude that will smother her once she has done so. Breathing is almost painful, for her throat hurts, her chest is tight and her stomach is working hard to make sense of an inordinate amount of adrenalin. Sourness permeates her mouth but swallowing is difficult. She paces the room, chanting, stopping still every now and then to bite a nail, scratch her neck, tug at her hair, alternately slap or stroke herself.

Fuck fuck fuck fuck what have I done oh God what have I done Max oh my God Max Max Max.

What about what he's done, Polly?

No no no ssh ssh music quick music what though what.

INXS, very loud and gloriously inappropriate, provides temporary distraction.

Go away, Miss Klee. Stop tapping at the door. I'm not going to tell you what day it is. I'm not going to turn the volume down.

'It's eight o'clock, Sunday March 30th,' says Polly suddenly, pinching away the brown tips of her spider plant leaves almost vindictively. 'No, it's *almost* eight, that's good, that's good. I bet Max'll phone in the next half hour. Yup. Yes.'

He doesn't.

'He'll be here, then, nine – nine fifteen.'

It's nearing ten and he isn't.

Polly is on the verge of panic; she can feel it welling, like a drum roll becoming ever louder and more frenzied, like a bottle being filled from a too-fast tap. If she doesn't keep her mouth closed, she'll scream; if she cries, she will be unable to stop; if she stops to think, she will implode. So she paces; pacing's safe. Up and down the five stairs, in and out of rooms, into the toilet for no reason, opening the fridge door for no purpose.

Oh Godjesus fucking fucking Christ. What is going to hap-pen? What happened? This wasn't supposed to happen. Max wasn't meant to be unfaithful. I never thought .he would. Didn't know he could. Has he done it before? Might he do it again? Why hasn't he come? Called? Written? Maybe he's not sorry, maybe he wants me no more. No no no, it's not to be over. It can't be. That wasn't the idea, the plan.

Polly can't quite see that a relationship oughtn't to be con-structed by plots and schemes. She had duped herself that her cleverly hatched plan was essential to the survival and progression of her partnership with Max. Never did she con-sider that this very strategy, intended, albeit deludedly, as a secret olive branch to herself, could ultimately detonate and destruct the very thing it was supposed to nurture.

I don't understand. I'm so tired, I can't sleep.

Yes you do and yes you can.

See, she's fallen asleep in a crumple by the patio doors. She'll wake at two in the morning and drag herself to her bed, just about managing to kick away her shoes before collapsing, unwashed and dazed, fully clothed, on the naked mattress.

This time three days ago was when I caught them.

Though she woke early, Polly was alert and felt utterly in control. Her thought process, though rapid, was at last lucid and constructive; the conclusions she drew upon, logical and reasonable. She had conversations with herself, sitting demurely on her settee. In lengthy rehearsals in front of the mirror, she envisaged what she might say to Max, practising the inflections she'd use and the correspondingly appropri-ate facial expressions.

'Zoe,' she said aloud at lunch-time, looking out to the patio, 'I asked her if she felt four things – rejected, cross, insecure and untrusting.'

Buster wound himself around her legs and butted her shins as if to say 'And? And?'

Polly heaved him into her arms, squeezed him hard until he protested. She apologized to him but deposited him beside the catflap, giving a shove to his reluctant flank until he grumbled his way outside.

'I *rejected* Max,' Polly continued to herself alone, 'and felt *cross* with him for being – well, for not being Chip, I suppose. *I* made *him* insecure and untrusting.' She pressed her cheek against the patio door and then knocked her forehead against it. 'All of this is of my own making.'

She went to the bathroom and sat with her back to the bath, a towel wrapped around her knees.

'Heed Kate's words – I must remember: heed Kate's words. HKW. HKW,' she chanted. 'She told me – no she *warned* me that it should be a guilty, precious, sacred secret that neither revenge, a fight nor the passing of time must allow me to reveal.'

She felt desperately lonely.

This is when you need family. Who do I have?

Megan – in lieu of the Fyfields, she came closest. Polly dialled her number.

''Sme.'

'Hullo you.'

'You free?'

'Er. Yes. Er. Sure.'

'Yes? Sure?'

'Dom's here – but we can chat.'

'Oh. No no, don't worry, I'm fine.'

'You OK?'

'Fine fine.'

'Tomorrow?'

'Yes yup.'

Polly replaced the handset and cried hard, holding her cheeks and rocking.

Bitch, doesn't she care? Not even Megan? It's because of another bloody Fyfield. Can't she see how I'm so alone? That she's all I have? I bet she knew all along about Max and That Carter Person. I've been duped.

'Well, I've had a total shag fest myself, actually,' she cried out loud, hearing instantly how pathetic she sounded.

254

Tit for tat. That's stupid. What are her tits like? Better than mine?

She knew it was self-pity, that she was currently a snivelling wreck in creased clothes with red-rimmed eyes and lank, dull hair who'd eaten little but junk food at odd hours. Strangely, to feel so wounded and alone was actually rather cathartic.

Where is he? Why hasn't he at least rung? He doesn't want me, does he?

Buster came by, but for the first time Polly stretched out her leg to keep him at bay.

I'm terrified of the future because I have no idea how it will be. I always took care to know, practically organize, the immediate, the short-term, the long-term future. I always thought of things as phases and because I believed in the future I knew they would pass. But I'm caught here, I'm slap bang in the thick of it. I can't see out and I can't see beyond.

Later, in the early hours of the fourth morning, Polly sat up in bed and felt a wave of exhilaration course through her blood.

'Of course!' she exclaimed in a whisper. 'Forgiveness, capital F! Hurray! Yes indeedy! I – Forgive – Max. I forgive you, darling boy. Now let's get on with things, greet the day and welcome the future. It's easy – as soon as he knows I've forgiven him, we can move on. I must let him know. It's time.'

Will Max forgive you?
  Polly?
  Have you even atoned?

TWENTY-EIGHT

'*P*olly? Max here.'

'Hullo.'
'We need to talk.'
''Kay.'

That was it, in its entirety. A telephone call of less than sixty seconds on the fifth morning. Two lines each. Twelve minutes ago. A total of nine words.

This time fifteen minutes ago we hadn't yet spoken, reasons Polly as she attempts to eat a banana, *and he'll be here in forty-eight minutes' time – an hour minus the twelve minutes just past, you see.*

She throws the banana away, spitting out the chunk that she put in her mouth. She gags.

Why did he say 'Max here'? Why did he have to introduce himself? As if he was talking to someone he didn't know very well.

Polly feels panicky, she shuffles back from the kitchen to the sitting-room, a little hunched.

I only said two words. 'Hullo' and ''Kay'. I should have said more. Maybe I should quickly phone him and say some more. Let him know everything's OK, all is forgiven.

She stares at the phone and is rendered unable to do anything but sit, hugging herself, for the next fifty-one minutes.

He's late. Bastard.

At first, Max and Polly found it difficult to look at each other directly; afraid of both what they might see and what they might not see – in case they saw what was missing, for fear of seeing what might be no longer there at all. But when Max snuck a long look at the back of Polly as she boiled the kettle for unwanted but politely accepted coffee, he brimmed with an emotion so raw and painful that he choked and shivered. Similarly, when Polly caught sight of his legs she let her gaze linger, as if it rested on nothing in particular, while she was overwhelmed by the knowledge that she loved this man and what on earth could she – was she – to do about it?

'I think we should take time out.'

No no no! Not that. You didn't just say that, Max. 'Time Out'? What? The phrase is too American for you. So you didn't just say it. You didn't mean it.

'What?'

'Polly – I think we need some space. Don't you?'

No no.

'No no.'

'I think you do.'

'I don't, Max. I don't. Everything will be fine. I forgive you – everything. I just want it to be like, to be like. Just – be. Don't look at me like that.'

'Look, I just feel we need time apart to work out why what happened happened. You cannot forgive me so easily, or so quickly.'

'I can – believe me, I just can.'

'Polly – how on earth can you? I went with another woman.'

He's looking at me like I'm an idiot. He seems irritated with me. Mustn't sound desperate.

'Doesn't matter how, I just can. It doesn't matter – honestly. What happened. Doesn't matter.'

257

She's not thinking straight. And she must.

'Yes, but it *does*, Polly. In five years, my eyes had never wandered – let alone my affection. Certainly not my hands. Never my commitment. I never even *wondered*. Certainly never desired. And suddenly I'm having sex with another woman.'

Don't say that. You don't sound like Max. I don't want to hear.

'There's something behind it, Polly – come *on*. You've been different too. There's something there. Or something not there. I don't know. And that's what we need to ascertain.'

Heed Kate's Words.

'No no. Doesn't matter, darling boy. Forgive and forget. I can do it, Max. Done it.'

'How *can* you forgive me so easily.'

HKW.

'Because I want to.'

'Why?'

HKW. HKW.

'Because.'

'Because what?'

'Nothing.'

'What do you mean "nothing"?' Max said, the irritation in his voice loud and clear.

'I mean I understand. And everything. So, let's just move on.'

'How *can* you understand? Hey?'

Heed Kate's Words. Heed Kate's Words. Heed them. Hard.

'Nothing.'

'But Polly – *I* can't move on. Not yet. I'm sorry. I don't believe in your forgiveness. Just yet. I'm sorry.'

'Max. Max.'

'Don't cry. Please don't cry. It doesn't help.'

'But I want to marry you, Max. And you me. You said so. You asked.'

'Maybe it was rash. I mean, all of this has happened only since marriage has been mooted.'

'Stop it. You sound so – hard.'

'I'm having to be, Butt— Polly. There's no way I'm going to marry you, feeling like this – about myself, about us. Absolutely no way.'

'What. Are. You saying?'

'I'm saying that we need time apart.'

'No we *don't*.'

'Polly. Jesus. I *need* time apart. Space. I *don't* want to be with you just now. I can't. I *want* to be on my own for a while. Without you. I'm sorry. And I'm sorry if you think I'm a bastard. I'm not. I think it's for the best.'

'What can I say? Can't I say something? Do something?'

'Nothing, actually.'

'*Noth*ing?'

'No.'

Please don't say no.

What did they look like as they spoke? What did they do? Max sat still and looked at Polly directly, scouring her face and trying to lock on to her darting, smarting eyes. Polly fidgeted; changed position on the settee, sat cross-legged on the floor, fiddled with the rim of her sock, scrutinized the freckle pattern on her left arm, paced over to the patio door and pressed her body against it. As Max made to leave, he kissed Polly's forehead and told her that, believe it or not, he loved her. She tried to hurl her body against his, to hold on tight for ever and ever, to make the moment last, to make him stay. But Max held her wrists and kept her from him, keeping his lips against her forehead all the while. His eyes closed throughout, not that Polly could see. She tried to make Max hold her hand. Max merely allowed her hand to rest over his. He couldn't hold hers, he didn't dare; he'd never let go if he did.

Max realizes that he has to let go. He sees how he and Polly have drifted until just their fingertips have been touching, and then not all the time. He realizes how easy it had been

259

for him to have been pulled away. By Jen, though might it
have been by whomever? Led to somewhere different. He
thinks he probably would like to be back with Polly but he
knows it will entail a journey. He needs to rest a while, to
prepare. Find a map. A compass.

Polly thinks it's an easy, logical solution to forgive Max. We
know that repenting and atoning for her own actions will be
far more difficult. Therein lies the key – until she has, there
is no way Max can believe in her forgiveness. It strikes her
too that he has not formally apologized for his own actions
and, though she is relieved that he is not blaming himself,
and though she firmly believes it is indirectly her crime, her
fault, that caused him to stray, she is worried by it too.

Did she drive him away?
Did he enjoy it?
Does he want to do it again?
Is that what he wants?
Maybe not Jen specifically – but there again, not Polly
either?

Belsize Park
8th April

Darling Megan,
*Please don't think me a coward for writing rather than
phoning or visiting. Well, maybe I am a coward but I feel,
for the first time in my life, an overwhelming need for
space and distance. How odd, when I am at my most
lonely, most aware of how alone I am in the world, I have
also an insatiable need to be on my own. I was horrified
when Max came to me this morning and asked for the
same. But, a few hours and many tears later, reluctantly I
suppose I can see some sort of sense in it.*
*I am acutely aware of your blossoming relationship with
Dominic and am terrified that my current situation might
make you, or him, or you both, back off. Please don't. I
adore you both and want only for your happiness.*

260

I can't write. I'd only ramble on. Anyway, I have a plane to catch. I'm going back to the States early. I don't think I really want to but I wouldn't trust myself not to pester Max if I remain in London. Here, the pain of him being so near yet so far is hideously intense. So, I'm off.

I want him, Megan, of that I'm sure. At the mo', though, he doesn't know quite what he wants. That hurts. I really don't want him to be hurting. But I really can't bear the thought of him not wanting me.

I'll be in touch. Promise. Love me, Meg, have faith in me and keep your fingers crossed for me. Hey?

Polly

PS. Could you look after Buster till term starts?

Belsize Park
8th April

Dear Dom,

You know me well. You know what I mean.

Making your brother happy for the rest of his days will be my life's ambition. Promise. Believe me.

Polly

Megan showed Dominic Polly's letter to her. He read it, he absorbed it. He couldn't not let Megan see Polly's letter to him.

A relationship must be built on trust, on sharing, on honesty.

Megan's brow twitched. 'What does she mean?'

'I don't really know,' Dominic lied easily.

Sometimes it's kinder to be imperspicuous with the truth.

Max showed no one his letter from Polly. Not even us, I'm afraid. He hasn't spoken to anyone either. He has packed his Beetle and has already headed off to I don't know where.

SUMMER

The lovely evening summer breeze
The warbling of a meadow lark
Moonlight in Vermont
Moonlight in Vermont

Karl Suessdorf & John Blackburn, *Moonlight in Vermont*

TWENTY-NINE

*P*olly did not approve of the name Woods Hole; it was clumpy and prosaic. The harbour village, though arguably not picturesque enough to warrant a truly poetic title, was treating her well and she wished to raise it above the plain, ugly-sounding name it was known by. Consequently, as she picked at an oversized blueberry muffin while sitting on a bench near the quayside, she mulled over more agreeable, if less appropriate, names.

Vineyard's Reach perhaps? Because this is where one meets the boat to and from Martha's Vineyard. Or Cape's Gate, because you could call this the very base of Cape Cod. 'Wood' is too dull, 'Hole' sounds unpleasant. How about Timber Dell. Maybe not.

'I'm waiting for Josephine, Miss.'

What? Who? Who are you? Oh. You want to sit down. Right here on this bench. My bench. But there's an empty one just there. Look. No? Never mind. Here.

With a little more drama than was perhaps necessary, Polly lugged her rucksack off the bench, propped it against her knees and smiled cursorily at the elderly man before focusing with intent on the blueberry muffin. She did not feel like talking. After all, she did not know a Josephine and she did not know this man.

'She'll be on the next ferry,' he continued, thick-skinned but with conviction. Polly crumpled the muffin bag, wedged it nonchalantly between the slats of the bench, nodded politely and then busied herself scanning the horizon. She wasn't sure what for.

Certainly not for Josephine, whoever she may be.

'Will you be taking the next ferry?' the man asked, his voice pleasant, lilting and light. Polly glanced at her watch. Yes, she was taking the next ferry but it was not due for another two hours.

Dilemma.

She wanted quiet.

She wanted to know no one.

But a question had been asked and it needed a reply. If she answered truthfully, she would have no excuse in leaving the bench, the man, Josephine. If she lied, then she had no reason to be sitting on the bench at all. If she lied, she would have to move before the ferry came in, before Josephine arrived. If she lied and moved, she would miss the ferry altogether. This man would have Josephine and she would have nothing but a two-hour wait until the next boat.

'Yes,' she responded in a polite voice, inclining her head though leaving her eyes put, 'I'll be taking the ferry.'

He nodded and seem satisfied. Under his breath and against the breeze he chuckled and it rather alarmed Polly. Her eyes disobeyed their surface indifference and cast themselves over to the man, cataloguing.

Elderly. Grandfathering age, she reckoned. Shabbily dapper, a slight frame enclosed neatly by a crisp brown suit, an open-neck shirt with just a glimpse of vest beneath. Shoes were slip-on and polished studiously, soles jet black, the tan uppers shiny, reflecting.

How his face belies this neatness; all wrinkled, warted and creased! Brow carved deep with the furrows of maybe seventy-odd years; under it, eyes blue and milky, heavily hooded by papery lids. White wire for eyebrows, unkempt and independent as tumbleweed.

Polly thought she'd snatched merely a furtive glance, but when his eyes met hers she realized she must have been staring quite a while. She smiled quickly and a little too widely, hoping it would deflect or serve as an apology. He returned it, and she saw how his teeth were good – his own, for sure; too idiosyncratic to be dentures, nicely overlapped here and there.

'You know the Vineyard?' he asked. Polly shook her head keeping her manufactured smile in place. 'Know the Cape?' he furthered. Polly twitched her nose and lips to say no. 'Live in Boston?' he suggested, raising those eyebrows at her, imploring Polly to converse.

And would that be such a hardship? After all, with her muffin finished, there was little to do in the long wait for the ferry.

'No, I'm not from America at all, actually. I'm English. I live in London, though I was born in Leicestershire.'

He seemed delighted and tendered a slightly arthritic hand, liver spots and all.

'You know, in all these years I never heard it said,' he chuckled, 'I'd always presumed it was *Lie Sester Shyre.*'

Polly's smile became generous at once. 'Not to worry,' she said, 'I always thought Chicago was in the state of *Ill In Wah.*' He appeared quite happy with that.

'*Ark Anz Us,*' she elaborated, tipping her body towards him.

'*Bow Shomp,*' he countered, nudging Polly gently. They shared a little laugh which turned into a unified sigh at nothing in particular. The sea lapped lazily at the edge of the harbour, licking away at the concrete as if patiently attempting to naturalize it. It lulled them into a chatty silence for a while.

Here they are still. Polly rather likes this man, he reminds her that she is grandfatherless and she reckons he'd do the job very well indeed.

'Well,' she says with an exaggerated look at her watch and a slap of her knees, 'still an hour and a half to go. Would you like a coffee?'

'Me?' He is absolutely staggered. Polly nods. He seems a little flustered and darts his eyes from her face to yonder and then back again. 'Or maybe tea?' she suggests, 'if you prefer.'

Do I not look kind and sincere?

'Coffeecoffee,' he whispers, eyes wide as an eight-year-old's. Off she goes and orders. The vendor, who has obviously seen with whom she is sitting, shakes his head and smirks but proffers nothing more than two steaming cups. Polly finds it rather disconcerting so she looks over to the bench while she waits for her change.

She observes him with tenderness; lost at sea, waiting for Josephine to arrive.

They blow on their coffee and sip contemplatively, content now with each other's company. The man's spectacles and Polly's sunglasses have misted up; great blooms of fog with each blow into the cup. They agree, their voices apparently lubricated by blindness, that the coffee is very good. Polly tells him the blueberry muffin was so too; he says he knows.

'Who is Josephine?' Polly asks in her Great British bid to make polite conversation.

'Josephine,' he announces, 'is who I am waiting for.' This is a little cryptic though his voice is nothing but loving.

I oughtn't to pry, being British and all.

'Leicestershire,' he enunciates correctly in a nicely rounded way, repeating the word but enquiring no further.

'I've sort of run away but not quite,' Polly suddenly hears herself saying, finding herself searching his face for approval or otherwise. 'You know, things to think about. Not knowing where to start. Hoping this might be as good a place as anywhere.' His conciliatory nod is bolstering. 'You know,' she continues, believing he very well might, 'needing a little time. Some space. Escaping a mess of my own making really.

270

Setting free; being released yourself. Seeing where you might wish to alight after a solitary journey?'

I'm rambling. Ssh. I should be saving up my thinking for some lonely, conducive beach. I can't start here, not in Woods bloody Hole.

'Well,' the old man says, wiping his glasses on the knee of his trousers, 'the Cape'll help and you're wise to be going over to the Vineyard. Yup.' He winks. Polly replies with a small grin.

And who is Josephine? Polly asks if she lives over on the island. The man's wince, however, cuts sharp, though he corrects it at once. 'Not any more,' he says a little too lightly. 'She's coming back now, on the ferry you'll be taking over there.' Polly nods liberally though she is none the wiser.

'Is she your wife?'

'No.'

Best not to pry.

Here she is! Bunting and all, smelling deliciously diesely, heaving herself to harbour.

'Here she is!' Polly and the man exclaim to each other in a congratulatory sort of way. Polly wriggles in against her rucksack.

'Can you see her?' she asks, watching his pale, dilute-blue eyes scan and scour the figures on deck, on the gangplank, 'Josephine? Is she there?' But he is too busy combing the throng to answer.

Now the deck is deserted, the gangplank bare and the passengers have dispersed. Where is she? He turns to Polly. 'I'm waiting for Josephine,' he tells her, failing in his legible wish not to appear disorientated and down. She shifts and shunts to redress the cut and strain of her rucksack. She feels concerned and she feels for him. She is cross with Josephine.

'Why don't I take the next ferry? I could wait with you,' she suggests in a sing-song sort of way.

'No no!' he counters politely, 'the Vineyard awaits *you* – it's where you need to be, having come from Leicestershire and all.'

'Well, if you are sure, but it wouldn't be any trouble, I should enjoy your company a while longer.'

'Really, Miss. Go. I'm waiting for Josephine, she'll be here soon. Perhaps on the next ferry.'

Polly shuffles and then wishes him well. He says 'good luck' and takes her hand in both of his but his eyes are elsewhere, watery and pale, forever scanning.

The distance between them is chugged away and Polly calculates that she must now be just one of many hanging over the railings waving the harbour farewell under a bellow of foghorns and the calling of gulls. She watches his figure diminish and a part of her wants to be back with him, on the bench, sharing gentle half-silence. But she is keener to find her own aloneness out on the island. Resolute, she turns her back on the land and tries to breathe normally against the buffeting, salty gusts.

Anyway, no doubt Josephine just got up late and missed the boat.

*   *   *

The degree to which American society is orientated towards the car saw Polly taking an *en suite* room at a pretty guesthouse in Oak Bluffs for less than the price of a Youth Hostel experience ten miles away. She *was* headed for the Youth Hostel, for she had deemed a certain frugality necessary for constructive soul searching. However, there was no bus to the hostel and a taxi there would add twice the price to that of the accommodation itself. When Polly realized that the cost of bike hire on top of the hostel tariff amounted to a dollar more than a guesthouse, she swiftly ditched the notion of dorms and duties for the promise of comfort, privacy and breakfast at Laverly's Lodge.

After all, it'll be much, much easier to gather my thoughts and see through to my soul after a good night's sleep and a hearty breakfast.

'Hi honey, you want to stay?' asked a plump woman in a sequin-encrusted T-shirt, 'I have a real pretty room available.'

The room really was pretty; oak floorboards, walls a gentle blue, a plump bed, windows on three sides with sea views from two, and a pair of chairs set as if deep in conversation.

'It's perfect,' Polly enthused, 'I'll take it.'

'Well, isn't that nice?' the landlady beamed. 'I'm Marsha, honey.'

'With the CIA?' Polly asked.

Look where I am, Max. Oh, I wish you could see me. Wonder where you are. Are you trying to imagine? Like me? Hope so.

This is something of a first, Polly. You didn't seem to think of Max at all when you arrived at Hubbardtons. You didn't seem to think much of Max, full stop. All you thought was that he'd be there, back home, for you, whatever you thought, dreamt or did. So why should he hear you now? Your modified thinking might just be happening too late. Anyway, why should he listen at all?

Shut up. I'm speaking to Max. I've just been for a stroll around the village and now I'm back in my room. You'd look fine in this room, Max. It's breezy and sunny and summer is coming into focus. I think I'll hire a bike tomorrow. I think I'll go to the little tapas sort of place for supper. Maybe not – I've bought a bumper bag of Hershey Kisses from the gas station. It's strange chocolate, not unpleasant but decidedly un-Cadbury's too. Who says that kisses look like this?

Oh my God, Max, might we never kiss again?

'Hi.'

'Hullo.'

'Want to eat?'

'Please.'

'Sure. This table OK?'

'Lovely, thanks.'

'Can I get you a drink?'

'Please. Um, beer.'

'Sure. I'll go fetch the menu.'

I don't really drink beer – but didn't Kate say it's life saving?

No, Polly, she said it was life changing.

'Cute,' Marc informed Bill, with a faint pelvic thrust, as he placed Polly's order for a beer and fetched a menu. Neither waiter nor barman (brothers, and joint owners too) were used to seeing a lone female of Polly's calibre sitting at the window table quite so early in the evening or the season. Though year round, solitary women came to eat at their establishment, the age of such patrons invariably amounted to more than Marc and Bill's years combined. The brothers had become adept at distinguishing between writers, artists and women of independent means but, while they were sure that this young thing fitted into none of these categories, so too were they puzzled as to who and what she was. And why, of course, she was here. *Here* here: in Martha's Vineyard and at their restaurant.

'Heck, it's early . . .' Bill reasoned, flicking his wrist to regard his watch while he sliced lime and raised an eyebrow at his brother.

'And we ain't busy . . .' Marc colluded, humming thoughtfully into a menu.

They're talking about me, mused Polly, wondering whether she could change her order for a Coke instead.

Now they're both coming over. Mind you, it is early and I am the only diner.

'You English?' asked Bill, placing a cold bottle of beer right before Polly.

'Yes,' Polly replied, smiling vaguely at the beer bottle.

'Just arrived?' asked Marc, shifting the bottle to one side so as to place the menu directly in front of Polly.

'Yes,' she confirmed, staring hard at the menu so as not to giggle.

274

'Right,' said Bill, pausing, nodding, then returning to the bar.

'Sure,' said Marc, nodding, straightening the salt and pepper pots before making a slow retreat. Polly appraised them in a glance: lean and fit physiques, each an easy six foot; skin and hair showing all the signs of vitality which a life by the sea bestowed. Thirty? Thirty-five? Twenty-eight? She wasn't sure.

'You some kind of writer or artist?' Marc tested while he took her order.

'No,' Polly told him.

'Independent means?' he persisted, hands on nattily aproned hips.

'I wish,' Polly laughed, liking him and his hips and his searching, mocha-coloured eyes.

'I'm Marc,' he shrugged.

'Hullo,' said Polly.

'That's Bill,' he motioned with a flick of his head which implied the target wasn't worth much consideration.

'Your *brother*,' Polly elaborated with a wry smile at Marc and a purposefully considered look in Bill's direction.

Marc twitched his face becomingly. 'How d'you know? You a psychic or something?'

'No,' Polly said, 'but I can tell a brother and his sidekick.'

'So,' said Marc, knowing it must be wit but not as he knew it, 'you're a . . .'

'Teacher,' Polly assisted. His eyes lingered involuntarily on her collar bone.

'Sure,' Marc laughed as if it had been on the tip of his tongue. Her collar bone too. He bowed to Polly, hands still on hips, and, with a click of his tongue and a tip of his head, implored her to 'enjoy'.

The slice of lime was on the tip of Polly's tongue and, though she had no idea what to do with it, she had even less inclination to ask. The lime was wedged into the neck of the bottle; a familiar sight from adverts at the cinema, but though such mini films extolled the beverage, they never quite explained the connection with the lime, what one was to do with it and how. Neither Marc nor Bill seemed to be watching and, in as nonchalant a way as possible, just in case they were, Polly made a swift attempt to sip the beer through the lime from the neck of the bottle. None reached her mouth though a cold fizzy streamlet coursed down her chin and along her neck.

Damn.

With what she hoped was panache, again lest it should be witnessed, she then forced the lime down the neck of the bottle and into the body of beer.

Ha!

However, when she attempted another swig, the lime blocked the flow and all Polly achieved was a dry and very audible slurp.

Bugger.

Marc and Bill looked over. Polly grinned sheepishly while they smiled broadly, a full quota of straight white teeth apiece.

'My fault,' Bill insisted as he brought her another bottle with lime on the side this time, 'the lime was too – you know, like, firm.'

Polly nodded and smiled in gratitude. Marc arrived, hot on Bill's heels, with vegetarian burritos and Polly nodded and smiled in gratitude some more.

They hovered until she sipped the beer and deemed it lovely, and tasted the burritos and proclaimed them fantastic. The brothers took this as a cue to draw up chairs and sit at Polly's table. They didn't ask. She didn't offer. She didn't mind. There was something ingenuous and warm about the men and she felt safe and comforted by their company.

'Dig in,' she said, pushing her plate forward. They declined politely, munching away at a bowl of tortilla chips instead. Without consulting Polly, or offering her the consultation of the menu, they then brought a catering-size tub of chocolate-chip ice-cream to the table along with a jug of coffee.

'Dig in,' said Marc, in a daft accent but with a lovely smile.

'Dig in,' said Bill, in a daft accent but with a comely twinkle to his eyes.

Polly dug in playfully, feeling flattered and pampered. 'Where's the loo, please?' she asked, much to the brothers' unbridled amusement. When she returned, they were gone and her table had been cleared. She sat quietly, enjoying the peace. It was still light outside and she intended to stroll along the waterfront before she turned in for the night. The brothers were soon back behind the bar, observing her discreetly. Polly cleared her throat.

'Can I have the bill, please?'

Bill came forward brandishing a triumphant grin.

'Sure.' He sat down at her table again and stretched his arms leisurely above his head.

I love the inside of men's elbows.

Marc shuffled menus in the background in a noisy and supremely irritated way. Polly glanced at Bill, whose elbows were still on display and who was regarding her dreamily. She shot her gaze over to Marc to find thunder across his brow.

'Oh God!' she exclaimed. 'Ha!' Spontaneously, she held Bill's wrist, gave it a squeeze and burst out laughing. 'Bill!' she wheezed, virtually out of control.

'Yeah?' he said.

'Can I have the Marc, please!' she squeaked, one hand at her nose in a futile attempt to gentrify her mirth. Marc came over. 'I meant,' she stammered, gasping for air, 'the, you know, whatsit.' Marc and Bill regarded Polly. 'The thingummy,' she said while the brothers consulted each other silently, as if acknowledging the girl's glorious daftness and attractive incomprehensibility. 'The, um, check!' Polly cried triumphantly, writing in the air illegibly with an invisible pen.

'Sure,' Marc shrugged.

'No problem,' said Bill.

Polly was still laughing hysterically, and snorting

involuntarily every now and then, as the brothers left to prepare the bill. When they returned with it, they found her
sobbing her heart out, her head buried into her arms across
the table. They didn't say a word but drew chairs either side
of hers. Her torso was shaking convulsively. Marc placed his
hands over hers. Bill laid his arm about her shoulders. There
they all sat until Polly was still. Tearstained, she raised her
face eventually, sheepishly lifting the corners of her mouth.
Bill and Marc tightened their clasps on her, blinked slowly
and nodded sagely.

'Sorry,' Polly croaked at last. She rummaged in her bag
and brought out a tissue and her credit card which she
placed with the bill and handed to Marc. They brothers took
her sonorous nose blowing as a signal to leave her and see to
the finance. They were back a few minutes later, returning
her credit card.

'We didn't want your money,' said Marc.

'We only wanted to know your name, Miss P. E. Fenton.'

'Polly,' she said holding a hand out to each man.

'I have to cook tomorrow afternoon,' Marc apologized,
'you want me to show you around in the morning?'

'That would be lovely,' said Polly.

'I got to fetch supplies in the morning,' Bill explained,
'you want to go for a ride in the afternoon?'

'That would be lovely,' said Polly, shaking hands formally
as she bade them good night and left for her lodgings.

'Teacher my ass,' said Bill kindly once Polly was out of
sight.

'Yip,' Marc agreed, 'that's one soul searcher. Soon in the
season, hey?'

'Christmas comes early,' marvelled Bill.

'Share?' asked Marc.

'Sure,' said Bill.

Polly finished the Hershey Kisses when she returned. The
chocolate, unnecessary even in a small amount on such a
full stomach, made her sweat a little and a headache loomed.

278

She interrupted the conversation between the two chairs, taking one to a sea-facing window which she flung open. There she sat, in the dark, until she wasn't sure when, listening hard to the universal language of the sea. Although acutely aware that there was turmoil in her life, Polly felt that the here and now was a safe and nourishing place to be.

THIRTY

Max had never been to Cornwall, which was precisely why he chose to go, much to the protestations of his Beetle and the utter exasperation of Dominic who had no idea of his brother's whereabouts. Dominic phoned the farm in Herefordshire where their childhood summers had been spent, also the cottage rental company in Wiltshire through which he and Max had organized great weekends; he phoned most of their London friends enquiring in a most roundabout way so as not to alarm them or inform them of more than was necessary and, in a final bid, he tried Max's art college friends who still shared the same student house in Birmingham, bought as a consortium and ever being renovated. Despite a sore ear and a soaring phone bill, Dominic was none the wiser two hours later. At precisely that time, Max was emerging from the sea, shaking water from his ears and shivering with delight as his wet body was licked all over by the constant breeze of early summer. He ploughed through the shallows and made for shore, boxer shorts gaping, nose running and eyes stinging; slightly breathless; exhilarated.

Once dry and dressed, Max strode out over the cliffs,

believing his legs could take him wherever he wanted to go right there and then. The blisters, however, an estimated five miles later, came as something of a nuisance. He continued on, telling himself that pain was gain and likening himself to a self-flagellating monk.

If there was something ablutionary about the discomfort, there was also a certain catharsis in unleashing a torrent of fulminations into the privacy and vastness of the landscape about fifteen minutes later, when he could hobble no more. Easing his shoes away, Max peeled his socks back gingerly and invited the sun and wind to soothe the sores. There he sat, near the edge of a cliff, watching the fulmars and gulls, glancing every now and then at his shredded feet, not really thinking about anything but feeling quite peaceful; pleased that he should be.

Unbeknown to Max, he was being watched intermittently from the window of a nearby cottage. He had not seen the building, partly because its vernacular provided a certain camouflage, partly because his focus had been commanded exclusively by the sea. Nearing tea-time, however, Max was observed with his head in his hands, his shoulders slumped, obviously oblivious to sea and surroundings. The kettle in the cottage was put to the boil; a tea bag, a splash of milk and three sugars were placed in a capacious handmade mug.

'Afternoon.'

Max lifts his head from his hands, turns his cheek and, without eye contact, nods cursorily in the direction of the greeting.

Piss off.

'Cuppa?' enquires another voice.

What? Shut up.

Immediately, Max feels a hard nudge to his back, as if being reprimanded for his surliness. He twists his torso and regards the intruders. A man, perhaps his age, a toddler with a freckle-spattered face and a riot of deep auburn curls, and

281

a goat who looks rather as he remembers his grandmother: tottering and with a good beard.

'Afternoon,' the man repeats.

'Tea?' the child asks while the goat stares at Max icily, lest he should chance upon further ungrateful thoughts.

'Afternoon,' Max responds to the man. 'I'd love a cup of tea,' he smiles at the child. 'Hullo,' he doffs his head to the goat.

'Gar bra,' says the child seriously.

'That's nice,' Max replies, not understanding a word but presuming his phrase to be the most suitable response.

'She said "Barbara",' the man explains to Max, 'the goat.'

'Right,' Max laughs a little, 'the goat. Called Barbara. Right.'

The man hands Max the mug of tea and then squats on his heels, squinting out to the sea, expertly absorbed in his own thoughts. The goat ambles away a polite distance to urinate. The girl flops down on to the grass next to Max and lays her tiny, pudgy hand on his thigh.

''Sot,' she warns him sternly, eyeing the mug, 'blow.'

Max blows and then takes a sip. It is scalding indeed, and very sweet. Nectar.

'Where've you come from?' the man asks, having let Max sip in silence for a decent period during which he chanced upon the state of the stranger's feet, 'John o' bloody Groats?'

'Feels like it,' Max said, before conceding London.

'You walked? From London?'

'No no, I drove. I left at four. Ay Em. Oh God, to – I don't really know where. I found a nice beach and swam this morning. What's the time? *Five?* Shit.'

The child fixes Max with a stern look.

'Sorry,' he says, pushing his fingers lightly through her curls while she shakes her head furiously and laughs.

'Where's your car?' the man asks.

'No bloody idea,' Max replies immediately, looking vaguely to his left, aware that no amount of brain racking will help him remember.

'Where are you staying?' the man furthers.

'Er—'

'We have room – stay with us,' the man continues non-chalantly. Max, conditioned in London reserve, shakes his head.

'Nah,' he says, 'I'd better find my car and make tracks.'

'With those feet!'

Everyone regards Max's feet, including the goat who has returned from her ablutions.

'Stay with us,' the man repeats with a shrug, 'we can find your car in the morning.'

'You sure?'

'Sure.'

'Well, if you're sure. That would be great. Thanks.'

'Yee ha!' the girl cries and scampers off, pursued by the goat.

'Nanny goat indeed,' the man chuckles, offering his hand in welcome and to aid Max to his feet, 'I'm William Coombes.'

'Max Fyfield,' says Max, grasping William's hand in more gratitude than he could know.

'Your daughter?'

'Genevieve,' confirms William, setting a slow passage back to the cottage, as if he always walks at that pace, regardless of whether his guest is blistered to buggery.

Max's feet are indeed burning but the downy grass underfoot, coupled with William's affability, seems to lessen the discomfort somehow.

'I'm a potter.'

'I'm a draughtsman.'

Their approval of each other's calling warranted a generous measure of whisky each, which they sipped amiably while watching Genevieve smear her supper over her face.

'I read somewhere that babies have taste buds on their faces,' Max reasoned. William raised his glass.

'Have you any kids?'

'No,' said Max, 'how long have you been married?'

'Oh, I'm not married,' William said easily.

'Single parent?' Max asked earnestly.

'No. I'm incredibly unsingle, in fact. Just very unmarried too. You?'

'Nope.'

It was the concerted way in which Max pondered into his whisky that decided William not to pry, but afforded him a glimpse to the possible reasons for his guest to have been pounding the cliffs and gazing far beyond the sea.

'Where is your non-wife?' Max asked, his voice rough from a deep slug of liquor. He regarded his watch. Gone six o'clock.

'She's at work. In St Ives,' William explained with touching pride. 'She'll be home quite soon actually.'

'St Ives,' Max mulled, wondering if it was where his Beetle was.

'Doubt it – bastard to park there,' said William, somehow reading his guest's mind.

'Will she mind me being here?' Max asked, looking around the kitchen and liking it. 'The mother of your child?'

'Chloë?' said William. 'Not at all.'

'Hullo?'

'Hey Dom, it's me.'

Dominic covered the mouthpiece, mouthed 'Thank you God' at the ceiling and grinned at Megan who smiled back, woozy with sleep. It was half eight on a Sunday morning, after all. Dominic cleared his throat.

'You wanker, where the fuck are you?'

'With friends,' his brother replied, not in the least offended.

'I was coming on to the "with" part. How about the where bit?'

'*Welsh* Where Bit?' Max joked.

'You in *Wales*?' Dominic asked, stunned.

'No,' said Max, knowing it too early for his brother to have noticed the pun, 'Cornwall.'

'What? I didn't know you had friends in bloody Cornwall. Didn't know you've ever been.'

'Neither did I. And I hadn't.'

'Oh God, you haven't joined some nutty cult or something?'

''Course not.'

'You're not going to sea?'

'Nope. Feet firmly on the ground – at last. Just having some space and peace. Staying with mates.' There was silence the other end. 'No offence,' Max added quickly.

'None taken,' said Dominic, offended. 'Keep in touch, yeah?'

'Will do,' Max assured him. 'Oh, er, any news?'

'No news,' said Dominic, peeling his ear for his brother's reaction; hearing nothing.

'Right,' said Max. 'Bye for now.'

'Take care,' said Dominic.

'Will do,' Max replied.

Dominic snuggled up against Megan, in whose embrace he could not doubt his standing nor the strength of her affection.

Max had been with William and his family for two days. They had retrieved his Beetle yesterday, after a short search, and it was now parked in front of the potter's cottage. They had been generous with their antiseptic and plasters, their home and their attention, and they had implored him to stay as long as he liked. Just then, he thought he very probably would.

Three days ago I did not know of the existence of this place, nor of its inhabitants. Now it feels more like home than any other place I've known. Apart from Polly's bosom. Shut it. Stop it. Block her out.

It occurred to Max, as he washed up from breakfast, that these were not merely people he had met; swiftly they had become much much more. He looked around. It was silent; serene. Chloë had gone to work and William had taken

Genevieve to Tumble Tots before visiting an elderly potter with whom, he'd warned Max, he'd no doubt spend more than the prescribed morning.

These are good friends and they are also my friends. I've been thinking how everyone back home is connected to me only via Dominic or Polly. Take the protagonists out of the situation and where would I stand? I'd not thought – I'd rather not. But here, I am accepted and liked just because I'm Max Fyfield. They are aware that I have a brother but they don't know him. I haven't mentioned Polly at all.

Cornwall has become Max's Vermont. I think it's healthy, beneficial, for Max to garner his own slice of anonymity. Here, he need be no one but himself; he can push the burden of his commitments and habits and the expectations of others to one side and lie down, unencumbered, on the cliffs. He's entitled to enjoy the here and now. He deserves to put Polly and London to the back of his mind. Let him imagine how good life could be for him right here, from this point forwards.

Max takes a cup of tea out to the garden, greeting Barbara cordially. The clarity of the morning promises a glorious afternoon.

I think I'll borrow William's bike and cycle into St Ives. Tell Chloë I'll fix dinner tonight. Pick up some wine.

The sea parades its unequalled collection of diamonds. Max believes they belong to him. Dream-soft clouds blush their way across an otherwise uninterrupted blue sweep of sky. Tiny wild violets sing out for attention and the faint scent of coconut comes in gentle wafts from the gorse. There is not a soul in sight. Max finds himself smiling broadly and it makes him laugh. He salutes the day with his mug of tea.

God, I feel good. This has provided me with the reality check I had no idea I so needed. Maybe I've felt where the buck stops. Maybe I've found where it is to start again. Good friends. A beautiful land. New beginnings.

THIRTY-ONE

*O*n the Fyfield Scale of *Looks, they rank high, very,* Polly thought on waking. *However, what they score in appearance, they forfeit in terms of Fyfield charisma.*

She giggled and rose from the bed.

There again, which is the more preferable?

These, I'm afraid to say, are Polly Fenton's wakening thoughts.

Polly was excited and a little relieved that it was finally morning and a decorous time to rise. She had slept with the window open and the chill night air had woken her intermittently, during which times she had lain in the silence, half-focusing on the vague shadows of the room, still half-inhabiting dreams in which a blurred Max and Dominic were readily exchangeable for the vividly recalled Marc and Bill. She was looking forward to seeing the brothers again.

I know.

Polly really should be soul searching; deep in thought at the very least. Wasn't that the reason for her leaving England early, for coming to Martha's Vineyard in the first place?

It still is.

But it's easier to think about seeing Marc before lunch and Bill after?

Yes.

Is this just your impulsive nature, or is it cowardice?

Both. I freely admit it.

Devastated by Max's rejection, but simultaneously excited by this new attention?

Takes my mind off things.

I thought you intended your mind to be solely focused on 'things', on what has happened, on what could be?

I'm not shirking. I've tried but thinking on it all too concertedly makes it irrevocably real.

So, instead, some strange reordering seems to have taken place within Polly's psyche and I think it probably happened while Marc and Bill solicited her, with their Hershey-coloured eyes, over the chocolate-chip ice-cream last night. Polly, it appears, has changed the way in which she views her past and considers her future.

Chip wasn't so much a crime I committed, more of an affliction.

I couldn't help it.

It wasn't really my fault.

You're deluded, but you're hardly going to hear me if you're not prepared to listen to yourself.

'Lovely,' Polly said, tasting the cinnamon doughnut Marc had bought her, looking about her at the sweet gingerbread harbour houses of Vineyard Haven, candy coloured and made of confection surely.

'Sure is pretty,' Marc agreed, tracing his eyes from Polly's, down her cheeks to her lips before taking stock of her as a whole, 'and it sure beats Pittsfield.'

'Pittsfield?' Polly asked, looking away while hitching up the sleeves of her T-shirt to her shoulders. Marc had done the same. It was not yet eleven but the sun was parading its warmth already. 'What's Pittsfield?'

'Not what but where,' Marc corrected. 'It's my home town. Massachusetts.'

Polly tipped her head to regard him. 'You're not an islander? Not a Vineyarder?'

Marc raised one side of his mouth into a wry smile. 'Nope,' he said, 'but I reckon another couple of years and I should achieve honorary status.'

Polly was at once disappointed and yet intrigued, realizing she had presumed Marc and his brother to be somehow part and parcel of some Vineyard Experience; laid on for her, placed there for her delectation and company.

'How did you come here?' she asked. 'Was it the draw of Martha's Vineyard specifically, or merely the desire to leave Pittsfield?'

'Boat,' Marc shrugged, regarding her wryly.

Polly twitched her nose and raised her eyebrows, glimpsing brain behind the brawn now that she had Marc out in the open and away from his double act; a depth behind his eyes that the restaurant lighting and her self-preoccupation had prevented her seeing the night before.

'Via Brown,' he continued.

'Brown what?' said Polly.

'Brown, Rhode Island,' Marc replied.

'*Brown* Brown?' Polly asked, trying not to sound incredulous or look too impressed.

'An Ivy League kinda green, actually,' he qualified with a smirk.

'Blimey,' said Polly, as much at Marc's clever quip as at his hallowed alma mater.

To her delight, conversation and smiles flowed easily from Marc while she was able to deflect questions which threatened to burrow too deep. He had majored in Political Thought, but running a restaurant was a long-held goal and an honoured promise to his late Italian grandmother. No, Polly wasn't much good at soccer. Yes, she was enjoying her stay. He had lived on the island for six years and intended never to leave. No, she hadn't seen much of the United

States at all. He had. Maybe she'd spend a week or two touring once term ended. Had she returned early precisely to visit the Vineyard? Sort of. He had travelled Europe extensively, but he'd never been to England. Maybe he'd come and visit the UK – you. That OK? Perhaps. Did she miss home? Was she content over here? Wasn't it unsettling to trade jobs and countries just for a year?

No. No. And no.

'Do you know, I like it here,' Polly told Marc, now sat up high next to him in his Jeep, while they drove slowly through stately Edgartown, 'I like the people and the pace.'

'It's a pleasure to have you,' Marc said, wondering at what speed to pace his seduction while Polly wondered quite when he was thinking of having her. The salacious smile which met her when she cast a glance over to him quite took her off her guard. It seemed to steep everything in reality and the familiar scent of danger came seeping through. She wound down the window, gulping fresh air, concentrating hard on the surroundings instead, wondering where Carly Simon lived.

It came as no surprise to discover, striding along Catama beach that afternoon, that Bill had studied History at Harvard; though it was a revelation to learn that, at thirty, he was actually two years younger than Marc.

'That's cos i'm worldly wise, Miss Fenton, and my brother's grossly immature.'

'I beg to differ,' Polly enunciated sweetly, knowing Bill would like the sound of it. 'I think your brother's jolly nice,' she said, looking to see whether Bill liked the sound of that so much.

What are you doing, Polly?

I don't know really.

'Yeah?' said Bill, holding out his hand to help Polly over a dune.

'You're not too bad yourself,' she furthered, facing the sea with her hands on her hips, her eyes closed because she did not need to see that Bill certainly liked the sound of that. She drank in the fortifying sea air in deep, measured breaths and wondered quite what it was that she was going to do.

Polly returns to Laverly's (armed with a large bag of 90 per cent fat-free sour-cream-and-chive flavour potato chips, a litre bottle of caffeine-free diet Coke), she sits on the swing on the veranda passing time with an elderly artist who spends each spring on the island. They are interrupted by Marsha who informs the gentleman that there are two telephone messages for him. They part, bidding each other a pleasant evening.

Polly goes directly to her room and sits quietly on the edge of her bed, her legs swinging. She retrieves a jar of Marmite and smears generous daubs over the potato crisps with her finger. She munches thoughtfully and swigs the caffeine-and-sugar-depleted Coke directly from the bottle. She goes over to the window without the sea view and cranes her neck in a futile bid to locate the boys' restaurant. She knows where it is. She knows that it is there. She just can't quite see it. Just beyond her field of vision.

She looks down below. The swing on the veranda remains empty and almost motionless. She can hear vacuuming. It's a little irritating. She goes to the bathroom and regards the taps. She needs a bath. She doesn't want one just yet. She sits on the edge of the bath and squeezes a tiny glob of tooth-paste on to her tongue to counteract the pervading potency of the Marmite.

No one's phoned me.
That's because no one knows where you are.
There's no connection here with anything in my life.
That's what you wanted, what you've actively sought out.
I could do anything and no one I know would ever know.
That's right.
I could be murdered and no one I know would know. God, I'm desperately confused. No one is aware of that.
They might just as much presume you to be having the time of your life.

But I'm not.

How would they know?

Do they even care?

Polly!

I could have sex all night with Marc and Bill simultaneously and no one need ever know.

You could.

And it would be perfectly legit – Max having given me the shove.

You could see it like that.

I have absolute freedom at my fingertips.

You do.

It's an enormous responsibility.

It is.

Twenty-four hours later, and the very second that Bill's lips touched hers for the second time, Polly opened her eyes, pulled away and realized exactly what it was that she was doing.

'I'm sorry,' Bill said, suddenly looking around him as if there might be spectators in the flower-strewn pasture he had walked Polly to that morning.

'No,' Polly qualified, '*I'm* sorry.'

'What for?' murmured Bill, pulling her close against him and bringing his head to hers again. Polly leant back until the two of them were posed in a tango-style clinch.

'Please?' Polly implored. Gently, Bill set her straight. And then she set him straight. 'I think you're completely gorgeous – stuff of my dreams – but there you must stay.'

Bill smiled slyly, plucked a long stalk of grass and, tracing it lightly over her nose and lips, said he had the power to make dreams come true.

'It's just,' Polly said, pressing her hand against his chest to keep him at bay, 'I thought I wanted it but I know now that I don't. Actually.'

Bill regarded her with an expression that blended hurt, irritation and persistent desire.

292

Oh God, thought Polly fleetingly, *am I going to be all right here? Am I going to get out of this? Nobody knows where I am.*

She stroked Bill's biceps in what she hoped was a soothing and non-sexual way. 'Sorry,' she whispered, in what she hoped was a beguilingly sweet voice.

'How come you changed your mind?' Bill cleared his throat and held her wrist, slipping his thumb along to the palm of her hand where it toyed with an invisible clitoris. Polly moved her hand until she was giving Bill a very English handshake instead.

'I think I've broken up with my boyfriend,' she said, still shaking his hand.

'You only think?'

'I'm not sure – it appears it's up to him.'

'So you rebounded all the way to the Vineyard? He must've screwed you something bad.'

'Not really,' said Polly, smiling at a bizarre image of herself being catapulted across the Atlantic, before reflecting on the fact that Max had never screwed her, only ever made love to her.

'You sure?' said a voice, bringing her back to the day in hand.

Oh. Bill. You.

'About?'

'Me?' he said, hands on hips, licking his lips leisurely, lasciviously.

Polly nodded apologetically.

'If you guys have split up, what's the big problem?' Bill persisted, eyeing her tits and rearranging his balls most unselfconsciously. 'No crime in it now – you being a single, free agent and all.'

'I slept with someone else – a bloke in Vermont,' said Polly, hoping the statement itself would suffice, though Bill's lust-laden smirk told her otherwise. 'And Max, my – shit, my *ex* – he slept with someone back at home,' she continued in a rush. 'Not that she's from back home. She's my

American exchange. It's horribly messy and all rather muddled. He doesn't know about me but I practically came across him.'

'Whoah whoah there!' Bill laughed, holding his hands up in mock surrender, 'that's some story.'

'It's not a story,' Polly remonstrated, sucking down a sob.

Bill held his surrendering pose, backing away slightly. 'Don't worry about it,' he assured her. A no-strings fuck was one thing – a knot of someone else's emotional baggage was another.

'Sure?' Polly asked, relieved.

'You bet,' he said, relieved.

'He'd never know,' Marc said suddenly while he and Polly strolled through pine on the way to a beach later in the afternoon. Polly was quite taken aback as they had been chatting so nicely about inane things. 'He needn't find out,' Marc said again, with more of a desirous growl this time, pulling her towards him and slipping one hand down to grasp her buttock. Polly wriggled but Marc held on tight.

Oh God. I can just see it: 'Corpse in a Copse'. Maybe if I just let him kiss me, he'll let me survive.

She allowed Marc to kiss her; her lips, though, remained staunchly motionless. No amount of his energetic tongue-dabbing could alter that. It was rather a turn-off.

'Beach?' said Polly, swiping her mouth with the back of her hand.

'Sure,' Marc replied, running his tongue along his teeth and then offering his hand which she studiously ignored. He ran the back of his hand along her hair and Polly praised its inherent gloss that caused Marc's fingers to slither off it so quickly.

'Bill told me,' he continued, walking on, 'about all the stuff going down? You and that guy? Sounds pretty shitty.'

'I suppose it is,' Polly said, flopping down on to the sand, lying on her side, propping herself up with an elbow.

'So you came here to chill out?'

'Suppose,' said Polly, squinting under her hand and turning her head away from the sun and from Marc.

'I won't tell if you won't,' Marc said teasingly. Polly turned to him, he was leaning back on his elbows, pushing his hands into his jeans pockets, rearranging an impressive hard-on rather obviously. She turned away quickly, not knowing whether to be appalled or to giggle.

'C'mon,' he implored, 'no one need know – ain't that notion exciting?'

'Yes,' said Polly, holding tight on to his eyes, 'very.'

'There you go,' Marc exclaimed in a very gravelly voice. Turning on to his side, he prised her legs apart with his knee and wedged it up against her crotch.

Oh God: 'Body on the Beach'.

'I didn't mean to flirt,' Polly said, not daring to move. She shook her head, and then shook it again at herself. 'Well, I did, I suppose. But now I don't want anything more. Truly I don't.'

'Sure you do,' Marc persisted, hovering a ready-cupped hand over her right breast.

'I don't, I assure you,' Polly said, grabbing his hand and holding it steady. They lay quietly for a few moments, her hand against his wrist, his leg still between hers, then she tapped his thigh like a mother waking a child.

'Sorry,' she said, opening her legs to free herself and sitting up, smiling at the sand and her silhouette. 'But, do you know, I *don't* want it. I *did*—' she qualified somewhat hesitantly, tucking her hair behind her ears only for it to flop back, 'I think. Yesterday – this morning even. With either of you – both of you, even. But I don't *now*. I really don't.'

Marc grabbed his balls in a rough caress. Polly's breasts heaved in momentary panic.

Am I going to be OK?

'Well, shit,' he said despondently, adding a 'y' between the 'i' and 't' for emphasis, shaking his head in frustration. 'You sure?' he tried, with a wheedling smirk, an obvious wink and a lot of lip-licking.

'Perfectly,' Polly confirmed. He regarded her sternly, observed her breasts remorsefully and finally gave a theatrical sigh in the direction of his cock. He stood up and helped Polly to her feet. They made their way back to his Jeep, Polly a few steps ahead of Marc.

'Great ass!' he tried, one final time.

'Thanks,' said Polly, over her shoulder.

Marc held the door for her and then settled himself behind the steering-wheel. He slapped it hard. 'Bang goes my bang,' he rued. Polly jerked and regarded him warily. He was quick to smile broadly and put her at her ease. 'I guess sucking face is out of the question too?' he probed, nudging Polly gently in the ribs until she accepted his smile, his words and his intentions as harmless and convivial.

Thank God.

Well done, girl.

Polly is out and about with the morning birds, having hired a bike, positively rickety, but fun all the same. Her boat doesn't leave until this afternoon. It's bliss to be by herself. She cycles along deserted lanes with the hush and rustle of the long grass damping down the sporadic squeaks and cranks of the bicycle. Her destination is Gay Head, about which Bill had waxed lyrical while purple prose had tumbled from Marc's lips. She is nearing there now. And it is lovely, magnificent even. Polly feels good and solitary, as she hoped; alone but not lonely. She stands awhile and wonders if this feeling is the desired effect she has sought. She rather thinks it is. Pleased with her conclusion, she turns her interest outward. There is something over there, a statue perhaps. She nestles the bike down into an eiderdown of grass and explores on foot.

Bronze. About four foot high, streaked and striated pale green-grey with the years. A little girl, about five years old, Polly reckons. The flutter of her pinafore dress caught motionless in bronze, a grasp of flowers in one hand, a hankie in the other. She wears little cobbley ankle boots, laced up tight and finished with a bow. Her face is not of anyone known and yet its inherent innocence seems to speak for all children. Polly catches her breath as the sightless eyes see right through her and beyond, way over the dunes, to the sea. And beyond.

Is it you?

Yes, it is me.

Josephine.

1950–1956.

So she was six. Polly bows her head in respect and bewilderment and wonders why she is so close to tears. She looks about her and spies primula, cow parsley and some plain but pretty grasses. Gathering them together, she binds them as best she can.

Here, Josephine, for you. From him.

'Excuse me,' Polly asks Marsha later, bags at her side, ready to settle her check having returned the bike and washed her face, 'could I ask you something?' she ventures, knowing full well that she can because Marsha is amenable and chatty and has looked after her well these past few days.

'Sure, hon,' the landlady says, 'go right ahead.'

'Who's Josephine?' Polly asks in quiet tones, 'who was she?'

Marsha appears frozen in time and caught in remembered grief. She shuffles a little and asks 'Josephine?', but Polly knows full well that she knows who she means. 'Little Josephine Bauer?' Marsha asks quietly through slanted eyes; testing, perhaps.

Polly nods, as if she knew her surname all along. 'Who died. When she was six.'

With a tired, sad shake of her head, and a swipe of hands over her apron, Marsha gazes at a point not yet visible to Polly and speaks.

'Little Josephine Bauer – a prettier petal you could not have found. Always full of joy – folks even nicknamed her Joysephine, you know, like a New Yorker would? She found a boat. I mean, hell, they're not hard to find, this being an island and all. But, though we drum it into all our kids not to horse around in the water, somehow this boat was just too pretty for the little girl to resist. She wanted to follow her daddy to work. Wanted to go over to the Cape. It wasn't a sea-worthy vessel, just a small boat for rivers and ponds, the type for playing in of an evening. Honey, Fate had moored it loosely in a little cove – and where was the Lord when Josephine climbed in? That's what I want to know. I still ask. Where *was* He? Only the boat was found. We searched for days. For months. Some folk are still searching.'

'Waiting for Josephine,' Polly murmurs; 'poor little mite,' she says, cringing at how insufficient it is.

'Her pop, old Sam Bauer, well, it drove him out of his mind and right off the Vineyard,' Marsha continued while swiping Polly's credit card through the machine. 'His waking hours became Pain, his sleep Purgatory. His heart all but died. He's never returned. Please sign.'

Polly signs and embraces Marsha instinctively. It is time to go.

Sam, Sam, why didn't I stay? Take the second boat which Josephine would not have been on anyway?

Polly is sailing back now, anxious to see the land loom for she knows who will be waiting.

I'll wait for Max.

They are nearing the harbour and Polly's eyes dart agitatedly to locate him. She can't yet see him but she knows he will be there, waiting. Like he was yesterday. And the day before. And the day before that, when she had waited with him. She feels wretched that she is just one of the many passengers causing him torment for not being Josephine.

There he is, over there. In blue today, a hat too. Older, more fragile than I remember; really so papery.

Polly smiles in his direction, trying hard to hold on to his pale eyes. He is too involved, searching for someone else, to recognize or even notice her.

I can hear him now and I don't want to.

'I'm waiting for Josephine,' he says to no one in particular.

Polly's eyes prick so she shields them with sunglasses. She turns her head away and merges anonymous, useless, with the crowd.

Maybe the next ferry.

She walks on without looking.

THIRTY-TWO

*W*hen Polly left Martha's Vineyard early, convinced that her true home and heart could only ever be with Max, Max himself had been in Cornwall for five days and had started to take great interest in the property pages of the local paper, placing the tip of a felt pen gently against the newsprint every now and then and watching the red dot blot.

'Are you looking to rent or buy?' William asked him, as he laid the table for lunch and removed a peeled clove of garlic away from Genevieve's eager reach.

'I know a gorgeous sail loft in Downalong that's available,' Chloë added, tucking her wayward corkscrew curls behind her ears so she could bend low over the soup to taste it.

'To rent or buy?' Max asked.

'Rent,' Chloë said.

'Shame,' said Max.

Soup was dished out and contented slurping confirmed its excellence.

'Are you leaving London,' Chloë started tentatively, 'because you want to live in Cornwall—'

William finished her sentence for her: 'Or are you buying in Cornwall so you don't have to return to London.'

'Ay, there's the rub,' Max said, nodding slowly and concentrating hard on the salt and pepper which were contained in the tiniest bowls he had ever seen.

And there's the nub, William and Chloë told each other in silent glances.

'No hassles this end,' William assured Max, passing him more bread and butter.

'You stay as long as you like – we love having you, you're part of our family,' Chloë added, giving him a gentle poke in the ribs.

'She's called Polly and I love her and I hate her and I've no fucking idea what to do,' said Max loudly, poking Chloë back before taking another slice of bread.

Whether in utter pity for his plight, or pure disgust at his language, Genevieve suddenly threw up copiously. A flurry of activity followed. Only once the three adults had brandished damp cloths and sympathy, and Genevieve had fallen asleep while William carried her upstairs, were they able to retire to the sitting-room with huge portions of treacle tart and a mammoth scrabble session. Max's revelation was left well alone.

'Polly,' Chloë said quietly in the garden two days later, as if considering the aural qualities of the word alone.

'Fenton,' Max elaborated, taking the hammer from Chloë and fixing the gate himself with a couple of very forceful, well-aimed clouts.

'Does Polly Fenton know you're in Cornwall?' Chloë persisted with effective artlessness.

'Nope,' said Max, bashing fence posts that were just fine. Gently, Chloë took the hammer from him and gave it to Genevieve who lugged it off to the studio where her father was at his potter's wheel. Chloë and Max heard a faint 'Ow – careful!' from William, and they laughed.

'Shall we go and see what the sea's up to?' Max suggested.

'Heavens,' Chloë said with elaborate gravity, 'I haven't checked on it since yesterday lunch-time. We *must.* Quick.'

They walked with purpose through the garden and out to the cliffs beyond.

'Well, that's a relief,' said Chloë, regarding the shimmering water below. They sank down on to a knoll of downy grass and watched the gulls play.

'Peregrine!' Chloë gasped.

'Where?' Max replied, swivelling his neck and searching hard.

'Gone,' said Chloë.

'What the fuck am I going to do? Jesus. Fuck it,' said Max.

'Get a cure for your Tourette's?' Chloë reprimanded gently.

'I'm sorry,' said Max with a shrug, 'I don't really swear much, actually.'

'Just on special occasions?' Chloë asked with kind leniency.

'Special,' Max said softly.

'Want to talk?' Chloë asked.

Max snorted again, shook his head and regarded her directly. 'That's what *I* usually say – I've never been asked that question because I've never needed it.' Chloë cocked her head and nodded, to comfort and encourage. 'Know something?' Max continued, holding on to her eyes in earnest. 'People presume me to be stronger than perhaps I am. *"Want to talk?"* – those words! How often have I offered them to a troubled friend with a beseeching face? And how great is the responsibility to be good old strong Max!'

Chloë looked at him and nodded her head. 'Well?' she said.

'Well what?'

'Talk? Want to?'

He smiled at her with gratitude laced with an air of resignation. 'I am not allowed to feel weak. Not me.'

'Allowing yourself to feel vulnerable is a massive statement of strength,' Chloë responded, laying her hand on his shoulder. 'Do you denigrate your friends for being feeble when they come to you in times of need? Do you denounce them as weak? Is weakness a failing?'

302

'A friend in need—' Max started, 'is a burden!'

'Bollocks!' Chloë exclaimed to Max's surprise. 'And I rather think you'd employ that very word if one of your friends said that to you.' With that, she evidently found something of utmost interest on the horizon and Max was afforded a few moments' reflection.

'Chloë, I wouldn't know where to start,' he said resignedly, his head dropping visibly under the weight of it all.

'Try a single word,' she suggested.

'Difficult.'

'Another?' she persisted.

'Polly.'

'Fenton?' she asked, as if to double-check as much as to elicit.

'Yup,' Max confirmed.

After half an hour, Max could manage sentences of four to five words. An hour later, he had furnished Chloë with all the facts, and quite a few of the associated feelings.

'What is it that you want, Max?' Chloë asked.

'I want to feel strong again – because, and it's bloody difficult for me to admit, I *was* weak – weak-willed.'

'And strength comes only with solitude and a small Cornish cottage all to yourself?'

Max did not respond. He stared down at the sea and imagined he saw dolphins.

Yes, actually. Maybe. I like being here. Away. I like it that Polly's not here – I like it that I'm so much more than just her boyfriend and Dominic's brother here.

'What is it that you'd like to happen?' Chloë asked after a careful silence.

'She's extraordinary,' said Max, as if it was quite a reasonable answer to Chloë's question.

'You want to be back with her,' Chloë said quietly, as a statement.

'America has changed her,' Max said despondently.

'You sure?' Chloë probed, 'I don't think so.'

'How would you know?' Max retorted, snatching at the

grass and finding it too short and tenacious to pull up. 'You don't even know her.'

'No,' Chloë conceded measuredly, 'but I have a hunch that it might only be a phase, a temporary aberration. It's not America's fault – though her being there may have expedited it. Anyway, what about bad patches in the past? How did you deal with them?'

Max jerked and frowned. He had no answer. Chloë laughed. 'You hadn't encountered any bad patches before?' she said incredulously.

'No,' Max said slowly, suddenly just as incredulous. 'No. I suppose not.'

'Might not this be all it is?'

'I don't know,' he shrugged, a certain light now filtering from behind his eyes and smoothing the creases on his brow. 'How would I know? What I do know is that my proposal of marriage – too bloody hasty in retrospect – seems to have had the opposite effect of the secure, happy-ever-after seal I presumed it was to provide.'

'But marriage aside, Max,' said Chloë, physically brushing the notion away, 'are you content to let the relationship lie – more than lie, *die* completely? Without finding out? Without another try?'

'No!' Max exclaimed, holding hard on to a tuft of grass to steady himself against a strong sensation of falling. 'But look what I've found out.'

'Well,' Chloë triumphed, 'I think you're extremely lucky that, in all your years together, this is the first bad phase. Heavens, boy, seal it up and use it as a stepping stone to a higher plane – use the knowledge, the experience, to strengthen your relationship from hereafter.'

'You sound like a preacher,' Max teased, running his fingers through the grass as he did Polly's hair.

Just as shiny. As soft. But green, of course.

'Well,' said Chloë, plucking a single blade with ease and sucking its sweet shoot, 'if proclaiming what you believe is preaching, then yes, I bloody well am.'

'Don't swear.'

'Sorry.'

'How do *you* know?' Max asked, regarding her slyly, 'how can *you* be so sure?'

'Know what?'

'About all – this—' he said, waving his hands impatiently and pulling a rather fetching grimace, 'stuff. You know: love, loss, loathing, lust, and all the other "L"s in between?'

'How do you *think*?' Chloë laughed. 'From experience, of course.'

Max looked at her, stupefied.

'Experience?'

'Heavens, I had practically packed my bags for Scotland, never wanting to see William again and vowing only ever to use *plastic* crockery – *that's* how bad things had become.'

'You and *Will*iam?' Max stared at her, his eyes darting all over her face in utter disbelief.

'The Max and Polly of West Penwith,' Chloë shrugged. 'Us. The very same.'

'Exactly,' said Max.

'Exactly,' said Chloë.

'Um, exactly what?' Max asked after a pause.

'Doesn't that make you feel better, more positive, hopeful?'

Max considered quietly before humming and nodding and beaming a strong smile at Chloë which she had hitherto never seen, but of whose existence and capability she had remained quietly confident. Max stood up and breathed operatically. He turned to Chloë and held his hand out for her. She took it gladly and he shook it gratefully.

'Thanks,' he said.

'What are friends for?' she replied, brushing his gratitude away along with one of her auburn curls. As they headed back for the cottage and lunch, Max asked about the bad patch she and William had gone through.

'I refused to marry him and he refused to live together.'

'And you're now living together happily unmarried,' Max marvelled.

'Exactly,' said Chloë, 'blissfully.'

'Now there's a thought,' Max said as they neared the kitchen door. 'One more thing – Genevieve – was she planned or, um, flunked?'

Chloë laughed. 'Meticulously – flunked.'

Max stayed on for a few days more. He stopped looking at the property section and, when he wasn't wedging clay for William, or helping Chloë, or conversing at length with Genevieve, he drew. He went through pencils at an alarming rate, often resorting to biro and the backs of shopping lists, not from choice but necessity. Max drew the cliffs, the goat called Barbara, the corner of the kitchen, Genevieve asleep, the back of Chloë's head, William working at his wheel. He drew his car, Chloë's bicycle, his healed feet, Genevieve's hands. He constructed still-life arrangements: one featuring his walking boots, Genevieve's teddy and an onion; another, a selection of broken pottery, the telephone and a banana. He went to Mousehole and drew boats. He went to Penzance and sketched tourists. He went to a play at the Minack Theatre and filled a sketchbook with drawings of the actors, the spectators and, later, the entire story of the play itself. He drew fish. He drew gulls. He drew a puffin with fish dripping from its beak, from memory.

Drawing was both cathartic and liberating. It was something Max had put on hold, that he had deemed an unaffordable luxury once he had left college and become a graphic designer. His only enduring concession to his love of drawing had been in relabelling himself a draughtsman. If he drew, in recent years, it had been only as rough preliminaries for commissions. Now Max was drawing again; subjects of his choice, on a scale in size and time which he defined. Some vast sketches he completed in ten minutes (Genevieve shell seeking); others little larger than envelopes took whole days (the puffin). All were united by his free and lucid style, their construction grounded in intuition as much as technique.

On the morning he left Cornwall, Max gave a drawing to each member of the household, including Barbara the goat. He and William shook hands firmly, laid a hand on each other's shoulders and then fell easily into a close embrace. He kissed Chloë gently, his hand in her hair, his cheek pressed against hers.

'Keep drawing,' she said.

'I will.'

'Come and see us again,' she said.

'I will.'

'Bring Polly next time,' she said.

All the while, Genevieve clung to his left thigh and it took both her parents and the promise of chocolate to prise her away and unravel her clenched fists into farewell waving for Max.

'Don't fuck off,' she sobbed after him.

But it is indeed time to leave, Max concedes out loud to his car as they cross the border into Devon.

'I mean, poor Dom. And Megan. And my clients.'

And Polly.

How are we going to get you two together again?

Bloody Polly Fenton. I've been cursing you for not being more like Chloë – all serene and calm and measured in emotional output. I've been wishing you could smile gently instead of grinning like a child; that you might laugh softly instead of so hysterically that you snort. I've been bemoaning the fact that you're not taller, more substantial, more, I don't know, proper-grown-up-woman. And yet I'm not thinking specifically about Chloë, certainly not about Jen to whom I have given very little thought.

I'm talking about your scampering and sudden tears, the way you squeal and become overexcited or overtired. Recently, I have wanted you to trade your fluffy bedsocks and what you call your 'bunny jimjams' for black lace and painted toe nails. God, sometimes it feels like I'm with a little girl. We shouldn't talk in baby voices, it's pathetic and nonsensical. Why are you so Marmite-centric in your taste? Couldn't you develop? And I wish you wouldn't love your bloody cat quite so obsessively.

But.

Polly bloody Fenton. I miss hearing you laugh and cry, feeling you clinging to me like a limpet. I quite fancy a meal where both soup and subsequent stew are flavoured with the ubiquitous Marmite. I want Buster to sit at the table, or more specifically on the table, with us while we eat: I want you to fall asleep, head in my lap, while I watch the ten o'clock news, then see you all bleary and tiny, when I wake you so you don't miss the 'And Finally'. I want to observe how gloriously petite and beautifully put together you appear when in a crowd. You're sexy in your fluffy bedsocks and nothing else. Your energy is infectious; your emotional deluge often as nourishing as it is sometimes exhausting. You put the colour in my life. Often, you're too bright and noisy. But maybe my life would be a silent monochrome without you.

Bloody Polly bloody Fenton.

I slept with someone else.

I asked you to marry me.

What on earth did I mean by either?

Can I figure this out?

THIRTY-THREE

Martha's Vineyard was an indisputably beautiful place but Polly wished she had never been. It hadn't been a holiday, or a retreat. She perceived it now as a rather surreal episode from which she had certainly learned. Still, though, she felt cluttered within. Normansbury, however, really rather a plain town and even more so in the rain, seemed the most wondrous place to Polly when the bus finally deposited her there after a circuitous journey from Woods Hole via a night in a particularly drab hostel in Boston.

'I'm here,' she rang Kate from a call box.

'I'm right there,' Kate replied while Polly swooned to the sound of her voice.

While she waited, Polly found a bench by a red oak tree, under which only the most persistent drops of rain could manage their way through. As she sat, soothed by the rhythmic swish of wheels on wet tarmac, she realized she was glad of the rain because it confirmed the distance from Martha's Vineyard.

There it was sunny. Yesterday too. Last week, in fact.

I wish I hadn't met Bill and Marc. I don't want to know about Sam Bauer and Josephine.

I just wanted to be a tourist. I just wanted to be on my own.

Just then, it wasn't possible for her to see that she had choreographed the development of her entire stay. Instead, the sight of two dogs humping, swiftly followed by the unmistakable sound of Bogey barking encouragement at them, provided Polly welcome distraction. She left her preliminary ponderings on the bench under the great oak and walked defiantly to Kate's car, into which she jumped and started chatting about absolutely nothing and nineteen to the dozen at that.

'How was the Vineyard?' Kate finally managed to interject as they pulled up outside her house.

'Yes,' said Polly in a rather different voice while she unloaded her bags and took great interest, with fingers and eyes, in the seam of her rucksack.

I had the opportunity – just to be a tourist – but I designed my stay otherwise.

I had the opportunity – with Bill and Marc – but I chose not to.

I had the opportunity to comfort Sam Bauer in some small way. I didn't.

'Tea?' Kate asked, hovering at a tactful distance and suggesting Polly reload her bags unless she intended to carry them to Petersfield House herself later.

'Please,' Polly replied, careful to tap at her temples to suggest utter empty-headedness rather than a mind racketing with confusion.

'So,' said Kate, slathering Marmite over Marcia's pumpernickel, 'you're early.' Her careful tone was one of kind observation and Polly hoped that a nod in reply was all that Kate required at this stage.

'How's Max?' Kate asked. And why shouldn't she? Polly swallowed hard on a chocolate-chip cookie but all she could taste was the lingering bitterness of forbidden fruit.

Mind you, that quick taste cleared my hunger, gave me a

metaphorical gut ache that will enable me to refuse it, steer clear, if ever I come across it again.

'No more Max,' Polly answered bravely, with a meek smile.

'My God,' said Kate, quite shocked.

'Doesn't want me back,' Polly shrugged, resigned, her eyes flat and the colour of mud.

'Does he *know*?' Kate whispered.

'No,' Polly replied with sad irony, 'all he does know is that he doesn't want me.'

The women put cookies into their mouths so that they did not have to talk.

Jeez, poor kid. What can I say now?

'You have plans?' Kate asked. 'Before summer term? Still a week off.'

'Not really,' Polly said slowly, twisting in the chair and seeing if there was anyone new on the Fridge of Smiles.

'You could go upstate – have a scout, go walk? Middlebury is real pretty. You could go right on up to the Northeast Kingdom – or take back roads right into the Green Mountains – Vert Mont itself, you see?'

'Oh yes,' Polly marvelled, wondering how, if words were her thing, she had not figured this out previously. 'Maybe,' she added.

'You could borrow a car,' Kate furthered.

'Maybe,' said Polly, 'or maybe just the bike.' She looked at her watch and stood up, 'I'd better make a move.'

'Sure,' said Kate. It was excruciatingly uncomfortable; they were being reserved, a distance that was anathema to both.

It was strange being alone in Petersfield House. Polly visited each room in turn, smiling at the variety of belongings left strewn on beds or draped over chairs or propped in corners; vestiges of the girls' personalities and guarantees of their imminent return. Her apartment was more tidy than she remembered leaving it, which unnerved her for some reason. She unpacked quickly and draped a few of her things about, whistling all the time to suggest that the silence didn't bother her, before sinking into the couch and staring at the phone, biting her cheek, for over an hour.

Having dialled Max but hung up just as soon as she heard a peep of a ring, and having called Megan and let it ring until a mechanized voice suggested she try later, Polly locked up Petersfield House and returned to Kate without warning or explanation.

'Mind if I stay?' she simply asked, somewhat sheepishly, while holding up her toothbrush for emphasis.

'*Mind*?' Kate exclaimed, as if even the thought that she might was an insult indeed. She touched Polly's cheek and Polly took her hand, kissed it swiftly before they fell into an easy embrace. Great Aunt Clara's bed was welcoming and occurred to Polly, just then, to be the safest bed she knew.

What am I going to do with mine? In Belsize Park? Will burning the sheets be enough? Will I actually be able to sleep in it again? Will I ever sleep in it alongside Max? Oh God, might I never share sleep with Max again – in whatever bed?

Suddenly, an image of her bed with Max and Jen in full shag, shunted itself uncompromisingly across the entire panorama of her mind's eye. She sat bolt upright and switched on the light, breathing fast and feeling, for the first time, that she was nearing the verge of pure panic, dangerously close to the cliff edge of emotional chaos.

Are they? Max and Jen? Doing it? I left early – did Jen go back to England early too? Was it all planned and premeditated? What are they doing at this precise moment? And are they doing whatever together?

It no longer mattered to Polly whether her bed was the location; the notion of their possible continuing coupling was enough. She shuddered violently until it dispersed the image.

Did my behaviour really drive him to it? Or does Max just not fancy me any more? Or does he just fancy her more?

Polly recalled Jen's height and exaggerated it, devising a physique of statuesque proportions. She added a stunning bust, a supermodel's abdomen, a dancer's legs and a porn star's pussy. Polly glanced down her nightdress (little roses, Marks & Spencer cotton), scratched her stomach and punched her thigh harder than she thought she was going to.

Is that why I'm so desperate to be back together? Because the thought of him with another woman is so excruciating? Because the notion of him simply not wanting me is so appalling?

She hugged her knees and rocked herself. Her leg throbbed.

Would I be feeling like this if I had never found out about the two of them?

She left the bed and pressed her cheek lightly against the portrait of Cézanne's gardener. The cold glass was as comforting as the old man's hand on her head might have been.

Did Max use the same techniques on Jen? Did she kiss like me? Taste like me? Different? Better? Oh God, she must've made him come. Someone else made my Max come. He came within someone else. Or maybe she swallowed for him. Or perhaps both. And more. All night, even. Should I be using the present tense?

An image, known so well, of Max's face during orgasm, the sound of him, the smell of him, grabbed Polly and made her choke. She took her nose to the old curtains and breathed in the mixture of mothballs and dried damp, the smell of time. She pressed the material hard against her face, opening her mouth wide into a vast, dry, silent wail. Her body heaved. She made no noise. She was too distressed to cry, too desolate to go in search of Kate's promised shoulder. She tasted dust. She had a funny taste in her mouth.

If I hadn't slept with Chip, would Max still've slept with Jen? Is this divine punishment? God, I wish I'd never set eyes on the bastard, what a stupid waste of time it all was. Chip bloody Jonson can go to hell – because that's where he's landed me. It's all his bloody fault.

Polly crumpled herself into a muddle under the window. A draught seeped through and coursed an unrelenting path up her vertebrae. She felt freezing and in pain and caught in a vacuum of absolutely no idea what to do or what was going to happen to her. She could not move. Eventually, she crawled over to the bed and heaved herself back up into it. Shoving her face into the pillow, she tried to cry, she was desperate to cry, but her throat stung too much and her tear ducts remained defiantly shut. She was denied the absolving comfort of weeping. It seemed not even her body was there for her.

*   *   *

'No Tupperware, thank you,' said Megan. She shut the door to Dominic's flat leaving Max, stupefied, staring at the brass 'B' of his own front door. He knocked again.

'Jehovah? We're Zoroastrians here,' said Dominic, looking Max directly in the eye. 'Sorry. Goodbye.'

Again, the door was shut on Max. Puzzled for only a moment, he then left the building, returning half an hour later and giving three hearty raps at the door. Megan and Dominic looked at each other and over to the television and *Coronation Street*; they looked down at their lazily entwined limbs and up at each other's faces again. They looked over to the door when three fresh raps rang out, raised eyebrows at each other and grinned.

'What?' Dominic shouted in convincing irritation on his way to the door.

'We've *got* double glazing,' Megan remonstrated, following close behind him.

'Pizza delivery,' called a voice of Afro-Itali-Asian origins. It was, of course, Max. 'American Hot, Four Seasons and Gardener.'

'Giardiniera,' sang Megan in operatic Italian, coming forward to embrace Max but then taking charge of the three brown boxes and turning on her heels instead.

'Thanks, mate,' said Dominic, reaching into his pockets, pressing a small amount of small change into Max's hands, turning away but not quite closing the door. Soon all three of them were ensconced on the sofa with home-brew, pizza and *Eastenders*. Perfect. Familiar. Max been away? Has he? Cornwall? Really? Didn't notice. Anyway, he's here now. Welcome back. Cheers.

Max's week passed quickly. His backlog of work seemed to have grown disproportionately to the time he had taken off, but he immersed himself in it and the clients were pleased. He also took over Buster's welfare from Megan, which entailed visiting the cat's flat in Belsize Park daily. Jen was nowhere though her return was imminent. She was, however, in the thoughts of Max, of Dominic and of Megan. All felt silent guilt; dreading seeing her again but eager to as well, just to allay fears and calm consciences.

The flat was, however, thick with Polly; her presence a permeating vapour inducing Max to sit awhile, in the silence save for Buster's purring or protestations; to remember, to think, to try to decide what to do.

Polly's week, however, passed at an insufferably slow rate. Though she timetabled her days to the very moment of closing her eyes at the end of each, still they dragged and she suffered. Cycling, hitherto merely a pleasurable and relaxing leisure pursuit, now became a quest for physical fitness; the crucial mental application it required doubling as a welcome preoccupation from other thoughts. The harder she cycled, the more taxing the routes and the longer the excursions, so the days passed just fractionally quicker: time trialing indeed. Polly had stayed only the one night with Kate, moving back into Petersfield House the next morning, early enough to have a full day on the bike too. Mostly, she chose the unsurfaced roads many Vermonters are keen to preserve, soon supporting their cause strongly herself: the dinks and ruts and constant rough surface necessitated utter concentration and she was glad for juddering and wobbling to preoccupy her mind entirely. It was just what she needed. She didn't have to think about anything other than staying on and getting up that hill.

The land looked beautiful. It was also strangely private; summer's verdant lushness appearing not to have the touristic pull of fall's burning bright. Polly was grateful for the solitude. Intermittently, during each outing, she'd say 'Hi, little fella' to the chipmunks, whom she refused to regard as being as common as the squirrels in Britain. She learned to distinguish between the red spots of the brook trout and the purple spots of the brown trout. She saw a skunk and her heart bled for it for, though it appeared lonesome and unloved, she didn't want to venture near enough to it to offer her friendship.

During her Tour de Vermont, she came across very few people. Two men busy at work in the orchards (standing with hands on hips, paunches out, gazing in reverence at their trees) gave her invigoratingly tart apples and a woman she passed, hoeing a vegetable garden, invited her in for lemonade, cookies and a chat.

'You English? How wonderful!' Polly's host was so wide-eyed and happy of the fact that Polly found herself putting on her best vowels and most gracious adjectives.

'What'll I call you?'

'I'm Polly, Fenton. How do you do.'

'Polly Fenton – isn't that just fine?'

'I say, is it? Thank you. And you?'

'I'm Ian.'

'Ian?'

'That's right, Ian Paisley.'

'Ian? Paisley?'

'Yes? That's me – you OK, hon?'

Polly left soon after that, fearing that the woman was slightly loopy and possibly a little dangerous too. In the early hours, however, Polly awoke with a start.

'Ann,' she said, sitting up in the dark, 'Ann. Bloody Ann of course. It just sounds like Ian.'

Polly made a ten-mile detour via Ann Paisley's house the next day so that she could be nicer to her; she took her some sour windfall apples and was careful to incorporate the

316

lady's name into her sentences. They didn't talk about much, just sat on Ann's veranda with the lemonade and the apples and the company, allowing the day to pass them by.

* * *

'I think,' said Max, while he sucked up a strand of spaghetti sonorously, leaving a dribble of tomato sauce on his chin like a frighteningly trendy goatee, 'I might pop over to the States.'

'That's nice,' said Megan, trying to sound nonchalant and not desperate for details.

'Mmm,' agreed Dominic, slurping a strand of his spaghetti but suffering a not-so-becoming blotch of sauce to his cheek, 'when?'

'I don't know,' said Max, raising his glass and toasting Delia Smith.

'Delia,' said Dominic.

'La Smith,' said Megan.

'Maybe soon,' Max continued, 'maybe not. Depends on work. Depends on flights. Depends on money.'

'I have a friend in the travel business,' Megan said helpfully.

'I can lend you a bob or two,' Dominic added.

Max regarded his wine. 'Depends how I feel,' he said quietly. Dominic moved the conversation round to cricket and Megan saw to the dessert.

THIRTY-FOUR

'*Middlemarch*,' said Polly, proudly holding up her own beloved Penguin classic which was so well thumbed that it fanned out slightly, rather like a bouquet, 'by George Eliot.'

She waited, grinning at her class; the first lesson that term and it was wonderful to be amongst them again. Right on cue, Laurel Lap-top raised her hand.

'Miss Fenton, what are his dates?'

'Ah ha,' said Polly, wagging her finger and realizing how she loved her job. '*He* doesn't have dates at all – George Eliot being a *nom de plume*, a pseudonym.'

'So what's the psycho's name?' AJ asked, so proud of his pun that he had dismissed with hand raising altogether. The class gave him a reverential chuckle.

'Ho,' said Polly fondly, 'what a wit you are, young master Harvey.'

'AJ,' AJ said quietly, looking a little uncomfortable, wondering if Miss Fenton would renege on their pact.

'Marian Evans,' Polly replied to his great relief, if utter incomprehension. Marian Evans he could take, Anthony Jerome he could not.

'You could say,' Miss Fenton continued, clearing her

throat for she was about to sing, '*didn't shave her legs and then she was a he.*' This was greeted by a raucous chorus of Lou Reed aficionados imploring Miss Fenton to take a walk on the wild side. 'I did,' she said, too quietly for her serenading class to hear, 'and I wouldn't really recommend it.'

After lunch, she gave her senior class their copies of *Mill on the Floss*. Having ascertained that Maggie and Tom Tulliver did not live anywhere near Lilliput and no, that wasn't Ted Danson either, but a guy called Gulliver by a guy called Swift which wasn't a pseudonym for someone called Doris, her class settled down to their work and afforded Polly a few moments' window gazing. The quadrangle below. Out over the hockey pitch. There, the sports hall, the gym, the athletic trainer's surgery. Big deal. So what? Anyway, the athletic trainer was now called Karen Crane.

'Get a vibrator,' Polly said to Lorna, her expression and tone deadly serious.

Lorna shook her head and cast a wry smile away from Polly. 'I don't know,' she mused.

'Get a vibrator,' Polly repeated with some urgency now, giving a quick stamp with her right foot for emphasis.

The teachers made their way to the memorial garden, positioned just before the school grounds petered out at the lower reaches of Peter Mountain. Here a collection of white birch trees were each adorned with a brass plaque bearing the name of a deceased alumnus. In the fall, the yellow leaves had blazed out against the white bark and Polly had learned their nickname, beacons of the forest. That these particular beacons also celebrated life seemed to Polly a most resonant commemoration and she found this small arboretum a peaceful, affirming place, whatever the season and leaf colour. Now she was going to save Lorna's life.

'Don't do it,' she said unequivocally as she and Lorna sat on the bench wedged out of a tree trunk and laid their lunch across their knees, snapping into their cans of Coke in unison. Lorna drank thoughtfully and then shrugged, smiling with a look of elation and anticipation that Polly knew very well. 'I think you're mad. Stupid. Really I do. *I'll* buy you a vibrator – an enormous, rippled, singing and dancing, multi-coloured one, if you like.'

'I don't need a vibrator,' Lorna qualified, 'it's not the sex, *per se*, that I'm after. It's just, kinda like – heck, you know, shit.'

Polly knew precisely.

'I guess,' Lorna continued, more serious now, 'that maybe I want to go fly free one last time before I make my nest with Tom.' She sighed satisfied, as if she had put her finger on a very sane idea.

'Don't!' Polly warned her, shaking her head and pursing her lips.

'Why not? Tom'll never know, I'll make sure of it.'

'Tom won't need to know,' Polly said with conviction, '*you* will. And that's enough to damage the relationship beyond repair.'

'You sound – I don't know,' Lorna laughed, 'like, well, like a teacher. A teacher in the faculty of Love And Life.'

'It happened to a friend,' Polly said, reading Lorna's words not as the light-hearted compliment intended, but as acknowledgement of a skill she'd rather not have.

'Yeah?' Lorna responded, interested.

'Indeed,' Polly confirmed. 'She had this incredible boyfriend – gorgeous, funny, kind – Mr Perfectomundo him-self, believe me.'

'And? Go on—'

'Well,' said Polly, chewing on her Caesar salad sub thoughtfully, 'she, my friend, threw it all away.'

'You don't say?'

'Yes I do. She bloody well did. She fancied a fling, swore that her boyfriend would never find out and that once she'd had her fill, she'd simply wipe her hands of the whole affair and get on with her life.'

'Way to go!' Lorna murmured approvingly, wondering if the friend was the Megan about whom Polly so frequently spoke.

'It was certainly one way to go,' Polly chastised, turning Lorna's praise on its head, 'because her boyfriend soon ended the relationship.'

'How did he find out?' Lorna asked, riveted enough not to have touched her sandwich.

'He didn't.'

'No? Hey? So?'

'He left her anyway.'

Lorna looked simultaneously horrified and confused. Polly concentrated very hard on the brass plaque of Marc Bakarat (Sausalito 1949–Saigon 1968).

'Why?' said Lorna slowly, beginning to grasp the gist and wishing that she hadn't.

'He left her,' Polly elaborated slowly, 'because her actions had changed her. No matter how convinced she was that they wouldn't, they did. It drove her boyfriend away and into the arms of someone else.'

'Oh my – can you just imagine?'

Polly did not answer that one directly. 'This girl, my friend,' she continued instead, 'tried to insist that everything was going to be fine, that she forgave him and all that; you know – let's just move on, wipe the slate clean, fresh start sort of thing.'

'But?'

'No go. The bloke was rightly perturbed by it all – you know men, thinking with their dicks and only contemplating their actions when their brains finally catch up.' Polly levelled the accusation silently at herself and shuddered. Lorna felt the chill seep across from her friend and into her. Polly's face was stony. It was also clearly legible.

'Polly?'

'Lorna.'

'Was it?'

'Yes. It was me. And I'm not my friend at all any more.'

Lorna, moved by the honesty of her friend's words, placed her arm around Polly's shoulders and murmured soothing things about everything turning out just fine. Polly removed Lorna's arm gently and regarded her at length before speaking again.

'*Among all forms of mistake*,' she said, '*prophecy is the most gratuitous.*'

Lorna took the gravity of Polly's tone very seriously. A few moments later, she burst out laughing. 'And what the fuck does that mean?'

Polly laughed a little. '*Middlemarch*,' she said.

'No,' Lorna corrected, with friendly sarcasm, 'late May.'

'It's from the novel – I'm doing it with the kids. And I take it to mean that we can't meddle with the future. Our actions in the present define it – however strongly we might predict otherwise. What you do in the present can truly jeopardize the way you see the future. If you take a risk, you must suffer the consequences being other than how you envisaged. You can't do something and think "It'll all be OK", or "This, this and that will happen" – because one's comeuppance for such arrogance is that very often it isn't.'

They continued with their lunch in silence, drinking from their cans rather noisily.

'Polly?' Lorna probed.

'I'm not mentioning names,' Polly all but warned her. 'The outcome is very different from that which I prophesied. I thought I'd have a quick and rather rampant fling and then find myself gladly in the arms of my Max who was spared from knowing anything about my pathetic escapade.'

'How *did* Max find out?' Lorna all but whispered.

'He didn't,' Polly confided with a pained smirk, 'he doesn't know.'

'You didn't tell him?' Lorna gasped, stunned. 'Once you knew that he'd done the self-same thing?'

'No,' said Polly defiantly, immune to Lorna's tone of utter disbelief.

'Maybe if you did, it'd even up the score?' Lorna suggested, as if it was advice that Polly had called for, or a solution she had not considered.

322

Polly smiled quickly and forlornly. 'I wanted a Secret,' she said very clearly, 'and secrets are for keeping.'

'Yeah, but—' Lorna reasoned.

'I can't break that contract with myself,' Polly said. 'What sort of a person would that make me?' She left the bench for Marc Bakarat's tree and peeled away a slither of bark. She brought it back and gave it to Lorna.

'Remember,' said Polly, 'that I've lost Max. He does not want me. Remember that, when you drop your knickers and Tom from your memory.'

Polly cannot sleep. Her advice to Lorna was also a form of confession. She has broken her secret by sharing it. This has brought her some relief but the weight of it all has not lessened: that her deeds are now known spells danger too. They would have been safer kept locked within. Where would that have left Lorna, though? Without Tom? Feeling like Polly? Burdened by a secret she'd rather not have?

Polly dresses and tiptoes down through Petersfield House, a dull symphony of creaking floorboards accompanying her footfalls. Out she goes, out into the night, back to the memorial garden; the beacon beeches pale and haunting, welcoming too. She snuggles down into the trunk-bench and folds her arms about herself protectively, a lonely embrace. It is very much night and as clear as day.

Blaming Chip alone has been but a deluded excuse.

Heeding Kate's words has been a convenient excuse.

I did what I did and I've been using Kate's advice – never to tell a soul – as an easy solution. A way out. I've sort of lain the responsibility with Kate, haven't I? 'Kate says it'll be OK as long as I keep it a secret.' I see the wisdom in her words – but keeping a secret does not mean that I'm entitled to ignore its existence myself.

She leaves the bench and wanders in between the trees.

'I was unfaithful to the man I love,' she tells Joseph Hanlon (1920–1994), 'the man I've taken for granted – his presence, his fidelity, his goodness.' She presses her lips gently against the bark and then dabs her tongue to see what brass tastes like. She pulls herself through the trees; circling, weaving, in and out, a slow folk dance of sorts; the dead folk and their living trees of remembrance lending a helping hand. She holds on to them and draws herself in between and around them all. She feels that they are assisting her; sometimes the trees themselves, sometimes the people they commemorate. She asks Mary Beth Stevens (1967–1993) if she died too young to have any regrets. Mary Beth Stevens seems to answer that she would rather have had more years even if it meant deeds she'd need to atone for. Polly doesn't quite understand so she hugs the slim trunk until it becomes a beech tree and Mary Beth is just a name on a plaque attached.

'What shall I do?' she asks, sitting on her heels and picking at bark. 'What *can* I do? What's going to happen to me?' She listens hard but hears no advice.

I had it all worked out – without really thinking, actually. There'd be Max. Max and me. Now there isn't. At all. I've lost sight of all I used to see. Now I don't even know what to look for.

'What's going to happen to me?'

The trees rustle very softly in night's slim breeze but no one answers her. No one can tell her what to do or what will happen. She daren't predict the future, not even what she would like to happen.

I did that before. Look where it landed me.

Having no inkling of her fate is fundamentally the most frightening thing. And it is very much a 'thing', not a thought, for it is her current reality and she has created it for herself.

THIRTY-FIVE

*S*o, Polly has started truly to see the error of her ways. Chip is in Chicago and no longer a member of our cast list. And Max feels that a trip to America might be in order. Eight chapters to go and everything is heading towards a neat and tidy ending.

As long as Max can book a seat. As long as he still wants to. As long as, if and when he makes it there, he and Polly are indeed reconciled. Two weeks have passed and Megan's travel-agent friend's number still lies on top of the Post-it pad, by the phone in the kitchen, becoming ever more sploshed as the days go by.

Anyway, am I not forgetting something? Of course. Forgetting some*one*. Jen. Not really a memorable character but a key figure in this tale none the less, and still a potential spanner in the works. Has she had enough Chips in her life for a nourishing diet of Max to be what she desires? Will she hold on to him a little longer, with his permission? Maybe she won't let him go, certainly not on a peace mission to the States, maybe she'll entice him to stay.

So, Jen remains on the scene – how can she not? In Belsize Park, cat- and flat-sitting for Polly and taking her classes?

And Polly torments herself that Jen may have appropriated Max too. Megan is a little concerned as well.

'I guess you guys know?' Jen had said through the corner of a smile which, though small, was delineated with triumph. 'About Max and I?' It was first break. First day of the summer term. Jen looked tanned and radiant, leaner than when she left, blonder too.

'Me,' Megan had replied with a swift smile that was wholly non-committal. 'Max and me.'

'You?' said Jen.

'Grammar,' shrugged Megan. The staff room was not a fitting location for such a conversation (well, with Polly, then perhaps; with Jen, certainly not) and, just then, Megan realized that she was not an appropriate participant.

Poor Jen Carter Woman. My loyalties are with Polly. I do not want the blonde statue to smile so connivingly. I will not help the foreign lesion. I don't want to know what's going on – if it is. Is it? Still? Should I tell Polly? Nope; change of slant.

'Chip,' Megan said with confidence, as if the name Max belonged to no one she knew, so why should she even consider it.

'History,' Jen replied, with a wink. 'Max has seen to that. I owe it all to him. Can't wait to see him.'

Megan cleared her throat but found neither voice nor idea what to say. She couldn't even say 'Max?' in a carefully contrived vague tone. Instead, she looked at her watch, rifled through a clutch of exercise books and did a good act at suddenly being most preoccupied with some fine detail of the Lower Fourth's homework.

'Catch you later,' said Jen. Megan watched her leave the staff room.

Is that a swagger? Sweet Mother Mary help us, Polly especially, for I think it is.

'Dom, I'm seriously worried; honestly, seriously – gravely.'

'Megan, inamorata fantastico, what on earth about?'

'Your brother – my alpha man supremico.'

'Max?'

'No, you.'

'Hey?'

'*You're* my main man magnificat. But I'm *worried* about your brother.'

'Max?'

'And Polly's locum.'

'Jen?'

'Yes. Worried. I am. Very.'

'Why?'

'Two things. Firstly, though I try to loathe her, to see her as the baddy, actually I feel for her, as well as feeling a bit guilty that we had some part in all of this. Secondly, I don't think once was enough for her – Jen. And I fear she has persuasively long legs, an influentially fit physique.'

'I know what you mean.'

'About her legs?'

'Idiot woman. I feel uncomfortable too.'

'Jen seems pretty set.'

'I don't think Max wants more.'

'You sure? Really? Thank God you think so. I was—'

'Er, so I'm sure it's fine and innocent that he's gone over to Jen's. I'm sure it'll be a perfectly platonic dinner. Megan? Hey? You OK?'

'I'm going home. Alone. How dare you? It's Polly's! It's *Polly's* place – not Jen's.'

As Max walked down Haverstock Hill to Belsize Park, he realized that the spring in his step was not so much in anticipation of seeing Jen, but from relief that Dominic had neither pried, nor judged, nor even employed anything but a totally normal tone of voice to say 'OK, have a good evening'. As he neared the Screen on the Hill, Max wondered about suggesting the Woody Allen movie currently playing. As he passed the cinema, he decided against it. He was looking forward to seeing her, looking forward to company. He nipped into Budgens in search of flowers, or chocolates, but eschewed the browning carnations and cheap selection box for a tin of condensed milk for Buster. Smart. Subtle.

When Jen heard the doorbell, much anticipated, though Max was absolutely on time, she gave a little jump, checked her reflection though she knew it needed no attention and then went to answer the door with her most comely smile fixed in place and for the duration of the evening.

'Hullo,' said Max, holding the tin of condensed milk aloft as if it was some password for swift entry.

'Hey there,' said Jen, taking it from him, placing a hand on his shoulder and kissing him softly right on the edge of his mouth.

'Evening, Miss Klee,' said Max as the old lady tottered her way down the stairs, obviously having been in as much anticipation of the doorbell as Jen herself.

'Please,' she said, 'to help me? What is this? What must I do? Should I phone this number? How much do they want me to pay?'

Max took her bundle of correspondence and leafed through it. Kindly, he laid an arm across her shoulders and explained that one was a bank statement two years old, another was a gas bill already paid and the pizza delivery service flyer needed no response unless she fancied a margherita with extra mushrooms. He led her back up to her flat, checked her radiators, unasked, and made sure she locked the door behind him. Emerging out on the landing, Max was faced with Mrs Dale and her face of thunder. She was livid enough not to speak – and why shouldn't she be, the communal lights had been on for at least five minutes. She knew so, even through the solid door to her flat. What are peep holes for?

'Drunk!' was all she could finally find to hiss. Max tried not to smile but when she followed this with a venomously spat 'you little sod', he could not help but laugh. However, the resultant whack from her bunch of keys, gathered together on a dangerously long shoelace like some cat-o-ninetails, was not expected and not amusing at all. Max was caught on the jaw bone and it hurt. Instantly, though, he knew not to touch his jaw or make a sound. He observed her with infuriating kindness while she panted with perverse excitement.

'You,' he said, in a calm voice, 'need help. I think I'll call Camden Council. But first, the police.' He had no intention of doing either but Mrs Dale wasn't to know and she scurried up to her flat in a whirl of colourful language muffled only once she had slammed the door. The communal light, however, remained on. Miss Klee, whose hearing was as sharp as her fleshless shoulders, was so excited that she ordered a pepperoni pizza by telephone and wrote a cheque to the gas board while she waited.

Jen guided Max into the flat.

'You live in a madhouse,' he marvelled.

'Here, let me see,' she murmured, her lips in line with his jaw. 'Does it hurt?' She took her fingertips to it and left them there.

'Ish,' Max reasoned, taking her wrist and gently removing her touch.

'You want I fetch you some ice?'

'Ice,' conceded Max, 'would be nice. Please.'

Jen went to the kitchen and Buster, having regarded Max most witheringly, sauntered over to the cat flap. With a hearty headbutt, he heaved himself through, a disdainful flick of his tail being his last communication to Max that night. Max was alone, just for a moment, but for long enough to wonder whether he was alone at Jen's or at Polly's. Jen appeared from the kitchen, as if to answer his conundrum. She had mashed the ice, though he had not heard, and presented it to him, wrapped in a tea towel.

'Here you go, poor baby.'

'Thanks, thank you. No, it's OK, I can do it. I know where it hurts.'

'I'll go see to the meal.'

'Lovely,' said Max, thinking fleetingly of the nape of Polly's neck until the sight of Jen's bottom, just about clad in a small token of lycra, brought him back to the present with a bump – in his boxers. He went over to the mirror to scrutinize the damage. His jaw looked no different but, catching sight of his eyes, he could see the true damage quite clearly. Jen's call that dinner was ready rescued him away.

The pasta was very nice, the wine crisp and light, the Häagen-Dazs predictable but welcome.

'So,' said Max, biting the bullet as he sucked on a lump of pralines and cream, 'how did it go? When you were home? Did you see him? Chip, I mean?'

Jen replaced the spoonful nearing her mouth and regarded Max squarely.

'Sure, I saw him – and realized what a total jerk he is. Damn hot to look at, but, like, a total no-brainer. I don't need him in my life.'

'No regrets?' said Max through a suddenly raised pulse.

'No siree,' said Jen, pulling her bottom lip very slowly through her top teeth.

'Good,' said Max, a little awkwardly, 'pleased to hear it. You deserve somebody really, you know, good.'

'Know what? I guess I do,' said Jen in a soft drawl, as if the notion was new and very appetizing. Her lips were wet. Max tried not to notice. 'I owe a lot to you, Max Fyfield,' she continued, venturing her hand to his wrist. Max tried not to hear and, as soon as Jen touched down, he took his hand to the back of his neck for an urgent rub of an imaginary itch.

'Coffee?' she asked, though she might well have said 'Cunnilingus?' for all Max's urgent protestations about it being late (just ten o'clock) and he was very full (supper had been Californian light) and that coffee might impede a much-needed good night's sleep (all caffeinated products were anathema to Jen). Max, however, had no excuses when a glass of juice was offered instead. Jen led him back to the sitting-room, swaying languidly as she went; Max followed, taking care to scrutinize the skirting boards and not the skirt. Kicking off her shoes, Jen coiled herself sinuously on the settee and patted the cushion for Max to sit himself beside her.

'And Polly?' Jen asked, after a few minutes of silence save sipping.

330

'In America,' Max stated.

'You guys OK? Sorted stuff out?'

'Well,' said Max with a sharp intake of breath, 'if you can call taking a break a way of sorting stuff out, then yes, I suppose we are OK.'

'I'm sorry to hear that,' said Jen genuinely, 'real sorry.' She laid her hand very gently midway up Max's thigh but he could not decipher between sympathy (with which it was intended), and desire (the intention he imagined). 'Oh well,' Jen continued, 'I'm sure things'll work out for the best, hey?' She gave his leg a friendly squeeze, misread by Max as a suggestive clasp. He left the settee rather quickly and fiddled with the first thing that came to hand, a plunger corkscrew with unfortunate thrusting action.

'Max,' Jen cooed, 'you seem awful tense. Something up?'

'Actually,' Max said clearly, 'yes.'

'Go ahead,' said Jen, relaxed and settled where she sat.

'Look,' said Max, taking his seat beside her again and taking her hand between both of his, 'I find you immensely attractive – a veritable magnet.'

'Wow,' said Jen, highly flattered and licking her lips with delight. Max paused, as often he did, enabling him to compose his sentence so that, when spoken, its meaning was not misconstrued. His pause, however, lasted long enough for Jen to interject.

'I owe so much to you,' she murmured with unbridled admiration, darting her eyes all over his face, his skin scorching wherever they alighted, 'I don't know how I'll ever thank you.'

'You can't,' Max responded immediately, 'I'm sorry, I mean, don't worry about it, you know?'

'Know what?' said Jen.

'I mean,' Max said, '*I* can't. I *can't*. It was a one off. I'm sorry. I don't want to – again.'

Jen regarded him unflinchingly, scanning and scouring his face, unsuccessful in raising his downcast eyes. Then she laughed. She giggled. It was unaffected and infectious and spread relief through Max until he ventured his eyes to hers, his soft gaze requesting her explanation.

'Oh Max,' Jen laughed, '*I* can't, also. *I* don't want to, either.' She took the corkscrew that Max still held and played with it subconsciously.

'Pardon?' said Max, wondering how best to interject and proclaim his intentions – or lack of – in black and white, capital letters, once and for all.

'What I owe to you,' Jen said slowly, her face open and her tone soft, 'is, like, my liberation, I guess.' She stood up and put her hands on her hips. Max noted that her legs were not quite so stunning without their high-heeled send off. Her knees were a little too knobbly, her calves rather straight, her ankles a little thick. 'If it wasn't for you – for that one night,' she continued, 'I couldn't have gotten Chip out my system, you know?' Max began a nod. 'You're my saviour and I love you,' she stated, raising her hands as if she was helpless to do anything about the fact.

'But,' Max stumbled, never knowing quite what an American truly meant when employing the word 'love'.

Jen continued as if she had not heard him. 'Back home, I met with someone from years back,' she elaborated, 'high school, in fact. His name is Jesse. I was in love with him at fifteen.' She paused, raised her eyebrows at Max, and shrugged her shoulders. 'I'm in love with him all over – yeah, and all over again!'

Max stared at her and heard the penny drop loudly in the sudden silence of the room. It released a laugh from the pit of his stomach. 'I was worried,' he said, 'that, well, I mean.'

'I know, I know,' said Jen, now nodding in harmony with Max. 'You didn't know how to say it was a one-nighter, right?'

'Right,' said Max, stroking his palms, back and forth, along his thighs.

'Should've come right out with it,' Jen shrugged.

'I know,' Max said, 'bloody English reserve and all that bollocks.'

'Hey, I meant, both of us. We're adults, hey? But, like, I

just feel so grateful to you,' she rushed. 'It's crazy, I love you now, you know? I didn't when we had sex – I just thought you were cute and all. But now, *now* I love you – cos like, because of you I have my life back.'

'And,' Max qualified, 'you have Jesse.'

Jen clutched at her heart and fluttered her eyelashes comically for a few moments before regarding Max sternly. 'And you?' she asked.

'Me?'

'What did you get out of it?' She sighed, placed the corkscrew back on the mantelpiece and took an orange from the fruit bowl, tossing it lightly from hand to hand. 'What did you get, Max? Jeez, you lost your girl, hey?' Max shrugged and nodded and focused on the cat flap.

'I think, actually, we may have lost each other,' he said, 'lost the knowledge of what we had, lost sight of what we could have had, somewhere along the way.'

Jen went over to him, perched on the coffee table and took his hands in hers. 'Go find her and find out,' she said unequivocally. 'Go find her,' she repeated in urgent earnest, 'and find out.'

With that, she bid Max good night, kissing him too, telling him she loved him, that he was her best buddy. Jen did not tell Max that Chip, utterly stunned not only by her survival but also by her discovery of a better life and love, had bragged most luridly about his couplings with Polly. Jen did not inform Max out of her respect for Polly.

Because Polly didn't yell at me, did she? That day, when she came back here? How come she didn't go right ahead and even up the score? Tell me she had screwed my then boyfriend? You know something, I might have. Actually, I guess I would have. But Polly Fenton did not. And you know why? Because she knew not to. And the pain she carries now, the weight of that burden, is probably far greater than that which we would have felt, had she told us. She's brave and she's good and she deserves Max back.

The light in the communal hallway remained on.

THIRTY-SIX

*M*egan was going to be late for school. Dominic had left for a shoot in Bethnal Green. Max still slept. Megan would not be going anywhere until he surfaced. There was absolutely no way that she was going to encounter Jen before she'd had the chance to verify details with Max first.

'I'm sorry,' she said over the telephone to the school bursar, 'I'm going to be late this morning. I'm waiting for the man to fix it.' She did not elaborate on what it was that needed fixing but the bursar did not mind; Miss Reilly was entitled to be late just the once. Megan replaced the receiver and boiled the kettle, making a cup of tea expressly for holding, not drinking. She looked at her watch. Assembly.

Come on Max, wake up.

She flicked through the brothers' address book and was pleased to see she could now put faces to most of the names. She looked at her watch. First period.

Max, bloody wake up.

She thought how Polly would still be fast asleep. Right at that very moment. Over the sea and far away.

Oh, to be able to predict, let alone generate, a happy ending. Isn't that what friends are for? Or to pick up the pieces.

Megan looked at her watch. Second period was half-way through.

Right.

Max was in the thick of a nightmare in which Mrs Dale was torturing him with light bulbs, keys and torrid abuse. She was coming very close, her hands suddenly metamorphosing into claws. As she grabbed him, he hurled her away with all the strength he could muster, busting through the shoelaces she had tied around his limbs.

'Fuck you!' Max hollered, propelling the loathsome hag away from him. 'Get away!' He grabbed both his hands into tight, punch-ready fists, stood over her, bobbing and weaving, and made to aim.

'Max!' she pleaded, using his Christian name and a soft voice for the first time.

Time to wake up, Max.

'Megan – what on earth are you doing?' Max said blearily, observing his brother's girlfriend sitting in a heap under him. 'What am I doing?' he said, rubbing his eyes. 'Oh God!' He dived into bed so the duvet swallowed his nakedness.

Megan blinked and blushed. 'What on earth were *you* doing?' she asked, scrambling to her feet and clutching her arm. 'Ouch.'

'Sorry, I thought you were someone else,' he said sheepishly, 'I think I'll have a shower.'

'Make it a cold one,' Megan suggested.

'What time is it? Bloody hell, ten to ten.' Max leapt out of bed and then back into it immediately.

'Towel?' Megan offered.

'Please,' said Max, 'isn't it Wednesday?'

'It is indeed,' said Megan, handing him a towel and demurely averting her gaze.

Max wrapped the towel about his waist and Megan noticed, quite objectively, that his torso was more toned than his brother's. 'If it's Wednesday and, oh God, five to ten, why aren't you at school?' Max asked.

'Because,' said Megan, 'I'm playing hookey.'

'You? Why?' Max slung his hands on his hips.

'Because,' said Megan, 'I have something to do. Correction: *we* have something to do.'

'We do?' Max ruffled his already sleep-tousled hair.

'Do we!' Megan confirmed, zapping up the blind and wishing Dominic was as tidy as Max. 'We're off to see Mr Fixit.'

'Who he?' Max asked, yawning and stretching and wincing at his reflection.

'He's my friend in the travel business,' Megan said, as if Max was dim, 'Muswell Hill. You're going to America.'

'I am?' Max's hands were back on his hips.

'Yes,' Megan confirmed, 'Standby, tonight. This afternoon, if we can make it.'

'I don't know,' Max deliberated as kindly as he could, though he felt a little irritated, 'I need to think about it.'

'No you don't,' Megan announced in her teacher voice.

'I don't think I'm ready,' Max persisted.

'Correction: you don't *know* if you're ready,' Megan continued. 'You have to go, Max. For her. For you. It's time.'

Max regarded her suspiciously and headed for the bathroom. Megan went to the kitchen and filled the kettle, making tea to drink this time. She looked at her wrist. It had two dark weals from Max's grab. She didn't mind that it hurt. But she hoped that the marks would disappear by the time she saw Dominic that evening.

'It is, isn't it?' said Max, bringing her out of a daydream and back into the kitchen. Wednesday. Ten fifteen. Max in a denim shirt, jeans, desert boots; clean-shaven and wide awake.

'It is what?' Megan asked.

'Time,' Max said, turning away.

Max and Megan stood in Muswell Hill Broadway and stared at each other.

'Oh my God,' Max said, slowly, his mouth remaining agape.

336

'We've got just over three hours to get you there,' Megan all but shrieked. They laughed in short spurts, staring at each other intermittently, overusing the Lord's name in vain; infuriatingly rooted to the spot though acutely aware of how much they had to do and how little time they had.

'Oh my God,' Megan gasped, one hand at her mouth, the other on Max's shoulder to steady them both.

'God,' Max agreed.

'Better bloody get going then,' Megan exclaimed.

'Better bloody,' Max agreed.

'It's all OK,' Megan said later, wrapping her arms around Dominic's neck and drawing him close for a long, steady kiss. 'Everything's going to be OK.'

'That's nice,' said Dominic, brushing her hair away from his lips and wondering to what she referred. 'Max around?'

'Nope, it's all OK,' Megan said, unbuttoning Dominic's shirt a few inches so she could kiss his chest and decide that she liked it much more than Max's anyway. 'He's gone.'

'Gone,' said Dominic, fighting to concentrate even with eyes shut. Megan murmured affirmatively while licking and nibbling at him.

'Where?' Dominic croaked. 'Gone where?'

'To America?' Megan replied, looking up from his chest with a shrug, as if Dominic should have known all along and not interrupted her unnecessarily.

'Has he?' Dominic jerked back a little, taking Megan's right hand and sucking her middle finger thoughtfully while she swooned. 'Has he? Max? America?' Dominic repeated, his speech a little muffled as he tried not to bite Megan's finger as he spoke.

'He has,' Megan confirmed, pushing both her hands into the back pockets of her jeans, knowing that such a motion would cause her breasts to jut and that Dominic would find his attention drawn magnetically to them. 'He'll be on the plane now, about half an hour into the flight. Five and a half

337

hours away from Boston. I'd say about nine hours away from Polly, in total.'

'Nice tits,' marvelled Dominic, 'I mean, nine hours.'

'I wonder,' Megan purred.

'I do too,' Dominic replied, a breast in each hand, a blouse and a bra in the way.

'What'll happen?' Megan said, encircling her hands over his wrists and urging a more energetic fondle.

'What'll be,' murmured Dominic, now very distracted, 'will be. What is apparent is that we have the place to ourselves.' Dominic motioned to the fluffy rug from Ikea slyly, eyeing Megan up and down suggestively. Megan licked her lips in reply.

Later, while they returned the furniture to its more usual locations, Megan told Dominic of Max's evening with Jen.

'It took me from here to Chiswick to summon the courage to ask him about it,' Megan said, 'and then it took from the Hogarth roundabout to Heathrow for Max to recount the evening.'

'That's lucky,' said Dominic, 'you might have had to change course for Gatwick, or even Stansted, if it hadn't been quite so innocent.'

'Exactly,' said Megan in earnest.

'He'll be landing in a couple of hours,' said Dominic, scrutinizing the clock on the video.

'Think everything will work out all right?' Megan asked.

Dominic pulled her close against him. 'Depends what you mean by "all right",' he said. 'Say the conclusion they draw doesn't correspond with our hopes?'

'Then that won't be all right,' Megan protested.

'But it will,' Dominic reasoned, 'really. If you think about it.'

*   *   *

Do I want to be on this plane? Making this journey? I don't know. I still don't know if I'm doing the right thing. I mean,

*going there; or coming here, rather – I'm less than two hours
away from landing. I do know that it's time. I do know it's
what I need to do. I just don't know what the right thing to
do actually is. I don't know what I want.*

'Sir, duty free?'

'No thank you.'

*Free from duty? Do I want to be? How will I feel when I see
her? Right now I feel very ambivalent. I feel a bit sick, too. I
hate planes.*

'Sir, tea? Coffee?'

'With caffeine?'

'Yes sir, unless you'd prefer it without.'

*Oh God. I don't believe it. Polly turns twenty-eight today,
I mean tomorrow, or is it yesterday? Hang on. No, I land on
her birthday. I forgot to send her a card.*

'Sir, more coffee?'

'Please.'

*I know, I could pretend that's the purpose for my visit – to
deliver her birthday card by hand. No, I can't; that would
give her the wrong idea and enforce affection. It would only
raise hopes. Hold on, does that mean I'm making this trip to
dash hopes, then? Anyway, is she still hoping for a reconcil-
iation? How would I know? We haven't spoken. We haven't
written. Not for nearly a month. How can either of us know
how things stand?*

'I just want things to be resolved.'

'Yes sir, more coffee?'

*   *   *

*I'm twenty-eight years old. Crappy birthday to you – crappy
bloody birthday to me. I am no longer in my mid-twenties. The
year after next I'll be thirty. Where will I be the year after next?*

'Hey, Miss Fenton.'

'Morning, Zoe – shouldn't you be in class?'

'Shouldn't *you*? Miss Fenton? You OK? Hey? Want me to
fetch someone?'

'It's my birthday and I'll cry if I want to.'

'That's a song, huh?'

'No, it's the truth.'

Miss Fenton cut a sorry figure as she turned from Zoe and made her way to class. It disturbed Zoe greatly to see her on the verge of tears. Teachers, like parents, don't cry, do they? Well, they shouldn't. Teachers are sort of parents anyway and, in the case of Miss Fenton, sometimes a whole lot better too.

'She shouldn't cry,' Zoe later reasoned in confidence to the clutch of friends she had gathered for a lunch-time confab, 'not on her birthday.'

''Specially not on her birthday,' Lauren agreed, casting her gaze over to where Miss Fenton sat, alone, seemingly transfixed by her full plate.

'You reckon she didn't get any cards?' Heidi asked, glancing at the teacher swiftly.

'Why else would you cry on your birthday?' Beth shrugged. They all shuddered at the thought of such neglect. 'Shall we go sing to her?'

'Like, right now?' Heidi asked. 'She might hate that.'

'It kinda might make her cry again,' Zoe pondered.

'Let's make her a party,' Johanna announced in a triumphant whisper with a quick clap of her hands, 'for the Petersfield House sisters.'

'And her classes,' Heidi interjected.

'Sure,' Johanna agreed, 'more the merrier, as she says.'

'Cool,' said Lauren. 'Guys too? Like, those she teaches?'

'Yeah,' said Johanna, who had her eye on Forrest but the misfortune to share none of his classes.

'Know what?' Heidi said, 'we should tell Ms Hendry — she's Miss Fenton's best buddy. She might help us get some stuff, you know?'

'Go to it,' said Johanna, with her trademark clap. The girls left the dining hall without looking over to Miss Fenton. They didn't want to raise her suspicions. Polly was oblivious to their presence anyway; in a world of her own, staring at a plate of food, not remotely hungry and yet feeling starved.

Lorna was horrified to learn it was Polly's birthday. You bet she'd help the girls organize a party. You bet she gave out exit passes and permission to miss study period. Lorna went in search of Kate and found her, paint-spattered, encouraging the sophomores to express their emotions by working beyond the constraints of brushes and paper.

'Use the walls,' Kate cried, oblivious to Lorna's entrance, 'use your hands. Feel your way. Kiss the colour – it's non-toxic. Watch. See? Yeah, kiss the colour. Embrace form and light. Blur the boundaries. Go ahead, guys, blur!'

'Mrs Tracey?'

'Ms Hendry!'

'You know you have blue lips, a green cheek and a yellow left eye?'

'Do I have a purple tongue, also? Should have – here—'

'Yup, you sure do.'

'You want to join us?' Kate asked, motioning to spare overalls on the pegs by the wall currently being painted.

'Want to join *us*?' Lorna qualified in a lowered voice, guiding Kate away from her throng and finding her hand turned orange in the process. 'It's Polly's birthday,' Lorna confided, 'and she's pretty low – thinks everyone's forgotten.'

'How can we forget if we never knew in the first place?' Kate retorted, visibly upset.

'I mean, her lot back home, you know?' Lorna explained.

Kate winced and then nodded. 'You want to come over this afternoon? Cook? Bake?'

'Sure,' said Lorna, 'that'd be great.'

'Half of three?' Kate winked before returning her attention to her class while Lorna slipped away. 'OK you guys,' Kate shouted, clapping and grinning effervescently. 'Stop the mural just now, OK. Tom, go fetch that humungous roll of paper, the stuff we use for stage sets? Good. Let's roll it out. Longer. More. Longer. Great. Now, let's make the mother of all birthday cards.'

THIRTY-SEVEN

*S*trange, Max ponders, standing on the bridge, his hand on the sign welcoming him to Hubbardtons Spring, his eyes drinking in the various sights of Main Street, *it looks not too dissimilar to how I'd envisaged. It's all very welcoming but do I actually want to be here?* He regards the sign again, as if to double-check, gives it a confident ping with his finger and strolls on into the town.

Diner on the left, looking just like they do in the films. Aroma-chiro-acu-herbal-zen sort of place on my right with a woman closing up under a trickle of wind chimes. Nice houses, all of them, even the most modest; set and settled like a friendly little group having a chat.

'Evening.'

Me?

Yes you, Max. It's Marcia, not that you'd know.

'Yes, hullo, evening – is Pleasant Street near?'

'Why sure – second right after the drugstore.'

'Thanks.'

'No problem.'

Hope not.

Pleasant Street lives up to its name for Max and, though

few of the houses are numbered, he seems to know instinctively which is Kate's from Polly's brief description in her very first letter. He walks past it, however, without changing his pace and continues to the end of the street. He sees the sign for the school at the start of a steep, tree-lined drive. A surge of adrenalin sears through his stomach. He turns back for Kate's but stands still a while. In front of him, Pleasant Street with its trees and homes and cars rolls down to Main Street. Beyond the fringe of trees, the river; just out of earshot. Then the hills, forever rising, interlocking. And above it all, the embrace of a temperate evening sky; a blush of pink, a vestige of blue, diaphanous cloud seeping across like a sigh; the moon, early, over there.

Max shakes his head and takes a deep breath. He yawns and shakes his head again. Why shouldn't Polly feel so utterly settled in such an apparently perfect place? It certainly compared highly with any of the places he had hitherto lived.

Apart from Cornwall, of course.

But everywhere he had ever known seemed now rather far away. Distant. Easy to forget, potentially.

You can't feel homesick in a place like this, can you?

He makes his way back down the street to the house he thinks is Kate's. The front door has no knocker, no bell, not even a letter-box. He doesn't want to hammer on the wood, the street is far too peaceful. He makes his way around the house, peering into windows as he goes, hovering momentarily by the steps leading up to the deck, assessing the back door. That's more like it. Ajar. Knock. Gentle push. Soft call. Hullo? Anyone home?

Kate is late because her selection of earrings is driving her mad. The decision, though, is important. There's a party to go to, a friend to support and only the best earrings will do. She chooses Mexican silver and wonders why it took her so long. They complement her nut-brown skin, her elegant neck, her cropped hair. But they don't go with her dress so she changes. She looks at the clock. She's not really late, not for Polly, but she's no longer early, as she had hoped to be, for Lorna.

'Clinton, that you?' Kate called, descending the stairs and expecting to see her husband back early from his run. She did not expect to come across a stranger engrossed in her fridge of smiles but she said 'Hi' all the same. The stranger, far more shocked and unnerved by her than she by him, scratched his head, mumbled a greeting and appeared generally but becomingly confused.

'Max?' she asked, eyes asparkle, face a little flushed, silver earrings dangling and glinting. 'That you, right?'

The man extended his hand. 'How do you do,' he confirmed and they shook on it heartily.

'Max, I'm kinda on my way out,' Kate explained, as if to a neighbour who had popped in unannounced for coffee and a chat.

'That's OK,' Max assured her with a hint of apology, 'honestly. Fine. I'm not going to be long.'

'Oh-my-God-Max!' Kate marvelled as her imagination tumbled, and reality dawned at last, 'Max, you're *here*.'

'Er,' Max laughed, looking about himself theatrically, 'I suppose I rather am.'

'I mean, *here*, today – Polly's birthday, hey?'

'Yes,' he said, 'it is. Today. I know.'

'She thinks you'd all gone and forgot,' Kate said.

'I did,' Max admitted. 'I remembered only on the plane.'

'You were coming anyway,' Kate stated, 'right?'

'Yes. Spur of the moment – but a good idea, I hope,' Max explained, presuming Kate to know about the situation between him and Polly, and actually feeling fine that she should.

'Could be,' said Kate warmly, 'and all. I got to go. It's a party for Polly.' She bit her lip and regarded Max quizzically, while trying to assess in an instant all the pros and cons of Max's entrance providing the biggest surprise of all. Max was doing the same. 'You want to come too?' Kate asked, squinting.

344

'I don't think so,' Max said, 'tonight's probably not the right time.'

'You sure?' Kate furthered, out of politeness though she tended to agree with Max. Max gazed at the fridge and focused on a photo which featured Polly in a group of people by a stack of timber. 'House raising,' Kate explained, 'last fall.'

'Polly building a home,' Max said quietly, 'in America.'

Kate stole a long look at Max, who was miles away and didn't see. She'd known him only a few minutes and yet, if she had had to pick from a long line of the most eligible partners for Polly, she saw how she would have chosen him without hesitation. Contemplative, strong, good. It was good that he was here. She was pleased; pleased too that he was how he was. Maybe he'd like to stay.

'You want to stay here?' she asked, bringing him back from his thoughts.

'No no,' Max answered. Then he thought back to Chloë and William's hospitality. Kate seemed to be offering much of the same. 'Well, perhaps I could. If you're sure. Just for a day or two. I'm not staying long.'

'Sure,' said Kate easily.

Max tapped his temples and pulled an exasperated face. 'I just boarded a plane,' he shrugged, 'without thinking.'

'Great that you did,' Kate praised. 'Listen, I got to go – but you know what? I think you should come along too, just for a peep through the window, just so you can see.'

Max backed away a step, trying to evaluate the benefits, 'Do you think so?'

'I know so,' Kate said, taking his arm and leading the way.

Forty minutes later, having absorbed a private glimpse of Polly, then returned to Kate's to introduce and then excuse himself to Clinton, Max stood in the centre of Great Aunt Clara's room, closed his eyes and breathed in the scent of Polly. He had just seen her, just left the sight of her, all ecstatic tears and squeals at her surprise party, and yet she was also right here in this funny old room too. He sat down carefully in the rickety chair and watched the lace panels waft and hover an inch or two from the windows.

Just the same. Looked no different – I don't know why I was expecting her to but I was. I suppose I thought that if she has changed, she'd look altered too. Oddly, it was more of a surprise to see her looking just the same. A bright button shining away and gleaming at all the people who love her, who have organized a party for her, who have made her birthday a happy one. Providing her with a feeling of family. She certainly looks very much at home out here, amongst them all.

'I didn't recognize her clothes,' he told Cézanne's gardener. 'I didn't know she had a pair of white jeans. Mind you,' he continued, to the vague reflection of himself in a window pane, 'this shirt is new too. From St Ives. She won't have seen it before.' He looked at Van Gogh's bedroom and then looked about Great Aunt Clara's. He went to his rucksack and rummaged through the clothes until he found his sketch pad. He sat down in the rickety chair, pencil poised, and wondered what to draw. The funny ornaments? Conclusions? A still life?

A life, still?

Polly went to bed a tired but happy twenty-eight-year-old.

They remembered. All of them. They said, 'How could we forget?'

She told herself that it mattered no longer that the other people she thought mattered had obviously forgotten.

I've just been given a wonderful party with cake and Coke and an enormous birthday card, presents too and kisses from everyone (apart from Johanna and Forrest, who were too engrossed kissing each other). I can hardly be ungrateful now, can I?

From Lorna to Jackson, Zoe to AJ, Polly had received their affection with open gratitude. Though she believed that she was truly at the centre of her life, that reality was undoubtedly right here, right now, in this place, with these folks, her mind kept returning to the loaded question of where were her cards from those in England.

Why not even Megan? Missing in the mail? Or just missing from her memory?

And still nothing from Max. Nothing at all.

Kate was surprised to find Max on the deck enjoying the peace and dew early the next morning.

'Morning, early bird,' she said softly, taking his wrist and finding that his watch read ten to seven.

'Morning,' Max replied, 'how was the party?'

'It was great,' Kate said, taking a seat alongside him and accepting his offer of a sip from his mug of coffee. 'You see her?'

'I did,' Max said, 'I saw her.'

'Looking good,' Kate stated. Max smiled. He didn't actually nod.

'How we gonna get you two together?' Kate sighed, 'I mean, like how are we going to get you two *together*, so that we can get you two together?'

'I don't know,' Max puzzled, 'because I just don't know anyway, if you see what I mean?'

'And she's teaching all damned day,' said Kate, lowering her gaze until it rested, quite happily, on Max's thigh. Her eyes travelled down his leg and alighted on the sketch book lying across his knees. 'May I?' she asked.

''Course,' Max replied.

Kate flipped through the sheets in awed silence while Max annotated them quietly for her. Puffin. Cornwall. My friends' daughter. Pigeon. My brother reading. Polly's cat. Bits of a bike. Great Aunt Clara's rickety chair.

'I got an idea,' Kate said, 'you want to help me take a class?'

Polly sought out Kate at morning coffee. 'That was such a smashing evening,' she said, hugging Kate and kissing her cheek. 'Thanks so much.'

'It was a lot of fun,' Kate responded, 'your birthday was just an excuse.'

'Yeah,' Polly rolled, as she had learned from the kids, 'right.'

'You want to come by and thank the artists for your card?' Kate continued. 'Walls are done and we've started on the ceiling. It looks so good.'

'Love to,' said Polly, 'I have a free period before lunch.'

'Did you see that guy?' Lauren asked Heidi, eyes agog.

'Mrs Tracey's new assistant?' Heidi gasped, holding her heart. The girls licked their lips and offered silent prayers.

'*See* him,' Zoe interjected, 'I, like, had two classes with him. He is just *too* nice.'

'What's his name?' Heidi probed.

'Mr Fielding or something – I don't know, I was so gone, man,' Zoe responded, feigning a faint. The girls laughed.

'Miss Fenton,' Lauren asked as their teacher came into the class room and started taking marked essays from her bag.

'Lauren?' Miss Fenton replied.

'You seen that new teacher? Know his name?'

'No and no,' said Miss Fenton, 'who and where?'

'A guy,' said Heidi, 'art.'

'I think he's English,' Zoe furthered, 'or Australian or something.'

'Oh yes?' Miss Fenton said, handing back essays, 'I'll check with Mrs Tracey later. These were diabolical.'

At ten past twelve, Polly made her way over the lawns to the art building. The main studio was empty, its walls defiantly white. The smaller studio was dark, with paintings by Manet projected on to the walls. The senior art history group sat in hushed reverence, witnesses to the execution of Maximilian; total silence save the whirr of the slide carousel. But no Kate.

Maybe downstairs, lots of wall space there.

'Kate!'

'Polly!'

They passed on the stairs, Kate appearing a little agitated and eager to continue her ascent.

'I came to thank your class,' Polly said.

'Go right ahead,' Kate said, looking steadily ahead of her, 'I got to be some place else.' She laid a hand on Polly's shoulder and then used it to lever herself on up the stairs. Polly made her way down and could already see a snatch of colour-festooned wall before she reached the bottom step. As she approached the room, the colour was almost audible and the light emanating from it seemed to seep along the corridor in a prelude.

'My God!' Polly exclaimed when she entered. 'Wow!'

Students on stepladders, students kneeling on the floor, students under the trestle tables, all stopped to observe her; their paint-sodden rags, sponges and fingers suspended. 'It's *marvellous*,' Polly gasped, crouching a little to admire the decorated underside of the tables. 'Wow. It's fan*tastic*.'

'You like it?' asked a student, with a face almost entirely blue which he pressed against a small, bare patch of wall.

'I *love* it!' Polly exclaimed, craning her head to admire the ceiling.

'So do I,' said Max.

Max?
Max?
Where?

Here.
I'm here.

Though Polly locates his voice as being behind her, she stares fixedly ahead, concentrating hard on the abstract shapes on the wall in front of her, finding that they make far more sense than the fact that Max is here in this room now. Behind her. Just over there. Her heart seems to be racing a relay between her stomach and her mouth, not knowing where to settle or how to slow down. Her mind is racing too

349

fast for her to catch hold of any sensible thought. She has no idea what to do. No idea what is happening to her. A hand is placed gently on her shoulder, close to her neck, a finger just missing the fabric of her T-shirt so that it alights on her skin. She knows the touch off by heart.

'Polly?'

Gentle pressure from the hand encourages her to turn.

'Max?'

It is.

Him.

Here.

'Mr Fyfelt, can I, like, dunk my shoe in the paint? I think the sole will give great texture.'

'Fyfield. And certainly you may – texture will give soul.'

'Max?'

'Mr Flyfield, what's the complementary colour of red? I forget.'

'Fyfield. Green.'

'Max?'

'Mr Fryfeel, can I go to the bathroom.'

'Fyfield, of course.'

'Max?'

'Polly.'

Kate appears and dismisses them with no more drama than if she had merely asked both of them simply to watch her class for a few minutes.

Off you go, both of you.

THIRTY-EIGHT

Mmm. Lovely. Can't you just see it? Max and Polly lying on a river bank, running fingers through downy grass and through each other's hair. So very Hollywood. Max and Polly gazing at the stunning landscape and deep into the soul of one another. Listen to the emotive, syrupy symphony in the background. Max and Polly kissing so gently in the privacy and protection of the maples. This is the stuff of Oscars. A lovely, cosy closing of our story at the very least. Max and Polly taking a moonlit walk, hand in hand, eyes locked into each other; smiles lit by their own brilliance and echoed by the platinum grin of a new moon. Fairy-tale magic. Max and Polly laughing. Happy, both of them. Together again. Happy now and happy ever after.

I love you.
And I love you.
The end.

Almost.
Not quite.
Not just yet.

* * *

Polly had no idea what to do once she and Max had left the art building. She didn't know where to look, what to say, how to feel or why, in the first place, Max was actually here.

Can you believe it? He's come! To me. I've had a glance or two but I'm too butterfly-flustered to gaze on him and really catch his eye. But I have more than caught his eye, haven't I – because he's all the way over here to be with me. Funny, but now that he's here, in Hubbardtons, he looks much taller somehow – I suppose I've been recalling him as more of the boy back home. Certainly not the man here now. Ssh! He's going to speak. He's taken my wrist – oh, blissful day!

'Go for a walk?' Max suggested. Polly nodded and set off in the direction her feet were already pointing. Conveniently, it took them out of the school grounds and along a narrow, steep lane, densely wooded.

'Surprised?' Max asked.

'Very,' said Polly, encircling both hands around Max's wrist.

'Stunning round here,' said Max in a flat voice at odds with his remark, 'I can see why you feel so settled and at home.'

'Settled?' Polly barked inadvertently, off her guard, quite taking Max aback.

Why are you here?

Maybe I wish I wasn't.

'Sorry,' Polly rushed meekly and walked on.

Oh God. There's an atmosphere – it's heavy and fragile simultaneously. What do I do now?

'Max?' she asked, stopping suddenly, now holding his right forearm between both her hands, tugging slightly. 'You here? Why are you here?'

'Don't really know,' he replied, his honesty slicing through Polly like a blade. He pulled his arm so that his hand caught hers and yet she was powerless to keep a hold.

'Oh,' said Polly, out of bewilderment, desperation; walked on because she didn't know what else to say. She held out her hand without looking at Max and her heart crept back up

352

her ribcage when he decided to take it. Within seconds, holding hands felt very odd, palms were uncharacteristically sweaty and neither of them held on very tight; as if too much pressure might indeed be too much pressure, as if touching with any conviction might be tempting fate or heading for disappointment.

Has he something to tell me? Good news or bad?

The path ended and pastureland opened in front of them. A fence. A gate. A felled tree trunk placed conveniently a few yards on. Down on it they sat and concentrated hard on the beautiful view.

'I'm sorry I didn't see you before you went,' Max said, regarding Polly who stared straight ahead of her, a vague smile fixed safely to her lips.

'Are you?' she said.

'No,' Max replied, with the same cutting honesty – the quality Polly loved best about him but now wished he lacked. 'Not really. I couldn't have.'

''Sokay,' said Polly, employing her trademark brightness to mask deep hurt. 'Don't worry. I understand.'

'Do you? Well, I think we need to talk,' Max said cautiously, '—although I don't really think we could have *then*, if you see.'

'No,' Polly concedes, 'and yes.'

'But now I'm here, I haven't a clue what to talk about.' Max chuckled softly, rose and stood with his back to Polly, looking at Vermont. Polly cupped her eyes and observed him.

New shirt. Nice. Suits him. Can't believe he's here. What does he want?

'What do you want,' Max asked, turning to her, towering over her, 'Polly Fenton?'

Polly couldn't reply for she had no voice and no true notion of the answer.

'Go for a walk?' she tried. Max smiled quickly but kindly and dropped to his heels. One hand splayed over the grass for balance, the other lolled over his knee. Though she scoured his face, his gaze remained fixed on a point beyond the mountains. Polly looked at his fingers instead but realized with some horror that the very sight of them made her want to cry. She blinked fast.

Can't cry, he might back off – but it might make him come closer. Don't know which any more. Too much of a risk.

'What do *you* want?' she asked Max quietly, hoping he wouldn't reprimand her for answering a question with a question.

'I don't know,' he said openly, taking his seat again beside Polly on the tree trunk. He looked at her. 'But I *am* over here,' he said, 'in Vermont. With you.'

Yes!

'Yes,' she marvelled, 'you are.'

'And I wouldn't be if—' he pondered.

Oh thank God, darling Max.

'—if nothing meant anything any more,' Polly finished for him, with a premature tone of triumph.

'I suppose so,' said Max. Polly sensed his shy smile but she dared not catch his eye.

'Yes,' said Polly. Very slowly she tiptoed shy fingers over his arm and walked them lightly down to his wrist. 'Hullo Max,' she said, making no attempt to mask the crack in her voice. Max looked out over Vermont again.

God, this could be so easy. She's so tempting. It could be so difficult.

There was so much to talk about that he could find nothing to say. 'You staying long?' Polly asked to a shrug from Max. 'Where are you staying?'

'With your friend Kate,' Max replied.

'In my bedroom?' Polly asked lightly.

'Great Aunt Clara's,' Max corrected, 'I believe.'

'Yes,' Polly confirmed, 'Great Aunt Clara's.'

This is horrendously awkward. What I really want to do is leap up and spin around and sing 'You're here, Max, you're here.' But, do you know, something's holding me back. Him. I don't think he wants me to.

'Listen, I have to make a move, I have a class,' Polly apologized, cursing the sight of her watch.

'Of course,' said Max, checking his.

You could always bunk off. I mean, Megan did. That's how I'm here. Prioritize, hey? Shouldn't you stay with me so we can try to talk a little more? I'm being manipulative. Her love for her job was one of the qualities I most admired in her.

'Walk with me?' Polly held her hand out a little way.

Oh God, you paused, Max. Say 'yes' right now, say you'll walk with me. Please want to.

'I think I'll stay here – if that's OK – jet lag busting,' Max said, rolling his sleeves up and turning his face, eyes closed, to the sun.

''Kay,' said Polly, shuffling a little and wondering about the penalty for a teacher skiving a class.

Go on, do it.

Can't.

'See you later?' Max said, eyes still closed but face inclined a little in her general direction.

''Kay,' said Polly. 'It's Formal Meal tonight, though.'

'OK,' said Max.

'After?' Polly suggested. 'Eight-ish? Better go.'

'Have a good afternoon.'

'You too.'

'Bye now.'

'Bye then.'

Polly felt most disconcerted as she wound her way back down to the school. She felt physically winded and held a hand to her diaphragm. She felt exhausted; the huge surge of hope that had nourished every cell in her body and filled her soul when she realized Max was in Vermont had suddenly drained away. Now she felt depleted, like a ragdoll in need of more stuffing. Because of course, Polly often gallops headlong to conclusions, leaping up and grasping at threads she is convinced are as strong as ropes, without really assessing the true facts often staring her in the face. That's why she falls. So far, she's always bounced. Maybe she needs to crumple so she can actually pick herself up. Predictably, Polly had decided in an instant that if Max had flown across the Atlantic to come to her, surely it could mean only one thing. A modern knight coming for her, coming because of her – his shining armour and his powerful white steed updated to twentieth-century aeronautical engineering. So what? The romance of it all was intact. Until, of course, Max started speaking.

He seems distant – and yet he is here.

Yes he is, Polly, and yes he is. Polly, of course, knows nothing about Max's journey to Cornwall, and the discoveries he made there.

Why didn't he want to walk back with me?

Polly doesn't know of Max's ambivalence on the flight over.

He says we should talk – but what about? If he was going to end it all, would he go to all this trouble? And expense? Wouldn't just a call or a letter do? No, that's not his style.

Feeling a little nauseous, Polly cursed Max's sense of duty, hating about him that which she had always admired.

Oh Christ, he's come here to dump me.

The notion chilled Polly so severely that she had to detour to her apartment for a jumper and was late for class as a result. She went in search of Lorna as soon as school finished. Lorna wore a maniacal smile and punched Polly quite hard on the biceps.

'Yo Fenton! Guess who's on *my* table at Formal Meal?'

'What?' Polly flustered. 'No, listen, something's happened.'

'You bet it has!' Lorna brandished.

'No,' Polly almost shouted and continued without pause for breath, 'it has, something really has happened. He's here. Max. Max is here. He didn't write and I wish he had. He's come from England. I want a letter instead, not him here. He's come over to, oh God, to finish. It. I know it. With me. You see? God. I want a letter.'

'Hey hey,' said Lorna, 'I know – I know.'

'You do?' Polly wailed, 'he *has*?'

'Whoah! What I'm saying is that I know he's *here* because he's on Kate's table at Formal Meal and she's invited me too.'

'You too?'

'Yeah,' Lorna said with a shrug, 'me.'

'See,' Polly said forlornly, 'see what I mean?'

Lorna embraced her friend. 'Crazy bitch,' she said affectionately, 'you're jumping to conclusions.'

'Better than grasping on to false hope,' said Polly, suddenly wanting to hit Lorna.

Polly hardly ate at Formal Meal. She put on a passable veneer for her table and joined in the conversation perfunctorily. She found her eyes disobeying her orders, by constantly darting over to Kate's table, circumnavigating it clockwise until they alighted on Max who sat with his back towards her. She did not catch his eye once and the laughter trickling over from Kate's table unnerved her. As the hall emptied, she hung back because she supposed she ought to. To wait. Till eight. Somehow, in the mêlée, she missed Max entirely and was soon left with just a trickle of loitering students who did not notice her at all. She was overcome by a desire to be utterly alone, she did not want Max to be there, she did not want to know a Max Fyfield at all.

I think it would be safer not to, much less complicated – to be all by myself instead, all on my lonesome.

Returning to Petersfield House, she walked slowly, half hoping that Max would in fact be there, half hoping that he would not.

What is it that I want?

As she neared, however, there was no sign of him and he appeared not to be inside either. Polly found herself to be bitterly disappointed.

What is it that he wants?

The girls were making noisy use of the last ten minutes

before study time, and Polly was able to creep to her apartment unseen. She phoned Kate.

'Kate? Polly. Max there?'

'No.'

'Oh,' said Polly, ''kay.'

She hung up before Kate had the chance to tell her that Max was on his way over. Polly stuck her head out from her doorway and bellowed, 'Study hour!' Her girls had never heard such a tone and they scurried to their work obediently. Polly shut her door and curled up on the couch, crying hard, wanting to cry silently, not wanting to cry at all; failing.

Fucking failing. What a fucking failure.

There was a knock at the door, to which she hollered 'study hour'. A few moments later, however, another knock.

'Study hour,' she whimpered under her breath, pulling herself up and sitting hunched, shoulders heaving. 'It's bloody study hour,' she whispered, 'go away and study.'

Knock knock.

'Who's there?'

'It's me. Max.'

'Why are you crying?' he asks, tucking her hair behind her ear and letting his hand cup her head.

'Don't know,' she sobs, taking her face away from the comfort of his chest only momentarily before barging it back, lest this should be the last time she can lie there.

'You sad? Happy?' he probes, slipping his hands down on to her shoulders, the remembered feeling of their shape greeting him once more.

'Yes,' she says, 'and yes.'

'Happy and sad?' he reiterates. 'Me too.' They share a sigh and stand very still. They hold on to each other, tight; Max breathing deeply into the top of Polly's head, Polly burying her face against him. His arms around her, one hand enmeshed in her hair; her arms locked together around his waist.

358

God, this is too tempting.
I can't hold on tight enough. He'll slip away.

'Shall we go for a walk?' Max asks, though he stifles a yawn
and tells himself sharply that he is not tired.

Polly looks unhappy. 'It's bloody study hour,' she cries,
sobbing afresh. Max blots her tears with his thumbs.

He used to kiss my tears away.

Give him a chance, Polly.

'Talk, then?' Max suggests before succumbing to a yawn of
prodigious proportions. Polly smiles at him and gives a
hearty sniff to wrap up her cry.

'You're bushed, my boy.'

'I am, I suppose,' Max concedes, rubbing his eye with the
back of his hand like a child.

I love him. Oh I do. I want to tell him. I want to touch him.
Go on then.

'Maybe you'd better go and have a long sleep.'

Oh, very romantic, Polly.

'We could talk tomorrow. It's sports afternoon so I'm free.'

Good girl.

'OK,' Max nods, 'you're probably right. I wouldn't want to
say something in a sleepy stupor that I might regret.'

What might that be? wondered Polly, unnerved, as she
showed him the door and bid him sweet dreams.

*He was tender just now, wasn't he? That must mean that
he wants me, that he wants to come back. That's why I could
let him go and sleep, you see, because he'll be back tomorrow. He said so.*

Polly took Max on a cycle ride to Grafton the following afternoon. The reason was twofold for she was as proud of her
increased fitness as she was of the area in which she was
living. Max was impressed by both and Polly liked the ambi-
guity contained in his frequently and breathlessly expressed
'Beautiful!' Was it in reference to the sight of her pert bottom
as she stood in her cleats and cycled up hill? Was it the hill

itself? Was it the hill that made him sound breathless, or the sight of her? Whichever, Max seemed to be enjoying his afternoon.

That's the main thing. He'll stay.

They filled a basket from the Grafton Stores and cycled on out of town to the cheese factory where they bought a chunk of Vermont Cheddar. They pedalled on a few miles until they found a picture-perfect shaded dell near to where Saxtons River and Turkey Mountain Brook meet.

'Fantastic names,' Max marvelled, unpacking the provisions and smacking his lips, 'Turkey Mountain Brook.'

'How about Pompanoosuc?' Polly suggested gaily, pointing it out on the map.

'Pompanoosuc,' Max repeated in a very odd accent but with great rhythm. They laughed.

'We could go to Dorset,' Polly suggested wide-eyed, 'or Peru. There's Weybridge too — or perhaps you'd prefer Manchester?'

'Manchester? I rather think not,' Max chuckled.

'Sunderland?' Polly pushed, 'Plymouth? They're all here, all in Vermont.'

'Ottaquechee,' Max enunciated carefully, scrutinizing the map.

'It's a river, a town and a gorge — pretty spectacular and not far from here,' Polly enthused. 'Perhaps we could go. I'm off duty from four on Saturday.'

Max flopped down on to the grass and rested his arms on his knees, map open and dangling in his right hand.

Did he hear me?

Polly laid her hand on his shoulder, because just at that moment she was overcome with affection for him. His slightly startled reaction, however, made her pretend at once that she was seeking only balance and she gave a convincing wobble as she took off her shoes.

'Harmonyville,' Max continued as if he hadn't noticed. Polly fell silent and cast her gaze over to him until he dragged his eyes away from the map and looked directly at her.

'Harmonyville,' Polly said, in a quiet voice but strong. 'You and I could live in Harmonyville.' Max looked a little confused and was about to return his attention to his current surroundings when Polly kept him focused. 'We could inhabit Harmonyville, Max – because, do you know, I think it's probably as much a notion, a spiritual place, as a real town in Vermont, U.S. of A.'

'Cheese?' Max offered, after a loaded silence during which he and Polly locked eyes.

'Please,' Polly said, wondering if she was allowed to feel somewhat triumphant.

Because he didn't flinch, did he? He didn't frown or even look away. Harmonyville. He didn't disagree. That's it. We're going to live in Harmonyville.

They ate their lunch, dangling toes in the water and feeling the not unpleasant sensation of just damp moss blush through their shorts.

'Polly,' Max said. Polly looked up. He cast his eyes away. She shuffled over to him.

'Max?'

'I don't see how you think we can make a go of things. Do you really *believe*?'

'Oh yes, I do, oh indeed, yes yes,' Polly rushed, almost before Max had pronounced his question mark. 'Certainly. No doubt. I'm positive. Definitely.'

'Hold on.' Max sounded a little irritated and his raised hand and diverted gaze compounded this impression. 'We can't just pick up where we left off, can we?'

Polly's brain worked hard.

God. Quick, a question – quickly, answer him.

''Course we can,' Polly said urgently trying to turn a blind eye away from the jumble of images rampaging across her mind: Chip, England last Christmas, Jen in her flat, herself running in hysterics to Kilburn, Dominic's eyes seeing right through her, a BGS class room, Mount Hubbardtons in the snow, the taste of grits, the smell of Buster's cat food.

'No,' she conceded quietly, 'I suppose not.'

'We can't,' Max stated, shaking his head resignedly, 'just not possible.'

God. Quick, a solution – think of something. Change his mind. Reassure. Persuade.

'New beginnings!' Polly chirped up, having blinked hard to dispel the intrusive images. 'A new start, a new phase.'

Max looked at her, grazing his teeth along his bottom lip. She could not read what he was thinking and her inability to do so, as much as wondering what it was that he was thinking, unnerved her.

I don't understand. Last night he was all tenderness – now he's distant. What does that mean – what can and should I do? Beg? Why is he here? What does he want?

She shuffled over to him, sat on her heels and placed her hands on his.

'I mean, think how young we were when we started out as a couple,' Max said clearly, 'and, as Chloë pointed out, we've had no real obstacles to test us, for us to contend with, nothing that provides a yardstick of our strength, of our true worth as a couple.'

Who the fuck is Chloë?

Listen to him, Polly.

'So now. Now? Well! Think about it, Polly. If we were to start afresh, might we not discover very different people from those we were so attracted to when we first started seeing each other?'

Polly looked away, desperate not to understand his point but knowing at once that what he had just said was horribly comprehensible and upsettingly, undeniably, pragmatic. A chipmunk appeared and seemed to smile at her. She looked back to Max and found him regarding her, as if in assessment. He shrugged and looked away.

Don't look away.

But I can't look at you.

Why not? Please do.

I don't want to.

'I don't know, Polly,' Max continued, 'but I *do* know that

362

things happen for a reason. Maybe we were coming to a natural end and it was all just, well, *hastened*.'

'But,' said Polly, the dawning of reality bringing with it a sensation of burgeoning panic, her heartbeat giving her a headache, 'I *do* love you.' Max looked away quickly, as if she had said the last thing he had wanted to hear.

Tough. I am going to say it loud and clear.

'I love you, Max Fyfield. I know I haven't treasured you enough. I want to be with you. Really I do.'

'I loved you – what we had,' said Max, looking sad and worryingly resigned too.

'Don't speak in the past tense,' Polly pleaded hoarsely, reaching out to him again. Max rose to his feet, though, and pulled his leg away from her just as soon as she'd encircled it with her arm.

'I think I have to,' he said, 'because, until I have a realistic sight of the tenable future – immediate and short term – I have no alternative.'

They cycled back in silence. Max leading the way.

THIRTY-NINE

Kate rarely ventured deeper into the labyrinth of Hubbardtons Academy than the Art faculty and the dining hall, which were set conveniently on the periphery. That night, however, she strode to Petersfield House with purpose. She knocked on the door to Polly's apartment and entered without waiting for a response.

'Polly?'

Kate marched in and out of the kitchenette and the sitting-room before coming across her, sitting in a hunch with legs akimbo, just outside her bedroom door.

'Polly? You OK?'

Polly raised a pale face and nodded unconvincingly.

'Listen, hon, you get yourself up, you hear? He's talking about leaving tomorrow and you have to save the day.'

'I can't.'

'Don't be so goddam defeatist. Yes you can. You have power. You are a woman.'

Polly looked at Kate suspiciously, wanted at once to giggle and sing her words à la Whitney Houston, but she knew fundamentally that Kate was wise and that her wisdom came from knowledge through experience.

'Tell him you love him.'

364

'I tried that,' said Polly, disappointed, 'it didn't seem to make much of a dent in his armour.'

'Nice analogy,' said Kate, 'but you don't need purple prose, you need to yell it at him. Mad Max – swear to God, he is – and you can do something about it.'

'How do you mean?'

'Let him see you so broken. Jeez, make the guy guilty. Men like to feel that they must protect us weak little ladies – it's the caveman shit and all.'

'Don't want to play games,' said Polly, hugging her knees. 'This isn't a game.'

At last. Well done, Polly.

'I know it isn't, and that's not what I mean,' Kate implored, crouching down and hugging Polly. 'I think – and I only just met the guy – but I think he needs convincing. I think you gotta be a little, say, *creative*. I believe it's all there, in him, but he's taken a knock and you know guys, they go into that old self-preservation, I-don't-need-this-shit mode.'

'Do you think so?' Polly asked, holding out her hand for Kate to hoick her upright. 'Really?'

'I know so,' said Kate.

'You do swear a lot,' Polly marvelled.

'What do *you* think?' Polly asks Lorna twenty minutes later, having recounted both her afternoon with Max, and Kate's visit.

'Three things,' Lorna says, holding up a corresponding number of fingers. Polly's wide eyes encourage her to dispense with tea-making and cut straight to the point. She leads Polly from her little kitchen and sits her down on her couch. Lorna perches on her coffee table and leans forwards to Polly.

'OK,' she says, 'three things: one, I'm in no doubt that Max does indeed love you, and love you deeply.'

'Yes?' gasps Polly as if it is the most fantastic, unexpected news ever.

'I do. Know why?' Lorna asks, answered by Polly's vigorous head shaking. 'Because he looked at me so so fondly all the way through Formal Meal.'

Oh yes? Bastard! I think he looked at Jen rather fondly too.

'Idiot!' Lorna chides, mind-reading. 'You know, it's like you want to love the people that love your partner, that your partner loves too?'

'OK,' Polly concedes, 'but what did he say? What d'you think?'

'Well, I felt he wanted to find out all about me? While mentioning you at any opportunity. I think he wants to get a hold on your life here – how you are, and how you are taken – you see? Make sense?'

Polly nods and her face appears to have warmed up a tone.

'Number two,' Lorna continues, 'Kate is right. Heed her words.' Polly jumps visibly but Lorna doesn't stop to check why. 'Kate is right,' she repeats with a shrug, 'he needs convincing and you gotta be creative – it shows effort born out of love and conviction – guys really don't need much more, hey?'

Polly nods again and looks hard at the palm of her left hand, as if jotting down points one and two.

'Three,' Lorna presses on, 'finally. Last and not least – I want to show you something.'

She takes Polly to her bedroom, motioning in the direction of the chest of drawers near her bed. 'Second down, left-hand corner.'

Obediently, Polly pulls the drawer but she sees only the neatest pile of crisply ironed T-shirts in the left-hand side. She looks over at Lorna, enquiringly. 'Shit,' Lorna laughs, stamping lightly, 'dig *deep*, girl.' Polly lifts one, two, three T-shirts. And then she sees it. Now she's smiling. Now she turns to Lorna and nods, a healthy grin lighting her face. She goes to Lorna and embraces her. They laugh.

Lorna has bought a vibrator. One of eye-watering proportions, no less.

*

''Sme.'

'Polly Fenton!'

'Is Dom there? You alone? Is it *Neighbours*?'

'No – yes – no.'

'How are you, Meg? I miss you. How am I?'

'I'm fine – how *are* you? Any, er, news?'

'What, like Max turning up out of the blue and into the heart of the Green Mountains?'

'Mmm, that kind of news, yes.'

'Max has turned up.'

'No? Really!'

'As if you didn't know, you dark horse – you and that bloke from *Holidays R Us*.'

'Just helping out a friend – me and that bloke from *Holidays R Us*.'

'Oh Meg, he's here and I love him. '

'*Holidays R Him*?'

'Max, idiot!'

'You don't say? Hurray! Hullo? Where've you gone? Hullo?'

'But – God – I don't think he wants me.'

'Polly – silly – why come all the way over to see you then, twit?'

'He is here, yes, but he isn't, if you see what I mean. He's distant like I've never seen him. That's new and frightening.'

'Go on.'

'He says we can't pick up where we left off – and we may have changed too much to make a fresh start. I think he wants to call it a day.'

'That, Polly Fenton, is totally beyond my comprehension – knowing you both as well as I do.'

'Really?'

'Honestly.'

'Then why is he packing as we speak?'

'Because, Polly, you're not there *unpacking* his stuff and making him want to stay.'

'I can't force him.'

'No, it's true, you can't. But you *can* make him *want* to stay.'

'Zoe?'

'Hey, Miss Fenton.'

'Studying OK?'

'Sure.'

'Am I interrupting you? Disturbing you?'

'No, not really – you want something? I done something?'

'Yes. No. I want to do something for which I need your help. It's highly illegal.'

'I think you need Beth, don't you?'

'No Zoe, it has to be you. I trust you, and only you, implicitly.'

Polly sat on the student's bed, reached for a very battered Mickey Mouse and hugged it close. Zoe twisted round in her chair and faced them both.

'Shoot,' she said, intrigued and just a little uncomfortable.

'I have to slip out for a mo' – can you hold fort?'

'How long's a mo'?' Zoe asked, eyes sparkling but not quite able to conjure a convincing image of her teacher buying drugs down some gloomy alley – not least because there was a veritable dearth of gloomy alleys in Hubbardtons. 'How long's a mo', Miss Fenton?'

'Potentially,' said Polly cautiously, 'the same length as a piece of string.'

'Boyfriend?' Zoe asked quietly, knowing instinctively. Polly nodded. Zoe regarded her with sympathy and affection and awe. 'Nice to be able to return the favour,' she said.

'Thanks a million,' said Polly, 'if anyone asks, *anyone*, I've gone to bed with a sodding headache.'

'Sure,' Zoe shrugged, 'sodding. No problem.'

'I owe you one,' Polly told her, handing Mickey Mouse over.

'No,' said Zoe, snuffling the toy's head, 'you don't.'

Polly creeps her way through the unlit sections of the school

368

grounds and takes the back route to Kate's. The light is on in Great Aunt Clara's room but it is also on in the kitchen and she doesn't want to be seen by anyone other than Max. She scurries over to Great Aunt Clara's window and looks in. No Max. There's no one there. But there is a bulging rucksack propped at the foot of the bed. Suddenly, Polly is subsumed with timidity and grief. Now she doesn't even want Max to see her.

I can't do it. I can't make him stay. It's too painful that he doesn't want to, that it's an issue at all. I thought he came here for me? Now he's leaving because of me.

She turns and faces away from the house, takes a few steps back along the path she's just trodden.

Come on, Polly – only a couple of chapters left and it is up to you entirely how they unfold, what will transpire, how it will end.

Don't pressurize me.

Don't be so dramatic. Just turn around and retrace your steps. Check the window and see if it's open. Unpack for Max. Tidy up.

The window is not locked and slides up with much less noise and difficulty than she anticipates. Polly springs herself on to the ledge and eases the mosquito frame open. It needs to come towards her and requires delicate balance and much breath-holding and lip-biting.

She's in. She's in Max's room or Great Aunt Clara's room or her old room – wherever – she's in. She cuddles the rucksack briefly before unpacking it as quickly as she can. It is not an easy task for each article of Max's clothing requires deep inhalation and a prolonged press against her cheek. His shampoo and Bic razors were purchased at the airport. Way overpriced. He's brought three novels, which Polly finds encouraging.

But not enough boxer shorts – only four pairs. Does that mean his ticket was booked for tomorrow anyway?

That's rich, coming from the girl who gives preference to

jars of Marmite over articles of her clothing when she packs for a whole term.

But only four pairs? Of boxers?

Yes, but look at all those socks.

Please stay, Max.

Do you want him to see you then? Tonight? Now?

God no!

Then hurry with your task.

'I think I'll turn in,' Max says to Kate and Clinton, stretching his arms above his head and then letting them drop gently so that they fall as an embrace around Bogey.

Quick, Polly.

'Sure,' says Kate.

'Night,' says Clinton.

Hurry, Polly.

'Night then,' Max says to the couple he's sure he's known most of his life. They send him to bed with their effortlessly generous smiles.

What? Hang on. Where's my stuff? Shit, the window's open – someone's been in. Pinched it. Fuck. Of all the things – in this little one-eyed town. I don't bloody believe it.

Max stood in the room and puzzled over what could have happened, and when, and what to do about it, what to do next. Going through to the kitchen, to alert Kate, seemed logical.

'Hey Max, insomnia already?'

'Sorry Kate,' said Max, scratching his head, wondering the best way not to alarm her, 'Clinton around?' Kate tipped her head and pointed to the ceiling. Right on cue, the sound of the shower whirred into action.

'Max, you OK?'

'I'm sorry to say this,' Max said, placing a hand supportively on Kate's shoulder, 'but you've just been burgled. My stuff's gone.'

'Burgled? Us? The Traceys? Here in Hubbardtons?'

She shouldn't be smiling – she's going to be devastated. I haven't even checked how much of my stuff has gone, let alone hers.

'The window wasn't locked – I have it open,' Max apologized, 'at night.'

'Never is – always is,' Kate confirmed. She slapped her knees. 'Come, then, let's go figure this out.'

Max pushes open the door to Great Aunt Clara's room and stands back so that Kate may enter first.

'All seems OK,' she says, circumnavigating the room and looking long and hard out of the window. (Max isn't to know that she is merely breathing in deep wafts of clear night air while gazing at the shadowy humps defining her beloved plants.)

'My stuff's been swiped,' Max says, holding up the clean palms of his hands for emphasis. Simultaneously, both he and Kate catch sight of a black strap trying to peep out unnoticed from under the bed. Max swallows the end of his sentence. Kate closes her throat on a swelling laugh.

'Hold on,' Max falters, venturing near it like it might very well be a snake. 'Oh.'

'Yours?' Kate asks as Max draws the rucksack out and holds it, a look of utter bewilderment settling across his brow.

'Um, yes?'

'Night night, Max,' says Kate lightly. She is well aware that he had packed. She also knows Polly very well.

'No, but really – I mean, I was packed and, you know, ready to go. Why would they leave my rucksack?'

Kate comes back into the room, goes over to the warped chest of drawers and pulls at the top one. She has a good look. She beckons Max over. As he nears, though, he knows what he'll find. His boxers, neatly folded. Pairs of socks nestling next to them. A drawer down, T-shirts and tops. He and Kate look over to the wardrobe and go to it together. Kate opens it and Max peers within. His trousers hang there. Shoes beneath them. He looks over to the small cupboard by the side of the bed. The three novels are laid neatly in a tiny spiral staircase.

'Looks like she doesn't want you to go,' says Kate, patting Max's shoulder and leaving the room.

'I'm not going – well, not today,' Max whispered up at Polly, standing beneath her window up at which he had just thrown a barrage of small stones to wake her. Polly gazed down at him and then glanced back into her room to locate her clock. It told her what she had already guessed from the silvery light and heavy dew; it was not yet six o'clock. She glanced in swift gratitude over to the memorial garden and then returned her gaze to Max.

'Good,' she whispered down to him, 'glad to hear it. Want to come up?'

'Better not,' Max replied, his voice breaking through his whisper, 'might get caught. Might get detention. Go back to sleep. I'll call by later.'

'What are you going to do?' Polly asked.

'Bit of sight-seeing,' Max replied, 'probably.'

It wasn't what Polly meant, but his answer was fine for the time being. At least he was staying. She watched him go and wasn't too worried that he did not turn to wave. At least he wasn't going. She returned to bed and hugged her pillow. Sleep caught up with her very quickly and she dreamt of Zoe.

Polly, sorry only to leave a note but I had a bus to catch. I've gone – away but not home. Just gone for a little potter by myself. Vermont appears to be a place for space and solitude which is just what I need. So I've gone touring. I hope that you understand. I don't want to go back to England just yet – so that's something, hey? I'll be thinking of you, of that you can rest assured. I am doing this for us. Anyway, I've never been to America . . .

Max

'No kiss?' Polly said to herself forlornly, on finding the note slipped under her door when she skipped back to her apartment at lunch-time, all energy and hope.

'Don't worry,' Kate assured her later, by phone, 'he's left a bunch of stuff in the closet.'

FORTY

$\mathbf{M}$ax phoned, two days later, from Woodstock. Polly worked hard at sounding fresh, fun and friendly.

He has to want to come back simply because he actively wants to be with me.

'Hullo. I've had the most brilliant day down the Quechee Gorge.'

'Have you? How lovely.'

'Spectacular.'

'Isn't it! Where to next? You could go to Stowe – that's where the Von Trapps live.'

'No, I'm headed for a place called Waitsfield.'

'Meant to be beautiful.'

'Not been?'

'No.'

Silence. Polly racked her mind for some interesting little quip, some banal comment about weather, some easy little piece of trivia to bandy. Max, though, had other ideas and beat her to it.

'Well, I'd better go – dimes don't last very long. I'll be in touch.'

*

Was I chirpy enough? Why didn't he stay on longer? Should I go and find him?

Four days later, Polly received a postcard from Max, from Montpelier. It was the first of ten that he was to send to her over the next fortnight.

'He's more of a Vermonter than you,' Lorna teased, an evening soon after, whistling at the scene depicted on the postcard from Lake Willoughby.

'Do you know what's so odd?' Polly said to her, taking the postcard and gazing on it, flipping it over and holding Max's writing next to her cheek.

'What?' Lorna asked.

The notion, though, had only just dawned on Polly and she was content to consider it by herself for a moment or two. Intuitively, Lorna realized, and busied herself looking through Polly's tapes with well-contrived interest.

'What's odd,' Polly began again, slowly, 'what's strange, is how the tables have turned.' She went over to Lorna and regarded her tapes. She selected Blur for the resonance of the band's name alone. 'I mean, last term, Max wrote to me endlessly and I hardly replied. I felt powerful and in control. Now? Now he's writing regularly again but I'm totally, I don't know, at his mercy? He's the one in control.'

'And that's something new?'

'I suppose.'

'Strange?'

'Yes,' said Polly quietly.

'I guess you've taken him for granted – or, at least, taken it for granted that you're the kooky, over-emotional one, and he's always to be the quiet soul that accepts you and excuses your temperament?'

Polly felt hurt and defensive but she bit her tongue, perhaps for the first time, and thought hard instead of reacting immediately. Humble pie was stuck in her throat anyway. She could only nod. Lorna pulled Polly's hair into a stubby pony tail, envying her its texture, its colour and sheen that

375

any French polisher would be proud to reproduce.

'I have to wait, I suppose,' Polly said in a deep, hushed voice, 'I suppose I just have to wait.'

'You patient?' Lorna asked while she continued to play with Polly's hair, scooping it through her fingertips, upwards from the nape of the neck, watching it fall back gently right into place.

'I'll have to learn to be,' Polly replied with her eyes closed. Weren't mothers meant to stroke hair to comfort? She'd seen it on adverts, films, buses and park benches. She was enormously relieved that Lorna continued to do so, for she acknowledged with certain sadness that she had no alternative.

Some days pass swiftly, others drag by, but Polly wears a brave face during them all. School is school and the daily routine, the fact that Polly has a timetable to follow, a role to fulfil, students dependent on her teaching, keeps her occupied and keeps her going. She loves George Eliot. She loves her job. She loves her students. Max has not phoned again. Lorna tells her not to worry, not to read anything by it, not to expect him to. Every night, usually in the bathroom and after she has cleaned her teeth, Polly recites to herself, 'Well, he hasn't phoned. I am not to worry. I must not expect him to.' When she wakes, she reminds herself that Max has left much at Kate's. (He's left a lot at Hubbardtons too, Polly.) It's reassuring. Kate has even invited her to peek in the closet for comfort.

It does cross her mind that Max might return in body only and not in affection, that he will come back merely to pack up and leave.

But I can't afford to dwell on it. I prefer to read between the lines of his postcards.

Max had been away for two and a half weeks when he phoned again. Lake Champlain. A phone box on the street outside the motel. The great expanse of water, walled by the distant Adirondacks on his left, Burger King on his right.

'Hullo.'

'Hey, Max.'

Silence. Come on, speak. Chat. Talk. Say something. He's in a phone box and dimes don't last long.

'Lake Champlain's fantastic,' he said, in a fairly monotone voice.

'Wish I could be there with you,' Polly said wistfully, though it came out suggestively.

'No,' Max warned, 'I have to be here alone.'

'Why?' Polly squeezed out in a tiny voice, suddenly wanting banal chat and not a loaded conversation.

'Because,' Max sighed, 'people who are supposedly madly in love shouldn't even consider infidelity, let alone go ahead and shag rampantly.'

Polly felt such a stab of pain that she was rendered speechless. Good job, really.

'I don't mean to be cruel,' Max said, somewhat startled at the feeling of power.

''Sokay,' Polly managed.

'What I mean is, in my mind, marriage means fidelity – in spirit and body. I mean, commitment on any level necessitates faithfulness and trust. Yes? Polly?'

'I'm here.'

Would it help if I told you about Chip?

Would that make it better for Max? Or just for you?

'In case you're wondering, it only happened once, Polly,' Max said strongly, 'but it certainly happened.'

Polly held the receiver away from her ear, Max grasped his tight.

'If it helps,' he continued, 'the act, the person, didn't mean much at all. But,' he cautioned, having listened carefully to Polly's pause, 'what actually *happened*, the fact that it did, means a hell of a lot, if you see. It changes what we had.'

'The fact that it *did* happen,' Polly quickly interrupted without knowing what she was to say next, 'and that I know about it, and that you and I, well, you know, *recently*.'

'Not a sentence, Polly, what do you mean?'

'I mean,' Polly continued, almost eagerly, 'our relationship hit rock bottom, hey? Right down there,' she elaborated, pointing for emphasis but with little point because Max of course couldn't see. 'But that's good,' Polly tried, 'it means there's now a flat base on which to build up again. The firmest of foundations. Do you see?'

Shit, this is all too much for a phone call. His money'll run out. Can't we talk about landscape and all things touristy.

'Money's run out,' Max lied, not that Polly could know. 'I'll be in touch.'

Polly listened thoughtfully to the tone buzzing through from the receiver for a few moments longer.

I hope it came out right. I hope he understands. I hope it's given him hope. I hope he's coming back soon. I hope I'm allowed to hope.

Max had been gone three weeks and Polly had suffered a fifth consecutive postcardless morning, when he returned to Hubbardtons just as suddenly as he had left. Polly was filling her plate from the salad bar at lunch-time when she looked up to see Max standing by the dining hall doors. In a bit of a blur, she handed her plate to whoever was on her right and walked through the tables to him. No one really noticed, apart from the sophomore with the plate of salad, who was unsure whether he was to guard it for the teacher or eat it himself. Lorna and Kate were sitting together at the far end; they had seen but they kept their gaze studiously diverted. Zoe had seen too, but took it as her duty to distract her fellow diners. Jackson saw, and was so despondent that when he swore quietly to himself, it came out as a rather loud 'Sheeyut'. Powers Mateland watched Polly, noted her expression, looked over to Max and was intrigued. Teachers have lives, teachers have feelings, teachers can exist without school.

'Hullo,' Polly said.

'Hiya,' said Max, slinging his thumbs into the band of his jeans.

'Want some lunch?' Polly asked him, wanting to touch him.

'Not hungry. Thanks.'

She took her hand to his arm, stood on tiptoes and kissed him lightly on the cheek. Powers observed everything from the corner of his eye – a skill honed by teachers and perfected by headmasters and deans.

'How are you?' Polly asked Max, at once transported away from her current surroundings and back into the safe world of her relationship. 'You look well – tanned and sparkly.'

Max returned her kiss, his hand momentarily cupping her head. Heaven.

'You look tired, my girl.'

Am I? Your girl?

'Am I? I mean, I am – it's exams soon.'

'Teaching this afternoon?'

Polly nodded.

Bugger, here I am. And that's what I do.

'Maybe we could meet up this evening?' Max suggested. 'If you're off duty?'

'I'm not, I'm afraid.'

'It's just – well, I'm going home tomorrow night.'

No!

He can't.

Please no.

Oh God.

'I'll think of something,' Polly says. 'I'll think of something,' she repeats, not sure who it is she is trying to convince. Max nods and leaves her.

'Where are we?' Polly asked her class while staring distractedly out of the window. 'What's going on?'

'Chapter 70?' Laurel said helpfully.

'*Middlemarch*?' Heidi prompted, as the class passed concerned glances around furtively, like an illegal note or a bag of candy, carefully out of the sight of the teacher.

'Miss Fenton?'

Polly dragged her attention back, thumbing through her copy of *Middlemarch*.

'Ah yes, who wants to read? AJ? Please do.'

'You want me to read the little poem at the top too?'

'Of course!' Polly exclaimed with an irritated tut she regretted at once but did little about. 'How many times have I told you – all of you – that those lines are often as loaded as the prose which follows?'

AJ read, smarting a little.

> *'Our deeds still travel with us from afar,*
> *And what we have been makes us what we are.'*

Polly went quite cold.

'Say that again,' she said quietly. AJ read it again, a slight shrug to the tone of his voice.

'Once more?' Polly requested, going over to the window so that she could see the sky while she listened hard. AJ obliged, his tone changing as he grasped the point of the verse.

'Pretty cool,' AJ said.

'Beautiful,' Laurel added.

'Neat,' elaborated Forrest.

'Real wise,' Heidi nodded.

'Isn't it just,' Miss Fenton confirmed and praised her class, 'absolutely perfect?'

It's not about apportioning blame. Myself. Max himself. Chip or Jen. What has happened has made me into the woman that I am. What has passed sees me now as someone ready for commitment, who's evolved from a self-centred girl wanting to play out fantasies. The experience of it, the lessons I've learned, will aid me in my journey hereafter.

Zoe gladly allowed her Dorm Mom to have a sodding headache again. All the Petersfield House girls had caught a drift of what was going on between Miss Fenton and that cute guy. They weren't going to cause any problems for her, they adored her too much. Anyway, their imaginations were hyperactive and the space Miss Fenton created enabled their conjectures to run riot. As soon as Zoe gave the all clear, they gathered together in her room, ate chocolate and hypothesized on what was happening in Miss Fenton's life. Their postulations ran into veritable novels, any of their proposed endings were plausible, all would make great reading. Our ending can be defined solely by Polly and Max.

Currently, they are sitting on Kate's deck. The house is empty as the inhabitants are at a lecture on the human aura and its implications for digestive problems, being held at the community centre in nearby Hanbury Falls.

'Can you imagine holding an evening similarly entitled in Swiss Cottage?' Max marvels, believing light conversation the best way to ease into his farewell.

'No,' Polly laughs bravely, 'maybe Crouch End though.'

'So, are *you* going to come back then?' Max asks, 'to England?'

Polly frowns. 'Of course,' she says, 'it's where I live.'

'Ah,' says Max, 'but is it your *home*?'

Polly looks over Kate's garden and wishes she was small enough to hide in one of the bushes.

She is about to hedge her bets.

Deep breath. Here goes.

'It's where I live,' she reiterates, 'but my home, Max, is with you.'

There. And you?

'Not wherever you lay your hat?' he chips in. (Actually Max, don't do that – just butt in, or interrupt or something.)

'I don't wear a hat,' Polly says clearly, 'but I do wear my heart on my sleeve – and I know now that it sometimes gets me into trouble.'

'Well,' Max says, as if in some long conclusion, 'we make mistakes so we can learn by them.'

'We do!' Polly enthuses, 'of course. I did and I have!'

Yippee, he's back. Same language. Same emotion.

'So have I,' Max continues.

'Darling Max,' Polly gasps, smiling, reaching out, 'my man.'

'Sorry Button,' Max says, holding her arms before she can sink against him, 'I can't do this. I'm just not convinced that we can work it out.'

She had never seen Max resolute. Not Max Fyfield, the man always open to suggestion, for whom consideration is a central element of his being. Max of the open mind and heart. Both, now, were closed against Polly. The end of a chapter, he explained to her, that's all.

FORTY-ONE

'*I*t can't be,' Polly said on first waking the next morning. 'It isn't,' she declared to her reflection in the bathroom mirror. 'I won't let it.' Her eyes were shot through the colour of mud and encircled with the darkness that comes from deep anxiety, disbelief and less than two hours' sleep. 'I know that he still does love me,' she reasoned to her toes as she slipped her socks on. 'Doesn't he? He does,' she told her shoes, slipping her hands into them and tapping the soles together while she thought what to do next. 'Doesn't he?'

Put my shoes on.

Ten minutes later, Polly was at the Dean's office.

'I'm dreadfully sorry,' she said to Powers Mateland, 'but I can't take my classes today.' Her arms were crossed over her breasts and she regarded Powers with a mixture of pleading and warning.

Please let me go. Don't ask.

'The whole day?' he enquired, with a disconcertingly passive expression.

'Yes,' said Polly, looking at her watch in a brazenly obvious glance.

'*All* your classes?' Powers probed.

'Every single one,' Polly defined.

Powers held the crook of his finger to his lips and looked at Polly. He'd been in love. Once.

'Sure,' he said, as if she had merely checked if she could teach her seniors out of doors.

'Thanks,' she said, as if that was all she'd asked for.

'Jackson?'

'Yo, Polly!'

'What time's your first class? Half ten, isn't it? Like mine?'

'Yup – you wanna go make love till then?'

'Nope. I want you to drive me to Normansbury for the airport bus.'

Jackson regarded Polly suspiciously. 'You *leaving*?'

'Nope.' She was twitching her lip and regarding him very directly.

'Now?' he said, looking at her in amazement.

'Please,' she said.

'What's in it for me?' he asked.

'Not a jot,' she confirmed. 'Can we go, please?'

God she was pretty when she was hiding the panic. Her twitching mouth, her glassy bottle-green eyes, petite nostrils flaring slightly with each breath, her hair swishing at the slightest movement of her head.

'Sure,' said Jackson, still blithely confident of his power of seduction.

Or else, I'm just one crazy sucker.

Max was not on the bus. In truth, Polly had only half hoped that he might have been. He had most probably taken the one an hour before. It didn't matter. What she had to say wouldn't sound right on a juddering bus and anyway, she'd probably feel too queasy to talk unless she was able to look out of the window and in the direction of travel.

Max wasn't on the bus because he was still in Hubbardtons, double-checking his rucksack and expressing heartfelt gratitude to Kate.

'Thanks for everything,' he said to her, busying himself with his bags so he did not have to catch her gaze which he could sense, hot and enquiring, on his cheek.

'Sure,' Kate smiled, 'it was fun having you here. You come back now.'

'Love to,' said Max truthfully.

'Come,' Kate said, nodding her head in the direction of the door, 'you have a plane to catch.'

Max's bus arrived at Logan Airport an hour after Polly's. He had been a little surprised that she had not somehow found her way on to it, but the landscapes of Vermont and Massachusetts provided ample distraction for him not to dwell on it. Consequently, when he heard a familiar voice arguing at the check-in desk, he was momentarily somewhat disorientated. He stepped back behind a pillar to listen. He couldn't see her anyway. The queue was long. Her voice, though, was quite clear.

'Listen to me,' Polly was shouting, 'I have to speak to passenger Fyfield.'

'Ma'am, I already told you, he hasn't checked in.'

'Well, can you check please?'

'Honey, that's all we do and I'm telling you, the guy has not been processed.'

'OK then,' Polly said in a chillingly curt voice, 'could you please ask your friends on the other side – you know, after passports and frisking.'

'Lady, if the guy hasn't come by here, he sure as hell hasn't gone through *there*.'

'But where *is* he?' Polly cried, her voice breaking with desperation and need.

'He has two and a half hours before his flight. Maybe he's just late.'

'Max,' Polly said, 'is never late.'

'Maybe he changed his mind and changed his flight.'

'No,' Polly said, resigned, 'he is hardly likely to do that.'

Max peeped out from the pillar. The queue forming behind Polly seemed much more interested in her dilemma than they were bothered by being kept waiting. Max smiled.

OK, Polly, let's make their day.

He walked up the queue, catching drifts of conjecture from his fellow passengers.

Wrong, wrong. This is fun, in a weird way.

He tapped Polly on the shoulder.

'Looking for me?'

'Max!'

There was a loud cheer from the queue. Even the check-in assistant looked genuinely pleased. 'There you go,' she said, 'next passenger, please.' The next passenger insisted that Max checked in first. Polly felt instantly wretched that he did so, though of course she had no reason to hope otherwise.

Please change your mind.

Polly, a man's mind is often far easier to change than a flight on a super-bucket-seat economy ticket.

'Window seat near the front,' was the first thing Max said to her as he led her away from the rapt queue. Soon enough though, an argument between check-in assistant and passenger, about lacto-ovo-vegetarian meals, provided the line with a new spectacle.

'What are you doing here?' Max said, not smiling but his look gentle.

'I,' Polly stammered, her eyes badly camouflaged khaki, 'I am just.'

'You are just?' Max asked. 'Is that a sentence, Polly?'

'I,' she tried again, 'came.'

'Yes,' he said slowly, 'you are indeed here.'

'I am going to say something.'

'OK,' Max said, slowly again, 'I'm listening. Do you want to go for a coffee?' He looked around the concourse and made to move away.

'No!' Polly shouted, grabbing his arm, breathing audibly. 'I want to tell you something. I don't want a coffee.'

'Tea? What, then?' Max asked. 'What is it?'

Polly shrugged. Max looked around the concourse again.

Oh God, is he looking a little irritated?

Polly feared she might cry so she turned away from him. And then spun back, just in case he had left.

My throat. My eyes. Can I do this? How do I do this?

'Please,' she implored, 'don't leave. I mean, for England, yes. Me? No. Don't. Let's stay.' Max looked from her shoes to his shoes in a non-committal way and raised his shoulders, though whether it was as a sigh or a shrug was hard to decipher.

'Please,' Polly said, tipping her neck so she could look up at his bowed face.

Max shook his head, 'Sorry.'

Polly gasped. Max refused to look because he was desperate not to hear. 'Polly,' he said, 'life's a journey and—'

'—I want to travel it with you,' she interjected in as controlled a voice as she could muster.

'Life's a journey,' Max persisted, 'we got off at the same stop – but we changed routes.' His eyes were very glassy, a sight Polly had never seen, though soon the deluge of her own tears obscured Max from view.

'*Our deeds still travel with us from afar*,' she croaked, blinking and gulping, '*And what we have been makes us what we are.*'

Max regarded her. Sternly. Then quizzically. He cocked his head.

'Say that again,' he said, locking eyes. She obliged, finding Max's gaze had burned away her tears. He hummed.

'And again,' he requested. She repeated the verse, her voice now clear as the light traversing his face.

'Is that what you believe?' Max asked her.

'Yes,' said Polly, 'at my very core.'

'Snap,' said Max, in utter amazement.

'Snap?' Polly queries. Max shrugs and shakes his head in apparent self-disbelief. He doesn't look particularly happy, he is frowning and looks utterly confused.

Snap? As in dragon or brandy? Snap out of it? What on earth? Hang on a mo' – snap?

387

'Snap?' she repeats, as if it is the first word she has learned.

'Snap,' Max shrugs, his eyebrows twitching bewilderment and relief simultaneously.

'Oh?' she says.

'I think so,' Max responds. 'Weird,' he marvels out loud but to himself, thinking he could desperately do with a coffee, wondering how on earth a line of verse could produce such clarity. 'It's like you've played your cards right and turned up the trump card no less — because it matches mine. Snap.'

'It is not a game, you know,' Polly says quietly, sternly, her brow deeply furrowed, her cheeks reddening with humiliation.

'Polly,' Max breathes, closing his eyes momentarily and swaying a little, 'am I glad to hear you say that.'

Now Polly doesn't know whether to frown or smile, the confusion threatens to cause a headache. Outwardly, the effort wrinkles her face and colours her eyes soft moss. Max can't help but cup her head and kiss. Polly looks terrified.

'Sorry,' he says.

What about? Exactly? This kiss? The past? The future?

He repeats his kiss and she is able to answer.

'Don't be,' says Polly.

They stand still and suddenly take note of where they are. Noisy departure hall. Plane to catch. Term to finish. Them — from this point on. So much to do, but where to start?

'Do you love and forgive me?' Polly asks.

'Yes and yes,' Max replies, 'you me?'

'Oh yes,' says Polly, 'and yes.'

They regard each other, frown and smile. Shuffle a little. Look away. Back again. Still here.

'You see, I forgive *me*,' Polly exclaims suddenly, 'because I've been most deeply repentant.'

'I've been livid with me too,' Max replies, 'but I'll accept my apology because I firmly believe my promise not to do it again.'

388

'It wasn't my fault,' reasons Polly, not passing the buck.

'No,' agrees Max, blaming no one, 'nor mine.'

'Remember the film *Love Story*?' Polly ponders, twiddling her hair whilst staring intently at Max's stomach, as if rerunning the film on it.

'Slushy bollocks,' Max responds, putting his hand on his stomach and tapping his fingers to see if he can make Polly blink.

'Actually,' says Polly, who's seen it a number of times, 'it was misguided and wrong – that stuff about love meaning you never have to say you're sorry.'

'Oh?'

She blinks and looks at Max directly, arms folded and lips pursed.

'Bollocks indeed,' she proclaims, '*dangerous*. Love means being strong enough – in yourself as an individual and in yourself as part of a partnership – to apologize.'

'Love,' interjects Max, 'means being committed enough to accept it.'

'I've come so close to losing what I know now to be my very lifeblood,' says Polly, tracing her finger over Max's torso for emphasis, 'you must see how I'll never risk that again.' Max does not reply. He lifts her chin and presses his lips against her forehead. He tucks her hair behind her ears and, in a luxuriously slow, measured gesture, dips his mouth to hers and kisses her very very gently.

'You used to make me feel whole,' Polly muses, 'but I see now how that's not the point. It's tosh about "two becoming one" – two halves don't make a whole.'

'No,' Max agrees, 'you have to be complete in yourself to be able to function as a pair.'

'Yes,' Polly nods earnestly, drawing a huge circle in the air for emphasis. Max makes a circle with his finger and thumb, takes Polly's hands and does the same and then interlinks the two. They stand there for a moment before the tannoy insists that passengers flying Virgin Atlantic to London make their way to the gate. Max undoes his fingers and changes the gesture to the firmest and most formal of hand-shakes.

'Great. At last. I can *leave* you,' says Max, suddenly so happy, finding confident amusement in his little jest.

'Yeah,' Polly retorts, delighted, 'just fuck off, would you?'

'I'm going.'

'Could you go, please.'

'I'm out of here.'

They laugh and marvel and sigh 'Oh dear'.

'See you soon?' says Max.

Why the question mark, Max? Are you unsure?

Well, it's odd, isn't it, I had it all figured out sensibly and bloody George Eliot's changed it all.

And Ryan O'Neill. And Polly Fenton. And you.

Polly regards her watch, squints at the departures board and looks long at Max while she sucks her lips and does mental arithmetic.

'About one month, one week, two days and six hours,' she elaborates.

'Nearer to seven,' Max interjects, 'hours. With head winds, I think.'

Polly punches him lightly on the chest, 'It's soon enough.'

Max catches her fist and takes it to his face, burying his nose in her palm, pressing his lips at the base of her hand.

I remember that smell.

Swiftly, he pulls her close against him. He traces a route from her forehead to her mouth and then replaces his index finger with his lips. His kiss is planted deep, sown into her soul, and she drinks him in.

Is this happening? Are you really holding me as close as it feels?

I won't be letting go again.

'Will you write?' Max asks.

'Swift bloody air,' Polly laughs. 'Now bugger off.'

* * *

Max last saw Polly the day before the day before yester-day. She's written Swiftair and he's just received it. He'll reply today and send it tomorrow. She'll have it in about three days.

Maybe she'll have written again by then.

She will have, Max, you can count on it.

FORTY-TWO

*S*o, here we are Polly, you're only a couple of days from the end of term and we're just a few pages from having to let you go.

It's July. It's been pouring with rain – it's going to mean a late fall but it will be more brilliant and lasting.

And you won't be here to see it.

No. I'll be in England. But I'll know that over the sea and not so far away, autumn is enriching the souls of all who bear witness to it.

You said 'autumn'.

Yes, autumn. In English. I'm having to start my packing, you see – it's going to take far longer to wrap up my emotions than my clothes and belongings.

It's been some ten months.

The time of my life – and I mean that with no flippancy. I've been lost and found and I've done it myself.

What'll you miss?

The people. The peace. The pace.

You can visit.

We're going to.

You said 'we'.

Yes, and you didn't make me.

*

Polly found it amusing that the farewells were utterly without the Hollywoodization and accompanying soaring violins and heavenly angels' chorus that she'd anticipated. There was no misty-eyed 'I love you'-ing, no heartfelt pleas not to leave.

But there *was* AJ, giving her his baseball cap and saying 'It kinda sucks that you won't be here next year' to a chorus of 'Yes siree'-ing from his classmates. There *was* Lorna, offering wide open arms for a very public embrace in the dining hall. There *was* the key to Petersfield House, placed in a box with a ribbon, and on which were tied little messages from her dorm daughters. And there was Kate, popping in to ask what time they should leave for Boston. In the station-wagon with the fake wood panelling. With the dog called Bogey. On the Interstate. Huge trucks. Pretty planked houses and tree-clad mountains out of the window. Full circle.

Polly saw how, in the grand scheme of things, in Hubbardtons, at Hubbardtons, she really was quite superfluous. It was a bitter sweet acknowledgement for her.

I can leave because they can let me go.

On the last day of term, the students were far more preoccupied savouring the diminishing hours with their buddies, packing at the very last minute and then failing to hide the excitement on seeing their folks draw up to collect them.

'So long, Miss Fenton.'

'Yeah, like, thanks for everything.'

'Keep in touch, Miss Fenton.'

'It's been pretty cool in your class.'

'I'll miss you.'

'See ya round.'

'Send my love to the Queen, hey?'

'Toodle pip,' said Miss Fenton, in fine form and to smiles all round. 'Have a super duper summer,' she said, kissing her vowels splendidly and much to the gratitude of all those to whom she said it. 'Cheerio.'

*

'Bye you.'

It's Lorna. Polly's friend and sworn-in penpal. She'll never usurp Megan and yet Megan won't really know quite how much Lorna has meant to Polly. As Lorna says, 'It's, like, we've done *stuff* together.' Not just piggy-bank raiding in Manchester. They've grown during this year and, though they'll selflessly take no credit, each has been fundamental to the other's development. Lorna has a vibrator. Polly has humility. Both have the men they started with and, at last, they are deserving of them.

'Bye bye.'

It's Polly. Touching Lorna's cheek and slipping one arm around her friend's shoulders, another around her waist. Pulling her in close and holding on tight, then letting go. Smiling fondly. Letting go.

'All set?'

It's Kate. Polly looks around her apartment at Petersfield House, it is as bare as the silence throughout the building. She is the last to leave. She's been dawdling; she's needed to.

I've had to say goodbye to the view from each window.

And to ponder at just how far the athletic trainer's office now seems to be, way over the sports field.

Very distant. Pretty nondescript.

And you've been into each of the rooms, standing still and bidding farewell to each of the vanished girls.

Daughters mine.

And now Kate's come to take you back to England.

Mother mine.

'All set?'

'Yup,' says Polly, taking a last, long look around; to commit it all to memory though it is all locked deep there already, to hide tears that prickle. 'Time to go home.'

*   *   *

Once again, Polly did not tell Max which flight she was on, she told him two days' time. Yes, she wanted to surprise him. But she also had an appointment to keep. It had been requested two days ago and Polly had agreed to it immediately.

Belsize Park. Just the same. Where's Buster? There he is, on the corner of the street, glowering at the tiny tabby from over the road, far too preoccupied to give Polly much more than a cursory glance, and a slightly reproachful one at that. Here's the house. Communal light is on but all is quiet in the entrance hall. No post. Invasive smell of cabbage from Miss Klee's landing. Quick, quick. Get in.

The flat is beautifully clean and tidy. A large pile of post is on the book shelf. Polly flips through it, nothing is so interesting that it can't be opened later. It's not yet eleven in the morning. She has Max to surprise. She has an appointment to keep. She has to unpack. Freshen up. Her bedroom is fresh and airy, the sash windows are down a few inches at the top, the bed is stripped, the mattress upended, the pillows look plump. The washing basket is empty. The bathroom is spotless. A new tablet of Pears soap. A new roll of toilet paper. Fresh towels.

Have I really been gone? Was I ever not here?

She'll unpack later. She's been sitting on the edge of her bed, gazing out of the window thinking of nothing specifically with her mind whirring and full. It's now noon. Max is up the road, tantalizingly close, blissfully unaware of her arrival, her proximity. Off she goes.

* * *

Polly was hovering by the intercom to Max's studio. She so wanted to sashay in, wrap herself languidly around him and plant a luxuriously controlled kiss first on his forehead, then on his lips; as long planned and frequently imagined. Standing there, in Hampstead at lunch-time, her adrenal gland in overdrive, she knew resignedly that she was probably capable of no more than hurling herself at him,

395

clambering all over him, whilst squealing and weeping far too much to kiss him with anything other than a deluge of clumsy bashes.

'Want to save me a job?' said a voice, at once recognizably Dominican and right behind her. Polly spun round.

'Dom!' she cried. 'Inic!'

'Welcome home, Pollygirl,' he said, as if she'd merely returned from a weekend away. He was standing before her, brandishing paper sandwich bags and a huge smile. But not for long. Soon, the bags were on the pavement, the coffee was spilt, and Dominic was prising Polly's arms away from his neck to avoid imminent asphyxiation.

'You're wearing shorts,' was all Polly could think to say in her excitement. Dominic looked down at his legs and splayed them, Chaplinesque, in a little jig.

'Yup,' he said, 'it's summer.' He gave her heavy sweatshirt a gentle tug. 'Jet lag?' he asked.

'Just arrived,' Polly confirmed. Dominic picked up the sodden sandwich bags and raised his eyebrows at her. 'Just happy to see you,' she reasoned apologetically and in her defence.

'Great to have you back,' said Dominic. He pressed Max's intercom.

'Hullo?' came Max's voice. Dominic put his hand over Polly's mouth to silence her excitement and could feel the vibration of her breath against his palm.

'Fancy something tasty for lunch?' said Dominic into the speaker, while winking at Polly. The door buzzed open in reply. 'Off you go,' he said to Polly. 'See you later, perhaps. Concert at Kenwood tomorrow night – fancy it?'

'I'm back,' Polly said to him, incredulously.

'Er, yeah,' said Dominic, wondering why she was stating the obvious.

'I'm *really* back,' Polly repeated, 'back home. For good.'

Dominic regarded her and smiled. 'I'm glad,' he said, nodding. He held open the door for her. In she went.

*

'Boo!'

Max remains with his back to the door, sitting at his work.

'Boo?' he says.

'Boo!' says the voice. Slowly, he turns. There she is, looking simultaneously radiant but exhausted; a vision and yet right here, standing in the doorway, holding her face in her hands. She's wearing a short skirt and the hemline is quivering, no doubt the baggy sweatshirt conceals a flurry of goosebumps. Her cheeks are a little flushed, her eyes are an extraordinary muddy green. It's not possible to detect whether the strange twitching of her lips is involuntary or not. Her right ear is holding her hair away from that side of her face and she is fiddling with a lock on the left side. She takes a strand and sucks on it, to give her lips something else to do, to give herself an excuse not to talk because she has no idea what else to say.

'Hullo,' Max says. Polly makes a strange, sharp noise in reply and holds the sodden sandwich bag aloft. 'Want to come in?' Max asks. She shuffles in a few steps, still brandishing the bag, her tongue tip pushing away the frond of sucked hair.

Come to me, Polly. Run and jump all over me. Bash my face with your manic kisses. It's your trademark. It's you.

Polly obliges almost instantly.

'Hey Button,' Max murmurs, stroking her back, her head and brushing strands of her hair from his mouth, and soggy crumbs off his drawing board.

Polly wipes her nose vigorously against his shirt. He kisses her damp cheek and dips down to her mouth. Their lips meet. Now they both know that she's home. They crumple down to the floor and their bodies lock together. There they stay, very still, very comfortable, incredibly relieved, immensely pleased, utterly exhausted.

'Welcome back, Mister Benn,' Max says a little later. Polly regards him for a moment or two and then laughs.

'As in *Watch with Mother*?' she asks. 'Little chap in a suit and bowler hat?'

'Yes,' says Max, 'and yes.'

'Who'd toddle off to the fancy-dress shop in his lunch hour?' Polly continues, delighted at the memory flooding back. 'Put on fancy dress and then have a quick adventure?' Her voice trailed away as she grasped the point.

'Yes and yes,' Max says.

'And then he'd find himself back in his suit and bowler?' Polly asks. 'Same old Mister Benn?' She falls silent and leafs with awe through Max's sketch pad. She looks a while on a beautiful portrait of a ringleted sleeping child.

Wasn't there was an adult version of Mister Benn? A film for grown-ups. Brief Encounter?

'Don't really know where we've been, or what costumes we've worn,' she murmurs, 'but I know I'm Polly Fenton,' she says, 'and I *know* that what defines me, deep down, is intact. I like what I find there. I'd like to share. It's good to be back, Max.'

'And you like the idea of being sensibly, blissfully and happily unmarried to me?'

'It's a very sound idea.'

'Fancy going to Cornwall for the weekend?'

'I'd love to, I've never been.'

'Nor,' Max remembers, 'had I.'

'Miss Fenton?' It was Jayne Greene from the Upper Fifth. 'I thought you weren't coming back till next term?'

'Some welcome, Jayne Greene,' Polly retorted. 'I've just come off the plane and I simply couldn't wait a whole summer before I saw you again.' The pupil was quite happy to believe her and swaggered off across the playground as if her teacher had not been away at all. Polly made her way through the old house which was home to the sixth-form block, up four flights of stairs to the four small attic rooms converted into music rooms. Cramped but sound-proofed. Bookable by a list kept on the piano in the main hall. A student entered one with a saxophone. Polly waited a few moments but all she could hear was a distant, subdued tune. All that jazz. Whatever. Room number 4. A quick knock and enter straight away.

'Hi, Polly.'

'Hullo, Jen.'

The women shake hands, formally, but for some time. They don't flinch from the sight of each other.

'When does your flight go? Tonight?'

'Uh huh, I have a cab picking me up from school at four. Can you believe Mrs Elms allowed me to miss the last three days of term?'

'No,' marvels Polly, 'it's unprecedented – she must have a soft spot for you. Or else you paid her substantial sums?'

'Or else, she can't wait to see the back of me?'

'I don't think so,' Polly says, 'from all accounts, I hear you've been a tremendous success. e e cummings,' she whistles in admiration. Jen takes the compliment graciously. Polly looks suddenly horror-struck.

'God,' she says, 'you don't think I'm expected to come back for these last three days of term, do you?'

'No one's said so,' Jen assures her. They laugh, both aware of the dire consequences of the proximity of a term's end, let alone a year's end, on the girls' behaviour. They laugh again; both knowing full well that Polly will be at assembly at 8.40 Monday morning. Sitting, no doubt, by Megan.

'So,' says Jen.

'So,' says Polly.

'You're back.'

'I'm back.'

There is an awkward pause during which Jen wonders if she should say sorry. Should she tell Polly that she'd spoken to Chip? That she knew? For her part, Polly wonders whether she should assure Jen that everything is fine, that she holds no grudges, that she had slept with Chip anyway. The women finish the silence with a meek smile apiece. Jen

399

shrugs and looks out of the dormer window over the roof-tops of BGS.

'Do you know Mister Benn?' Polly asks.

'What, the big clock?'

'No, no, not Big Ben, *Mister* Benn?'

'That guy who creeps around the science block?'

Polly laughs and shakes her head. 'We're deluged by your bloody *ER*, *Friends* and *Northern Exposure* – fine televisual viewing, I do concede – but you mean to tell me that Mister Benn has not made it across the Atlantic?'

'Nope,' says Jen, 'who the hell is he?'

'Oh,' Polly replies, 'just a chap on TV I think you'd like. We both have a lot in common with him.'

'We do? Is he on video?'

Jen continues to look out of the window. The netball court cum tennis court cum playground. The tree sitting defiantly at its centre. She is looking forward to the space and structure of Hubbardtons.

'It was – it was so—' Polly pauses, stuck for words, halted by the lump in her throat. 'And I'm back now. And you're about to return, too.'

'Polly,' Jen says, turning to her and regarding her unflinchingly, 'I'm, like, sorry.'

'For what,' Polly replies but not as a question at all. 'You have nothing to apologize for. In fact, I thank you, Jennifer Carter. I wouldn't have wanted things to have worked out any other way,' she continues, with conviction. 'Through experiences, one learns. And oh, how you grow from what you have learned.'

'So so true,' Jen agrees.

'Thanks for asking me,' Polly says, touching Jen's arm, 'thanks for suggesting that we meet.'

'Hey,' says Jen, holding up her hands in surrender, 'thank you for coming – I'm so so pleased that you did. And thanks also for Buster – I'm going to miss him a lot.'

'What a year,' Polly enthuses, 'it was a bloody huge, brilliant year.' She sighs wistfully and very much in the past

400

tense. In her mind's eye, the people who have inhabited her recent life stand in line. Kate with a jar of Marmite. Marcia with the CIA. Mikey McCabe – ha! remember him! Chip – whom she now had no need to forget. Her Dorm Daughters. Those brothers, in aprons, from the Vineyard. AJ in his baseball cap. Turned back to front. Lorna and her vibrator. Jackson. Powers. Laurel and Lauren in salopettes. Josephine in bronze. Charle(s). The men who gave her windfall apples. The sales assistants in Manchester. There they all stand, in a line, outside Jojo Baxter's unfinished house. It's a curtain call. They are as actors in a favourite play, one in which Polly had a bit part. They are taking a bow. And another. They exit stage left.

Polly blinks. She's in a music room at BGS that smells vaguely of gym shoes and toasted sandwiches. She's standing next to Jennifer Carter, who's a lot taller than her but completely on the same level. She stands alongside Jen, looking from the tiny window, sharing the view. Polly touches Jen's shoulder and then places the back of her hand gently against Jen's cheek. Jen takes her hand and holds it. They share a private, generous, congratulatory smile and bring their foreheads together.

'What a year,' Polly marvels in a whisper. 'Do you know, I wouldn't have had it any other way – because I certainly wouldn't be where I am now,' she says.

'Exactly,' Jen marvels, liking it that they stand so close. 'But, know what? If the opportunity arose, I sure as hell wouldn't do it again,' she adds, smiling broadly and nudging Polly.

'God no,' Polly responds, her hands to her face, her eyes dancing and dark, 'neither would I.' ×